**Praise for these other novels in the bestselling
Joe Ledger series**

PATIENT ZERO

"Plenty of man-to-zombie combat, a team traitor and a doomsday scenario add up to a fast and furious read."
—*Publishers Weekly*

"An enjoyable read and one that's hard to set down."
—*Fangoria*

"Heated, violent, and furious . . . as palatable as your favorite flavor of ice cream. [A] memorable book."
—Peter Straub, *New York Times* bestselling author

"*Night of the Living Dead* meets Michael Crichton."
—Joseph Finder, *New York Times* bestselling author

DRAGON FACTORY

"Excellent . . . Expect this straight-ahead thriller to hook action-crazed readers and inspire them both to seek out the first Ledger book and eagerly anticipate the next installment."
—*Booklist*

"Eager readers can look forward to one more volume in this humorous, over-the-top cross-genre trilogy."
—*Publishers Weekly*

The King of Plagues

Jonathan Maberry

St. Martin's Paperbacks

THE KING OF PLAGUES

Copyright © 2011 by Jonathan Maberry.

All rights reserved.

For information address St. Martin's Press, 175 Fifth Avenue, New York, NY 10010.

ISBN: 978-1-250-09283-0

Printed in the United States of America

St. Martin's Press Trade Paperback edition / March 2011
St. Martin's Paperbacks edition / August 2016

St. Martin's Paperbacks are published by St. Martin's Press, 175 Fifth Avenue, New York, NY 10010.

10 9 8 7 6 5 4 3 2 1

This is for the brave men and women of the U.S. Armed Forces. Politics aside, if you're wearing the uniform in these troubled times, know that there are a lot of people who appreciate and respect what you do. Come home safe.

And, as always, for Sara Jo.

Acknowledgments

As Joe Ledger's biographer (ahem) I rely heavily on the brilliance, insight, experience, and patience of a variety of experts. Thanks to Dr. John Cmar of the Infectious Disease Department of Johns Hopkins University Hospital; Dr. Steve A. Yetiv, professor of political science, Old Dominion University; Dr A. M. Dodson, FSA, Research and Teaching Fellow, Department of Archaeology and Anthropology of the University of Bristol; Dr. Pawel Liberski of the Department of Molecular Pathology and Neuropathology, Medical University of Lodz, Poland; Philadelphia police officer Bob Clark; the men of the 1/111th Infantry Battalion–Recon Platoon, with Thirty-sixth Brigade–Iraqi Army Recon; Marie O'Connell, Jackie Szambelak, and Dr. Barry Getzoff; Michael Sicilia of the California Homeland Security Exercise and Education Program; Walt Stenning, Ph.D., former head of psychology at Texas A&M University; Michael E. Witzgall; Ken Coluzzi, chief of Lower Makefield, Pennsylvania, police department; the International Thriller Writers; authors David Morrell,

Gayle Lynds, Sandra Brown, John Gilstrap, Jason Pinter, and Eric Van Lustbader; George Schiro, M.S., consulting forensic scientist; Greg Dagnan, CSI/Police/Investigations Faculty–Criminal Justice Department, Missouri Southern State University; Peter Lukacs, M.D.; Ted Krimmel, SERT; and Suzanne Rosin, winner of the "Name Joe Ledger's Dog" contest.

And special thanks to Javier Grillo-Marxuach, Michael De Luca, and Matthew Snyder; Fran and Randy Kirsch, Charlie and Gina Miller, Arthur Mensch, Sam West-Mensch, and Greg Schauer; Geoff Strauss; Nancy Keim-Comley, Janice Gable Bashman, and Tiffany Schmidt; and Rachel Stockley and Ian Graham.

And, of course, Michael Homler, Joe Goldschein, Matthew Shear, and Nadea Mina at St. Martin's Griffin and my agents, Sara Crowe and Harvey Klinger.

And to the wonderful staff at the Starbucks in Southampton, where much of this book was written (yes, I do believe I'll have a refill).

Prologue

"Unless you do exactly what you're told," whispered a voice, "we'll kill your wife and daughter."

The words dug into Trevor Plympton's brain like railroad spikes. He sat on the chair, wrists bound to the armrests with plastic pipe ties, ankles tied to the wheeled feet of the chair. A hood over his head let in no light. He was lost in a world of darkness and fear. And those words.

He could barely remember what had happened. He'd taken the elevator to the basement parking garage, clicked open the locks on his Vauxhall Astra, felt a sharp burn against the back of his neck and then nothing. When he finally woke up he was already lashed to the chair. He'd cried out in alarm, tried yelling for help.

A heavy hand belted him across the face. A savage blow, made worse by the absolute surprise of it. He couldn't see it coming, could not even brace against it or turn away.

Then the whispering voice.

"W-what . . . ?" It was the best response he could

muster. Nothing made sense; the world was a confusion of disorientation, fear, and pain.

"Did you understand what I said?" asked the voice. A male voice. Was there an accent? It was hard to tell with the whisper.

"Yes," Plympton gasped.

"Tell me what I said."

"T-that you'd k-kill my family—"

A hand clamped onto Plympton's crotch and squeezed with sudden and terrible strength. The pain was white-hot and immense. The grip was there and gone, as abrupt as the snap of a steel trap.

"That's incorrect," said the voice. "Try again."

Plympton whimpered and then suddenly flinched, imagining another grab or blow. But there was nothing. After a handful of seconds Plympton relaxed a little.

Which was when the hand grabbed him again. Harder this time.

Plympton screamed.

"Shhhh," cautioned the whisperer. "Or next time I'll use pliers."

The scream died in Plympton's throat.

"Now," said the whisperer, "tell me what I said."

"You . . . said that . . ." Plympton wracked his brain for the exact words. "Unless . . . I did exactly what you said, you'd . . . kill my wife . . . and daughter." The words were a tangle of fishing hooks in his throat. Ugly words, it was impossible that he was saying them.

When the hand touched him again it was a gentle pat on the cheek. Even so, Plympton yelped and jumped.

"Better." The man smoothed the hood over Plympton's cheek.

"W-what do you want me to do?"

"We'll get to that. What concerns us in this minute is whether you will agree to do whatever I ask. It will be easy for you. It will be just another day at work."

"At work?"

A million dreadful possibilities flooded Plympton's mind.

The whisperer said, "I'm going to remove the hood because I want to show you something. If you turn your head, your family will die. If you yell or try to escape, your family will die. Do you understand me?"

"God," Plympton said. Then, before the whisperer could punish him again, he said, "Yes."

"There won't be a second warning."

"I swear."

The whisperer placed his hand on Plympton's head, fingers splayed like a skullcap, and then slowly curled them into a fist around a fold of the hood. He whipped it off so violently that it tore a handful of hairs from Plympton's scalp.

Plympton almost screamed with the pain, but the warning was too present.

"Open your eyes."

Plympton obeyed, blinking against the light. As his eyes adjusted he stared in shock and confusion.

He was in his own apartment, tied to the chair in his own office. The desk before him was neat and tidy, as he'd left it, but the computer monitor had been turned away. *No reflection,* he thought with bizarre clarity.

Plympton could not see the man, but he could feel

him. And smell him. An odd combination of scents—
expensive cologne, cooked meat, gasoline, and testosterone. The overall effect was of something large and
powerful and wrong behind him, and with a jolt Plympton realized that he'd started to think of his captor as a
thing rather than a person. A force.

"I want you to look at some pretty pictures," the
stranger whispered.

The man's hand came into Plympton's peripheral
vision. Thick forearm, thick wrist, black leather glove.
The man laid a photograph down on the desk. The hand
vanished and returned with a second picture, and a third,
and more until there were six four-by-six-inch photos on
the green desk blotter. What Plympton saw in those pictures instantly separated him from the pain that still
hummed in his nerve endings.

Each picture was of a different woman or teenage
girl. Three women, three girls. All nude. All dead. The
unrelenting clarity of the photos revealed everything
that had been done to them. Plympton's mind rebelled
against even naming the separate atrocities. To inven-
tory such deliberate savagery was to admit that he could
embrace the knowledge, that his mind could understand
them, and that would be like admitting kinship to the
devil himself. It would break Plympton and he knew it,
so he forced his eyes not to see, his mind not to record.
He prayed with every fiber of his being that these things
had been done to these women after they were dead.

Though . . . he knew that wasn't true.

The arm reappeared and tapped each photo until it
was square with the others in a neat line.

"Do you see?" the whisperer asked. "Aren't they beautiful? My angels."

"God. . . ." It was all Plympton could force past the bile in his throat.

"See this one?" The whisperer placed a finger on the corner of the third photo. One of the teenagers. "She was the same age as your daughter."

"Please!" Plympton cried. "Please don't hurt my daughter! For the love of God, please don't hurt my little girl. . . ."

Pain exploded in Plympton's shoulder. It was only after several gasping, inarticulate moments that he was able to understand what had just happened. The whisperer had struck Plympton on a cluster of nerves in the valley between the left trapezius and the side of his neck. It had been fast and horribly precise. The whole left side of his body seemed to catch fire and go numb at the same time.

"Shhhh," cautioned the whisperer. After a long moment the man patted Plympton's shoulder. "Good. Now . . . I have two more pictures to show you."

"No," sobbed Plympton. He closed his eyes, but then the whisperer's lips were right there by his ear.

"Open your eyes or I'll cut off your eyelids, yes?"

Plympton mumbled something, nodded.

The whisperer placed two more four-by-six photos on the desk, arranging them in the center and above the line of six photos. A strangled cry gurgled from Plympton's throat.

The photos were of his wife and daughter.

In the first photograph, his wife was wearing only a

pair of sheer panties and a demi-cup bra as she leaned her hips against the sink and bent close to the mirror to apply her makeup. Her face wore the bland expression of someone who believed she was totally alone and who was completely absorbed in the minutiae of daily routine. The picture had been taken from behind so that she was seen from the backs of her knees to above her head, with the front of her from hips to hair in the mirror. Plympton's heart sank. Laura looked as pale and beautiful now as she had when they'd first met twenty-two years ago. And he loved her with his whole heart.

That heart threatened to tear loose from his chest as he looked at the second picture.

His daughter, Zoë. Fifteen years old and the image of her mother, except that instead of mature elegance Zoë had a lush coltish grace. In the photo, Zoë was naked, her young body steaming with hot water as she stepped out of the shower over the rim of the tub, one hand raised to push aside a shower curtain that had a pattern of swirling stars. Plympton saw his daughter in her unguarded nakedness and it awoke in him a hot fury—an inferno of murderous rage that flooded his arms with power. His whole body tensed, but then the whisperer said, "We have someone watching them both right now. We are watching them every minute of every day. We have their cell phones tapped. We're in their computers. We know their passwords, their travel routes, all their habits. Six times each day I have to make calls to tell my people not to kill them."

As fast as the rage had built in Plympton it was gone, leaving only a desolated shell of impotent anger.

The whisperer said nothing for a whole minute, letting

those words tear through the chambers of Plympton's mind and overturn all the furniture and smash out every window. Then the whisperer reached past Plympton and slid two of the photos out of the line of six. He placed one next to the picture of Laura, the other next to the picture of Zoë. The woman in the first picture was about Laura's age; she had the same basic coloring. The same for the photo of the girl next to Zoë's photo. He did this without comment, but the juxtaposition was dreadful in its eloquence.

"Now," said the whisperer after another quiet minute, "tell me again what I told you."

Plympton licked his dry lips. "Unless . . . I do exactly what I'm told you'll kill my wife and daughter."

"You believe me, yes?"

"Yes." Tears broke and fell, cutting acid lines down Plympton's cheeks.

"Will you do what I want?"

"Yes."

"Anything? Will you do absolutely anything that I want?"

"Yes." Each time Plympton said the word he lost more of himself. All that remained now was a frayed tether of hope.

"Good."

"If . . . if I do," Plympton said, dredging up a splinter of nerve, "will you leave them alone? Will you leave my family alone?"

"We will," promised the whisperer.

"How do I know that you'll keep your word?"

There was a pause, then, "Are you a man of faith, Mr. Plympton?"

It was such a strange question, its placement and timing so disjointed, that Plympton was caught off-guard and answered by reflex.

"Yes," he said.

"So am I." The whisperer leaned close so that once more his breath was a nauseating caress on Plympton's ear. "I swear before the Almighty Goddess that if you do what we want—and if you never talk about this with anyone—then I will not harm your wife or daughter."

"Don't fuck with me," Plympton snarled, and heard the man chuckle at the sudden ferocity in his voice. "You said 'I.' I want your word that none of you will ever come near them. Or harm them in any way."

"I so swear," said the whisperer. "And may the Goddess strike me down and curse my family to seven generations if I lie."

Goddess? The word floated in the air between them. Even so, as weird and grotesque as the promise was, Plympton—for reasons he could not thereafter understand—believed the whisperer. He nodded.

"What . . . what do you want me to do?"

The whisperer told him what he wanted Plympton to do.

"I . . . can't!"

"You can. You promised." There were no more blows, no grabs or taunts. The photos and the value of that strange promise were enough now to have established a strange species of trust between them.

Even so, Plympton said, "If I did that . . . I'd be arrested. People could die—"

"People *will* die," corrected the whisperer. "You have

to decide if they will be people you work with and patients whose names you would never know, or if they will be your lovely wife and daughter."

"They'd never let me. . . . That facility is too well protected."

"Which is why we came to the one person who is positioned to bypass that security. You weren't picked at random, Mr. Plympton."

The whisperer touched the photo of Plympton's daughter, drawing a slow line along the curve of her thigh toward the damp curls of her pubic hair.

"All right! God damn you! All right."

The whisperer withdrew his hand. "I'm going to put the hood back on your head. Then I'll cut you loose. You will sit there and say the names of your wife and daughter aloud one thousand times before you remove the hood or stir from that chair, yes? I will know if you betray our trust. You know that we're watching. You know that we can see what goes on inside this house. If you move too soon, then I will know, and I will not make the calls that I need to make in order to keep your loved ones alive."

Plympton sat there, weeping, trembling.

"Tell me that you understand."

"I understand."

"You are the architect of your own future, Mr. Plympton. Like the Goddess Almighty, you can decide who lives and who dies. It feels glorious, doesn't it?"

"Fuck you."

The whisperer laughed.

Then he pulled the hood over Plympton's head.

Trevor Plympton sat in an envelope of darkness and

despair and said the names. When the knife cut through his bonds he flinched as if he'd been stabbed but otherwise did not move.

"Laura and Zoë."

He said their names one thousand times. Then he said their names another hundred times. Just to be sure.

After that he removed the hood. The apartment was empty. The ugly photos were gone. The photos of his wife and daughter were gone. The hood and plastic cuffs were gone. Except for the Taser burn on his neck and the aches from the torture, this might all have been a dream.

He went into the bathroom and splashed cold water on his face.

"God help me," he whispered.

Part One
Seven Kings

*Lycurgus, Numa, Moses, Jesus Christ, Mohammed,
all these great rogues, all these great thought-tyrants,
knew how to associate the divinities they fabricated
with their own boundless ambition.*

—DONATIEN-ALPHONSE-FRANÇOIS, MARQUIS DE SADE

Chapter One

Park Place Riverbank Hotel
London, England
December 17, 9:28 A.M. GMT

"Are you ready to come back to work?" asked Mr. Church.

He didn't say hello, didn't ask how I'd been. He got right to it.

"Haven't decided yet," I said.

"Decide now," said Mr. Church.

"That bad?"

"Worse. Turn on the TV."

I picked up the remote, hit the button. I didn't need to ask which channel. It was on every channel.

"Okay," I said. "I'm in."

Chapter Two

The Royal London Hospital
Whitechapel, London
December 17, 10:09 A.M. GMT

I stood in the cold December rain and watched thousands of people die.

The Hospital was fully involved by the time I got

there, flames reaching out of each window to claw at the sky. Great columns of smoke towered above the masses of people who stood shoulder to shoulder with me as dozens of hoses hammered the walls. The smoke was strangely dense, like fumes from a refinery fire or burning tires, and there was a petroleum stink in the air.

"Back! Back!" cried a firefighter, and I turned to see that there were too many people and too few police . . . and we were all too close. I could feel the heat on my face even though I was in the middle of the street. "Get the hell back!"

I looked at the firefighter. He was running toward us, waving us back with both hands. Then I looked up at the building and knew at once that he wasn't doing crowd control. He was shouting a warning. The building was starting to collapse. I turned to run, but behind me was a tight-packed sea of people. They were staring in numb shock as the wall slowly leaned out toward them. Maybe they didn't see it, or didn't understand what was happening. Maybe the very fact of a spectacle this vast had hypnotized them, but they stood their ground, eyes and mouths open. I grabbed a man in a business suit and shook him and then slammed him backward.

"Move!" I screamed.

The crowd snarled at me. Ah, people. No sense of self-preservation in the face of disaster, but give them a chance and they'll bark like cross dogs.

Fuck it.

The firefighter was getting closer, louder, but the roar of the fire was louder still. Then something deep inside the building exploded. A heavy *whuf!* made the whole front of the building bulge outward in our direction.

That did it.

Suddenly the whole crowd was backpedaling and stumbling and finally turning to run as the entire façade of the Royal London Hospital bowed slowly outward and fell, the ancient timbers and brick defeated by the inferno heat. Hundreds of tons of burning brick slammed onto the pavement. A gigantic fireball flew at us across Whitechapel Road, chasing us as we dove behind the fire trucks and ambulances and police cars. People screamed as cinders landed on their skin. Splinters and chips of broken brick battered the crowd like grapeshot. The firefighter was struck between the shoulder blades by a burning chunk of stone the size of a football. He pitched forward and slid all the way to the curb, his helmet flying off and his hair immediately beginning to smoke. The falling rain hissed as it struck his back and head, but it wasn't strong enough to douse the fire.

I leaped the small wrought-iron fence and pelted in his direction as embers fell like meteorites all around me. I whipped off my anorak and slapped it down over him, swatting out the fire. The smoke was thick and oily and filled with dust despite the rain. I yanked my sweater up over my nose and mouth, grabbed the fallen fireman under the armpits, hauled him to his feet, and then staggered out of the smoke with him. A second firefighter saw us and ran to help.

"He's alive," I said as I lowered the first fireman to the ground.

I backed off as a team of paramedics appeared out of the crowd. The second firefighter followed me.

"Is that everyone?" he yelled.

"I don't know!" I bellowed, and turned to head back into the smoke, but he caught my arm.

"Don't do it, mate. The rest of the wall's about to come down. Nothing you can do." He pulled me backward and I stumbled along with him.

He was right. There was a low rumbling sound and more of the wall fell, chasing the onlookers even farther back. The firefighter—a young man with a cockney voice and a Jamaican face—shook his head. "Whole bleeding thing's going to go. Can't believe I'm watching the London die."

The London.

A familiar nickname for the hospital. Not the Royal London, not the Hospital. The London, as if that name, that place, stood for the old City itself.

We stood there, watching helplessly as the oldest hospital in England died. There was nothing anyone could do. After I'd gotten Church's call and turned on the TV, I'd rushed out immediately, caught the first cab, and screamed at the man to get over to Whitechapel. The traffic was so thick that I had run the last six blocks. The press was already calling it a terrorist bombing. If that was true, then it was the worst in British history.

The firefighter shook his head. "Look at it. Survived the Blitz, survived everything, and now this. *Poof.* Gone." He looked at me, his eyes glazed with the enormity of it. "They put a billion pounds into expanding it. Over twelve hundred beds since the renovation, and with this round of flu you know they'd all be filled. More than two thousand staff on-shift. Doctors, nurses, orderlies . . . I know a lot of them. . . ."

"What happened?" I asked sharply, hoping to snap him back to the moment.

He wiped soot from his face. "Dunno for sure. They're saying it was bombs."

" 'Bombs'? More than one?"

"That's the report we got. Five or six explosions. Big ones, and almost at once. Then the whole place was fully involved. That last blast was probably the heating oil in the subbasement. But those others . . ."

"What's with the black smoke?"

He shook his head. "Mystery to me, mate. Smells like a rubber fire, don't it? The fire investigators are going to have to sort that out, because that's definitely oil smoke. Makes no sense."

"How many people got out?" I demanded, looking around for someone who had been in there, someone I could ask questions of. If this was a terrorist attack, someone had to have seen something, and the sooner we could get a jump on it the better.

"Out?" The young firefighter's bleak eyes shifted away to the fire, and then down. "No one got out that I heard of. Place went up too fast." He spit saliva that was clouded with black grit onto the debris-littered pavement. "At least it was quick."

I hoped he was right about the last part . . . but he didn't sound all that convincing.

A line of police officers worked their way between the apparatuses, pushing spectators back across the street. The rain slackened to a drizzle and news crews crept from their vans to do stand-ups. I recognized the young woman nearest to me. Kimiko Kajikawa, from the BBC. I'd seen her read the news every night at six.

This was the first time I'd ever seen her without her legendary unflappable cool. She looked like she'd been crying, and I imagine that it was the numbers that were hitting her. If the firefighter was right and the bombs had caught everyone unawares, then we could be looking at something like thirty-two hundred dead in a single moment. Maybe more. Nearly as many as had died in the fall of the Towers. If all those beds were full, then it could be even worse.

I felt tears burning in the corners of my own eyes.

All those lives. All those people.

And all of those families. How many of them were watching Kajikawa right now? Jesus Christ.

Since signing on with the Department of Military Sciences I've seen far more than my fair share of death, but nothing on this scale. And even though the flames and smoke hid all of the bodies, I could *feel* the death. It was like a huge dark hand had reached inside me and was squeezing my heart. I turned to the people around me and saw expressions on their faces ranging from confusion, to disbelief, to shocked awareness. Each was processing the enormity of this at the speed their mind would allow. I could almost see how this was gouging wounds into the collective psyche of everyone here, and anyone who was watching a news feed. Each of them— each of us—would be marked by this forever. The moment had that kind of grotesque grandeur.

I edged closer to hear Kajikawa.

". . . we'll be following this story as it unfolds," she said. Her voice was steady, but the hand holding the mike trembled. "So far no one has stepped forward to take responsibility for the bombing at this landmark

teaching hospital. Established in 1740, the facility pro-
vides district general hospital services for the City and
Tower Hamlets and is also the base for the HEMS helicopter ambulance service. Hospital authorities say that
nearly all of the twelve hundred beds were occupied as
of yesterday."

There was a commotion to my right and I turned to
see a tall, harried-looking man in a black uniform fighting his way through a sea of TV and news service
microphones.

"Fire Commissioner Allen Dexter is on the scene,"
said Kajikawa as she hustled over to join the throng
around the man.

"Commissioner Dexter," shouted a Reuters reporter,
"do we know how many casualties yet?"

Dexter's lip curled in irritation at the typical callous-
ness of the question. It was clear from the different
shapes his mouth took before he answered that the words
he said were not the first ones on his tongue: "Not at this
time."

"Can you speculate for us?" the reporter persisted.

The commissioner slowly faced the hospital, which
was an inferno from foundation to rooftops. When he
turned back, his pale eyes were bleak. "We have not yet
identified anyone who was in the building at the time
of the blasts and who since escaped."

The reporters were too jaded to be stunned by this.
They screamed questions at him, but Dexter turned
away as a wave of police officers surged forward and cut
him out of the pack.

"There you have it," Kajikawa said, turning back to
face the camera. "This is quickly becoming the worst

hospital disaster in British history. And if this is a terrorist attack, then it could well be the worst ever." She said it with what almost sounded like pride. Somewhere between her earlier tears and now she'd made a huge internal shift from "human being" to "reporter." Maybe the cameraman had said something to her, or maybe she did a mental review of reporters whose careers had been made by great human suffering. Like Dan Rather and Walter Cronkite breaking the story of JFK's assassination, Wolf Blitzer with the first Gulf War in Kuwait, and Anderson Cooper during Hurricane Katrina. Or maybe being in the thick of the throng of reporters reminded her of the most sacred rule of journalism: "If it bleeds, it leads."

I thought it was vulgar.

Kajikawa was still working it. "We do not yet have word about how many of the hospital's eight thousand staff members were on duty today, but as the building continues to burn out of control, hopes for a happy outcome are likewise going up in smoke."

Jesus.

Chapter Three

The Royal London Hospital
Whitechapel, London
December 17, 10:46 A.M. GMT

I found a relatively quiet spot in a vee formed by two fire trucks parked at right angles and called Church. I told him what it was like at the scene, and remarked on the dense oil smoke that was turning the entire sky black.

"Odd," he said. "Perhaps it is intended as a symbolic touch. A statement."

"On what? The Mideast oil wars?"

"Let's add that to our list of questions."

"What do we know about this attack?" I asked.

"Too little. Benson Childe, my opposite number in Barrier, called to ask if we'd heard anything from our networks. We haven't. Nothing credible, anyway. Half a dozen fringe groups have issued statements claiming responsibility, but they are the ones who do that for everything. I've had our people trolling through FBI, CIA, and Senate subcommittee records, reports to the President, speculation from our own analysts. So far we have a lot of enemies and there is no shortage of threats against us and our allies, but nothing that specifically targets this location or date. No one has identified a specific political or religious motivation for this, so the Brits are holding off on calling this a terrorist attack."

"From where I'm standing it doesn't look like anything else. I worked a lot of fires when I was a cop, Boss, and this isn't bad wiring or someone smoking in bed. There's going to be more collateral damage than we had at Ground Zero. Maybe a higher body count, God help us."

"Yes. Which means that the whole world is going to be looking at this, and that's why the Brits are taking their time in putting a label on it. They don't want to kick off a rash of hate crimes. For the moment the verbiage is 'national tragedy.'"

"Anything from Al-Qaeda?"

"Not so far, but expect something. If this isn't their play, then they'll reach out to praise whoever did it."

"What about our other sparring partners? The Cabal? The Kings?"

"There's not enough of the Cabal left to orchestrate this. As for the Seven Kings . . . that may be more likely."

"Why? What's been happening while I've been off the radar?"

"There have been some clashes. Our informant is still feeding us useful intel. We've had several dustups with the Chosen."

"Sorry I missed the party," I lied. In truth, I wasn't looking to jump back into any firefights with the Kings' field troops.

We had learned about the Seven Kings a few weeks after my first mission with the Department of Military Sciences. Mr. Church had received an anonymous phone call from a source even MindReader was unable to trace. The call had come in on Church's private line, a number known only to key people: the President of the United States, a few people in government, the heads of the top counterterrorist organizations belonging to our allies, and the team leaders of the DMS. Either one of them was the mysterious caller or the caller had managed to learn that private number or the caller had the technology to hack into Church's coded phone. None of those options was particularly comforting.

He was able to record the call, however, and played it back for us. . . .

Chapter Four

"I want to speak to Colonel Eldritch."

Eldritch was one of a dozen different names for the man I knew as Church. None of them were his real name as far as I knew.

"Who is this?" Church asked.

"A friend." The caller spoke through a voice-distortion system that made it impossible to tell if it was a man or a woman.

"Your ID is blocked. My friends don't need to hide their identities."

"Then consider me a new friend."

"What is the basis for our new friendship?"

"A shared interest in the security of our nation."

"Will you tell me your name?"

"My name is of no importance. What *is* important is who I represent."

"Who is that?"

"A group of loyal Americans whose actions are always in the best interest of America."

The caller had not said *in the best interests of the American* people.

"What do you want?"

"There is a new and grave threat to this country."

"What is the nature of this threat?"

"It is a group called the Seven Kings of the New World Trust."

"Who are they?" asked Church. "And what is their agenda?"

"Chaos," said the caller.

"What kind of chaos?"

"Total. Global. Apocalyptic."

"Excuse me," said Church, "but this is bordering on being a crank call. If you are a loyal American as you claim, and if there is a threat about which you have knowledge, then please give me the facts in plain and simple terms."

There was a sound that might have been a short laugh. "For reasons that I do not care to explain, I cannot give you too much information on the Seven Kings. Perhaps I will be able to share some information from time to time."

"Will you give me something now?"

"Yes. Something that will save American lives." The caller gave Church the location of a Hamas cell operating in Washington, D.C., that was being funded by the Seven Kings. "This group plans to strike tomorrow during the afternoon rush hour. Many people will die, including key members of Congress. You can stop this."

"That's it?" Church demanded. "You speak of a group dedicated to global chaos and the downfall of our country and all you give me is a single terrorist cell? How do I know I can trust you?"

"You'll find the cell."

And then the caller disconnected.

Chapter Five

We followed up with recon and verified the cell's existence. Fourteen hostiles and enough weapons and explosives to start a war. Or tear the capital apart.

I led the hit.

D.C. had been in the crosshairs since long before 9/11, so there are fifty kinds of counterterrorism protocols built into the infrastructure and dozens of agencies are tasked with gathering intel. It's all supposed to be shared. Politicians aren't supposed to lie, either.

Our people used MindReader to hack everyone else's database and dump everything into one massive pattern-recognition search. By collating information from a dozen different agencies we learned that much more was known about this matter than any one group believed and the reason everyone who needed to know *didn't know* was because red tape and departmental pissing contests reduce the flow of interagency intel to a dribble. Guys with prostates the size of soccer balls can piss a heavier stream.

It fell to the Department of Military Sciences to put the pieces together and put boots on the ground. Thanks to MindReader.

When Mr. Church formed the DMS he built it around a computer system that was several generations ahead of anything else known to exist. MindReader was designed to look for trends and the software was very carefully crafted to take into account some factors that might otherwise be missed, and although computers can't generalize or make intuitive leaps, this one came pretty damn close. Its other unique feature was that it could intrude into virtually any other computer system without tripping alarms. When MindReader backed out, it rewrote the target computer's software so that there was no record that it had ever been hacked. It was a highly dangerous system, and Church guarded it like a dragon.

So less than five hours after the mysterious call—from someone whom everybody except Church was already calling Deep Throat—disconnected we had snipers on rooftops, choppers in the air, a satellite re-tasked to do thermal scans, and Echo Team ready to kick in the doors.

The cell was located in a small frame house on Ninth Street in the Penn Quarter section of D.C. Lots of foot traffic, lots of tourists. We parked the van around back and halfway up the block. We were not wearing our usual combat rig—unmarked black BDUs, helmets, and ballistic shields. Too many civilians and no way to know who was a spotter for the bad guys.

I wore a Hawaiian shirt over jeans. We all wore vests, though, but these were the latest generation of spider silk bulletproof vests with carbon nanotubes filled with nanoparticles that become rigid enough to protect the wearer as soon as a kinetic energy threshold was surpassed. Stuff that's not on the open market yet, but Church has a friend in the industry and he always buys us the best toys.

I strolled down the street with Khalid Shaheed, one

of my newest shooters. Khalid looks like a schoolteacher and came to the DMS by way of Delta Force. A good guy to have at your back.

We pretended to argue about whether Brooks Robinson should be considered the greatest Orioles player of all time rather than Cal Ripken. I used a prearranged cue word to escalate the argument into a shouting match just as we passed the front of the target house. Shouts escalated into shoves and soon the front door opened and a man wearing a blue sports coat stepped out onto the porch.

"Hey!" he yelled. "Stop that. . . . Get out of here!"

He had a Palestinian accent, and Khalid turned to him and in brusque Palestinian Arabic told him to mind his own business. Actually, Khalid told him to have anal sex with a three-legged dog. Nice. The man began screaming at Khalid and soon they were nose to nose. The door was still open and I could see other faces appear at the windows and in the doorway.

My sunglasses had a mike pickup built into the frame. I whispered, "Go."

Instantly the rest of Echo Team hit the house. Big Bob Faraday, a former ATF field man who was built like Schwarzenegger's big brother, kicked the back door completely off its hinges. Top Sims, my second in command, swarmed past him with Joey Goldschein at his heels. Joey was our newest member, a good kid, six months back from Afghanistan. They bellowed at the top of their lungs as they moved through the empty kitchen and into a side hall.

"Federal agents! Lay down your weapons!"

The adjoining dining room was filled with men, most

of them crowded around a big oak dining table that was covered with bricks of C4 and all the wiring needed to blow the whole house into the next dimension.

You'd think that people would be disinclined to initiate a firefight when there's forty pounds of high explosives lying right there on the table. You'd be wrong. Lot of crazy people out there.

Suddenly it was the O.K. Corral.

Out front, the man arguing with Khalid turned sharply at the noise from inside the house. He never saw Khalid pull open his loose Orioles shirt and pull his piece. Maybe the man heard the shot that killed him, but I doubt it.

Khalid and I both had the whole team yelling in our ears about explosives and armed resistance. Deep Throat's intel had been solid.

Khalid and I opened fire together, hammering the front windows and the doorway. The men were so tightly clustered that there was no way for us to miss.

Then the dead were falling and the others were backpedaling into the house. We jumped up onto the porch and I covered Khalid while he reloaded. Then I had to duck behind the brick wall between window and door as a hail of heavy-caliber bullets ripped through the frame. There were screams and blaring horns from the street behind us, and I knew that backup teams were closing on the house. The Hamas team was in a box that we were nailing shut. It was up to them whether the box was a container or a coffin.

Khalid and I both yelled in Palestinian Arabic for them to lay down their arms. The only answer was a renewed barrage of automatic gunfire.

"Flash out!" I barked into my mike, and then pulled a flash bang out from under my shirt and lobbed it through the doorway. Khalid and I covered our ears and squeezed our eyes shut. The blast was huge.

"Go! Go!" I snapped, and Khalid spun out of his protective crouch and rushed inside. I was right behind him. He fanned left; I took the right. There were five hostiles in the living room, but all of them were down, rolling around on the floor, screaming but unable to hear their own voices. Flash bangs blow out the eardrums and temporarily blind the unwary. We kicked weapons out of their hands and kept moving. The firefight in the dining room was still hot and heavy. I saw Top Sims in a shooter's squat behind a breakfront that bullets had reduced to little more than splinters and shattered crockery. Big Bob and Joey were firing from the hallway entrance.

I tapped Khalid and he nodded and took up a shooting position from the living room doorway while I peeled off and headed for the stairs. From the sound of it there was a second firefight up there. The team's other big man, Bunny—a moose of a kid from Orange County—had been on-point for the second-floor entry, and he had former MP DeeDee Whitman on his wing.

"Green Giant, this is Cowboy. On the stairs and coming up," I barked into the mike.

"Join the party, Cowboy." Bunny's voice sounded relaxed.

Then DeeDee added, "Stay away from the windows. Chatterbox is enjoying himself."

"Copy that, Scream Queen."

Chatterbox was our last team member. His real name

was John Smith, and the DMS had headhunted him away from LAPD SWAT. He was one of those silent, introspective types who looked like a beatnik poet from the Village but who was the hammer of God with a sniper rifle.

I tapped the command channel and keyed over to Smith's frequency.

"Chatterbox, this is Cowboy. I'm on the second floor. No window shots until I give you the word."

" 'K,' " he said.

I peered around the wall at the top of the stairs and looked right into the eyes of a dead man. He was sprawled on the floor with a black bullet hole above his left eyebrow and a look of profound surprise stamped onto his face. The whole back of his head had been blown out. John Smith at work. I've seen a lot of great shooters in the military and on the cops, and I've met a few whose accuracy bordered on the supernatural. But John Smith was a Jedi. He was spooky good. If you're unlucky enough to step into his crosshairs, then you'd better be right with Jesus.

I leaned farther out into the hall and saw that most of the second floor was an open-plan studio. There were two more men slumped like rag dolls. Automatic weapons lay near each one. Three other men knelt beside the windows, weapons in hand. They were probably too smart and too scared to try to return fire after three of their brothers had taken head shots. It was a tough nut to crack, because a sniper is the most feared man in any battle scenario.

The second most feared is the guy who sneaks up behind you.

I ducked back onto the stairs and whispered into the mike. "Cowboy to Chatterbox. I'm moving into the field of fire. No shots until I give the word or fifteen seconds is up. Copy?"

" 'K,' " he said again. Guy never shuts up.

I took my Beretta in a two-handed grip and then I was up and moving, rounding the corner, entering the open room, running fast as I cleared the corners with a flick and then fanned the barrel back to the shooters, taking the one farthest from me first with two in the head and shifting to the next gun without a pause. The other two shooters started to turn, but I shot the middle guy twice through the side of the head and the impact sent him crashing through the broken window.

The third guy was almost in kicking range and he was moving at lightning speed, swinging his AK-47 up, turning toward me, finger already inside the trigger guard. If he'd had a handgun instead of a long gun he might have beat me to the shot, but I put the first one in the center of his chest, then raised the gun fourteen inches and put the second one through his forehead. Double tap. All six shots fired in less than three seconds and my head ringing with thunder.

Then John Smith's voice was yelling in my ear, "On your six! On your six!"

I ducked and spun to one side as a hail of bullets burned through where I'd been standing. Four shooters were crowding into the doorway and I had no idea where the hell they'd come from. The first two banged into each other trying to get through the doorway, and I was already coming up out of my jump and roll. I killed them both with five shots between them. I moved like a son of a bitch, rushing in but to one side, firing one-handed as I tore a fresh magazine out of my pocket. The bodies in the doorway fell face forward just as my slide locked back. The third shooter kicked his way into the room, starting to turn as he cleared the doorway and the bodies.

Shit. No time to swap out the mags, so I dropped my Beretta and drew the Rapid Response Folding knife from its sheath clipped inside my jeans pocket. The RRF has a wicked little 3.375-inch blade that locks into place with a snap of the wrist. What it lacks in weight it makes up for in speed, because at only four ounces it moved as fast as my hand. No drag at all.

I bashed the rifle aside with my left and whipped him across the throat with a very tight semi-circular slash. Blood exploded outward in a hydrostatic jet. I faded left and took a hard leap past his shoulder, and drove the point of the knife into the face of the fourth shooter. The blade caught him beside the nose and I punched it all the way through. He screamed and his finger clutched around the trigger, sending half a magazine into the legs of the guy whose throat I'd cut. I gave the knife a quarter turn and yanked it out, then plunged it back into his throat.

He collapsed over the tangled legs of his comrade.

I tore the knife free and wiped it clean on a dead man's sleeve, then retrieved my Beretta and swapped out the mags.

My heart was hammering in my chest and I could smell my own sweat mixed with the copper stink of blood. There hadn't been time to be scared before now, but it was catching up to me like a son of a bitch.

I tapped the commlink. "Chatterbox, Green Giant—center room clear. All hostiles down. Repeat: All hostiles are—"

"*Get out!*"

It broke into the team channel. Top's voice. Screaming.

"Hostile with a vest! Hostile with a vest! Out–out–*out*!"

A vest.

Jesus Christ.

We all knew about those vests. Anyone who had been in Iraq or Afghanistan knows about suicide bombers who follow the compulsion to strap on forty pounds of high explosives and turn the day into red nightmare.

Suddenly we were all yelling and running. I ran for the window and went out like I was Superman. Maybe a drop of fifteen feet to the street. There was a huge black noise behind me, and just as I cleared the window I felt myself lifted as if wishing I could fly was making it so.

As if.

The force of the blast threw me out over the street. I pinwheeled my arms, and my legs mimicked running as I flew. There were cherry trees along the curb. In one of the weird moments of clarity that happen in the middle of a crisis, I knew that the leaves and branches were going to break my fall, but I wasn't going to like it one bit. Behind me the fireball burned the air and ignited the leaves and sucked all the air out of my lungs. Then the tree curled its branches into a fist and knocked me out of all sense and understanding.

* * *

I WOKE UP in an ambulance. Top and Khalid were with me, both of them covered with soot and blood-stained field dressings. Top told me the news.

One of the hostiles had come up out of the cellar wearing a vest packed with bars of Semtex. Everyone on Echo Team had taken cuts and burns except John Smith.

I started to say that we'd gotten off lucky, but something in Top's face stopped me.

"What—?" I asked.

"Joey," he said. "He pushed Khalid out the door, but he caught his foot on a throw rug and went down. He got up, but he was one step too late."

Joey Goldschein had been the only one of my team left inside when everything went to hell. He was six months back from his second tour in Afghanistan. He deserved a longer life.

That was our first encounter with the Seven Kings.

AFTER THAT, DEEP Throat came to Church with dribs and drabs of intel. My part in the Seven Kings affair slowly evaporated as I became involved in several un-related cases. Other DMS teams worked on it, and it's both sad and frightening to say that there are always multiple threats chewing at the fabric of our society. Vultures and predators, sharks and parasites, bent on destroying us in order to satisfy their own political agen-das. I don't say that they do this to satisfy their religious agendas, because I'm either idealistic enough or cyni-cal enough to believe that religion is deliberately mis-used as a label for greedy sons of bitches whose real objective is wealth and power. Sure, the freedom fighter in the trenches may think that God wants him to strap C4 to his chest and walk into a post office, but until the so-called religious leaders do that themselves I think it's a scam. And they're scamming their own loyal followers as much as they're scamming the rest of the world. I think this was true during the Crusades and it's true now in the Middle East. I seldom trust the guys at the top.

The real bitch was that despite having clashed with groups supported by the Seven Kings, we didn't have a frigging clue as to who or what the Kings were. It was like fighting an invisible empire . . . and yes, I know that sounds like an old movie serial. But there it is.

Chapter Six

The Royal London Hospital
Whitechapel, London
December 17, 10:52 A.M. GMT

Church said, "The Kings have been busy during your 'vacation.'"

"Deep Throat been calling his BFF again?"

"I see isolation and contemplation haven't matured you. Pity," Church said. "We've had five additional tips. Three out of five of the tips resulted in action taken. We recovered prisoners in several of the raids, but none of them were above street level. They knew the name Seven Kings but nothing else of substance."

"Did Deep Throat warn you about today?"

"Not specifically. He said, 'Watch out; the next one will be epic.' However, if this is a Seven Kings attack, it would be their first hit on foreign soil."

"That we know of."

"Yes."

"You any closer to finding out who Deep Throat is?"

"No. But I have some friends in the industry working on this."

The blaze looked even hotter than before. The crowds surrounding the Hospital had to number in the thousands.

"I don't think there's any doubt that this is a terrorist hit," I said.

"Even if no one comes forward to take credit for this, we're likely to see a rise in hate crimes."

I agreed. After 9/11 there was an insane wave of violent hatred toward Muslims even though we were not—and never had been—at war with Islam. Echoes of the Japanese internment camps. Xenophobia is one of humankind's most embarrassing traits.

I said, "Destroying a medical complex of this size had to have taken enormous and very detailed planning. Can't have been a matter of someone walking in the front door with a C4 vest or a car bomb in the parking garage. This place is massive and it all went up at once. Someone put some real thought into this and—"

Church interrupted me. "How are you doing?"

Church is borderline heartless, so the fact that he was asking made me stop and do a quick self-check. I realized that I was speaking way too loud and way too fast. I took a deep breath and let it out slowly, and in doing so I could feel how much of it was stale air that had been turning to poison in my chest.

"I'm good," I said more slowly.

He didn't comment. He wouldn't.

"Dr. Sanchez will be on the first thing smoking."

"I don't need a shrink," I began irritably, but he cut me off.

"I'm not sending him to hold your hand, Captain. Dr. Sanchez has a great deal of experience with post-traumatic stress, and much of that can be ameliorated if dealt with from the jump."

That was true enough. Rudy was an old friend and he was my own post-trauma shrink before he became my best friend. Since we both signed onto the DMS he'd been the voice of reason and everyone's shortest pathway to a perspective check. Even, I suspected, for Church himself, though Rudy refused to discuss it.

Church said, "You'll liaise with Barrier and offer them any support you can. Barrier knows that anything they tell you will be processed through MindReader, and they're comfortable with that. They don't have anything as sophisticated, so we may get some hits before they do."

Barrier was the global model for effective covert counterterrorist rapid-response groups, and it actually predated the DMS by several years. Church had tried to get the DMS in place first, but when Congress wouldn't green-light the money he served as a consultant to the U.K. to build Barrier. When that organization proved itself to be an invaluable tool against the rising tide of advanced bioweapon threats, the Americans finally got a clue and Church built the DMS. The Barrier agents I'd met were every bit as good as our guys, most of them having been handpicked from the most elite SAS teams.

However, hearing the name Barrier inevitably conjured the image of Grace Courtland.

Damn.

Maj. Grace Courtland had been Church's second in command at the Warehouse, the DMS field office in Baltimore. She was a career military officer and the first woman to join the SAS as an active operative, and the permanent liaison between Barrier and the DMS. She was tough, smart, and beautiful, and she was my direct superior in the chain of command. At the end of August, against all common fucking sense, we fell in love. That was wrong in a whole lot of ways. Rudy tried to warn me, but I brushed him off and told him to mind his own business. And yes, I know that as he was the DMS shrink this *was* his business, but when was the last time someone falling in love listened to good advice?

Grace and I knew that a love relationship, no matter how discreet, made us fly too close to the flame. As agents of the Department of Military Sciences we tackled the deadliest threats imaginable, so personal entanglements could only end in trouble. In our case, it ended in disaster. We faced off against a threat so huge that books will be written about it. At the end of it, the good guys won and I lost. I lost Grace. She died saving us all, and I think I died, too. Part of me, anyway.

Since then I've knocked aimlessly around Europe with my dog, Ghost, a specially trained DMS K9. We got into a couple of scrapes together while doing some unofficial stuff for friends of Mr. Church. I hadn't actually quit the DMS, but I didn't want to return to the Baltimore Field Office. Grace would not be there. The place would be full of echoes, of shadows and memories. Of ghosts.

Originally, I had come to Europe on a hunting trip. The bastard who shot Grace escaped the bloody resolution of that case. He escaped and went into the wind. As a going-away present, Mr. Church left me a folder full of leads, travel documents, and money, and, without ever saying so, his blessing.

Ghost and I went hunting, and after many weeks we ran our prey to ground. There's an unmarked grave on one of the Faroe Islands off the coast of Denmark. I pissed on it after I hand-shoveled the dirt and rocks over what was left of the body.

It didn't bring Grace back, but I believed that somewhere—maybe in Valhalla—her warrior's soul approved.

Ah . . . Grace.

Damn it.

Church apparently got tired of the silence on my end of the phone and plowed ahead. "Your current credentials will get you into the investigation. I advised the President and Prime Minister about your participation. And . . . I'll likely be on the same flight as Dr. Sanchez. Do you want me to bring Jerry Spencer as well?"

Jerry was the top forensics man I knew. He'd joined the DMS at the same time I did. His genius was in walking a scene and letting the evidence talk to him.

"Absolutely. As soon as the ashes are cool enough to walk, I want Jerry in the smoke. It should all be over by the time he gets here, because at this point it doesn't look like the fire department is doing anything but containment on this. It's all going to burn down. What's my play?"

"Be available to the Brits. They'll tell you what they need."

"Where's Gog and Magog? Shouldn't they be on this?"

These were the two DMS teams permanently stationed in Great Britain. Gog was based at the Regent's Park Barracks on Albany Street in London; Magog was hosted by the forty-eighth Fighter Wing at the Lakenheath RAF base in Suffolk. I worked with both of them on my second mission after signing on. We tracked a network of Iranian terrorists who were selling yellowcake by the hundredweight to terrorist groups. That's not something you serve at birthday parties. It's a uranium derivative used in the preparation of fuel for nuclear reactors. Look it up in *Terrorism for Dummies* and you'll see that there are all sorts of things you can do with it.

"Gog is dealing with a critical matter in Prague. Magog is in Afghanistan dismantling a Taliban bioweapons team. At the moment you're the only senior DMS agent in the U.K."

"Swell."

"The London counterterrorist offices have both accepted my offer of your services."

"Why would they want my help?"

"Because I briefed them on the Seif Al Din, *Mirador,* and Jakoby cases. I'll send them a report on the Seven Kings, and will send all recent data on them to your BlackBerry."

"Good. You know," I said, "of the big-event terrorist

attacks we've seen—the Alfred P. Murrah Building, both World Trade Center attacks, the London subway bombings—they were all one and done, followed by a lot of gloating via the Internet. Don't get me wrong, I'll throw myself into this with a will, but unless this is one of our playmates, then I'm just another pair of boots on the ground."

"I'm no more psychic than you are," said Church, "but I believe that there is a clock ticking somewhere. Maybe the Kings, maybe Al-Qaeda. Besides, terrorism notwithstanding, this is a crime and you're a cop. Work the crime. Somebody has to have survived. Somebody has to know something."

"Any chance you can send Echo Team over here?"

"They are out at Area 51 and—"

"Wait—what? There's an *actual* Area 51? That's so cool."

Church sighed. "At times you're as bad as Bug and Dr. Hu. Yes, Captain, we have an Area 51 and no, Captain, there are no UFOs there. Nor are any alien autopsies being performed there."

"Damn."

"It is, however, a classified area, and Echo Team is providing backup for Lucky Team out of Vegas and the intelligence investigators from Nellis. Possible security breach, but so far no fireworks."

"Crap. Can you send them my way when they're finished kicking E.T.'s ass?"

He grunted. "Why? They're not investigators."

"They can handle door knocks and Q and A."

"I'll see what I can do." He paused. "Bottom line, this needs to be handled with precision. We dropped the ball on 9/11. We reacted too slowly and often the wrong way. We have to do better this time."

"'We'? This isn't the U.S.A.," I reminded him.

"How does that matter? This is an attack on humanity. There are sixty million people in Britain."

Wow, I really was off my game if I walked into that.

"What if Al-Qaeda or one of the other usual suspects steps forward to claim responsibility for this?"

"Best-case scenario, we establish some fresh leads that will maybe result in a useful joint Barrier-DMS action."

"Worst case?"

"We lose the thread of this and have to wait for something else to happen."

I looked across the road to where one of the brand-new towers was crumbling, the charred bones of the building collapsing under its own deadweight. More of the black smoke billowed up and turned a horrible morning into the very dead of night.

"Damn . . . ," I breathed.

Church must have been watching the same thing on the news. I heard him sigh.

"Welcome back to the war, Captain."

Chapter Seven

CNBC: Breaking News Report
December 17, 10:55 A.M. EST

TRANSCRIPT OF THE FINANCIAL NEWS REPORT
In the wake of the devastation in London, the Dow Jones Industrial took a drastic 7.19% dip and there

are Wall Street rumors that the White House may suspend trading and close the New York Stock Exchange until the initial panic has subsided. This echoes the events of 9/11 which saw the NYSE closed for several days following a period of losses in the stock market. Airlines and tourism industries are also expected to be affected due to fears of another attack.

In a preliminary statement issued a few minutes ago, SEC chief Mark David Epstein cautioned investors not to engage in a "flight to safety," reminding everyone that panic produces a decline in financial markets but that the markets typically recover. "While there is certainly reason to be concerned over the events in England and around the world," he said, "the best course of action in financial terms is inaction."

Epstein is expected to make a more detailed statement tonight following the President's address to the nation.

Interlude One

Fair Isle, Scotland
The Shetland Isles
December 17, 6:31 A.M. GMT

Rafael Santoro moved silently through the shadows of the garage. He came up behind Dr. Charles Grey and touched the blade of a knife against the man's cheek.

"No sound," murmured Santoro.

The scientist stiffened. Not so much from shock or surprise, but like a man who is suddenly aware that a long-dreaded but inevitable horror has finally come.

Santoro bent close to whisper in the scientist's ear, "It's time."

Grey began to tremble. "Please . . . God! No. . . ."

"Yes," said Santoro. "You know what you have to do. You promised that you would do it."

Grey started to turn, but Santoro pressed the knife into his flesh. Santoro did not break the skin, but he made sure that Grey could feel the edge, could feel the quiet appetite of the steel. Santoro was an artist of supreme delicacy with a blade. With fast or slow cuts he was able to sculpt a victim into a masterpiece of crimson art. It was one of the many talents that made him so valuable to the Seven Kings, and to his patron, the King of Fear. Fear and the blade were both aspects of Santoro's personal religion.

"I can't," whimpered Grey. "Don't you understand that? What you ask is impossible."

"Nothing is impossible if the Goddess wills it to be. That is the nature of faith, yes?"

"'G-Goddess' . . . ?" Grey stammered. "I don't understand. . . ."

Santoro leaned forward, rising onto his toes so that his lips were an inch from the back of Grey's neck. "You told me that you were a man of faith, Dr. Grey. Do you remember? That first day when fortune brought me to you? When I showed you the pictures of those angels."

"Angels . . . ?" The pictures that this man had shown him were not of angels, but he understood what Santoro meant. Grey gagged at the thought of such horrors being described as angelic. They were images out of hell itself.

The blade was an icy promise on his flesh. "Are you saying now that you were lying to me? Lying about faith?"

"No! No," pleaded Grey. "That's not what I meant. . . ."

"Then tell me what you meant, Dr. Grey. Tell me that you believe the All is capable of everything. Everything."

"Y-yes. . . ."

"Say it," Santoro growled. He raised the knife from Grey's cheek until the beveled edge filled his vision.

"Yes," Grey said hastily. "I believe, God help me, I believe, but—"

With a snarl, Santoro withdrew the knife and with his free hand grabbed Grey's shoulder and spun him violently around.

"*God* may believe you, but you are a piece of shit in the eyes of the Goddess!" Santoro wore a black mask, but through the eyeholes his eyes blazed with dark fire. He then snatched Grey's right hand and slapped the knife into his sweating palm.

Grey sputtered with confusion and looked dumbly down at the vicious weapon he held. It had a six-inch double-edged blade and a handle wrapped in red silk thread. It looked as much like a tool of ritual as it did an instrument of destruction.

"Do you know what faith is, Dr. Grey?" Santoro asked quietly. When Grey shook his head, the small man smiled. "Faith is my shield; it is the armor that covers my flesh and soul. I am a man of faith, Dr. Grey.

I know that the Goddess protects me. I know that she has forged me into her sword."

"I . . . I . . . ," was all that Grey could manage.

"If you are a true man of faith, Dr. Grey, then you will believe that the Goddess lives in you. *Use* that faith. Prove its existence to me and to yourself. Cut me."

Grey looked at the weapon in his hand. His face twisted into a mask of horror as if he held a squirming scorpion.

"Do it," insisted Santoro.

"I—can't . . . No . . ."

"Do it or I will go into the house and find young Mikey and show him the knife. Would you like that, Dr. Grey? Would you like to watch? I will leave you one eye so that you can see it, and I will leave you most of your tongue so that you can scream. You will want to scream."

Grey suddenly stabbed at the small man. He saw his hand move before he felt his muscles flex, the dagger point glittering as it tore through the shadows toward Santoro's smiling mouth.

But Santoro was not there.

In the gloom of the garage he became a blur. He pivoted on one foot and shifted so that the stabbing knife pierced only empty air. His hands flashed out, striking and striking and striking, the movements unspeakably fast, the blows hideously powerful. He struck Grey in the groin and the floating ribs and the solar plexus and the throat. Santoro pivoted like a dancer and struck Grey in the kidneys and tailbone and between the shoulders. Then the scientist was falling, falling, all in a fractured second. His arm still reached for the stab, but his body crumpled within the cocoon of blows.

He collapsed onto the cold concrete floor of the garage, gagging, gasping for air with lungs that seemed incapable of drawing a spoonful of breath. His mouth worked like a dying fish, making only the faintest squeaks.

Santoro stood above him, composed, relaxed, not even breathing hard. He knelt and picked up the knife, cleaned away the surface smudges on Grey's shirtsleeve, and stood. The knife vanished into its hidden sheath beneath Santoro's jacket.

"When you can breathe again," he said, "I suggest you spend some time on your knees. Pray to the Goddess, yes? Pray for forgiveness for the sin of doubt."

He bent over and knotted his fingers in Grey's hair and jerked the man's head viciously back.

"And pray that *I* forgive you. Pray that I will leave young Mikey alone. And intact."

Grey managed to squeeze a single word out of his tortured throat.

"Please . . ."

Santoro bent closer still, lips against Grey's cheek. "Will you do what you have promised to do?"

Grey nodded.

"Say it."

"Yes!" Grey gasped weakly. Tears streamed down his face. "Yes. . . ."

Santoro opened his fingers and let Grey slump to the floor. "We will be watching, Dr. Grey. When you do what you have promised, you will have help."

Grey raised his head at that. "H-help?"

"At work. You will not have to do this alone. You are never alone."

As the reality of that sank in, Grey buried his face in the crook of one arm and wept.

When he stopped sobbing and looked up, Santoro was gone.

Chapter Eight

Park Place Riverbank Hotel
London, England
December 17, 11:43 A.M. GMT

I went back to my hotel to change clothes. My dog, Ghost, met me at the door with a tail that stopped wagging as soon as he smelled me. Shepherds have extremely expressive faces, especially the white ones, and Ghost gave me a "hey, even I don't roll in stuff that smells that bad" look; then he lay down with great dignity in front of the TV and licked his balls.

I stripped and showered the stink of oily smoke from my skin and hair, and then leaned my forehead against the wet tiles and tried not to think about what was inside that smoke. Four thousand people. That was the current estimate.

I cranked up the hot water and tried to boil the reality of that out of me.

Four thousand.

God.

I have a little bit of religion. Not much, but enough to make me believe that there's something bigger than all of this, and some reason that we're all struggling through it. But on days like this, my faith takes a real beating. Or maybe it's not my faith in God that gets pummeled. Probably it's faith in my fellow man. I know I'm more than half-crazy, but it takes a whole lot of bat-shit insanity to want to blow up four thousand people. In the three and a half million years since our furry forebears started walking upright we've had more than enough time to clean up our act and get the Big Picture. The fact that we're still killing one another doesn't speak to an inherent ignorance or perceptual deficiency in the species. We *do* know better, so stuff like today is pure, deliberate evil. There's no religion, ideology, viewpoint, or political exigency that can justify mass slaughter of the innocent. Not one.

Feeling bitter and hurt by what was happening, I toweled off, dressed in my least wrinkled suit, ran a brush through my hair, and headed for the door. I was expected at Barrier headquarters for a briefing. Ghost was sitting in my path.

"You're not coming," I said.

He cocked an eyebrow. I don't know if that's something all dogs do or if Zan Rosin, the DMS K9 trainer, had taught Ghost the trick just to piss me off. I suspected that it was both.

"Move."

Ghost did. He got up and moved closer to the door. He sat down again and looked up at me with the biggest, saddest brown eyes in town.

We had this argument a lot. He usually won.

He did this time, too.

Chapter Nine

The entrance to Barrier was via the Vermin Control Office. Cute.

I produced my credentials and a separate set for Ghost. The receptionist barely batted an eye at the eighty-five-pound shepherd at my side. A rat-faced man who looked very much like he worked for "vermin" control came and led us through a series of interlocking offices until we finally emerged into the actual offices of Barrier. When we're out in public Ghost plays the role like he was trained. He walks to one side and slightly behind me, head up, ears swiveling like radar dishes, nose scooping in trace particles of everything around him. A well-trained dog is a wonderful companion. Loyal, smart, and they don't talk.

"Captain Ledger?"

I turned as a tall, hawk-faced man came striding across the lobby toward me.

The man looked like a typical ex-military: thin, with great posture and eyes that were fifty degrees colder than his smiling mouth. I figured him for ex-SAS and maybe ex-MI6. He looked to be about sixty-five, but I'll bet he could give me a run for my money over an obstacle course.

"Benson Childe," he said. "Director of this band of thieves. We were told to expect you." He looked down at Ghost and held out a hand to be sniffed.

Ghost looked at me for permission and I gave it. I use a combination of hand and verbal signals. With a stranger, a twitch of my little finger means it's okay for him to approach. Ghost took the man's scent and filed it away. I was pleased to see that Childe didn't try to pet the dog. It indicated he understood K9 protocols.

"I hope I can be of help," I said. "This is a terrible tragedy."

"Yes," he said as he led us into his private office. "By the way, Captain, your reputation precedes you. I've heard some very good things."

I laughed. "Somehow I can't imagine Mr. Church gushing about me."

"Hardly. The Sexton isn't one to gush. His brief on you was short but colorful."

The Sexton. Another of Church's names. I've heard people refer to him as Colonel Eldritch, Mr. Priest, Deacon, and Dr. Bishop. I wonder if any of them was close to the mark.

"No . . . Grace Courtland told me about you."

Grace. Dammit. Hearing her name now felt like an ambush. I tried to keep it off my face, but Childe's eyes searched mine and I saw the precise moment when he saw and recognized the particular frequency of my pain. He nodded to himself, an almost imperceptible movement. Was he confirming a suspicion, or simply noting my reaction?

I nodded but said nothing, not trusting my voice. Ghost must have sensed something, because he rose and moved slowly to stand partially between me and Childe. I scratched Ghost between the shoulder blades. If only dogs really could stand between us and our own inner pain. All dogs would be saints.

Childe discreetly cleared his throat. "I think we'll be able to find a use for you, Captain," he said. "Grace said that you were a detective before you joined the DMS. And I believe you've worked several large-scale terrorist cases since."

"A few."

"That will be useful, because we have a laundry list of terrorist cells believed to be operating in the U.K. and an even longer list of persons of interest. My computer lads are coordinating with your lot to run their profiles through MindReader, but your personal experience may be invaluable."

"We have any candidates yet?"

"Not as such. However, we have people collecting eyewitness accounts at the fire scene, and inputting everything from actual observed data to hunches. With MindReader able to collate all of the random factors for us, we're approaching this from the standpoint of 'no detail is too small to count.' "

"Smart. Devil's in the details."

"Too bloody right it is," Childe agreed. He looked at his watch. "In ten minutes we'll be meeting with the Home Secretary and various divisional heads of our counterterrorism departments." He went to a sideboard and poured brandy from a decanter and handed me a glass.

"Before we go in there, I have something to say, and something to ask."

"Okay."

He sipped his brandy and said, "Grace Courtland."

I took a second before responding, "What about her?"

"I recruited Grace out of the Army and into the SAS," he said. "She was the first woman to serve in the SAS, as I'm sure you know. From the moment she entered the Army anyone with eyes could see that she was a cut above. Not just a cut above the other recruits, but a cut above anyone. Male or female. She was born for this kind of work. Sharp mind, natural leader. Very probably the finest soldier I ever met, and believe me that's saying quite a lot. I brought her into the SAS initially to prove a point, to show that modern women can handle the pace, endure the hardships, and hold their place in the line of battle, even at the level of special operations. Grace more than made my case. I know that you fought alongside her, so you must have seen how she was in combat. Fierce, efficient, and yet she never lost that spark of humanity that separates a warrior from a killer. Do . . . you understand what I'm saying?"

I nodded.

"When Mr. Church formed the DMS and requested that Grace be seconded to him as the liaison between his organization and ours, I was proud of her . . . but I resented the request. Grace was mine, you see." He studied my eyes. "She was like a daughter to me . . . and no parent could have ever been prouder of a child than I was of Grace."

"A lot of people cared about Grace," I said, keeping my face and tone in neutral. "You made your statement. What's your question?"

"Tell me, Captain Ledger, were you with Grace when she died?"

When I didn't say anything, Childe edged a little

closer. "Church tells me that one of your strengths is that you seldom hesitate, and yet you're not answering me."

"It's not hesitation," I said. "I'm just wondering how much trouble I'll get in if I tell you to go fuck yourself."

Ghost caught my tone and growled softly at Childe.

That amused him. "Why the hostility?"

"Why the question? I've been waiting for one of you guys to take a shot at me for what happened to Grace."

"That's not my agenda," he said, heading me off before I got a full-bore tirade going. "My question is straightforward: were you with her when she died?"

"Yes," I said. "I was."

"And did you care for her?"

"She was my fellow officer."

"Please, Captain, this is off-the-record and just between us."

He had no right to ask and I was under no obligation to say anything that wasn't in my official after-action report. But his eyes were filled with an odd light and the defensiveness I felt was my own, not the result of any kind of attack on his part.

I said, "Yes."

"I know this is a lot to ask . . . but how much did you care?"

"Why?" I asked, and my voice was a little hoarse.

He closed his eyes. "It's . . . important to me to know that at the end, when she was dying, she was with someone who truly cared about her."

I said nothing.

Childe turned away and sipped his brandy. "Grace was alone for most of her life," he said softly. "She'd lost all of her family, her husband had walked out on her, and her infant son died shortly after birth. Grace was always alone, and it would destroy me to think that she died alone. Thank you, Captain." He turned back and offered me his hand.

I took it and we shook.

Then Childe looked at his watch. "Time to go."

Interlude Two

Agincourt Road
London, England
December 17, 12:24 P.M. GMT

The man in the city suit and bowler hat stepped into the doorway of a men's tie shop, his face raw and red from the bitter wind. He dug a cell phone out of his pocket and punched a speed dial. The phone rang twice and then a voice with a distinctly Spanish accent said, "Yes?"

"The bloke you told me to follow . . . he's just stepped inside the pest control office."

"You are certain of his identity, yes?"

"Of course I am."

"Good."

"What do you want me to do?"

"Nothing. Go back to work. Others will handle this."

"But I—"

"Go back to work."

"Is this it? Am I done now? Will you bastards leave me alone?"

The Spaniard laughed softly. "You may hear from us," he said. "From time to time."

He was still laughing when he hung up.

The man in the bowler hat closed his eyes and cursed silently to himself. Behind his eyes he saw the photographs that the Spaniard had shown him. Photographs of what the madman had called his "angels."

"God help me," the man whispered. The contents of his stomach turned to sewage and he had to take deep breaths to keep from vomiting. He stepped cautiously out of the doorway, afraid of falling down. He cast one look at the doorway to the Vermin Control Office, then turned away and hurried home to his children.

Chapter Ten

Barrier Headquarters
London, England
December 17, 1:37 P.M. GMT

"The Prime Minister has authorized that the Threat Level be raised to 'exceptional.'" The Home Secretary, Julian Welles, sat at the head of the table and looked for reactions to his news. No one offered any, so he continued. "We are five hours into this. What do we know?"

The gathered men nodded; a few sighed. I kept my face neutral. Ghost lay beside my chair, and I'd given him the commands for down and quiet. A muted plasma screen showed the scene at the hospital. Most of the building had collapsed by now, and they were using deluge cannons to knock down the remaining flame-shrouded walls rather than let them topple into the streets. One corner of the old building still stood, though, and the news cameras kept returning to it, as if its stubborn refusal to yield meant something more than a vagary of physics. The streets around the hospital had all been evacuated—a process that started in earnest once the first of the new towers fell, kicking out massive gray clouds of billowing smoke. 9/11 might be over a decade ago, but even the average guy on the street knew about the dangers of breathing in that dust. It was more than debris—the fire and the pressure from the collapsing buildings had vaporized people.

There was an untouched plate of sandwiches on the table. No one had an appetite.

Welles was a small man who exuded a great degree of personal power. He had an aquiline face, a hooked nose, and black hair combed back from a high brow. A casting agent would have looked at him and said, *Sherlock Holmes.*

"We don't know anything for certain," said Detective Chief Inspector Martin Aylrod, head of the National Public Order Intelligence Unit. "The hospital has taken a number of threats from animal rights groups who want to stop the animal testing that's part of the cancer research center. But . . . our initial background checks on known members resulted in what you'd expect. Vegans with too much free time and only the most minor political connections, and even then they seem tangential. Even so, I've ordered all of our staff to report for duty to do comprehensive interviews, and we'll share our information with the general pool."

Welles turned to the only woman at the table, Deirdre MacDonal, a fierce Scot with a bun so tight that it had to hurt her brain. She ran the National Counter Terrorism Security Office, a police organization funded by, and reporting to, the Association of Chief Police

Officers, which in turn advised the British government on its counterterrorism strategy. "What have you got, Deirdre?"

She scowled. "Too much and damn all. We're monitoring a laundry list of microcells and splinter groups, but none of them has ever demonstrated the capabilities to do something like this. Or anything even close to this."

"Has *anyone* taken credit for this?"

MacDonal snorted. "The whole daft lot of them are queuing up to take credit. We've even had nine separate calls from people claiming to be Osama bin Laden himself. And one from Saddam bloody Hussein."

"From beyond the grave, no less."

"He claimed that the man they hanged was a clone."

"Ah," said Welles, and shot a look at me. "Would the DMS have any opinion on that?"

"I'll pass it up the line, but I doubt if Saddam was alive he'd be calling to chat."

"I daresay. Who would benefit from this?"

Childe cleared his throat. "Hard to say, especially if you look at the staff and patient demographics. There are a fair number of Muslims, Christians, Jews, and others. The hospital isn't particularly political. No one of political or religious significance is associated with it or incarcerated as a patient. If this is a political statement, it's more obscure than it needs to be."

"Yes," agreed the Home Secretary, "and our press statements will reflect a neutral and nonaccusatory attitude until such time as we know at whom we should point our finger."

Childe nodded.

The Home Secretary eyed the group. "Has anyone received a credible threat of *any* kind? Something we can act on?"

Deirdre MacDonal said, "There have been several calls made to local precincts, but none of them are likely. Most are local nutters who regularly take credit for everything from the latest drive-by shooting to conspiracies by secret societies. Freemasons, the Illuminati, bloody space aliens. Barking mad, the lot of them."

"None of them bear investigation?" asked Welles.

She sighed. "All of them do, Home Secretary, and we have teams running each one down, but we don't expect any of them to actually be directly related."

Welles looked at me. "Was anything phoned in to any of the American agencies?"

"Same as you have here," I said. "A lot of groups and individuals trying to take credit but no one who stands out. We're processing everything as fast as we can, though. I'm sure a pattern will emerge."

"You're sure or you're hoping?" asked MacDonal.

"I'm sure and I hope I'm right," I said, and that squeezed a smile out of her pinched face.

Welles steepled his fingers. "Do we think that this might be related to any of the upcoming holiday or charity events? Or is there any indication that the scheduled events may become targets?"

"Excuse me, sir," I said, "but as I'm here more or less on vacation, I haven't been paying attention to the social pages. Which events are most politically sensitive? Doesn't the Queen give a Christmas address of some kind?"

"That's a fair question, Captain," he said. "And Her

Majesty usually touches on politics, and in recent years that's been Afghanistan and Iraq. The broadcast is on Christmas Day but is actually taped beforehand."

"Do people know that?"

"Yes," answered MacDonal. "Which puts it low on the list of likely targets."

"There are large gatherings of people at Trafalgar Square and the South Bank on the nights leading up to Christmas," said Aylrod. "The tree lighting has already passed; that was the first Thursday of this month. But there are several scheduled events for caroling. A bomb at either place would do untold harm, and if timed to Christmas . . . well, the religious and political implications are there to be seen."

"Bloody wonderful," said Welles sourly. "Put people on both events."

"What about the Sea of Hope?" asked MacDonal.

"What's that?" I asked.

She smiled. "I would have thought you knew about that, Captain, as it's really an American event. It's a big international fund-raiser for humanitarian aid for those countries suffering from diseases of poverty."

I nodded. Although I didn't know much about the fund-raiser, I certainly knew about the epidemics. Lately AIDS, malaria, and tuberculosis—the classic diseases of poverty—had taken alarming upsurges in Africa, with comparable spikes from the new Asian flu in Malaysia, another new strain of mumps in the poorer sections of Ireland, dengue fever in Bolivia, Brazil, and Paraguay, and a stunningly potent new strain of meningitis that was burning its way through West Africa.

"The event takes place aboard the SS *Sea of Hope*,

one of those absurdly large Norwegian cruise ships," Welles said with disdain. "There will be plenty of speeches and appeals for humanitarian aid from nations, corporations, organizations, and individuals. Prince William is nominally in charge of our end of the project and will be giving the keynote address; however, the Bush twins, Chelsea Clinton, John Kerry's daughters, and a few other political offspring are part of the board of directors. It's all part of the Generation Hope campaign started by the eldest Obama girl."

"Wow," I said, "that would make it a prime target. Is the ship docked here in London?"

"No. It touched at Dover last week to take on supplies and has since sailed for Brazil. The fund-raiser cruise starts on the twenty-first, but the centerpiece is the concert on the twenty-second. A rock concert that will be simulcast to arenas and movie theaters worldwide. U2, Lady Gaga, the Black Eyed Peas, John Legend, Taylor Swift, a laundry list of others are aboard, and others will perform at venues in forty countries. A portion of all ticket sales to be donated, et cetera. All very noble, but also a logistical nightmare."

I blew out my cheeks. "As I said, that would do it."

But Childe shook his head. "Whereas I agree that it would be a terrorist event of epic proportions, it's probably too big. If a shipload of celebrities and the children of world leaders were successfully attacked there is no ideology on earth that would protect the perpetrators from the wave of retribution. It wouldn't be a snipe hunt like what we've been doing with the bloody Al-Qaeda—this would be a unified front of overwhelming revenge. Any nation that could be proven to have supported such an action would be disowned by its allies and attacked by everyone else."

"I'm inclined to agree," said Welles.

"Besides, the ship doesn't return to England at all," Childe said. "The concert is held at sea and afterward the ship docks in Rio de Janeiro for a private after-event party for the celebrities and their families. It's bloody hard to attack a cruise ship, especially with the escort that will be sailing with it. The frigate HMS *Sutherland* will be with them as soon as Prince William is aboard, and they'll be joined by the USS *Elrod*. And a couple of subs—one of ours, one of yours—will be ghosting them."

MacDonal gave a fierce shake of her head. "Terrorists can't attack ships at sea. They don't have the resources for it and we've already provided for the unexpected. It's the same reason that there have been no attacks on presidential inaugurations, the Queen's public events, and so on. Too much security makes failure too likely, and failure weakens their message. My concern is that we are investing so much time and energy in the *Sea of Hope* that we are, in essence, distracting ourselves from other potential targets like the London Hospital."

I nodded. "Even so, we have to be prepared for a group that isn't sheltered by a specific government. A group willing to take a big risk no matter how ill considered. We need to make sure that the cruise ship is searched and searched again. Inside and out. Divers to check for mines attached to the hull, bomb sniffers inside, chemical analysis of the food and water."

MacDonal looked at me. "Your man, the counterterrorism expert Hugo Vox, has overseen this since the beginning, and his consultant Dr. O'Tree is here in London to dot all the *i*'s and cross all the *t*'s. By the time the royals are aboard, everyone on that ship will have been vetted by Vox."

That was reassuring. To have been "vetted by Vox" was the highest level of clearance. Grace Courtland had been vetted by him. I hadn't met Vox, but he was one of Mr. Church's most trusted colleagues.

"We'll keep our eye on it nevertheless," concluded Welles, "but for now let's return to the London. What have we learned from the actual fire—?"

Deirdre MacDonal suddenly held up her hand as she bent over her laptop. "Excuse me, Home Secretary, but I believe we have something. My lads have been reviewing the CCTV feeds from the area and they've just red-flagged something. You'll want to see this." She looked hard at me. "You as well, Captain Ledger."

She tapped some keys and transferred her video feed to the big screen monitor. "This is a bit of footage from the video traffic camera mounted on the wall across from the entrance to the parking garage. This bit here starts at three twenty-two A.M."

We watched an empty stretch of brick wall for a few seconds and then there was movement as a man walked purposefully along the street. He wore jeans, gloves, and a dark hoodie pulled up and zippered so that none of his face was visible. The man stopped, looked up and down the street, then removed two small cans of spray paint from his pockets and sprayed the wall. He wrote a word in black ink, overlaid it with a red number, and then used the red paint to capture it all inside a circle.

"Son of a bitch!" I said. Beside me I heard Benson Childe fairly snarl; most of the others gasped.

It was the logo of the Seven Kings.

Interlude Three

The Seven Kings
December 17, 1:37 P.M. EST

The wall was filled with life. Floor to ceiling, wall to wall, images of people in all their colors and costumes were animated by individual urgencies and passions. Newsreaders and statesmen, talk-show hosts and market forecasters, media experts and the man on the street. A hundred flat-screen OLED monitors brought every aspect of the crisis into the chamber. The seven men who sat on the ornate high-backed chairs were silent. The seven others—five men and two women—who sat beside them in less ostentatious chairs were equally silent. The voices that filled the room spoke from Wisdom Audio speakers, their many languages and dialects blending and swirling in the soft shadows of the chamber. A Tower of Babel, chatter and noise, and yet all of it saying the same thing. Everyone, on every screen, was absorbed in the event. The whole world shared this moment.

The Royal London Hospital was gone. As the fourteen silent people watched, the last stubborn wall yielded to the fiery Mephistophelean fingers. The foundation blocks, blackened from hours of inferno heat, cracked to hot ash, and the tower canted sideways. As it crashed down, imps and demons of pure flame capered in the clouds of smoke that billowed up.

That was how the King of Plagues saw it from his place at the table. Fire and heat. Melting flesh and screams from within a world of burning torment. He closed his eyes and felt an almost orgasmic rush.

On the screens, the whole world paused in horror, as if there had been some hope built into the mortar of that last corner of the old building. As if its resistance somehow meant that the whole event was not comprehensive, that it was poised to occur rather than already seared into today's page of history. But as it bowed in inevitable defeat, the world's voices coughed out a collective and broken sigh.

Acceptance is a terrible, terrible thing.

Each screen showed the thick pall of oily black smoke that erupted from the burning building. It was so dense that it blotted out the sky and turned day into night.

There was another moment of silence as the jackals of the media took a breath. Not in reverence, but in order to begin a fresh tirade that would be equal parts hysteria, greed for ratings or copies sold, and mindless chatter to fill airtime until someone fed them something of substance to report.

He turned to his fellow Kings. Three to his left, three to his right. He looked at the Conscience who sat beside each King. Every King and every Conscience smiled.

The King of Plagues recited a passage from Exodus, changing it only slightly to suit the moment: " 'And the Lord said unto Moses, stretch out thine hand toward heaven, that there may be darkness over the land, even darkness which may be felt.'"

Into the silence, the King of Plagues said, "Beautiful."

"Beautiful," they all agreed.

And truly, to each of them, it was.

Interlude Four

Four Months Ago
Nouveau Visage Center for Cosmetic Surgery
Beverly Hills, California

The Burned Man had a hundred names in a hundred places around the world. His own name had been left behind when he had been forced into hiding, and over the last eight weeks he'd changed names weekly, often daily, relying on identities that had been carefully put in place over fifteen years. He had millions of dollars in numbered accounts, and safe-deposit boxes in forty countries filled with cash, jewels, and bearer bonds. As long as he was never identified he could remain free and live well for the rest of his life, and he was still a relatively young man. He had been forced to leave behind a fortune worth many billions, and a name that had been on short lists for the Nobel Prize and a knighthood.

Now . . . ? His downfall had come through no fault of his own but through betrayal, and since then he had become infinitely careful. And infinitely bitter. When his name was mentioned these days, it was always accompanied by words like "terrorist," "mass murderer," and "most wanted."

Escaping with his life had been immensely difficult,

and even his injuries were mild compared to what they might have been. He knew that he should be grateful to be alive and free and rich.

He was also a very careful man. Before his accident, it would have amused him to know that the authorities were looking for him in all the wrong places. Now it was a simple fact of life, the result of the careful planning that would have to be routine forever.

He felt no guilt for what he had done. When the pain from the surgeries flared, or the memories of his flesh melting as he struggled to escape the explosion, the Burned Man vented his anger by wishing he had done more harm. When he unwrapped his bandages and stared into a mirror at the ruin of a face that had once been on the covers of over five hundred magazines worldwide, from *Forbes* to *National Geographic,* his anger became an almost physical force—a burning ball of hatred that he wished he could spit out at the world.

The pills and the booze and the plastic surgeries helped, but only in the way that morphine helps to hide the pain of a cancer but does not remove the tumor. They did not take away the deep loss and sense of betrayal that hung burning in his mind every minute of every day.

He lay on a chaise lounge by the pool in the recovery pavilion of Nouveau Visage, the most exclusive, confidential, and expensive center for cosmetic and reconstructive surgery in the United States. Even after weeks, much of his face was still wrapped in surgical dressings, as were the tips of his fingers. A tall glass of sparkling water garnished with cherries and mint leaves sat sweating on a nearby table, and movie stars in robes and bikinis lounged around him. Guests almost never spoke to one another. It was part of the mystique of "we were never here" that made the place so exclusive. Even the invoices sent by the billing department were in code so no secretary or IRS agent could sell secrets to the tabloids. The items on the Burned Man's bills were for personal training, spiritual counseling, and financial advising. There was no trail to follow.

He sipped his drink, wincing only a little at the effort.

The Burned Man wondered if he was becoming addicted to surgery, a phenomenon he knew inspired many of his fellow inmates to return here at least twice a year without really needing to. Since he had checked in, the doctors from this facility—and specialists he'd paid exorbitant amounts to have flown in—had repaired the burns, done skin grafts, reshaped his ears, performed a complete rhinoplasty, augmented his chin, reassigned fat to give his body a new shape, and even transplanted a new eye to replace the one that had been boiled in his head during a geothermal explosion. When the bandages came off and the surgical bruises healed he would be a totally new man. A Swiss surgeon even had replotted the whorls and loops of his fingerprints using a radical new procedure that cost $1 million per finger. The downside was that it would have to be repeated every two years, but that was a small price to pay for his freedom. As long as he was careful not to leave DNA where it would come to the attention of the authorities it was likely he would never be identified and never be caught.

The tissue grafts and the new eye had been provided by his friend and former lover Hecate Jakoby, and they were a perfect match to his own. They should be— Hecate was one of the world's leading genetic designers and she had grown them especially for him in case of just such an emergency. Hecate had done the same for the Burned Man's companion, who sprawled on the adjoining lounger reading an L. A. Banks novel and sipping a Bloody Mary.

"May I freshen your drink, sir?" asked the pretty nurse, and when the Burned Man nodded she bent and retrieved his glass, giving him a generous and deliberate view of her cleavage. The nurses had a private bet that the Burned Man was one of the British royals and all wanted to bag a duke or a lord.

The Burned Man admired the view and gave the nurse as much of a smile as his bruises and bandages would allow. His good eye twinkled and his lips and teeth were perfect.

"Lovely girl," said the Burned Man once she was gone.

"She's a cow with fake tits," murmured the other without looking up from the page.

"I'd like to shag her, not marry her—," the Burned Man began, but a cell chirped softly on the table between the loungers. His companion picked it up, flipped it open, and said, "Hello?" with complete disinterest and maximum boredom.

"I want to play a game," said the voice at the other end.

The companion stiffened, which the Burned Man caught. They bent their heads together to listen.

"Who is calling?" said the companion in a banal secretary's voice that was entirely unlike his own.

"That isn't the response we agreed upon. I'll hang up in five seconds."

The Burned Man and his companion shared a look that was equal parts wariness, surprise, and intrigue. There was no one else within earshot, and the noise from the artificial waterfall was an excellent sound blocker. The Burned Man nodded.

"Very well. What game would you like to play?"

"Horse racing."

Horse racing. The Sport of *Kings*. Sweet Jesus.

Toys looked like he wanted to run, but the Burned Man smiled and took the phone. "Assure me that this is a secure line."

"It's secure, Sebastian." The man had a lot of Boston in his vowels.

"I don't know that name," the Burned Man lied. "Why are you calling me?"

"First, tell me how you are. I've heard some alarming reports. Sebastian Gault—third most wanted man on eighteen international police lists."

"Fourth," Sebastian corrected.

"Third. Janos Smitrovitch had a heart attack in his hot tub last night."

"Third then. Thanks for sharing. Now please bugger off—"

"Ah, c'mon . . . be civil for Christ's sake. Can't you squeeze out enough enthusiasm to shoot the breeze with an old friend? At least tell me how you are."

Sebastian Gault—the Burned Man—sighed. "Oh, I'm just peachy. I feel like a new man," he said dryly.

Speaking hurt less this week than it did last and the physical therapy had gone a long way to restoring the mobility of his jaw and neck muscles, but the discomfort was always there. The doctors said that some pain might linger forever. Gault was learning the skill of eating his pain. Each bite made him more bitter and less forgiving.

"And Toys?"

Gault turned an inch toward his companion. Toys smiled.

"The same."

"He still listen in on all your calls?"

"Yes," said Toys. "Someone has to weed out the cranks and bill collectors."

The American laughed. "Thank god you haven't changed. The world would be a much dimmer place."

Gault cut in irritably, "What's this about?"

"Ah . . . it's about destiny, my friend."

"Whose?"

"Why, yours, of course. This is a big day for you guys."

"No, it isn't. Today we plan to have seaweed wraps and then I think we'll each get a massage. That's as much destiny as I want, thank you very much."

"I doubt that's true. What happened to your dreams of empire? I remember you telling me how you planned to make a king's fortune, how you were going to reshape the world by forcing the U.S. out of the Middle East in a way that would put tens of billions in your pocket."

"It was hundreds of billions," Gault said with a touch of frost, "and if you read the papers you'll know that things didn't quite work out as planned."

"Yes, but we are so impressed by the scope and subtlety of your plan. It should have worked. It would have, had you placed less stock in true believers and more in practical cynics like Toys."

Toys leaned back and gave his friend a charming eyelid-fluttering smile.

Gault covered the phone and hissed at Toys, "Tell me, 'I told you so,' again and I'll smother you in your sleep."

Toys mimed zipping his mouth shut, but his smile persisted.

Into the phone Gault said, "Tell me again why we're having this conversation? And try for once not to be so sodding cryptic. And . . . who is this 'we' you're referring to? Or has the Dragon Lady gotten back into the game?"

"Ha! I'll tell her you called her that. She's killed for less. We've both seen her do it."

"The only excuse your mother needs for killing someone is that the day ends in a *y*. She's the most lethal bitch I ever met."

"But you love her."

"Of course," conceded Gault, which was true enough. Right around the time Gault first made the cover of *The Lancet*, Eris had begun summoning him to wherever she was staying for long weekends filled with every kind of sybaritic excess. Although Eris was twenty years older than Gault, her sexual appetites were more ferocious than his, and that was saying quite a lot. Even Gault's late, lamented Amirah—that treacherous witch who was the reason he was swathed in surgical wraps—was less of a bedroom predator than the American's mother. More than once Gault had thought about marrying Eris. If she'd been younger or, perhaps, saner, he might have. Even so, the memories of being the fly in her erotic webs were so potent that he felt a serious stirring in his loins.

He said, "How could I not?"

The American laughed again. He had a bray of a laugh that came from deep in his chest.

"Tell me what this is about," Gault prompted.

"I'll do better than that, Sebastian. We'll show you. Get dressed and pack your stuff. I'll have a car outside in twenty minutes."

"You don't even know where I am."

"Of course I do," said the man. "Nouveau Visage . . . in the pool area. You're on the fifth chaise lounge; Toys is on the sixth. Oh . . . and don't bother with the fresh glass of sparkling water the nurse is bringing. They're charging you for Bling H20, but it's only Perrier."

He disconnected.

Gault sat there, letting his body pretend a posture of relaxation while his good eye cut right and left around the pool area. Beside him, Toys clicked his tongue.

"Well, well," Toys said softly. "That's unnerving."

"Son of a bitch."

"Trite as it sounds to say it—especially coming from me—I feel violated."

"Everyone who meets that son of a bitch feels violated," Gault said. "And for good reason."

They looked around, making it casual, faking some conversation and genial laughter, but neither of them could spot the spy or spy camera. It made Gault itch all over.

Still . . .

"Why did he call? How did he know where we were?"

" 'We,' " Toys echoed.

"We," Gault agreed. He stood up. "Let's go back to our suite," he suggested.

"To search it?"asked Toys.

"No," said Sebastian Gault. "To pack."

Chapter Eleven

Barrier Headquarters
London, England
December 17, 1:50 P.M. GMT

"Who the bloody hell are the Seven Kings?" Detective Chief Inspector Martin Aylrod looked at the screen and then at me as if this was somehow my fault.

However, Deirdre MacDonal turned to him in surprise. "Good God, Marty, don't you read *any* of the reports I send you? They're that terrorist organization the DMS and Barrier have been crossing swords with since—"

"Well," Childe interjected, "it's really just the DMS. We've only provided support, but this is the first evidence of them being here in the U.K."

"Which doesn't answer the questions of who they are," insisted Aylrod. "Christ, Benson, you look like you're about to pass a kidney stone."

I said, "We don't actually know *who* they are. In general terms they're a secret society supposedly modeled along the lines of the Illuminati."

"More like SPECTRE," muttered MacDonal. "A lot of James Bond supervillain nonsense."

"They're a bit more than that," Childe said dryly.

"What do you mean," demanded Welles.

I told them all about Deep Throat and the cryptic info he'd fed us. "Hard to tell if they're a genuine secret society or a criminal group using that as a PR campaign to make themselves appear ancient and powerful."

"They blew up a sodding hospital," snarled Aylrod. "That seems pretty effing powerful to me."

"Sure," I agreed neutrally, "but that's today's news. Until now they've been like Professor Moriarty—behind-the-scenes and supposedly tied to a lot of stuff, but really frigging hard to connect with any certainty. And they like using pop culture to build their mystique, so it's really hard to pin down anything clearcut about them. There's a ton of stuff about them on the Net, and a lot of conspiracy theorists have tied the Seven Kings to a zillion ancient groups and prophecies."

"What are their politics?" Welles asked.

"Your guess is as good as mine, sir. Deep Throat said that they're dedicated to chaos."

"'Chaos'?" Welles said dryly. "Could you be a bit more vague?"

I smiled and spread my hands.

Aylrod said, "And your lads have had run-ins with them?"

"Quite a few." I gave them the highlights. "Their street-level soldiers are called the Chosen. The odd thing is that the Kings have so far worked with extremist groups among the Shiites, Taliban, Al-Qaeda, and a Sunni group. Yes, I did say Sunni."

"So, they're opportunists," suggested Welles. "Working with whoever will work with them?"

"Or manipulating any group they can to further their own aims," I said.

"Clever," said Aylrod. "Have you managed to interview any of these 'Chosen'?"

"Sure, but these street-level guys are just that. They're members of isolated cells so far removed from the policy level that they genuinely don't know anything beyond a couple of words and names. Nothing that connects us to anything useful. So far we've been able to determine that the Chosen are the ground troops. There's a group that's a big step up from them called the Kingsmen. The DMS had one tussle with them, and they are very, very tough hombres."

"How tough?" asked Aylrod.

"Man for man they could hold their own against the SEALs or the SAS. Smart, resourceful, superb level of training, and they're equipped with the latest and the best gear."

"Who's training them?"

"Unknown."

"Any of them in custody?"

"So far none have been taken alive."

"Pity," said Welles.

"Yeah," I said. "We're anxious to have a meaningful chat with one of them."

"What else have you learned?"

"Not much. There's someone called the Spaniard who acts as a liaison between the street teams and the Kings. He's known to be utterly ruthless and to have a special love of torture with knives and edged weapons.

But that's all we have on him. Everyone we've heard of
who has run afoul of him is dead. I saw one of his victims. Not a pretty sight."

Aylrod said, "Any leads through the equipment they
use?"

"No. It's either Russian or Chinese made or stolen
American stuff. The street teams are more likely to
have AKs; the Kingsmen came at us with M4A1 car-
bines and a couple of HK416s. Those HKs are state-
of-the-art-Delta Force weapons."

Aylrod nodded gravely, then pointed to the screen.
"What happened after the logo was painted?"

"He walked away," said MacDonal. "The camera at
the corner caught him, but then he vanished. Looks like
he either entered the hospital or somehow slipped away
out of sight of the other cameras. We have someone
searching the camera feeds in an expanding grid to see
if he shows up anywhere else."

The Home Secretary nodded. "Assessment?"

MacDonal pursed her lips. It made her look like an
evil librarian. "The person in the video may or may not
have been part of this Seven Kings group. He could have
been a gangbanger given a few quid to paint that on the
wall."

"That was a grown man," Childe observed. "Not a
teenager."

"How can you tell?" asked Welles.

"General build and the way he walked. He was confident and careful, but not furtive."

I nodded. "And he's painted that logo before. He
wasn't tentative about it. He wasn't trying to figure
out what to write or how to write it. He did it as

quickly and smoothly as if he's done it plenty of times before."

"A gangbanger would be just as quick and smooth," MacDonal said.

"Sure," I agreed, "but as Mr. Childe pointed out, this was no kid."

Welles said, "Any clue as to why this group calls itself the 'Seven Kings'?"

Benson Childe shook his head. "We helped the DMS with the research on that, but so far we haven't struck gold. There are over three hundred thousand hits on that name on the Internet. A boat storage facility and a real estate developer of that name, both in Florida; the Seven Kings Relais hotel in Rome; a mystery novel called *The Brotherhood of the Seven Kings* published in 1899; a tomb of the Seven Kings in Andhra Pradesh, India; a punk rock band of that name; and even a town here in London."

"Where in London?" asked Welles.

"It is a suburban development in the borough of Redbridge, part of the Ilford post town. We have people out there, but so far that image has not been found on any walls."

"We'll send this out to all stations and departments," concluded Welles. "And I believe that we'll be using Captain Ledger as an advisor. He's asked to be part of the hospital investigation and I think that would be a wise choice. Moving on. What do we know about the actual fire?"

"The fire is still too hot for a proper analysis," said a frail-looking man with watery brown eyes who sat next to Childe. Unlike the others, he hadn't given me his card. "But from gasses collected at the site the fire investigators have verified the presence of nitrates, and in great quantities. This was definitely a bomb. Or, more precisely, several."

"How many, Darius?" asked Welles, and that fast I knew who the frail man was. Darius Oswalt, Director General of MI5. I knew him by name and reputation, but the mousy physique didn't match the legends I'd heard. I expected a Daniel Craig type, not someone who looked like a low-level chartered accountant.

Oswalt spread his hands. "We've looked at the CCTV feeds from the moments leading up to the explosion. Witness reports vary between four and nine blasts. However, we estimate that there were fourteen."

"Fourteen?" gasped Welles.

"No one reported that," said Aylrod.

"Not surprising," said Oswalt. "But the CCTV images of Whitechapel Road show fire erupting from multiple points when the 'first' blast happened. We believe that all of the bombs had been set to detonate at the same time and were positioned to do the greatest possible structural damage. Considering how much of the complex has already collapsed, I think it's a safe bet that many of the charges did, in fact, simultaneously detonate. As for the mistiming? There are always some x-factors when it comes to the wiring and setting of the digital timers. The blasts all happened within four seconds of each other, though, so it's as close as may be. How the terrorists managed to smuggle fourteen bombs, give or take, into a building with moderately good security—well, that's the real question, isn't it?" He paused and from the look on his face it was clear that he had a bomb of his own to drop. "Based on the CCTV footage, we can make a pretty good guess as to the time the perpetrators intended all of the bombs to go off."

"What time?" I asked, and everyone leaned forward, caught by Oswalt's grave tone.

The MI5 man sucked his teeth for a moment, eyes introspective.

"According to CCTV," he said slowly, "the bombs detonated at precisely eleven minutes after nine this morning."

"Bloody hell," murmured Aylrod.

I closed my eyes for a moment and felt an old ache in my chest.

The bombs had gone off at 9:11.

Interlude Five

The State Correctional Institution at Graterford
Graterford, Pennsylvania
December 17, 1:51 P.M. EST

He sat in his cell and smiled at the shadows. The cockroaches were his friends. The spiders, too, and he read great mathematical truths in the subtle intricacies of their webs.

The guards feared him. The gangbangers never messed with him. They'd tried during his first week, but never again. Longtime inmates gave him space in the mess hall and would walk out of their way so as not to step on his shadow during afternoon exercise. The multitude of the Aryan Brotherhood mythologized him, ascribing biblical powers to him and endlessly arguing over hidden meanings in his most casual comments. Men had been shanked over such disputes. The Jamaican and Haitian convicts thought that he was some kind of white *bokor*. The Muslims thought that he was a demon. The madmen among the prison population thought he was a god. Or an angel. Men had been killed for speaking ill of him.

In truth, Nicodemus took no sides among the thirty-five hundred prisoners within the walls of Pennsylvania's largest maximum-security correctional facility. He would not allow himself to be tattooed with gang markings or colors. He did not deliberately sit with any one group or another. When asked why by a wide-eyed and fatuous young Latino fish, Nicodemus had closed his eyes and said, "Because I belong to all of His people."

"Whose people? God's? People say that you think you talk to God. Or maybe the Devil. But that's just bullshit, isn't it?"

Nicodemus merely smiled and did not answer. A week later Jesus Santiago was found dead in the laundry room. His tongue had been cut out and the numbers 12/17 were carved nine times into his flesh on his chest and back. The medical examiner concluded that Santiago had died from a heart attack. He was twenty-one years old and had no history of heart trouble.

Nicodemus told the prison psychiatrist that he knew nothing of the young man named Jesus Santiago. "No such person dwells within my mind," he said. "I cannot see him with my left eye, nor do I see him with my right."

"You were seen speaking with the boy," prodded the psychiatrist, Dr. Stankevičius.

"No," said Nicodemus. "I was not."

"A guard saw you."

"If he says so, then he is mistaken. Ask him again."

When the doctor asked Nicodemus if he knew the significance of the numbers 12/17, the little prisoner smiled. "Why ask a question to which you already know the answer?"

"I don't know the answer, Nicodemus. Why don't you tell me?"

"Time is not like a ribbon stretched from now until then. It is a pool in which we all float."

"I don't know what that means."

"Search your mind. Dive into that pool."

That was all that Nicodemus would say. His eyes lost their focus and he appeared to go into his own thoughts.

After the session was over, Dr. Stankevičius searched through the folder for the eyewitness report by the guard who had been walking the yard that day. The report was gone. The psychiatrist requested that the guard be brought into his office, but the officer in question had not reported for work that day. When Dr. Stankevičius pressed the matter, he learned that the guard had been transferred to a facility in Albion, at the extreme northwest corner of the state. No attempt to contact him either through the system or via personal telephone or e-mail was successful. Two weeks later the guard was fired for being drunk on duty and went home, put the barrel of his great-grandfather's old U.S. Cavalry revolver into his mouth, and blew off the top of his head. He left a suicide note written in tomato sauce on his bedroom wall. It read: *For sins known and unknown.*

That same week the file on the death of Jesus Santiago, the young Latino, vanished from Dr. Stankevičius's locked office. When the doctor attempted to locate the boy's record on the prison server, it was gone.

A month later, on the day of the devastation at the Royal London Hospital, Dr. Stankevičius had the guards bring Nicodemus into his office. The psychiatrist was sweating badly when he made that call.

Neither guard touched Nicodemus as they ushered him into the doctor's office, and though they both towered over the stick-thin little man, he exuded much more power than they did. Dr. Stankevičius noted that the guards kept their hands on their belts near their weapons.

Nicodemus stood in front of the desk, his hands loose at his sides, head slightly bowed so that he looked up under bony brows at the doctor. Nicodemus had eyes the color of toad skin—a complexity of dark greens and browns. His skin was sallow, his lips full, his teeth white and wet.

"Have a seat," offered Dr. Stankevičius. He could hear the tremble in his own voice.

"I thank you," Nicodemus said in the oddly formal way he had. A guard pushed a chair in front of the desk and the prisoner sat. He leaned back, folded his long-fingered hands in his lap, and waited. His eyes never left the doctor's face, and Nicodemus's lips constantly writhed in a small smile that came and went, came and went.

"Do you know why I asked you to visit me today?" began the doctor.

"Do you?"

"What is that supposed to mean?"

"It means what it wants to mean, sir. We each derive our own meaning from life as we fly through the moments."

"Are you aware of what has happened today?"

"I am aware of many things that have happened today, Doctor. Saints and sinners whisper to me in my sleep. Dumas speaks truth to me in my right ear and Gesmas tells only lies to my left ear. Please be specific."

Stankevičius did not recognize the two names Nicodemus had mentioned, but he wrote them down. Then he leaned forward. "Jesus Santiago, the boy who was killed . . . the numbers twelve/seventeen were cut into his skin."

Nicodemus said nothing.

"Why do you think someone did that?"

Nothing.

"Did you do that?"

"No, sir, I laid not a hand on that child. Anyone who says that I did is a liar in the eyes of the Goddess and will be judged accordingly." '

Stankevičius wrote down "goddess" but did not comment.

"Did you arrange to have it done?"

"What people do is theirs to explain or justify."

"Do you know who did it?"

No answer.

"Why 'twelve/seventeen'? Why those numbers?"

Nicodemus said nothing.

"Do you know what today's date is?"

"Time is a pool, Doctor. Today is every day."

"Please answer the question. Do you know what today's date is?"

"Yes," he answered, his writhing lips twisting as if fighting to contain a laugh. "As do you."

Dr. Stankevičius stared at him. He licked his lips. They were dry and salty. He knew that he should end this line of conversation right now and call the warden, but he felt compelled to talk to this man.

"Did you have advance knowledge of what was going to happen today?"

Nicodemus beamed. "I am but a voice in the wilderness crying, 'Make straight the path.' I am neither the right hand of the Goddess nor her left hand. I am a leaf blown by her holy breath."

The psychiatrist opened his mouth to ask about which goddess the prisoner referred to, but Nicodemus continued. "This is an important and blessed day in the history of our broken little world. Grace is bestowed upon those who witness such events. We need to lift up our voices and rejoice that we are living in such times as these. Future generations will call these biblical times, for with every breath we are writing the scriptures of a newer testament. The Third Testament that chronicles a new covenant with our Lord."

"You mention a 'goddess' and you mention the Lord. Would you care to explain that to me, Nicodemus?"

The prisoner laughed. It was a disjointed, creaking laughter that rose in rusted spasms from deep in his chest. The sound of it chilled the doctor to his marrow.

"The Goddess has heard the call of seven regal voices and has awakened," Nicodemus said softly. "She is coming. Not in judgment, Doctor, but to stir the winds of chaos with her hot breath."

"How do you know this?" asked the doctor.

"Because I am not here," said Nicodemus. "I am the fire salamander that coils and writhes in the embers at the Goddess's feet."

He did not say another word, but his eyes burned with a weird inner light that Dr. Stankevičius could not look into for more than a few seconds. After several fruitless attempts to get more information from the prisoner, the doctor waved to the guards to have Nicodemus taken back to his cell.

When he was alone, Stankevičius pulled a handful of tissues from the box on his desktop and used them to mop the sweat from his face. He tried to laugh it off, to dismiss the strangeness of the moment as a side effect of the terrible tragedy in England that was rocking the whole world. His own laugh was brief and fragile, and it crumbled into dust on his lips.

He sat at his desk for several minutes, dabbing at his forehead, staring at the chair in which the prisoner had sat. The echo of that laugh seemed to linger in the air like the smell of a rat that had died behind the baseboards. Stankevičius had been a prison psychiatrist for eleven years, and he had worked with every kind of convict from child rapists to serial murderers and, during his days as a psychiatric resident, had even sat in on one of Charles Manson's parole hearings. He was a clinician, a cynical and jaded man of science who believed that all forms of human corruption were products of bad mental wiring, chemical imbalances, or extreme influences during crucial developmental phases.

But now . . .

He licked his lips again and reached for the phone to

call the warden. He told him the bare facts, allowing the warden to draw his own inferences. When he replaced the receiver he continued to stare at the empty chair.

He believed—wholly and without a shred of uncertainty—that he had just encountered a phenomenon he had always considered to be a cultural myth, a label given to something by minds too unschooled to grasp the overall science of the human condition. Stankevičius had no religious beliefs, not even a whisper of agnosticism.

And yet . . . He was sure, beyond any doubt, that he had just met true evil.

Chapter Twelve

Barrier Headquarters
London, England
December 17, 2:22 P.M. GMT

This was turning into one bitch of a day. The images of the burning Hospital were now overlaid with an image of the mocking logo of the Seven Kings and the film loops of the towers crumbling into dust on a sunny New York day. I felt enormously out of place and thoroughly impotent. The bad guys were killing people and I was taking meetings.

Jesus.

I cut out of the conference as soon as I could. They let me use an empty office so I could make some calls.

Church answered on the third ring. He doesn't say anything when he answers a phone. You made the call, so it's on you to run with it.

"Seven Kings," I said. He made a soft sound. It might have been a sigh, but it sounded more like a growl.

"How sure are you?" he asked quietly.

"Very." I told him about the video. "Deep Throat let us down on this one."

"Yes," he said. "By the way, did you note the time of the explosion?"

"Yep. No way it's a coincidence."

"I don't believe in coincidences. Expect the newspapers to catch on soon."

"That's going to be a shitstorm, Boss. Is this a Kings/ Al-Qaeda operation? Are the Kings showing support for Uncle Osama? Or is this some attempt to hijack the 9/11 vibe to make this one even worse?"

"All good questions in need of answers. We've been in a holding pattern with the Kings for months."

"Balls," I growled. "This is how the military must feel after more than a decade trying to find bin Laden."

"Not all problems have quick solutions. The longer you're in this business, the more you'll come to know that."

He was right. Even though my first few missions with the DMS were insanely difficult and dangerous, they had ended quickly. A few days or a week tops. I guess it's because something has to be in motion and have gained traction before it comes onto the DMS radar, which means we usually have to fight the clock to keep the Big Bad from doing whatever it has cooked up. The Kings thing was different. It was huge but vague. It was like trying to guess the size and shape of the Empire State Building by standing four inches away from the wall at ground level. Perspective was all skewed.

"In the short term," Church said, "the authorities are going to have to work some spin on the 9/11 connection."

"Hate crimes," I said.

"If you've been reading the reports I've been sending you, then you'll be aware that there has been a marked increase in hate crimes here in the States for a couple of months now. Someone has been waging a very dangerous propaganda war on the Net."

"Yes, teacher. That's connected to the Internet thing. The Goddess and all that."

"All that, yes."

"Tied to the Seven Kings?"

"Unknown but likely. Recent posts have called her the Goddess of the *Chosen*."

"The Chosen, huh? Uh-oh. I must have missed that."

"Skimming your reports isn't the same thing as studying them."

I declined to share the comment that occurred to me. Instead, I said, "Have the Net postings mentioned the Kings? Or Kingsmen? Or the Spaniard?"

"Not so far. MindReader will flag any that do."

"I wish we knew more about the frigging Kings. I mean, kings of *what*? Did anything ever come out of my suggestion that it might be an alliance of the states that sponsor terrorism?"

"There are too many ways to build a list of only seven who want to harm the United States."

"It's always tough being the popular kid in school. What about something biblical? Wasn't there something about the Book of Revelations?"

"I think that's more likely, but there also are too many

ways to interpret the religious significance of the number seven, including something from the Book of Revelation," he corrected. "And yes, I think that's likely. Most scholars agree that the seven kings in Revelation are allegorical references to seven nations. The prophecy says that five of the kings are known, so the scholars contend that they are Babylon, Medo-Persia, Greece, Pagan Rome, and Papal Rome, or possibly Egypt, Assyria, Babylon, Medo-Persia, and Greece."

"Are you reading this off the Net?"

"No."

"So you just happen to have that memorized?"

"What's your point, Captain?"

"Nothing, Boss. But you're intensely weird."

"So I've been told. The fiery destruction we saw today certainly had an apocalyptic quality."

"You have any friends in the prophecy industry?"

"Funny," he said without humor. "I have some contacts who are experts in symbology, particularly as it applies to terrorism."

"MindReader come up with anything yet?" I asked.

"Nothing immediately useful."

"I thought that doohickey could find anything."

"One of these days I'll have Bug explain to you how computers work. You can't program it to look for 'bad guy' and expect it to cough out a name. MindReader looks for patterns, but you need the right search argument. It's all about choosing the right key words."

I grunted. "Yeah, yeah, I know. I'm just frustrated."

"That's a club with a large membership. What else have you got?"

I told him about the *Sea of Hope* discussion.

"I agree that it would be high profile," he said, "but enormously difficult. However, I'll pass along your concerns to the team overseeing security. In the meantime, we got something unusual from the warden of Graterford Prison. Homeland took his call and rerouted it to me."

"Graterford in Pennsylvania?"

"Yes. He told me about a dead prisoner with the numbers twelve/seventeen carved nine times into his skin, and a current inmate who seems to have unusual personal knowledge of the incident. A very strange character named Nicodemus."

"Nine times?"

"Yes."

"Any traces of an eleven?"

"Add the digits."

"Oh," I said. "Crap."

"I put a request into the Department of Corrections for Nicodemus's records, but that will take too long, so I directed Bug to hack the system. We should have everything within the hour. You can access the material from your laptop, but I'll have the highlights sent to your BlackBerry."

"Who is this fruitcake? He have any ties to terrorist groups?"

"None of record. But then again, not much is known about him prior to his arrest, which occurred in 1996. He was arrested at the scene of a multiple homicide in Willow Grove, Pennsylvania."

"Who'd he kill?"

"It's not entirely clear that he killed anyone, although he was convicted of multiple homicides. There are no eyewitnesses, so the case was built on strong circumstantial evidence, and he offered no defense."

In '96, a mother and her teenage daughter were about to enter Gifts of the Magi, a store that sold items for the Catholic market. Nativity scenes, pictures of Jesus, stuffed lambs, icons, that sort of thing. As the mother began pushing the door open she looked through the glass and saw a man standing a few feet inside. He was covered with blood. The mother saw several other people lying on the floor or slumped over the counter.

She pulled her daughter away and called the police from the Barnes & Noble in the same strip mall. When the first responders arrived, the man was still standing there. He made no attempt to flee or resist arrest.

There were four victims. The woman who owned the store, her disabled vet of a husband, and two customers. All of them had been stabbed repeatedly.

"Here's the challenging part," said Church. "All four victims were stabbed with the same knife, and from the wound profiles it's clear that it was a double-edged British commando dagger. However, no weapon was found at the scene. All of the area drains were checked, rooftops searched, trash picked through. There are no traces of blood outside the store, suggesting that the perpetrator never left the premises, and Nicodemus was drenched in blood. All of the experts agree that had he left the store he would have left a blood trail."

"Weird."

"Very."

"He could have handed the knife off to an accomplice who was not bloodied."

"Of course, but it was the first of a number of unusual elements associated with the case. You'll enjoy this."

"Okay . . . hit me."

"During the booking phase three separate police cameras malfunctioned. The fingerprint ten-card went missing. When his clothes were collected, bagged, and sent to the lab in Philadelphia, the police courier had a fender bender and at some point while he was arguing with the other driver his car was robbed. The only thing taken was the evidence bag. When they ran him through the system, his fingerprints were not in AFIS, and to-day when we ran them through the military fingerprint banks we got nothing; however, he was wearing a Ma-rine Corps Force Recon ring when he was arrested."

"Did they do DNA on him?"

"Yes, but no one can put their hands on the results. I'll get a court order to take a new cheek swab."

"Have Jerry Spencer take the swab when he gets back from London. He doesn't make procedural mistakes. He thinks the chain of evidence is holy writ."

"As is appropriate. Spencer's on the plane with me, by the way. He's sleeping and said that if you called I was not to wake him. He said that he needed sleep more than he needed to talk to you."

"What a guy." Jerry still resented my bullying him into foregoing early retirement from Washington PD and signing on to the DMS. Even though it was a big pay bump and nobody shot at him anymore, he would rather be entertaining trout on a quiet lake somewhere. "Eventually I'd like Jerry to look over all of the origi-nal evidence collection procedures from Willow Grove, the State Police, the Sheriff's Office, and the DOC. I know a lot of guys from that area. They don't make a lot of mistakes."

"No," Church agreed.

"Somebody should get eyes on this Nicodemus character. Can you reroute Rudy? Send him to Graterford?"

"He's sitting next to me and our plane just touched down at Heathrow; however, I can get him on the next outbound flight to Philadelphia."

I heard a brief muffled conversation as Church explained my suggestion to Rudy. Rudy's voice went up several octaves and he said something about me in gutter Spanish involving fornication with livestock. He's a mostly charming guy. Real class.

"He said he would be happy to," said Church.

"So I heard."

Ghost was looking at my phone with great interest and thumped his tail enthusiastically. He probably had heard Rudy's voice.

"As for the stateside phase of this," Church said, "I'm passing the ball to Aunt Sallie." Aunt Sallie was Church's second in command. I hadn't yet met her, but she and Church had history going back to the Cold War days and she was supposed to be a wild woman. "She'll coordinate with domestic agencies and keep a line open to our friends in NATO and INTERPOL."

"Okay, I'm heading back to Whitechapel to join the door-to-door of the neighborhood. Somebody may have seen something like delivery vans. They had to have brought a whole lot of explosives in. And I'll want to talk to staff members who weren't working today. Somebody has to know something."

"Good. I've also brought Hugo Vox in on this."

"Vox the T-Town guy?"

"Yes. I've asked him to put together his groups of consultants. He's built several think tanks of strategists, novelists, and screenwriters. Thriller novelists mostly. David Morrell, Gayle Lynds, Eric Van Lustbader, Martin Hanler—authors of that stripe. Their novels are built around extreme and devious plots and are usually so well thought out that some in our government have decried them as primers for terrorists."

"Yeah, I heard a lot of that after the Towers. People were making comparisons to *Black Sunday,* that book by the *Silence of the Lambs* guy."

"Thomas Harris. And, yes, there are striking similarities. The authors are vetted by Vox, of course. We're hoping the authors will come up with scenarios that we can use for programming MindReader's searches."

"Worth a shot. Maybe we'll get lucky."

"One of these days you'll have to tell me where you continue to find your optimism," he said, and disconnected.

Interlude Six

T-Town, Mount Baker, Washington State
Four Months Before the London Event

Dr. Circe O'Tree lived in Terror Town.

Her office was tucked away in a corner of a sprawling jumble of blockhouses built as extensions to what had been a ski chalet prior to 9/11. The office was never warm and she could hear gunfire all day long.

Circe spent most of her day on the Internet, cruising

Web sites and social networks, reading thousands of posts, making notes, updating lists, and fighting the onset of early cynicism. At twenty-eight she still believed it was possible to remain idealistic and optimistic about the better nature of the human species despite all of the evidence that filled her daily intake of information.

"Knock, knock," said a voice, and she turned to see her boss, Hugo Vox, standing in the doorway. He held two chunky ceramic mugs of steaming coffee and had a box of doughnuts tucked under his elbow. "You ready for a break?"

She pushed her laptop aside. "Like an hour ago. My eyes are falling out."

"You look as tired as I feel," said Vox as he handed her a mug. "I've been doing Webinars all day with the DOJ and there's only so much red tape I can eat before I want to shoot myself."

He hooked a visitor chair with his foot and dragged it in front of her desk, then lowered his bulk into it.

Hugo Vox was a big man, son and grandson of Boston policemen, though he did not wear a badge himself. His father had been wounded on the job and retired early to write novels, and the second one had become an international bestseller, spawning a Robert De Niro movie and a TV series that ran for six years. His next eleven novels had made the family rich. On the day the elder Vox, who had single-parented Hugo, won an Emmy for his show, he drove out to the estate of the mother of his son and proposed. They had been lovers in college, but her wealthy and aggressively classist parents had forced her to give up their baby. Now, as young forty-somethings (she had inherited millions after her parents—the com-

puter fortune Sandersons—died in a plane crash), they
settled down to form the family that fate and the class
system had once denied them. As a result, Hugo had
been able to afford Yale, and while still an undergrad-
uate he formed a staffing agency, specializing in security guards. He hired many of his father's retiree cop
friends. By the time Vox was out of grad school his
company was providing security for the United Nations
in New York and thirty other organizations with government ties.

By the time Vox was thirty he was a multimillion-
aire in his own right and his company, SecureOne,
had begun taking contracts from military bases, partly
to provide private security contractors and partly to
screen employees applying for positions in sensitive
areas. The catchphrase "vetted by Vox" identified
personnel who had passed SecureOne's ultrarigorous
screening process. He received a number of large military contracts to screen personnel for special operations and was soon putting the Vox seal of approval on
operators for Delta Force, the CIA, and similar covert
organizations.

The day after Vox's father died from lung cancer, the
planes hit the Towers. Vox was asked to head the team
that investigated the flight schools in which the Al-
Qaeda operatives had earned their pilot's licenses.
Vox's report put people in jail and it crushed several
companies whose standards for security were deemed
"criminally lax." If some people had previously wondered if Hugo Vox was too strict before 9/11, he was
thereafter seen as a role model.

In 2002 Vox created his first think tank. He reached

out to a select number of thriller writers—friends of his father—and brought them together to dream up the most dreadful and unstoppable kinds of carnage that human minds could concoct. Bombings, exotic bioweapons, covert takeovers, dirty bombs, plagues, and more. The authors gave him everything he wanted and then some, and Vox put it all in a report and brought it to the White House along with a proposal for a training camp in which the top counterterrorism teams in the United States and allied nations would run the scenarios over and over again until they had discovered or invented adequate responses.

The response from Homeland and the Oval Office was not exactly a blank check but close enough. Homeland leased land in Washington State and Vox bought the old White Trails Resort. Terror Town was born.

That was more than a decade ago, and now T-Town was the centerpiece for counter- and antiterrorism training. And now many key players in the War on Terror could boast of having been "vetted by Vox."

As online social networks flourished over the last few years, all manner of fringe and splinter groups had begun using resources like MySpace, Facebook, Twitter, and message boards for anonymous communication. Vox wanted someone to monitor these networks, someone with the credentials and the intelligence necessary to find even the most obscure clues that might reveal the presence of tangible threats. When Circe O'Tree's résumé had crossed his desk, Vox knew that he had found a perfect fit. Her reports had stopped a number of attacks and put some dangerous people in jail.

"So," Vox said, gesturing to her laptop with a jelly doughnut, "who's being scary today?"

"I've been tracking some spooky stuff with Israel and Islamic key words."

"Anti-Semitic stuff?"

"Not exactly. It's militant, but it *appears* to be more *pro*-Israel militancy. Let me read some of them." She opened a Word document and brought up a file. Circe wore half-glasses perched precariously on the end of her Irish nose. "Here's one. 'Why would God put a sword into the hand of Israel and forbid him to use it? It makes no sense to sit by while Jihad is waged against the Chosen People.' "

Vox grunted.

"And another one: 'As David did to Goliath shall Israel do to the giant of Islam.' " She adjusted her glasses. "On the surface these are anti-Islamic statements couched in pseudobiblical phrasing, but they have an—oh, I don't know—a sense of *meanness* about them. It doesn't feel like simple rants."

"Who's posting this stuff?"

"That's the thing; most of these are anonymous posts on Twitter, but they're from accounts started at places like cybercafes. They create an e-mail account, use that to open an account on a social network, and then either abandon it or log in from a different site. We've seen that kind of behavior before, Hugo. Remember all that 'war in heaven' and 'Armageddon in the shadows' stuff from a couple of years ago? This has the same feel. Careful and anonymous."

He grunted and nodded. "Yeah, sounds like it. Have you checked with our friends in the Bureau?"

"I did, and I got the usual 'we'll look into it' reply, which translates as 'ignore the rantings of the crazy lady.'"

Vox grinned. "How about Homeland?"

"Same thing, dammit." She cocked an eye at him. "Any chance we can bring it to the DMS? Maybe let MindReader—"

"Too soon," Vox said firmly. "Deacon's been very clear that he doesn't want to hear anything from us unless it's actionable."

"Okay." She felt deflated. "Let me collate what I found first. If I'm going to make a report even the DMS will accept, then I'll want to bring all of it."

"There's more?"

"Like this? Hundreds of postings, and thousands of places where these posts have been reposted and retweeted."

"Re*what*?"

"Tweeted. A post on Twitter is called a 'tweet.' When someone likes it and wants to pass it on, they 'retweet' it."

"Good God."

"I know it sounds silly, but Twitter has become the most powerful tool of business on the Net."

Vox smiled like a tolerant bear. He had coarse, thick features, a bulbous nose, and rubbery lips, but his smile was charming. "Tweets by terrorists. You can't say that this job isn't interesting, kiddo."

Circe nodded but did not smile. Unlike her boss, she was very beautiful, with dark eyes and foamy black curls; also unlike him, she seldom smiled. As much as genetics had been generous to her, life itself had not.

Less than a year ago her mother had been killed in a car accident, and Circe's younger sister had died in combat in Afghanistan the previous summer. She felt alone and adrift in the world, and except for a father she almost never saw, Circe had no family. T-Town had become her home and Hugo Vox had become a second father, but Circe was still adrift in the shadows of loss and grief.

"There's something else," she said, and pulled up another file. "Some key words have popped up in these postings. Not all of them, but enough of them to make me pay attention." She touched the screen and ran a plum fingernail down, pausing at different entries as she scrolled with her other hand. " 'Goddess,' or some variation of it, shows up in a lot of the entries. In the text, but more often in the usernames of the original poster or people reposting."

"Oh, Christ . . . not her again." Over the last few years various groups ranging from the CIA to the DMS had tracked a series of online comments from a person, or perhaps a group, called the Goddess of the Chosen. The posts were heaviest before and after catastrophic events. If there was a hurricane, a volcanic eruption, a terrorist bombing, or an airline disaster the Goddess would make a post claiming that the event had happened according to her will. So far the identity of the Goddess had not been established, and because she tended to comment on *all* disasters it was hard to qualify her political leanings. Vox rubbed his eyes tiredly. "Are you sure it's her?"

"Sure? No, but there are a lot of posts and most of them are using name variations: Goddessofthe7, Sacred-Goddess, Queen_of_All, which is a goddess reference;

and posts are using various names of goddesses from world myth. Demeter, Mazu, Mami Wata, Mórrígan, Nemain, Macha, Badb, and scores of others. Hundreds, really."

"How many posts have you been tracking?"

"Over forty thousand." When Vox's eyes bugged she said hastily, "Not personally—I'm using the Merlin pattern-search software from the DMS."

Vox grunted. "I didn't know Deacon let you have Merlin."

"He didn't. Grace did."

"Is it any good?"

"Well, it's not MindReader, but it's better than what we have."

"What else is popping up?"

Circe adjusted her glasses. "Some of the names may be randomly chosen from a grab bag of goddess names. But there are some that seem to have a political connection. Asherah, Anath, Astarte, and Ashima all show up as usernames. There is some evidence that that the Hebrew faith may have been polytheistic and those names are possible female counterparts of Yahweh. If that's true, then they were later removed as the culture became more male centric. Lilith also shows up. As does Ba'alat Gebal or Baaltis, who is essentially a pan-Semitic goddess. And Eris, Greek goddess of discord. That's 'Discordia' in Greek, which ties into the chaos concept. And—"

Vox held up his hands. "Okay, okay, I get the picture. Lots of goddess references. Tell me what you *think* about them. Is this the same 'goddess' you've been tracking?"

"Not sure yet. If so, Hugo, this is the first time the Goddess has made specific threats against Islam. Her usual rant is against what she frequently calls the 'sin of complacency.' Those are anarchical references supporting chaos as the natural path for spiritual growth."

"Which is horseshit."

"Well, arguing for an ongoing state of chaos is self-contradictory. But these new posts are clearly political, and they suggest that action should be taken, which gives them a whiff of militancy."

"A militant goddess cult? Is there precedent?"

"Not recently, but historically? Sure. There were goddess cults all over the world, and some of them have been quite violent."

Vox took a big bite of his doughnut and chewed noisily. "Okay. Write your report. Good work, kiddo. Keep at it." He pushed the box of doughnuts across the desk. "Keep the carbs. You earned 'em."

He heaved his bulk out of the guest chair and left, sketching a wave with his coffee cup.

Circe watched him go and then looked down at the documents on the screen. She chewed her lip for a moment, wrestling with some of the same doubts that had plagued her since she first noticed this pattern. Was it there? Or was the Merlin software simply too good at finding patterns in *everything*?

She bit a piece of a cinnamon doughnut, sipped her coffee, toggled over to Twitter, and dove back in.

Interlude Seven

Michael Hecht was not a Jew. None of his friends were Jews, and except for the accountant at the hardware store in which he worked part-time, no one he knew was Jewish. None of his uncles or grandparents had fought in Europe during World War II, and he had no connections to anyone who had been interned or murdered in the Nazi concentration camps. He had never been to Israel and did not know anyone who had. Michael Hecht did not even particularly understand politics. He had an I.Q. of 86 and had a C average in school. He never watched any debates and could not with any degree of certainty name anyone in state politics.

Michael Hecht also did not personally know any Muslims. None of them were among his friends, family, or co-workers. No Muslim had ever been rude to him, physically attacked him, done harm to people he knew or loved.

All of this information came out during Deputy Sheriff Jaden Glover's interview of Hecht following the twenty-two-year-old's arrest. Glover had known Michael all his life; he'd once dated Hecht's oldest sister, Maryanne.

"Why'd you do it?" Glover asked.

Hecht shrugged. He sat on a metal chair, his wrists cuffed to a D ring on the table. Another deputy stood by the door. Hecht had been Mirandized at the scene and again here in the station. He'd waived his rights both times.

"C'mon, Mike. You drove thirty-seven miles; you stopped to buy gasoline. You brought half a dozen of your mom's Mason jars with you. And rags. You even brought a lighter and you don't smoke. You had to have planned this."

Michael Hecht shrugged again. His face was smudged with soot and he had some tissue stuffed into his nostril to stem the bleeding from where the building caretaker, Kusef, had punched him.

"You went to all that trouble," said Glover, "and you put firebombs through all the windows. You burned the whole damn thing to the ground. What was in your head, boy? You upset 'cause Milt Ryerson's boy lost his leg in Iraq? This some kind of personal vendetta?"

Michael Hecht did not know what a vendetta was. "Shit, I didn't know Tommy lost his leg. Damn . . . that's fucked up."

Glover cut a look at the other deputy, who arched one eyebrow.

"You didn't know about Tom Ryerson?"

"Nah . . . I ain't seen him since graduation."

"Then why'd you set fire to the mosque?"

Hecht looked confused. "What's a mosque?"

"What's a— Judas priest, boy, that's what you just burned the hell down."

"It wasn't no mosque. It was a church. A raghead church."

"That's what a mosque is. A church for Muslims."

"Fucking ragheads."

"Do you have a reason to hate Muslims, Mike?"

"They're fucking sand niggers."

"You ever *met* a Muslim, Mike?"

Hecht looked away for a second. "No."

"Then why did you want to burn down their church?"

Hecht was silent for a long time, his face contorting as he tried to think it through.

"Come on, Mike . . . I'd like to help you here, but you got to be straight with me."

Michael Hecht leaned back and looked up at the ceiling. "Ah, man . . . I don't know. They're just fucking ragheads, y'know."

That was all they managed to get out of him. When the county detectives made a thorough search of Michael Hecht's house, they also searched his e-mail accounts and backtracked his Internet usage. Hecht was subscribed to hundreds of message boards. Over forty of them were devoted to the Goddess. The most recent posting Hecht had been to was the last in a series of linked messages on Twitter. The first one read: *The Chosen will not tolerate the impure touch of the Muslim.* The intervening posts escalated up from there in racial hatred, culminating with the one that had, apparently, sent Michael Hecht out into the night.

Fire purifies.

Michael Hecht was charged with one count of arson and fourteen counts of murder. His state-appointed defense attorney tried to build a case on diminished capacity, but by the time the matter went to trial the attorney knew that he was trying to sell a sympathy verdict in what had become a landmark hate crime case. The jury deliberated for fourteen minutes. Michael Hecht was convicted in a Powell County Kentucky court and sentenced to death. He remains on death row to this day.

IN NEW YORK City, a flaming whiskey bottle was thrown through the front window of the 117th Street mosque during evening prayers. Several congregants suffered minor burns, and only the swift and combined actions of Azada, a teenage girl, and three of her friends, who grabbed fire extinguishers, prevented loss of life.

No one was arrested for the crime; however, witnesses saw a black male, approximately thirty-five, wearing a business suit, running from the scene seconds after they heard the sound of the window breaking.

IN ATLANTA, GEORGIA, four white males and one Hispanic were arrested as they emerged from the Al-Farooq Masjid mosque on Fourteenth Street. The young men had emptied two five-gallon cans of gasoline inside the building and had stopped to light a rock that had been wrapped in a gas-soaked rag. Police cruisers, responding to a silent alarm triggered by the break-in, blocked the flight of the youths. All five were taken into custody. Fire department personnel worked with the caretakers of the mosque to clean up the building; however, early estimates were that it would cost forty thousand dollars to remove all traces of the gasoline and replace tapestries, books, and furniture damaged during the intrusion.

When detectives interviewed the boys, one of them admitted to having gotten the idea from the Internet. It was later determined that three of the five regularly followed forums and posts by the Goddess.

A week later the Catholic church attended by two of the boys was firebombed. No suspects have so far been identified.

Over the next month three mosques, two churches, and two synagogues were burned in Georgia.

WITHIN SIX HOURS of the Goddess's "Fire purifies" post, arson-based hate crimes directed at Muslims rose nearly 4 percent. At the end of six weeks, taking into account retaliatory attacks that included arson, drive-by shootings, rapes, beatings, and bomb scares, the incidence of anti-Muslim hate crimes rose 39 percent. Corresponding hate crimes directed at Jews rose 26 percent, and hate crimes directed at Christians of various colors and denominations rose 24 percent. The total number of victims directly connected to these crimes, according to the Department of Justice, numbered 43 dead, 175 wounded.

The day that CNN broke the story and showed those statistics, the Goddess, using the name Enyo, posted this comment on over sixty social networks:

I am well pleased.

Chapter Thirteen

Whitechapel, London
December 17, 2:41 P.M. GMT

Benson Childe arranged to provide me with a set of Barrier credentials that would be a master key to all levels of the investigation. He also authorized me to carry my weapon, which was useful, since I was already packing the Beretta 92F.

"A constable will meet you downstairs with the ID cards and other documents, and then he'll drive you back to the London, where you'll liaise with Detective Sergeant Rebekkah Owlstone. Her team is coordinating the door-to-door interviews of the neighborhood."

"Great."

We were in his office and he poured a cup of tea into a cardboard container and handed it to me. "Temperature's dropped out there. You'll need this if you're going to be pounding on doors."

I thanked him, and Ghost and I went out into the December blast.

JUST OUTSIDE I spotted three constables standing by the open door of a police car. They all turned toward me and the closest, a beefy guy, asked, "Are you Captain Ledger?"

I began to say "yes" when I heard a metallic sound and then a growl as Ghost suddenly bristled and stopped, his muscles instantly tense.

It took my brain a half second to process the sound I'd heard, because it was incongruous.

The beefy cop smiled at me and pointed a pistol at my face. The sound had been him quietly racking the slide.

He was almost laughing as he said, "Happy Christmas from the Seven—"

I threw the hot tea in his face. If you're going to ambush someone, don't make a speech first. It's a rookie mistake. He screamed as the scalding liquid struck him full in the eyes.

"Hit!" I bellowed to Ghost. He and I leaped forward together, me driving hands first into the left-hand cop and Ghost hitting the guy on the right like a white cannonball. Ghost growled deep in his chest and I saw teeth flash and then there were screams as he and the cop fell to the asphalt.

The guy I went for managed to bring his pistol up, but I'd planned for that and bashed his arm aside with my right as I drove the flat of my palm into his forehead. The gun exploded with a flat *crack!* My blow slammed him against the car, knocked his head all the way back, exposing his throat. I hammered his Adam's apple with both fists and he collapsed under me, gurgling wetly and trying to suck air through a crushed trachea.

I spun off him just as the window beside me exploded. Beef, half-blind and scalded, fired wildly in my direction, the bullets shattering windows and punching through the black paint of the police car. I rushed in and to one side, but he tracked me, probably only seeing shadows out of those eyes, but enough to swing the barrel toward my face. I came up outside his line of fire, took his gun hand in both of mine, and twisted sharply as I pivoted. In the dojo and in the movies the victim of a wristlock does a nice flip through the air. In the real world his wrist turns way too fast to act as a lever for his body, which means that the forearm bones explode inside his arm. His scream rose into the ultrasonic. I kicked Beef in the knee and as he canted sideways I kicked the other knee. He collapsed into a screaming pile of junk.

I tore my coat open and pulled my Beretta even while I dove for the front of the car. There were screams there, too, and the mean growl of a dog in mortal combat. I hit the hood on one hip and skidded across, landing on the far side and bringing the gun down.

"Off! Off!" I yelled, but Ghost was already backing off. His white muzzle was bright red with blood, most of it from the attacker's throat. Ghost looked at me with eyes that had gone from those of a pet and companion to those of a hunter-killer from ancient times. The primitive killer in me met the eyes of the predator wolf in him, and for a moment there was a shared awareness. Not adversaries. Members of a pack. The level of understanding that passed between us could never be taught.

"Back and down!"

He looked down at the dying man and growled low and evil . . . and then moved three steps away and sat.

There were shouts around us and I turned, sweeping the Beretta's barrel around. Another pair of cops and people in ordinary clothes. Whistles and yells.

I bellowed, "*Special agent!*"

I didn't know what else to say. Were these constables also assassins for the Kings? If so, the risk to innocent bystanders was about to jump off the scale.

The two cops drew their batons and closed on me in a nice flanking approach, yelling at me, ordering me to lay down my weapon. One of them was shouting into his shoulder mike.

Balls.

I pointed my gun at the closest of them.

"Freeze!" I barked. The sharp tone of voice and the

implacable presence of the gun slowed them from a run to a walk and then to frozen immobility.

To Ghost I snapped, "Set!" The command to get ready for a nonlethal takedown. Nonlethal as long as the guy didn't injure the dog, and then all bets were off.

"Freeze!" I yelled again. "These men are *not* police officers."

"That's Danny French!" snapped one of the cops, pointing to the man whose throat I'd crushed. "You murdering bastard!"

Crap. Okay, they *were* police officers. Now what?

The man I scalded moaned and sagged back. Dead or unconscious, I couldn't tell.

Ghost edged toward me to protect my flank. I could tell that the officers were going to try it. Gun and dog notwithstanding. For all they knew I was a mad cop killer.

"Stop!"

Benson Childe came running out of the building with a phalanx of armed Barrier personnel at his heels. I saw Deirdre MacDonal and Detective Chief Inspector Martin Aylrod following behind. Because they wore uniforms the street cops looked at them in confusion. The crowd was even more confused because guns were being pointed at cops and no one was pointing a gun at the crazy Yank with the dog.

Childe's men pushed the cops against the wall and frisked them. I didn't think they were involved—and was pretty sure they weren't—but I was in no mood to take stupid risks. I lowered my weapon and eased the hammer down. Childe didn't ask me to surrender it.

"Sit and watch," I said to Ghost, and he did just that.

The wolf was still there behind his eyes. I could feel the killer behind my own.

Childe leaned close to me. "For God's sake, Ledger, I *know* these men. What the bloody hell happened here?"

"Seven Kings," I said.

Chapter Fourteen

Over the Atlantic, Flight 7988
December 17, 2:42 P.M. GMT

Dr. Rudy Sanchez sat in his first-class seat and fumed. He disliked air travel at the best of times and definitely didn't want to be in the air when terrorist bombs were going off anywhere in the world. In the days following the attack on the World Trade Center, Sanchez had been one of a team of doctors who had descended on Ground Zero to help in any way they could. As a psychiatrist, Rudy saw firsthand the initial waves of post-event trauma that were the result of the attack. He saw the wound inflicted on the hearts, minds, and souls of the people working the site. The haunted eyes of police and firefighters who spent hours picking through the rubble to locate pieces of people who had been their friends or colleagues. The dreadful loss of confidence in the world in the eyes of the thousands of people who stood constant vigil at the fringes of the disaster. The strange blend of relief and guilt in the eyes of the survivors.

During the flight he'd listened to the constant buzz of frantic discussion aboard the United Airlines jet. Since 9/11, terrorism was part of everyday language. It had become so commonplace that jokes were made about terrorists. Books and movies had been made about it. And the thought that it was already that deeply enmeshed with ordinary life chilled Rudy to the bone.

And now he had the Nicodemus file and everything about this matter was unnerving. The file was strangely incomplete. There should have been hundreds of pages of it. Evaluations, transcripts, after-session notes, and a detailed record of the man's arrest, trial, and incarceration. Instead there were a few dozen pages of very general notes that might apply to any prisoner. Commonplace stuff. Worthless except for the very last set of handwritten notes taken a few hours ago by the prison psychiatrist, Dr. Stankevičius, and even they were cryptic. References to a "goddess" but without context to identify which goddess.

The overall thrust of Nicodemus's words had tended toward Judeo-Christian references, particularly with his reference to Dumas and Gesmas. They were variations on the spellings of Dismas and Gestas, the names of the two criminals crucified on either side of Jesus. But since those names were not in the standard Bible but in the highly apocryphal Gospel of Nicodemus, it seemed likely they were simply part of the overall religious delusion the prisoner had built up around himself. None of it tied back to either 9/11 or the London, at least as far as Rudy could determine. There was nothing else of substance in Stankevičius's notes.

Rudy was alone in first class. Since the bomb went off there had been a flood of seat cancellations. He used his secure access to open a video Web chat with Bug via satellite. A small box opened up, showing the face of the head of the DMS computer lab. Although his name was Jerome Taylor, even his own family called him Bug. He had been a computer hacker as a kid and came onto Mr. Church's radar when he tried to hack Homeland, believing that if he had the right access he could locate Osama bin Laden. Maj. Grace Courtland and Sgt. Gus Dietrich showed up at Taylor's door the following morning. He was offered a deal: work for the DMS or go to jail. When he accepted and was told about MindReader, he fell deeply and irrevocably in love.

"Hey, Doc!" he said brightly. The world could be in flames and Bug would still be jovial. Rudy wondered how Bug's mood would change if the Internet crashed.

"Bug," he said, "are you sure you sent me all of Nicodemus's records?"

"Yeah."

"Could you have missed something?"

"Could Oprah fit into Beyoncé's bikini?" He snorted and said, "Either they have a lot of his stuff stored on paper records or . . ."

"Or what?"

"Or someone's removed it."

"Can't MindReader tell if someone has been into the computer files? Doesn't it leave a handprint?"

"Footprint, and yes. Except there's no footprint here. From a computer standpoint nothing appears to be missing, and I've gone into the Willow Grove and Philadelphia PD databases, too. There's just nothing else there. We can't even verify his first name. If he has one."

"Hijo de puta."

"The fact that all of this is missing is deep magic. I'm

getting a Woodrow just thinking about how sexy this is, 'cause we're not talking about some pissant tapeworm. Someone's punked the system just like MindReader. And they've absconded with the treeware and—"

" 'Treeware'?"

"Paper. Actual we're-so-last-century printed documents. Somone in meatspace actually swiped the physical records as well. That's stuff *we* can do when we bring our A-game. No one else has anything like Mind-Reader, so I can't grok how they did this. Whoever he is, this guy's a freaking ghost."

Rudy disconnected and then called Mr. Church.

"Problem?" asked Church.

Rudy explained about the records. "Is it possible Bug missed something?"

"Bug doesn't make those kinds of mistakes."

"Then, that begs the uncomfortable question as to the possibility of a more sophisticated computer system than MindReader."

"Unlikely. It would have to have been designed and built entirely without a connection to the Internet or we'd have gotten a whiff of it. Or built with an operating system so different as to be unrecognizable as a computer to all other computers. It's doubtful something that exotic would be able to interface with the existing systems and networks."

"Deep Throat has a phone system that we can't understand or crack."

Church didn't comment.

"Coming at a time like this," said Rudy, "with terrorist activity ongoing, a mystery of this kind is more than a bit unsettling."

"Yes," Church agreed. From his tone of voice he might have been agreeing to a comment on the weather, but Rudy knew him as well as anyone at the Warehouse. There was an edge of strain in Church's calm voice.

Church disconnected and Rudy tapped keys to bring up the booking photos of Nicodemus. From the side he was unremarkable. Thin, slightly stooped, with a receding chin and thinning hair. An ordinary man. From the front, however, he was something . . . else. His eyes were a little too far apart, and the left was set higher and at a slight angle. His nose was thin and his mouth was a wet smile. Rudy enlarged the photo and stared into the man's eyes. They were cold and bottomless. Those eyes, and that smiling mouth, suggested a warped sensuality that Rudy found immensely distasteful, and a deep understanding of things that had no natural place in the human mind.

"Dios mio," Rudy murmured.

Interlude Eight

T-Town, Mount Baker, Washington State
Four Months Before the London Event

Circe O'Tree chewed on a plastic pen cap as she scrolled through the recent postings on Twitter. When she refreshed the page she had been watching, a new tweet popped up.

The Elders of Zion are not a myth. They live . . .
they wait. They will have justice.

She chewed her lip.

It was posted by one of the new accounts Circe was following. *Enyo.* Circe opened a browser and hit a saved link that took her to an online reference database of mythology. She typed in the name. The entry came up at once.

> *Enyo.*
>
> *A Greek goddess of war. She often accompanies Ares into battle. During the fall of Troy, Enyo inflicted horror and bloodshed alongside Phobos ("Fear") and Deimos ("Dread"), the sons of Ares. Enyo is responsible for orchestrating the destruction of cities.*

Circe frowned at the screen for a few seconds and then reached for the phone. Hugo Vox answered after four rings.

"Jesus Christ, woman, don't you *ever* sleep?" Vox growled, sounding like a sleepy bear.

Circe glanced at the clock and realized with a start that it was four twenty in the morning.

"I'm sorry, Hugo. . . . I completely lost track of the time."

"The White House had better be in flames," he said.

"I'm sorry," she said again, flustered and suddenly embarrassed by her impetuousness. "It can wait."

"No," he grumbled, "I'm awake now. What is it?"

She told him.

"Ah . . . Christ. Okay, I'll be right down."

While she waited, Circe toggled back to Twitter and refreshed the page. The comment had been retweeted

41 times. When she refreshed again a minute later there were 153. An enormous amount of posts, even for a social network as active as Twitter. Most of the posts were negative, decrying the comment and disputing the existence of the so-called Learned Elders of Zion. But more than a hundred posts offered support of the comment. Of those, only a third were goddess names. Circe did track-backs on many of them. Half were known agitators among the violent fringe of the conspiracy community. Some were frequent posters of anti-Islamic comments. The rest appeared to be ordinary people.

There were so many things about this that bothered her. First, the choice of a name that was clearly tied to violence and destruction. Over the last few weeks the Goddess had made a clear shift toward militancy, though choosing the name Enyo suggested a much more aggressive leap. The other troubling point was the Elders of Zion reference. Circe was sure she had something on that.

Ten minutes later Hugo Vox came into her office wearing gray T-Town sweats that were water stained. His hair had only been finger combed. He looked at her and then more pointedly at what she was wearing. The same blue skirt and blouse from yesterday.

"You didn't leave here all night, did you?"

"I got caught up—"

"Look, kiddo, while I admire the dedication you have for your job, you're young and pretty and smart and you should be out on dates on Friday nights . . . not locked up here with a computer and the kind of junk food *I* eat."

She made a face.

He sighed. "I know, I know . . . you don't like dating

guys in the service. How come, though? They're all good guys. Top of the line."

"And vetted by Vox," she said with a grin.

"Well . . . not vetted for dating you, but I could look into that."

"Thanks, Hugo, but I don't need a matchmaker. Besides, the guys here at T-Town pretty much ooze testosterone. They spend all day long shooting things and beating each other up. What would we talk about over dinner? Muzzle velocity and choke holds?"

"What about some of those bookworms you meet at signings? That literary agent of yours has a case of the hornies for you."

"Oh, please. He's a wiener."

Hugo grinned. "So . . . soldiers are too manly and the artsy crowd is too effete. Let me know when you find someone in the middle. I'm serious. You ever get off your ass and go out to have a real night off, I'll pay for dinner for both of you."

She mumbled something awkward and waved him to a chair. He was chuckling as he settled his bulk into it.

"Okay," he said, "you obviously found something. Thrill me."

She launched in, but before she was finished he held up a hand. " 'Elders of Zion'? What the hell's that?"

"The full name is *The Protocols of the Learned Elders of Zion,* which was supposedly the secret master plan by a group of Jews outlining how they would take over Europe and dominate the Christian world."

"How come I never heard about this?"

"Well, this is early-twentieth-century stuff. And it was proved to be a hoax."

"Then why the fuck am I not still sleeping in my god-damn bed?"

"Please, bear with me, Hugo. The *Protocols* were a piece of propaganda intended to implicate European Jews in a conspiracy that did not exist. Henry Ford, who was a notorious anti-Semite, used the *Protocols* in his campaign against Jews, and even Hitler trotted them out to support his racist insanity. Much of the material was directly plagiarized from writings of political satire to-tally unrelated to the Jews. But hatred of the Jews in early-twentieth-century Europe was stronger than com-mon sense; and later, following the establishment of Israel as a state, a renewed wave of anti-Zionism sparked new interest in the *Protocols* . . . and this hatred spread from Europe to the Middle East."

"So what?"

"The Goddess has just started posting about the Elders of Zion."

Hugo sat forward. "Okay, now you have my full attention."

"No one credible defended the authenticity of the *Protocols of the Elders of Zion*," said Circe, "So . . . why bring them up now? The Goddess's earlier militant remarks had been firmly directed at Islam on behalf of Israel. Maybe now she's trying to build a case that the *Protocols* are real."

"Yeah," Hugo said thoughtfully, "and that could get ugly, considering the lunkheads who gobble this shit up."

"Another possibility is that Enyo is someone *else* us-ing the same tactics as the Goddess in order to redirect anger back at Israel."

"Also potentially ugly." Hugo rubbed his eyes, then cocked his head at her. "Tell me straight, kiddo . . . rate this on a scale of one to ten, one being harmless freaks on the Net and ten being we scramble the DMS."

She chewed her lip some more. "Right now, I . . . I don't know. Maybe a five? But this is the kind of thing that can lead to real violence."

Vox snorted. "Violence against who? The Jews? The Muslims? I can't tell from this shit who the Goddess is really mad at."

"That's just it," Circe said. "Maybe it's both. Maybe she just wants to start a fight."

"To what end? She's got to be rooting for someone."

"Maybe not. Maybe she just wants to see things burn."

He peered suspiciously at her. "Isn't that a line from a Batman movie?"

Circe blushed. "It fits, though. Or it might fit. Some people groove on violence."

Vox grunted.

Circe said, "Look, remember last year, when the white supremacist group in Alabama started using message boards to make threats against Jews? There were a half-dozen synagogues torched."

"The people posting weren't the same ones who torched the temples. They were idiots following a bad idea."

"That's what I think we have here. Maybe the Goddess is a *movement* rather than a person. There are plenty of people who feed off that sort of thing. They don't actually have to be the ones throwing Molotov cocktails as long as they can watch the fire on TV."

Vox pursed his lips and considered. "You say you're at a five with this? When you get to a seven I'll give you assets; until then you're flying solo. But . . . update your Goddess report and send it to me. I'll make sure someone at Homeland pays attention to it."

"Thanks, Hugo."

"This is good work, kiddo. Even if this turns out to be nothing, this is very sharp stuff." He stood up and walked to the door, then half-turned. "You may not want to hear this—I know things are kind of weird between you two—but your dad will be proud of you."

Interlude Nine

McCullough, Crown Island
St. Lawrence River, Ontario, Canada
Four Months Ago

As promised, the limousine was waiting at the curb. A driver in traditional livery stood by the open door. A second man, identically dressed, stepped forward to take their bags. Both were slim, fit, and Korean.

Toys caught Gault's eye, flicked a glance at the driver, and then affected to scratch his ribs. Gault did not need the cue. He'd already seen the bulge of the driver's shoulder-rigged pistol. The other man, too. Nice cuts to their jackets, though. Most people would never have guessed either of the Koreans was armed.

Gault did not have a weapon. Toys, he knew, carried a knife in his left sleeve. Gault had seen his friend use that knife several times. Few surgeons were as precise or dispassionate.

Once upon a time Toys had been Gault's employee, a combination executive secretary, valet, and bodyguard, but that time had passed. Events had occurred that forever changed the dynamic of their relationship. Now they were more like brothers. Or fellow refugees. Gault was at least nominally the alpha of their two-man pack, but that position was held now by mutual consent rather than financial or personal power. In the same disaster that had scarred them both, Gault had discovered an emotional blind spot that had nearly proven fatal while Toys had demonstrated terrifying personal power.

They got into the car and settled back. The driver and the other man sat in the front with the Plexiglas screen closed. The limo was next year's model. Very expensive and nicely outfitted. Toys poked around and found unopened bottles of Cerén vodka—a superb El Salvadoran brand—and vermouth. Toys set about making martinis.

"Stirred, not shaken," he said as he handed one to Gault. It was a private joke. Although Toys loved watching the Bond movies—for eye candy of both genders—it irked him that Ian Fleming had his hero order his martinis to be made the wrong way. By shaking the mixture, the bartender created air bubbles that turned the martini cloudy. More crucially, shaking also caused the ice to release too much water, thereby bruising the flavor of the vodka. A perfect martini should be stirred gently for thirty seconds, then chilled properly and served stingingly dry and cold. Toys always made perfect martinis.

They sipped.

"What are the odds that this lovely car is bugged?" asked Toys. He said it in a normal tone of voice.

Gault smiled thinly. "I would be disappointed if it wasn't."

They settled back and sipped their drinks and said nothing else during the drive.

THE TWO KOREANS took them to a small airport and ushered them onto a private Gulfstream G550. Gault was impressed. He had planned to buy one of those for himself before his plans had gone to hell in Afghanistan. The sleek jet came with a $59.9 million price tag. It had a range of sixty-seven hundred miles and all sorts of lovely bells and whistles, and though it was designed to accommodate up to nineteen passengers in great comfort, Gault and Toys found themselves alone in the cabin.

The second Korean came in to attend to drinks and to take their orders for dinner, and when the food came it was superb. The first course was a crème brûlée of foie gras that they washed down with 1990 Cristal champagne, and that was followed by several small but delicious dishes, including tartar of Kobe beef with Imperial Beluga caviar and Belon oysters, and mousseline of *pattes rouges* crayfish with morel mushroom infusion. The accompanying wines—a 1985 Romanée-Conti, a '59 Château Mouton Rothschild, a '67 Château d'Yquem, and a '61 Château Palmer—inspired great respect from both of them.

"Well," said Toys as he sipped Hennessy Beauté du Siècle cognac, "I think we can submit a new definition for 'ostentatious.'"

"Mm. Are you complaining or commenting?"

Toys sloshed the deep-amber-colored liquid in his

glass. "This is two hundred thousand pounds a bottle. I'm not a cheap date, Sebastian, but they had me at the crème brûlée."

"You think they're trying to prove something to us?"

"Don't you?"

"Of course. And notice that we're both saying 'they.' Not 'he,'" Gault said. He sipped the cognac. It was delicious and it soothed the aches in his damaged flesh, but he would never have spent two hundred thousand on it. His devotion to brand names did not extend into mania.

"Well, to be fair," Toys said, "our American friend was always grandiose, but cultured . . . ? Not so much."

"And he has no excuse for it. He's new money, but he went to the very best schools."

"You're new money."

"Yes, but if you didn't know it you couldn't tell. You can tell with him. At a hundred paces, too. Table manners of a baboon, and he keeps his mouth open while chewing. And he has that thing where he speaks like a college professor one minute and a dockworker the next."

"You do know that he can hear everything we're saying."

Gault merely smiled.

"So," said Toys, rolling the cognac back and forth between his palms, "the question is 'why?'"

Gault shrugged. "A demonstration of conspicuous ostentation makes its own statement, don't you think? After all, no one *needs* to own a jet like this. There are plenty of less expensive aircraft that are more than opulent enough for the few hours their owners and their guests spend aboard them. To put it crudely, the price tag is a big 'fuck you' to anyone who can't afford it, and much more so to those who can almost afford it."

"Mmm," mused Toys. "Then tell me this, O mighty sage, why are we being treated to such luxury? He doesn't owe us a thing, not even sanctuary."

Gault merely shrugged. He was pretty sure he knew. He closed his eyes and remembered a sultry night a dozen years ago. He and Eris in a Belle Etoile suite at the Hotel Le Meurice in Paris. The two of them naked, covered with bites and scratches, the bed and nightstand wrecked, sheets torn and tangled, and the air heavy with the smell of wine, perfume, and sex.

"One day," she'd murmured to him as they lay together on the floor, their feet propped on the edge of the bed they'd fallen out of during their last deliciously ferocious bout of sex. And it was *sex*. No one could call what they did lovemaking. It was too violent and immediate and selfish for that, and it had served them each and satisfied them both. "One day you'll be a king, lovely boy."

Gault was propped on one elbow, his head resting in an open palm while he used his other hand to trace slow, meaningless symbols in the sweat between her heavy breasts.

"A king?" he mused, his voice still carrying some of the East End London of his youth. "No way that's possible, but I'd like a knighthood. That would be brilliant."

She shook her head. Her hair was snow-white, with subtle threads of lustrous brown sewn through it. Candlelight reflected in her eyes so that it looked like she was on fire inside.

"No, lovely boy. I have my eye on you. One of these days you'll be a king."

Sebastian laughed. "A king of what?"

"What would you like to be king of?"

"Not of bloody England. Too much nonsense and fluff."

"You could be the king of your own world," she said. "A king of the microscopic world of viruses and bacteria."

"Oh, very nice. Behold the leper king—"

"Shhhh!" Eris pressed a finger to his lips. "No. Not a king of the common cold or the king of cancer. One day I think you will be the King of Plagues."

He almost laughed again, but there was something about her tone when she said those words that stopped him. "The King of Plagues." Saying it as if it was a real title for an actual king. No mockery. This was not a joke to her.

Sebastian Gault had looked deep into her burning eyes. "Tell me," he had whispered.

And she told him. Not much, but enough. She broke off a delicious fragment of the truth and whispered it in his ear, and it was that seed, planted there in the shadows that smelled of their passion, that grew into Gault's dreams of empire. The many paths that led away from that moment in his life trailed away into infinite possibilities, but one—*that* one—was paved with gold.

The King of Plagues.

"And if I am a king," he whispered as he pulled her on top of him, "will you be my queen?"

"No," she breathed, her voice husky and dark, her

hand reaching down to guide him inside. "No . . . I will be your goddess."

Afterward, he had made love to her so hard that they both wept and ached all the next day. And each time an unwise step or movement speared pain through either of them, they remembered and laughed. It was not the sex that they remembered but the idea that had fueled it.

The King of Plagues.
And the Goddess.

THE FLIGHT WAS long and the crew did not inform them of their destination. From the duration and the angle of the sun, Gault judged that they were in southeastern Canada. Looking out of the porthole suggested east, and Gault was sure that they were still in America.

When the plane landed they were both relaxed and composed and accompanied the two Asians without comment or protest. The plane had set down at a large private airstrip by the water, and the boat ride across the river was quick and comfortable.

As the boat coasted to a gentle stop at the dock, Gault nudged Toys with his knee. Toys looked up to see a woman step out of the shade of the boathouse and into the bright sunlight. Even Toys, whose taste tended toward fashion models of both gender of the type once known as "heroin chic," lifted his eyebrows in appreciation. The woman was tall, slender, with snow-white hair that lifted and snapped in the breeze off the water. She wore skintight white sporting slacks and a bikini top that was little more than triangles of brightly colored

cloth. Her feet were bare and she wore silver jewelry at
throat, ears, fingers, toes, and navel. Sunlight flickered
around her as if the daylight kept reaching out with
quick and naughty touches. Her body was lithe and fit
and the only concession to makeup was a fierce red lipstick that was an immediate challenge.

"Well, well," murmured Toys. "Not exactly Snow
White, is she?"

"Good God," breathed Gault. "That's Eris."

"I thought you said Eris was his mother."

Gault laughed. "That *is* his mother."

Toys turned to Gault with a half smile, but he wasn't
joking. Then Toys took a second and longer look at the
woman as she walked toward them.

"If that's cosmetic surgery, I'll marry her doctor."

"No. Just bloody good genes and a refusal to age like
ordinary mortals. I don't know how old she is, but she
has to be in her sixties."

"You're killing my youth-centric sensibilities."

Gault laughed. As soon as the boat was tied to the
cleats, he leaped onto the dock and walked toward Eris
with his arms wide. She beamed at him like a happy
panther and hugged him fiercely, showering kisses
on him, even on the bandages. As Toys approached,
Gault gave him a look that said, *Well, she's not my
mother.*

Eris turned, graceful as a dancer, and gave Toys a
quick and frank appraisal. "Who is this delicious beast,
Sebastian?" she said in a husky voice that was English
with a soupçon of Boston. "Is this the clever one who's
been keeping you out of trouble all these years?"

"Sweetheart," Gault said, "meet Toys. Toys . . . this is

Evangeline Regina Isadora Sanderson. Lady Eris to the commoners and Goddess to those who really know her."

"Toys . . . mmm, now that's a name with real potential."

Toys took her hand and kissed it in a way that was at once elegant and filled with self-referential mockery. Eris gave him a wicked grin. At close quarters he could see that she was indeed older than she at first appeared, but no one would ever guess fifty, let alone mid-sixties. The bikini top was challenged to restrain abundance; her eyes were as green as a tropical sea and flecked with sparks of gold fire.

"Welcome to Crown Island," she purred.

"Thank you for having us," said Toys.

Eris eyed him up and down. "I haven't had you yet."

Then Eris hooked their arms so that they bookended her and led them toward the huge fortress of a building that was McCullough Castle.

Above them the sun was a furnace, and Gault wondered what was being forged in its heat.

GAULT AND TOYS were escorted to separate rooms.

"Divide and conquer?" Gault asked with a smile.

"Divide, yes, conquer—no, lovely boy. We want you to be comfortable. Travel is such a bore. Take a hot shower. Fresh clothes will be laid out. Someone will come to fetch you in an hour."

One of the two silent Koreans stepped up to Toys and led him down a side hall.

When they were alone, Gault took Eris's hand and led her a few steps away from the second servant.

"What's going on, love? This is weird even for you."

She laughed. "Mystery and intrigue is all the thing, lovely boy."

"I'm not the boy I once was," Gault said bitterly. He touched his bandages. "And I'm no longer 'lovely.'"

Eris shook her head. "Bruises will heal and you'll come to love your new face."

"I wasn't talking about my face," he said distantly.

"Oh, God, are we going to have a gloomy existential conversation in a drafty hallway?" But before Gault could reply, she kissed him lightly on the mouth. "Go and make yourself clean and pretty for me."

Chapter Fifteen

Breaking News: CNBC
December 17, 2:55 P.M. GMT

U.S. stock markets closed today after an apparent terrorist attack on the Royal London Hospital. The newly renovated hospital was completely destroyed, and early estimates number the dead at four thousand. That number is expected to climb.

Though the incident in London happened before the opening bell, trading went into full flight-to-safety mode as points were chopped off by panicking investors. Stock markets in Europe and Canada have also plunged.

SEC commissioner Mark David Epstein has not said when trading would resume.

Chapter Sixteen

The three assassins were, in fact, genuine London police constables. All three had clean records; none of them had known ties to extremist political or religious groups. In every way they were ordinary citizens, and that was the scariest part of it.

"I don't understand this," complained Benson Childe. "They're *good* men."

"My ass," I said.

We sat in his office on opposite sides of an open bottle of Clontarf single-malt Irish whiskey. Mac-Donal, Aylrod, and the others had just left to handle the aftershocks of the shooting and manage the spin control. Ghost slept under the table. I'd cleaned him up and calmed him, but he twitched in his sleep.

"The man you scalded with the tea is named Mick Jones. You broke nine of his bones. He's claimed that this was an unprovoked attack."

"He's a lying sack of shit," I said. "He was the one that said, 'Happy Christmas from the Seven Kings.' He was smiling when he said it. A happy guy doing a job he enjoyed. Probably one of the Chosen."

Childe frowned into his whiskey. "Well, as soon as he can be transported to a military hospital we'll see about opening him up. One of my lads, Spanton, will oversee the interrogation. He's a right bastard, too, so we should get something."

I wasn't chewed up with sympathy for the crooked cop.

Childe downed a heroic slug of whiskey and poured two fingers into the glass. "All this brings up ugly questions. How did the Kings know you were here for a meeting? Why do they want you dead? How were they able to corrupt three upstanding police constables? And what did they hope to accomplish by killing you? Understand, Captain, that while your DMS field record precedes you, I don't quite see why the Kings would target you above all others."

"Me, neither. I'm certainly not a key player in the Hospital-bombing investigation." I took a sip that was every bit as large as Childe's. I was fighting a bad case of the shakes. "I spoke with Church a few minutes ago and there haven't been any attempts on other DMS agents. Guess I hold the golden ticket in the Lunatic Lottery."

We sipped in silence. I wasn't sure how to read Childe. I knew Church liked and trusted him, but the Barrier director seemed decidedly chilly since the shooting. Granted, he knew the officers, but I wondered if the confusing nature of the incident made him doubt me.

Well . . . fuck him if he did.

He must have caught something in my expression, because he gave me a rueful smile. "We'll sort it all out, Captain. Here in the U.K. we have a longer history of dealing with terrorists and secret societies than your lot does. From Guy Fawkes to the bloody IRA. Half the time we never know what's really going on. We catch a few, kill a few, dismantle a splinter cell, but it's like cutting heads off a Hydra. Twice as many grow back and it's bloody impossible to say if we're doing any good."

"Better than doing nothing," I said.

He grunted and sipped. "It doesn't feel that way. It feels like all we're doing is pretending to maintain a shaky status quo while in reality things are slipping bit by bit into chaos."

I leaned forward and pushed the bottle away from him.

"Oh yes, very funny. That's not drink talking, Joe, and I'm not using this to wash down Prozac. I suppose it's a kind of battle fatigue. I've been in this for thirty-four years and I can't say with any certainty that I've won any wars. I've won my share of battles, but the war always seems to go on."

It was the first time he'd called me by my first name. A flag of truce? I finished off my whiskey and set the glass down.

"Before this happened I was going out to play cop. That still sounds like the best way to try and tackle this."

Childe looked at me. "After what just happened? Are you in any condition?"

It was a fair question. I'd fled to Europe because I didn't think I was in any condition to be part of this sort of thing. Or at least that's what I thought. Somehow the war always seems to find me.

"My vacation's over, Benson," I said. I clicked my tongue and Ghost instantly returned from whatever dark dreams were troubling him and was at my side. I bent and stroked his head.

Childe stood and offered his hand. "Stay safe."

I laughed, but I shook his hand.

We went outside into the cold. We were both hyper-vigilant, and though we saw nothing else the rest of the day, I could *feel* the eyes of the Seven Kings on me wherever I went.

Interlude Ten

T-Town, Mount Baker, Washington State
Three Months Before the London Event

Circe O'Tree perched on the edge of her chair and tried not to chew her lip as Hugo Vox read through the most recent version of what had come to be known as the "Goddess Report." Two or three times per page he reached into a ceramic bowl and took a handful of Gummi worms. He chewed steadily and noisily as he read, and except for the sound of shouts and gunfire from the counterterrorism range outside the room was quiet. The second hand on the Stars and Stripes clock on the wall seemed to crawl.

When he finished the last page he looked up expectantly. "This is incomplete. You got a lot of data here, kiddo, but I don't see any conclusions."

"That's what I wanted to talk to you about, Hugo. I don't know where to go with it. I just know that it's bad and it's getting worse."

He nibbled a Gummi worm and said nothing.

Circe took a breath and plunged in. "Ever since I started this I've been making connections and tracking patterns. The Goddess, the Elders of Zion, the covert and overt suggestions for violence . . . there's a lot of stuff here. The more the Goddess posts, the more the other Internet extremists pick up on it and repeat her comments, add to them, discuss them in chat rooms and on message boards. People are blogging about it, writing essays and magazine articles about it. Not just conspiracy theorists and shock journalists, either. And . . . it's spilling over into the real world."

She laid a copy of *The Grapevine* on his desk. The picture showed the fiery aftermath of a Pakistani mosque being destroyed by a bomb in a parcel that had been delivered a few minutes before prayers. Forty-three dead, eighty wounded. The headline read: *ISRAEL STRIKES BACK.*

Vox picked up the newspaper and sneered. "This is a rag. This is the same paper that printed Pat Robertson's comment that 9/11 was God showing displeasure at gays." He tossed it down on the desk. "I wouldn't wipe my ass with it."

She reached into her briefcase and brought out a stack of other newspapers and began stacking them on his desk one by one. *USA Today,* the *Arizona Republic,* the *Chicago Tribune,* the *San Jose Mercury,* and *The Fresno Bee.*

"Balls," he said.

"Every major newspaper has reported incidents that *could* be interpreted as hate crimes."

"Most of these papers retread each other's—"

She lifted a shopping bag that was filled with newspapers. "*Bahrain Post, Gulf Daily News, Cyprus Mail, Al-Ahram Weekly, Tehran Globe* . . . I could go on and on, Hugo. Want me to get the rest from my office?"

"Okay, okay, Circe, but we have to look beyond the

reportage. Have you established for certain that these crimes are related to the Goddess posts?"

"I don't know if it's even possible to prove that, but look at the timing." She unfolded a flowchart and spread it over the mountain range of papers. "See? The red line marks the first of the anti-Islam posts and here's the first of the *Protocols of Zion* posts. Now look at the blue line. Those are incidents of hate crimes. Look at the spikes."

"These are all hate crimes against Muslims?"

"No. Some are against Jews."

"*By* Muslims?"

"Not always. Some are from anti-Semitic and anti-Zionist groups composed of Christians and others, but—"

"So, we're seeing hate crimes go up, but they're not all specific to the message of the Goddess?"

"No, but—"

"This is supposition, Circe. I can surf the Net and build a case that the widespread popularity of Hello Kitty was responsible for the fall of the Nixon presidency." When she looked blank, he gave her a Cheshire cat grin. "Hello Kitty hit the U.S. in 1974, same year as Watergate. I bet I could do a flowchart and probably make a good enough case to get a book deal out of it."

"How do you *know* this stuff?"

He grinned and tapped his head. "I am filled with useless trivia. I'd clean the hell up on *Jeopardy!* Point is, kiddo, this data is interesting, but it still doesn't make your case."

"That's the thing, Hugo; with the Net it's almost impossible to collect hard, verifiable evidence. That's why groups like the Goddess *use* it."

"Say that's true, so how do we separate that out and give it more credence than the ten billion other equally well-documented conspiracy theories, lies, exaggerations, wishful thinking, and pure bullshit that comprise the World Wide goddamn Web?"

Circe sagged. "What are you saying, that we ignore it?"

Vox looked genuinely surprised. "Hell no! I really think you're on to something here, kiddo, but we're talking about making a case to the lunkheads in Washington who have an ironclad record for ignoring good leads and following bad ones."

"The DMS is different," she said.

"Sure, and if we take this to the DMS and we're wrong, D.C. will fry us. No one is supposed to bring *anything* to them unless it's verified to the highest possible probability, and right now that isn't how we can label this. Personal belief alone doesn't cut it." He took a breath. "In the meantime, what's your next step?"

She was momentarily flustered, then steadied herself with a breath. "I created a few e-mail accounts with goddess names and have posted responses phrased to coax a more definitive statement, but most of the posters are clearly not core to this. Unfortunately, I haven't yet gotten any responses that I can say are clearly from someone in the know."

"*If* someone even *is* in the know."

"If," she agreed reluctantly. "But I believe that the Goddess is real, and I believe that the group she represents poses a real threat."

"I hear you, but until we have facts we can't build a case for it being a clear and present—and therefore *actionable*—danger." He tossed the report onto the desk. "What do you suppose their motive is?"

"I don't know. 'Chaos' doesn't seem to be a profitable goal."

"I guess not." He tapped the report with a half-eaten Gummi worm. "You know, ever since you brought this to me I've been back and forth with the State Department, the FBI and CIA, and the Israelis. None of them think that this is coming from Israel. I mean, beyond the tension that's been going on since—oh, I don't know, Moses parted the fucking Red Sea, there isn't anyone in Israel who thinks Jews are involved in this at all."

She nodded. "The more I read the Goddess's Net postings the more I'm convinced they are designed to do the reverse of what they're saying, just like the *Protocols*. By pretending to support and justify Israeli aggression against Islam, they're actually trying to frame them as terrorists. The problem is . . . it might be working. Whether they blew up the mosque or not doesn't matter as long as the right people *think* they did."

"Which brings us back to the third-party possibility." He rubbed his eyes. "Keep on this. But maybe you can drop a bug in the ear of that British broad you're friends with."

"Grace Courtland?"

"Yeah. Get her take on it, but on the down low. Nothing official. If she thinks you have something, then I'll reach out to Mr. Church. But take it slow, kiddo. One step at a time."

Chapter Seventeen

Director Childe arranged to have me detailed to the Metropolitan Police unit working the neighborhood around the fire scene. When I explained that Ghost was, among other things, a bomb sniffer, that amped up my usefulness.

No official statement had been given about the three assassins, but rumors within the police department hinted that an American was involved and that the officers might be tied to a terrorist cell responsible for the London Hospital bombing. My name was not mentioned, and yet the constables I worked with treated me with distance and caution. Fair enough, because after what happened outside Barrier I didn't trust any of them, either.

Everyone in London was paranoid. Everyone had reason.

The search team to which I was attached was composed of more than three hundred officers and detectives, and a comprehensive door-to-door search was under way. Everyone was being interviewed.

First thing I did was visit the fire site. Jerry Spencer was already there when Ghost and I arrived. Jerry was in his fifties, with iron gray hair, an unsmiling face, and intensely dark eyes. His mouth wore a perpetual smile of disapproval and disappointment.

I held out my hand. "Jerry, great to see you. How was the flight?"

He eyed me like I was a side dish he hadn't ordered. "Joe," he said without inflection. He kept his hands in his pockets. Jerry looked down at my dog and grunted. Jerry didn't have any pets. I suspect he wasn't allowed to.

"Taking it back," I murmured as I lowered my hand.

"Heard they tried to make a run at you," he said.

"Yeah."

"Fuckers."

"Yeah," I agreed. I waited for him to say something else, maybe ask after my health and well-being. He started walking toward a pair of his assistants who were unpacking his gear from several large metal suitcases.

"Do we have anything yet?" I asked, falling into step beside him.

Jerry shrugged.

"And that means—?"

"It means fuck off until I call you and tell you I got something."

"Love you, too, man," I said, and clicked my tongue for Ghost. We left Jerry to it. Gloomy bastard.

I JOINED UP with the constables working the door-to-door. They partnered me with a very bright but also very young detective sergeant named Rebekkah Owlstone. She coordinated two dozen teams and together we met with thousands of residents; we asked tens of thousands of questions. We took names, dates, addresses, observations, speculations, rumors, unfounded accusations, political diatribes, opinions, and crackpot theories. What we didn't get was a solid lead of any kind. We kept at it through the rest of that terrible first day and straight through into the new day that dawned gray and bleak and devoid of promise. We were no further along than we had been the day before.

I called to check on the shooters, but so far the background checks hadn't popped up any leads.

We were chasing phantoms.

Interlude Eleven

The State Correctional Institution at Graterford
Graterford, Pennsylvania
December 18, 3:26 A.M. EST

Dr. Stankevičius sat upright behind his desk, his palms placed flat so that he could press against the blotter to keep his fingers from trembling. "You asked to see me, Nicodemus?"

Nicodemus stood between the towering guards, a man who was a dichotomy in flesh. His small stature and frail bones suggested weakness and vulnerability, and yet his personality and charisma were like a dark tower of steel and cold stone. He dominated the room and he hadn't yet spoken a single word.

"Please have a seat," said the doctor.

Nicodemus's lips writhed as he sat and there was the gleam of spittle at the corners of his mouth. "Thank you for taking time from your busy day, Doctor," he said softly.

"It is the middle of the night. What is it you wanted to see me about? Was there something you forgot to tell me yesterday?"

"I have had a dream."

"A dream?"

"Some would call it a vision." His eyes were half-hidden by the shadows cast by the bony overhang of his brow.

"What was the nature of this vision?"

"Revelatory. It is a time of great discovery, Doctor. The Imperial Eye has opened and the Eye sees what the Elders see, and it is well pleased. The Eye can see into the minds of the Elders and what it sees is deemed good."

"I—"

"Plagues will be visited upon the lands of Empire— and upon those who have broken faith with the Sons of Moses."

"What does all of this mean?"

"The voice you hear is mine, but the servant is a vessel through which the Goddess speaks for all to hear. It is the time for all who believe to rise and be counted. False prophets have been heard throughout the land, but paradise does not wait for the bringers of small fire. The true face of the All shines not on those who use the sickle to hew down the wheat staffs that grow in the field of the Goddess. The true face of the All shines upon those who have never strayed from the winding path that leads through the desert."

Dr. Stankevičius sighed and leaned back. "Nicodemus, I'm sorry but I'm not in the mood for this. You said that you had important information for me. If you have information regarding the murder of Jesus Santiago, then—"

Nicodemus suddenly leaned forward. The guards jumped in surprise and almost—almost—made a grab for him, but neither of them seemed capable or willing to lay hands upon the little man. Dr. Stankevičius recoiled from the wild look in Nicodemus's eyes. His eyes flared wide so that the whites could be seen all around the irises, but those irises seemed to have darkened from a mottled green-brown to a black as dark as midnight. It was a trick of the light, Stankevičius told himself.

A trick of the light.

"*They* are coming," whispered Nicodemus in a voice that was unrecognizable as his own and barely recognizable as human. It passed through the doctor's mind like a cold wind.

The room went still.

"How will you be judged when the Sons of the Goddess sit on their thrones? When the Elders reclaim what is theirs and the Goddess reaches out her dark and shining hand across the face of this world, will you stand with the wicked and be cast into everlasting perdition? Or . . . will you stand with the Chosen and be counted as a warrior of heaven?"

Stankevičius felt his skin crawl. When he exhaled he could see the vapor of his own breath. But that was impossible; the thermostat was permanently set at sixty-eight.

Nicodemus bent forward another inch so that now his eyes were completely hidden by the shadows of his pale, craggy brow.

"The Elders have appealed to the Goddess and she has sent her judgment."

"Wh-what judgment, Nicodemus?" stammered the doctor, his body suddenly wracked by a shiver. It was so cold in the room that his teeth hurt.

Nicodemus smiled so that his full lips were stretched thin over wet teeth. "She has sent Ten Plagues, just as the God sent Ten Plagues in His turn. The first was a rain of fire and ash that filled the streets of the new city. Woe to the children of the wicked that they did not listen, that their hearts were hardened as the Pharaoh's heart was hardened. But the Goddess did not harden the hearts of the wicked. Anyone who says that she did is a liar and blasphemer. The wicked need no help in hardening their own hearts. They are defiant in their iniquity."

"What are you talking about? What are these plagues?"

The guards edged away from him, their hands on the riot sticks hanging from belt loops. Neither of them looked at each other or to Dr. Stankevičius. Each was locked in his own private moment, each caught up in his own damaged reaction to this man.

Nicodemus sat straight, bringing his face down toward Dr. Stankevičius. He opened his eyes and for a moment—for a terrible single moment—his eyes were completely black. No iris, no sclera.

"Lo! And behold the rise of the Seven Kings. All shall fall before them!"

He blinked and his eyes were normal again.

A trick of the light, Dr. Stankevičius told himself. *Just a trick of that damned light.*

Nicodemus sat still and did not say another word.

After a few minutes Dr. Stankevičius ordered the guards to take Nicodemus back to his cell. When the door was closed and the sounds of their footsteps faded, Dr. Stankevičius rose and tottered toward his bathroom.

He stared for a long minute into his own bloodshot and haunted eyes. He sank to his knees as a wave of nausea slammed into him; then he flipped up the lip of the toilet and vomited into it. Again and again until his stomach churned and twisted on nothing.

Only a trick of the light.

Except that he was sure that it wasn't.

Chapter Eighteen

Whitechapel, London
December 18, 7:29 A.M. GMT

Next morning I caught two chilly hours' sleep in the back of a police car while Ghost kept watch, and then shambled to a pub for a late breakfast. Eggs, sausage, bacon, toast, and jam. I'm a big believer in the adage of eating breakfast like a king, lunch like a prince, and dinner like a pauper. Except that I tended to eat lunch and dinner like a king, too. That way there were plenty of leftovers for the mouth-on-legs that was Ghost.

I called Rudy, who was on the plane to America, and I woke him up. You'd never think that a civilized, cultured, and educated medical man like him could curse worse than Amy Winehouse on a bender.

"You kiss your mother with that mouth?"

"Where do you think I learned to curse?" he growled.

I'd met his mother and I could see his point.

"Why am I awake and talking to you?" he asked after a yawn so loud that I could hear his jaw pop over the cell phone.

"You hear about what happened yesterday?"

"Yes," he said, and that fast I could hear that he'd shifted gears. "Mr. Church said that you weren't injured. But . . . how are you feeling?"

"Paranoid, scared, angry, and frustrated."

"I can imagine," he said. "There's a lot of that going around these days."

"We're chasing phantoms."

"What?"

"Oh, it's just the feeling that keeps popping into my head. Trying to fight back against the Seven Kings is like trying to grab shadows. You can never put your hands on them."

"If I said, 'That's part of the spy game,' how much of a beating would you give me?"

I laughed. "Look, I called because I need to bang some ideas off of you before I bring them to Church."

"Sure," he said, and, "As you're so fond of saying, 'hit me.'"

I took a sip of coffee. "Okay, the way in which it was set up, the multiple bombs in key spots, suggests inside knowledge, and we're probably looking at someone in authority. Barrier estimates that the bombs had to be big, hundreds of kilos of C4 or something like it. The blast didn't have the signature of TNT, so we can probably rule out materials hijacked from a mining or demolition company. This is military grade, and that's very hard to come by."

"That's two points," Rudy observed. "The first being the access to the building and the probable authority to allow for materials to be brought in, or to cover up the fact that they've already been brought in. The second point being that the bombers had access to significant amounts of military-grade materials."

"Right. But on the first point, that suggests more than one person."

"Why?"

"Unless this was done in increments over time, it would take several people and some equipment to get all those explosives into the building. Hand trucks at least. And the materials would have to have been hidden, so maybe file cabinets filled with them. Or laundry hampers."

"File cabinets or hampers that no one cared to look in between the time they were brought in and the time the bombs went off," Rudy said. "That's not actually very hard for the right person to manage."

"Who would have that authority?"

"The hospital administrator and the first tier of assistants, of course. But to move objects in carts or hand trucks you have the head of physical plant, the senior janitorial staff, and the head of housekeeping. It's actually a longer list of people than you might think."

"That's what I was thinking. So we're probably looking at a minimum of two people working to bring the materials in under the radar of day-to-day operations."

"Or on the radar."

"Why?"

Rudy thought about it. "I've worked in enough hospitals to know that when new resources are brought in they're often distributed to appropriate departments but not immediately assigned to individual staff. There's always a paperwork lag. It wouldn't be unusual at all for new cabinets to be brought in and put in corners or disused offices or closets until they were assigned to the staff. And . . . another snag could be that they were brought in, but the keys hadn't yet arrived or someone had accidentally sent the wrong keys. That's a typical hospital snafu. At Mount Sinai we once had six brand-new cardiac crash carts sent, but the manufacturer had forgotten to ship the wheels. They sat in closets for almost two weeks before they were assigned to floors."

I drank my coffee and thought about that. Ghost made a noise very much like a person clearing his throat for attention, and I tossed him a sausage. He snatched it out of the air with the precision of a dolphin taking a leaping mackerel.

"That's good, Rude," I said. "Now, who would know the physical layout? Who would have access to the blueprints? Those bombs were placed at exactly the right structural points."

"Again, that's going to be a long list, Cowboy. Hospital plans are public record, and something as high profile as the London renovation would have drawn a lot of attention. There would be dozens of copies of the main layout available to civil engineers, the fire department, civil defense, and anyone in hospital management. If and when we get a list of suspects, you should look for someone with some kind of background in engineering."

"And someone with some military or demolition experience, too. That might be our hook," I said. "I think I'll have my friends here take a closer look at the building maintenance staff."

We swapped a few other ideas but got no other brain-storms.

"Go back to sleep, Rude. Maybe you'll wake up and find that this was all a dream."

He sighed. "That would be nice. And maybe Santa Claus will put Shakira under my Christmas tree. That's just about as likely."

He hung up and I set my plate down and let Ghost go to town on my unfinished sausage and toast. I was finishing my last cup of coffee when my phone rang.

"Do you have anything new?" asked Church.

I told him about my conversation with Rudy.

"That's useful. I'll discuss this with Benson Childe and we'll put some additional assets on those aspects of the background checks. What are you doing right now?"

"I was about to head back and put in a few more hours with the door-to-door."

"I may have to take you away from that later this morning."

"What's up?"

"Details are still sketchy, but this may be more of a DMS matter than police work."

"C'mon . . . what could be more important than what just happened?"

He said, "Something that hasn't *yet* happened?"

"Look," I said, "I'd like to stick with this thing if I can. Try not to need me on whatever else you have cooking."

"I'll use you as the situation demands," Church said coldly. "Keep your phone on." He disconnected.

I sat in the dark little booth for a couple of minutes, feeling the aches in bone and tendon and soul. I didn't want to be pulled off this part of the investigation. It kept me grounded on the level of real people rather than on the surreal level of Kings and governments. That was important because since Grace's death my connection to basic humanity had been questionable at best.

After she died I came here to Europe for the sole purpose of killing someone. My only companion was a dog. The guy I was chasing was one of the world's most dangerous assassins. I should have called for backup and didn't. I slaughtered the son of a bitch and it felt good. That's probably not a good thing from any psychological perspective. I was still dealing with grief and recovering from injuries received in the same battle that had killed Grace. I should have gone back to the States and spent time with my dad, my brother, and his family. In therapy with Rudy. Instead I got into fights, went scuba diving and skiing, spent hundreds of hours rigorously training Ghost, and even threw myself out of a couple of airplanes. That was my game plan for "relaxing and recharging."

So, I'm kind of a whack-job. That's not a news flash to anyone.

My disconnect didn't start with Grace, though. I went through some trauma as a teenager that fractured my psyche. At the best of times I have several people living inside my skull. There's the Modern Man, that part of me who clings to idealism, hoards his dwindling supply of optimism, and is frequently shocked at the dreadful things people are willing to do to one another. Over the last year, that part of me has begun to crumble. The other two aspects—the Cop and the Warrior—are teetering on a precarious balance. The Cop is probably the closest thing to a primary identity that I have. He's the well-balanced, astute, and emotionally controlled member of my inner committee. He's the part I trust the most, and it's his face that I show to the world. Most of the time. Sometimes—more and more often lately—the world has seen the face of my other self. The Warrior. Remember that TV show *Dexter*? He would have called it his "dark passenger." When I imagine what that part of me looks like, he's crouched down in the weeds with green and black greasepaint camouflage on his face, a red dew-rag tied around his head, and eyes that are both fierce and dead. He waits there, always ready, never sleeping, perpetually eager to take it to the bad guys in ugly and brutally efficient ways.

I closed my eyes and looked inside for some light, but there was nothing but shadows and dust.

So I threw some money on the table, absently tapped my left side to reassure myself that the Beretta was snugged in place, clicked my tongue for Ghost, and went back out to the war.

Chapter Nineteen

Area 51
Eighty-three Miles North-Northwest of Las Vegas
December 18, 4:31 P.M. EST

First Sgt. Bradley F. Sims—Top to everyone who knew him, and second in command of Joe Ledger's Echo Team—stood by the Humvee and squinted at the open hangar door. The sharp, evil-looking snout of an experimental fighter-bomber leered at him from the shadows,

its black skin absorbing the stray rays of sunlight
without reflection. Four other DMS agents clustered
around the vehicle, each of them in unremarkable DCUs,
the desert combat uniforms unmarked by unit patches
or insignia. Their agency logo—a black biohazard symbol with "DMS" above and "Department of Military
Sciences" below, was only used inside the Warehouse
and other field offices. They currently carried ID from
Homeland and the FBI, and Top had an extra set that
identified him as a special agent of the NSA. All legal
but not in any way accurate.

"Getting hot out here, Top," said the big man to his
right. Staff Sgt. Harvey "Bunny" Rabbit was six-seven,
and most of it looked to be packed onto his arms and
chest. Even with the three hundred pounds of muscle,
he had long, rangy limbs and the quick, agile balance
of a volleyball player, a game he'd played to Pan Am
Games level, missing the Olympics only because of the
Gulf War.

"It's a fucking desert, Farmboy," said Top. "Tends to
be hot."

Bunny took a pair of Oakley sunglasses from his
pocket and put them on. He was blond and pale, a
Scots-Irish mix with a few Polish genes somewhere in
his family tree. Top was a black man from Georgia.
Bunny was the second youngest man on Echo Team,
though he was third in command after Top. At forty-
two, Top was the oldest by ten years. The others—the
thin, dark, and professorial ex-SEAL Khalid Shaheed,
eagle-eyed and beak-nosed former MP DeeDee Whitman, and the laconic SWAT sniper John Smith—were
all in their late twenties or early thirties.

Six other vehicles were parked around the open hangar. Two from the base's own military police, one from the intelligence team based at Nellis, two DMS Humvees from the Casino, the Nevada Field Office located in an actual—though no-longer-operating—hotel casino. Lucky Team had gone inside with the military investigators, leaving most of Echo Team outside to bake in the sun. Only Ricky Gomez and Snake Henderson from Echo went in with the others. They lost the coin toss.

Echo Team was here to do some babysitting. Lucky Team was down three men following a raid on a Reno chemical lab that had turned into a firefight. The intel from the FBI had been weak, indicating that there were only five hostiles on-site, but Lucky had walked into a nest of thirty. By the time an HRT unit could roll, two DMS agents were dead and the team's former leader, Colonel Dolcyk, had taken a bullet graze on the forehead that would keep him in the hospital for weeks. The second in command, Leto Nelson, had rallied his team and laid into the hostiles like the wrath of God. They'd held their line until the backup arrived, killing eleven of the terrorists and wounding six others, but it had been a bad day for them. Echo was here to make sure it didn't turn into a pattern. When luck goes bad it can keep flowing downhill.

The operation itself was little more than a "look-see." Over the last three nights the surveillance cameras on the base had malfunctioned. Once could be mechanical failure; twice was an alert. Three times was deliberate action even to the most hesitant and short-budgeted military pencil pusher. On any other base the response would have been an increase of guard patrols and the installation of a secondary and covert set of cameras that would watch the standard security cameras, and a check-back of everyone who had access to the security office. But this corner of Area 51 was home to the Locust FB-119, the newest generation of stealth aircraft. Unlike previous generations, the Locust FB-119 was designed to be totally invisible to radar, building on a radical new design philosophy that was generations up from the faceted surfaces of earlier stealth craft. The Locust could also disguise its infrared emissions to make it harder to detect by heat-seeking surface-to-air or air-to-air missiles, and chameleon fast-adapting skin that immediately changed its underbelly colors to match the skies through which it flew, with a lag time of .093 seconds. Six Locusts sat in the hangar, ready for the last phase of tests before Senate approval for mass production.

If even a single photograph of the craft hit the Net or fell into North Korean, Iranian, or Chinese hands it could spark a new and ugly round of the arms race, because it would be clear to any aeronautics engineer that these birds were designed to deliver nuclear payloads.

Bunny squinted up at the unrelenting sun.

"December my ass," Bunny complained. "Got to be ninety."

"It's seventy-three," said Khalid, and under his breath he said, "Kisich."

"Hey, I heard that."

"But you don't know what it means."

"If I shoot you enough times you'll tell me."

Top touched his ear jack. "Go for Sims," he said, and listened for a moment. "Copy that, Snake. Sounds like it's Miller time. Tell Lucky Team that first round's on Echo—"

And the hangar blew up.

They saw it before they heard it. The windows above the half-open doors bowed outward and the entire roof leaped in a single unit above the building. A split second later the heavy *whump!* slammed them all backward. A massive ball of red-veined yellow flame mushroomed up from the building. Another blast followed the first less than a second later, and a third. The walls disintegrated, filling the air with debris as sharp as blades.

Top twisted and dove for cover, tackling DeeDee as he went, spilling them both into the open door of the Humvee even as the shock wave lifted the vehicle and battered it onto its other side. Bunny was plucked off the ground and slammed into Khalid and they struck the ground on the far side of the vehicle, both of them losing their weapons as superheated gasses blew them along the hardpan like debris. John Smith tried to run, but a piece of debris—a half-melted plastic bucket—struck him in the lower back and dropped him like he'd been shot.

The Humvee lurched over onto its side and rocked back and forth as gravity pulled Top and DeeDee down into an awkward tangle of too many arms and legs against the door of the passenger side. There were more explosions, one after the other, the force of them rumbling with earthquake power through the ground, rattling every bolt and fitting in the big vehicle. The windows shattered and a hail of gummed safety glass hammered them.

The long, slow *boooooom* of the last explosion echoed out across the desert.

Then there was silence.

To Top Sims the silence felt like it was filled with knives. He hovered on the edge of consciousness, agony stabbing through every bruised inch of him. Top knew he was hurt, but he could not tell how badly. His head throbbed horribly and there was warmth in his ears. Blood? He prayed that his eardrums hadn't been blown out.

He lay still for a moment, listening for the sounds of combat. The echoes of the blasts kept pounding inside his head. He worked his jaw and something clicked behind his jaw and one ear popped. He could hear. First his own labored breathing and then a muffled sound. Below him.

"DeeDee," he croaked.

She made a soft, hurt sound.

"Talk to me, soldier," he said as he tried to shift his weight off her. She was a strong woman, but his 175 pounds were smashed down on top of her 130, and at an angle that was doing neither of them any good.

"Can't . . . breathe . . . ," she said in a hoarse whisper.

Top reached up to grab the steering wheel and pulled his weight away from her. He heard her gasp in a lungful of air.

"Better," she said, but her voice was weak.

"I'm going to climb out. Got to see what's what. I'll be back for you."

"I . . . I'm good," she said without conviction.

Top reached up with his other hand, taking the knobbed wheel in both fists, then set his teeth and pulled. It was like doing a chin-up through a junk-cluttered manhole, and the strain on his muscles was incredible. Particularly on his left side, which had only recently healed from injuries from a mission down in the Bahamas back in August. As he pulled himself up he could feel the burn along the newly healed ribs and barely knit muscle in his shoulder. Top set his teeth against the pain and hauled.

"Top!"

He looked up as a big shadow moved above him, blocking out the sky. Bunny's face was streaked with dust and lines of blood, but his eyes were clear. He reached a hand down and knotted his fist in the front of Top's combat vest, then with a grunt like an angry bear reared back and hauled Top out of the Humvee as easily as Top might pull out a child. The huge muscles in the big young man's arms swelled like ripe melons as Bunny pulled. Top caught the edge of the frame and hoisted himself onto the side of the vehicle.

"You may be ugly, Farmboy, but right now I could kiss you."

"Buy me dinner and a movie first, old man." He wiped sweat from his eyes. Top's trembling fingers fumbled for his sidearm, but Bunny said, "We're not under fire, Top. No hostiles. No nothing."

"Got to get DeeDee out."

Bunny bowed down and thrust his head and shoulders into the Humvee. "Hey . . . DeeDee . . . how we doing down there?"

"Just fine. I'm down here doing my fucking nails."

Bunny snorted and took the hands that she reached up to him and pulled her out. She and Top hopped down onto the ground, dazed and unsteady.

"Report," gasped Top.

Bunny crouched atop the Humvee. "We're not under fire. This isn't an active attack. Khalid's winded. I landed on top of him. Smith's good." His blue eyes were hard as diamonds. "Top, Ricky and Snake were inside when it blew."

Top closed his eyes.

Ricky Gomez had been with Echo for three months, the longest active service besides Bunny. He'd proven himself in half a dozen tough assignments. But . . . Snake. God. This was only Snake's third day on the job. His first field op.

He was only inside because he lost a coin toss.

"Is Smith on-point?"

"Yeah," said Bunny. "His weapon was damaged in the blast, but I gave him mine and he's watching our asses. Sat phone's toast, but we have team radio. Smith's on channel two."

Top spit blood out of his mouth and tapped his commlink to the channel. "Rock to Chatterbox, come in."

"Go for Chatterbox," said Smith quietly. The link was bad, full of static.

"What've you got?"

"Zero movement, zero hostiles."

"ETA on fire and rescue."

There was a pause. "From where?"

"From the main damn building," Top snapped, but then he caught Bunny's eye. The big man shook his head, then nodded past the end of the overturned Humvee. Top staggered away from the vehicle and looked past it. The Locust hangar had been at the edge of the complex, the outermost of eleven buildings. Most of the buildings were empty as the base dwindled toward complete decommission, but there was a security shack, crews quarters, and the aeronautics lab. Four active buildings and seventy staff.

Or . . . there should have been.

Now all there was, as far as the eye could see, was burning rubble and towers of smoke that rose to the sky like the pillars of hell.

Area 51 had been wiped off the face of the earth.

Part Two
Driving Force

How can any act done under compulsion have
any moral element in it, seeing that what is moral
is the free act of an intelligent being?

—AUBERON HERBERT

Chapter Twenty

Mr. Church's phone rang. He looked at the screen display and saw that it was his aide. Sergeant Dietrich knew that he was in a meeting with Barrier and the Home Secretary and would never interrupt unless it was an emergency.

Church excused himself and stepped into the hall as he thumbed on the phone.

"Boss," Dietrich said in a fierce whisper, "Lucky Team and Echo Team have been hit." He quickly told Church about Area 51.

"God Almighty," whispered Church. "Is there anything to indicate that this is a Seven Kings event?"

"Not so far, but we don't have investigators on the scene yet. I called the Casino. They're pretty rattled, but they've scrambled some choppers."

"Notify all stations to go to Level One Crisis Alert."

"You want me to come get you?"

"Yes, but then we have to pick up Captain Ledger. The situation in Scotland looks like it's going south on us."

"Christ. What the hell's happening, Boss? Three Level Ones in twenty-four hours?"

"The Seven Kings are making their move."

"But *what* move?"

Church didn't answer. Instead he gave Dietrich a string of orders and then hung up.

Church stood in the empty hallway for two minutes as he worked it out in his head. Then he made several calls. The first was to the President of the United States. The second was to Aunt Sallie at the Hangar to apprise her of the situation.

Then he dialed the number for Hugo Vox.

"Deacon?" said Vox. "You get a break on the London thing?"

"We have a new situation, Hugo," Church said, and quickly outlined the problem.

"Ah . . . Christ! Is this more of the Seven Kings bullshit?"

"Too soon to tell, but it seems likely."

"What can I do to help?"

"Has your think tank come up with anything?"

"Nothing useful, but they're hard at it. Bug's been feeding us intel, but no one's come up with a good reason why that hospital should have been targeted."

"I was hoping for more by now, Hugo."

"I can go beat them with chains, Deke . . . but it won't make them think any faster. We need more data. Can I tell them about Area 51?"

"Yes, but if you do then the team has to be sequestered for the duration of the crisis. That could be hours, days, or weeks."

"They're not going to like that."

"Imagine how much I care."

Vox snorted. "Okay. Anything else?"

"Yes," Church said. "Is Circe still at T-Town?"

"No, the good Dr. O'Tree is in London. I've had her working on security for that silly boat ride thing for the last couple of months. Goddamn waste of resources."

"You disapprove of the Sea of Hope?"

"Of its intent? No, of course not, but they've asked for so damn much security that every agency is coming up short and my own crew is spread pretty thin. Bad damn timing for all this other shit to hit the fan."

"Isn't it, though?"

"And with the Hospital attack, the Brits are not only *not* thinking of canceling it; they've asked for more security. Shit, Deke, the Chinese army couldn't penetrate that thing. And it's only rock and roll."

"It's an opportunist's dream hit. It's the Prince of England and a lot of other celebrities."

"It's celebrities' kids. Inbred offspring of the rich and famous. The Paris Hilton crowd. Fucking bunch of privileged silver-spoon—"

"Really, Hugo? We have time for this?"

"Yeah, yeah, sorry. It's a sore spot with me. There's just too much going on in the real world for me to want expend any consideration for stunt events."

"Message noted. Now, back to matters at hand. Where's Circe?"

Chapter Twenty-one

"Captain Ledger!"

I turned to see Detective Sergeant Rebekkah Owlstone hurrying along the bystreet toward me. Owlstone was the coordinator for the team to which I'd been assigned. We were doing background checks on the Hospital staff and I was coming out of a house where the family of a dead nurse was lost in the horror of shared grief. The day was bitterly cold, with a raw wind that smelled of salt water and ash. Owlstone waved me toward the lee side of a parked delivery van. It was about a degree warmer out of the wind.

"What is it?" I asked.

Owlstone, a petite and pretty brunette from Hampshire, pitched her voice in a confidential tone: "We have a situation, sir. A pair of our lads—Constables Lamba and Pettit—have been interviewing the families of the janitorial staff, and they found something very curious taped to one of the apartment doors. Lamba took a photo of it with his phone and e-mailed it to me."

She produced her BlackBerry and pressed a button to bring up a picture of a standard apartment door: beige wood with metal numbers. A crooked sign read: HAPPY CHRISTMAS. Garland and lights framed the door. Owlstone pressed the "plus" button to enlarge the image to show a white index card taped just under a length of bright green plastic garland. A finger, presumably the constable's, held the garland back so that the note could be read.

In shaky block letters it read:

They are with Jesus. May God forgive all sinners.

"Christ! Have they entered the scene?"

"No," she said. "They notified me straightaway. I called it in and they told me to fetch you. Everyone else senior is too far away."

"Good. Let's go."

We climbed into her car, with Owlstone crammed next to me and both of us crowded by my hulk of a dog, and drove the three blocks to the apartment building. A constable was outside erecting sawhorse crime scene barriers. The apartment was on the top floor. Most of the doors in the hallway were decorated for Christmas, and more than half of them were ajar, with concerned and curious neighbors looking out at all the policemen in the hall.

A constable, with PETTIT on his name badge, stepped forward to intercept us.

"No one's touched the door, Detective Sergeant," he reported. "But the card fell down and there was something behind it that you need to see."

"What is it?" asked Owlstone, but I looked past the officer and I could feel the Warrior inside my head tense for fight or flight.

Someone had used red and black felt-tip pens to leave a message on the apartment door. A message, or a signature, no larger than a silver dollar. A number 7 overlaid atop the word "KINGS" and encompassed by a bloodred circle.

Son of a bitch.

"Captain," gasped Owlstone, "is that—?"

"Yes, it damn well is. Evacuate the building. *Now!*"

Owlstone hadn't been told to take orders from me, but she didn't argue. She spun and began shouting orders to the other bobbies.

I dug out my phone and called Church.

He said, "Seal the building. I'll tell the authorities here and advise that they certify this as a D-notice situation. We don't want that logo in the press; otherwise gangbangers will tag it on every wall in the country. And I'm sure Barrier will roll a team out to you."

"I don't want to wait that long."

"Then do what you have to do. I'll clear it so you're in charge of the crime scene until Barrier takes over."

Owlstone closed on me and lowered her voice to an urgent whisper: "What the hell's happening, Captain?"

"Call me Joe, and I think we just caught the first break in the London Hospital case. Barrier is on its way, but I'm in charge until then. Orders to that effect are being cut right now. Call in if you're uncertain; otherwise let's get to work. You okay with that?"

There was a flicker on her face that suggested she wasn't completely okay with it, but she nodded. A lesser person might have tried to fight that, because this was likely to be a career-making moment. Owlstone was too much of a good cop to play politics, and that elevated her several notches in my book.

"Floor's clear!" called Pettit from the other end of the hall.

I took a digital camera from my pocket and snapped off twenty frames, catching the symbol, the door, and the surrounding hallway. Then I bent and made a close no-touch examination of the door. I had Ghost sniff it, too, but he didn't give me the signal for a bomb. He did, however, give a quick double bark that he was trained to use when he was searching for missing bodies. Search and recovery dogs are trained to sniff out cadaverine, a foul-smelling molecule produced by protein hydrolysis during putrefaction of animal tissue. In other words, *eau de rot.*

Something in there was dead.

Chapter Twenty-two

Whitechapel, London
December 18, 10:28 A.M. GMT

"What's he found?" Owlstone asked, backing away. "Is it a bomb?"

"No," I said. "He's also trained to find bodies."

"Bloody hell."

"Time's not our friend, Detective Sergeant. We need to kick the door."

She nodded, but she looked scared.

"Backup," I suggested quietly, and she took a steadying breath and waved for Pettit and Lamba to join us.

"Okay, lads," she said. "Captain Ledger will kick the door; we'll cover and then clear the apartment in a two-by-two pattern."

They nodded and drew their guns. I drew back and kicked. The door flew open and I went in and left while

Owlstone covered my right. We moved fast, yelling for anyone who was there to lay down their weapons. But no one was there, and we all knew that going in.

"Clear!" yelled Pettit from the kitchen.

"Clear!" yelled Owlstone from what looked like a teenager's bedroom.

"In here! In here!" yelled Lamba from the doorway of the master bedroom. "Two down. Civilians! Two down. Get a medical team."

Owlstone made the call, but it was well past the point where medics could do anything. The woman and teenage girl on the king-sized bed were far beyond the need for first aid. Or any aid. Ghost sniffed the air near the bed and gave a brief whine.

Pettit checked the adjoining bathroom. "Gun in here! Plenty of blood, no bodies."

"Step out, Ed," ordered Owlstone.

Ghost suddenly *whuffed* softly and sat down by the hamper, looking from it to me and back again. I froze.

"What's he found?" snapped Owlstone.

"He's cross-trained as a bomb sniffer," I said, and the constables all took reflexive backward steps. "Don't worry; I don't think that's what he's found."

I was right. All we found in the hamper—after a very careful search—was dirty clothes. There was one set of coveralls with the name Plympton embroidered on the breast that Ghost sniffed, again giving us the single *whuf*.

"These must be Plympton's," I said, "and there must be nitrates on them. He probably had these when handling the explosives at the hospital."

Owlstone and her men looked greatly relieved. Me, too. I fished a red rubber ball out of my pocket and tossed it in the air so Ghost could leap up and catch it. He returned it to me for another toss and tried for a third, but two catches was the reward for finding something and he knew it. His tail thumped happily on the floor, though, and that image was grotesquely at odds with what lay on the bed four feet from where the shepherd sat.

The bodies lay straight and proper. Fully dressed, the woman in a neat red skirt, white blouse, and a vest with snowmen embroidered on it. She had a Christmas wreath pin on her left breast. Her hair was as neat as possible, given the conditions. Beside her was a teenage girl who looked like she would have been beautiful, had time and the cruelest of Fates given her a chance. Her eyes were closed, long lashes brushing perfectly smooth cheeks. She wore the skirt and blazer from an expensive girls' school, but she had earrings in the shapes of Christmas bulbs.

Both of them had been shot in the head. Blood trails led from the bed to the bathroom, and when I gingerly stepped past Lamba I could see that the ugly work had been done in there. The handgun, an old Webley top-break revolver, sat on the closed toilet lid. The gun was broken open, the bullets removed. The three spent shells stood in a precise line with the three unfired rounds. Bloody fingerprints smeared the casings and the toilet. The precision with which the rounds had been arranged was at odds with the smears of blood. Just as the neat and tidy positioning of the bodies belied the condition of the victims.

"Bloody hell," whispered Lamba. "What is this? Some kind of ritual?"

"Looks like a professional hit," said Pettit. "The sense of order is—"

"No," I cut in. "No . . . this is pain. I think the husband did this, and I think he made them as pretty as he could so that they wouldn't suffer any further indignities."

Pettit cocked an eye at me. "Are you a forensic specialist?"

"No," I said, but I didn't care to explain my thought patterns to him. I knew I was right. "There will be another note."

Owlstone said, "Okay, lads, you two take charge of the hall. No one comes in." The constables nodded, clearly happy to leave the apartment. I wanted to go with them.

Once they were gone, Owlstone called in to headquarters. She listened for almost a minute. "Yes, sir," she said crisply, and disconnected. Then she threw a calculating look my way. "Well, Captain, I just spoke to the Chief Superintendent, who said that we are to break investigative protocol and that I was to assist you in an examination of the crime scene."

"And you have a problem with that because—?"

"Mucking about with a crime scene before Forensics arrives is a great way to lose evidence."

"We could wait, but this is a matter of terrorism. The murder investigation is secondary. It's more important right now to find a lead to the terrorists than it is to build a court case."

"If we cock this it'll ruin me in the department," she warned.

"Me, too. So, let's not cock it up."

I gave her my very best "hey, I'm a blond-haired blue-eyed all-American guy" smile. That smile would charm the knickers off the Queen. Owlstone's eyes were cold and her mouth was a stiff line of disapproval, but . . . she nodded. And she kept her knickers on, which in light of that smile spoke to a great deal of self-control.

We turned and faced the bed.

The stupid smile I wore crumbled slowly into dust and fell away.

"Damn," I said softly.

Owlstone sighed, and we set to work.

Interlude Twelve

Near Shetland in the Orkney Isles
December 18, 10:21 A.M. GMT

Rafael Santoro pulled the folds of his coat around him and tried not to shiver. The jacket he'd worn around London was inadequate for the wind that blew like knives across the North Sea. His gloves, purchased to allow dexterity, were equally useless.

"'Ere, Father, take this 'fore you freeze."

Santoro looked up into the lined, weather-worn face of the captain of the hired boat. The man held out a battered tin mug of steaming coffee.

"Bless you, my son," murmured Santoro as he took the cup and buried his nose in the steam. He preferred tea, but now was not a time to be fussy. He blew on the scalding liquid and took a careful sip, but even then he burned his tongue. He winced.

"Aye, it's not very good," said the captain, misreading the wince, "but it's 'ot."

"It's fine, thank you."

The captain was a lumpy man with a Cockney accent and a bulbous drinker's nose webbed with purple veins. He lingered, clearly wanting something else. What now? Had the man noticed or discovered something? Did he want a bribe? Santoro looked up, hoisting a smile onto his face.

"Something—?"

"Well," began the captain, fumbling with it now that he was up to it, "you see . . . the thing is, Father, it's about wot 'appened in London. The fire and all. Those terrorists." He paused. "I try to be a good Catholic, Father, but I can't understand why God would allow this kind of thing to happen."

"God gives us free will, my son. He allows us to make our own choices. One day all of the wicked will be called to account for what they have done."

"Yeah, but that's just it, Father. Who would *want* to do something like this?"

Santoro smiled sadly and shook his head. *What kind of man indeed?*

After the captain shambled away, shaking his head in confusion, Santoro closed his eyes and drifted into a comfortable doze. The question had triggered so many memories, and as the boat rocked on the waves his dreaming mind drifted back to the very first event he had orchestrated for the Seven Kings.

Bombay, India
March 12, 1993

At 1:03 in the afternoon, a small man with a tidy mustache drove into the parking garage beneath the Bombay Stock Exchange, found a spot near the elevator, and turned off the engine. He sat behind the wheel for several minutes, pretending to read notes in a file folder as two carloads of employees from the exchange, returning from a late lunch, walked—laughing and talking—between the rows of parked cars, waited for the elevator, and then piled into the lift. When the doors closed, the small man got out of his car. He walked quickly up and down the rows to make sure that he was alone. When he was satisfied, he unlocked his trunk and pulled back the orange blanket that covered the unconscious Pakistani man.

The Pakistani was drugged but uninjured. Under other circumstances he would wake up in under an hour. He was dressed in the traditional clothing of a Muslim, a dark and formal *sherwani* and an embroidered velvet kufi. The small man bent and lifted the Pakistani out of the trunk, grunting and cursing with the effort. The drugged man was barely 140 pounds, but he was totally slack, and the small man had trouble pulling him over the lip of the trunk. It took four minutes to drag him to the open driver's door and another three to adequately position him behind the wheel.

By the time the small man was finished, he was bathed in sweat. He mopped his forehead very carefully so as not to remove the makeup. Though Rafael Santoro's own Mediterranean complexion was dark, he was not as dark as an Indian. He checked his watch. One sixteen. He smiled. Plenty of time. All that remained now was to close the car door and walk away.

He took the elevator to the lobby and walked out through the revolving door. He paused at a sidewalk stand that served *nariel pani* and drank the coconut water right there. So soothing after his exertions. He asked the vendor to scrape out the tender kernel inside, then strolled away, nibbling thoughtfully on it as he mentally counted the last three hundred seconds in his head to see if his calculations matched the digital timer in the trunk.

He felt the blast before he heard it. A deep rumble like a subway train rolling beneath his feet and then muted thunder filled the air behind him as the densely packed high-RDX explosives in the car detonated. He turned to see the shock wave ripple along both sides of the street like a waft of heat haze, shimmering in the air and blowing out storefronts and car windows. Santoro wrapped his arms over his head and dropped into a squat beside a wooden kiosk where brightly colored tourist scarves were sold. The shock wave passed him and fled down the street, and he peeked through an opening in his overlapped arms. He smiled at the beauty of it.

He turned as the crowds of people around him shook off their shock and ran toward the burning building. Santoro consulted his watch. His mental calculation had been off by less than fifteen seconds. The watch read: 1:30.

The crowd surged past him and he allowed the tide to pull him back to the scene of the disaster. He stood with the others and watched as the stock exchange burned, and when the flames leaped to the adjoining buildings Santoro hid a small smile. He stayed there for over an hour, and by then news that there had been a second blast was already being circulated. By the time he reached his hotel room and ordered a meal, the news stations were frantic with reports of bombings all across Bombay. The current estimate was eight, but Santoro knew that there would be more. Twenty had been planned. Some in cars, others on buses and even in the saddlebags of scooters.

Room service arrived and he ate a healthy meal of curry, flavored with coconut, tamarind, chili, and spices, with basmati rice. He tipped the boy and settled down to his meal.

He ordered a bottle of wine and sat with it in a comfortable chair. He was glad that he had not been one of the agents who had been ordered to leave a suitcase bomb in his hotel. He liked this place. Maybe next spring he'd come back here. He wasn't as fond of the Juhu Centaur Hotel or the Hotel Sea Rock, so he didn't mind when the increasingly shocked reporters told of blasts that tore through each of them. Other bombs destroyed the Plaza Theatre, the Nair and J.J. hospitals, part of the University of Bombay, and the Zaveri, Century, and Katha bazaars. He watched the news all day. He was mildly disappointed that the rail station bombs were found and defused before they could detonate. By day's end the tally was thirteen blasts that claimed 257 lives and left over seven hundred injured. A nice day's work.

He could not help but laugh as the police and various "experts" on terrorism discussed and debated the reason for the attacks. The air of Bombay was thick with paranoia.

Santoro showered, washing away the brown dye that made him look Indian. He would apply a fresh coat tomorrow before he checked out of the hotel.

He toweled off and got ready for bed. He knew that the whole plan would succeed. It was like clockwork. Long in the planning, subtle in the orchestration, deceptively simple in execution. A bread trail would lead the police toward a Muslim crime family who would take the fall. Lovely. There were no loose ends for the police to follow, nothing that would lead them back to Santoro, or to the men who had hired him to plan and execute what had been discreetly referred to as the Bombay Holiday.

Muslims had nothing to do with it. It was not part of any Islamic jihad. It had, in fact, nothing at all to do with any religious ideology and it made no specific theological statement. At least, not as far as Santoro knew. He was fairly insightful, and as far as he could judge, this whole thing was about what it was always about.

Money and power.

With that happy thought in his head, Santoro pulled up the sheet, snuggled into the pillow, and fell into a deep and untroubled sleep, content in the knowledge the world would never be the same again. The Seven Kings would be pleased. His last thought as he drifted off was, *The Goddess will love me for this.*

THE BOAT THUMPED down over a tall wave and Santoro jolted awake. He looked around, his hand touching the knife beneath his clothes.

The captain saw him and smiled. "Wind's picking up," he said. "We're 'itting some chop, but we'll be in port before it gets too bad."

"Yes," said Santoro, but he was agreeing to a different meaning entirely.

Smiling, Santoro took his iPhone out of his pocket and checked his text messages. There were separate notes of congratulations from each of the Seven Kings. Both the King of Fear and the King of Plagues asked him how things were progressing on Fair Isle. To both, Santoro sent the same message:

Crimson rivers will flow.

He could imagine the champagne corks popping as that was read aloud in the Chamber of the Kings. Just before the boat docked, Santoro received a message from the Goddess herself:

You are the beloved Sword of the Goddess.

The world swam around him and Santoro felt tears stinging his eyes.

He bent his head and whispered prayers of thanks and love to the Goddess, and prayed to her that he might soon be lifted from the flesh of a servant to the spirit of a god. *Her* God.

Her God and lover.

Chapter Twenty-three

Owlstone removed two pairs of latex gloves from her pocket and handed a set to me. I pulled them on and took my camera from my jacket. It's a special design that takes thirty-five megapixel shots at ultrafine quality, with a three-hundred-image capacity. A prototype from one of Church's friends in the industry. I clicked off a hundred shots, moving fast, trusting to the anti-shake function to capture everything. At least the forensics team would have some nice pictures to look at.

Nice.

Christ.

When I finished taking the pics I took a small cable from my pocket and connected the camera to my phone and then sent the images via satellite to Church, Benson Childe, Jerry Spencer, Bug, and Dr. Hu.

Photos on the bureau made it clear that the victims were the mother and daughter who had lived here. Laura Plympton, forty-one, and daughter, Zoë, fifteen. They'd both been pretty.

"Look at this," Owlstone said, her voice dropping into a whisper. She drew a cheap plastic pen from her inner pocket and touched the curled left hand of Laura Plympton. I came around to her side of the bed. I took my penlight and shined it into the dark hollow formed by her curled white fingers. "Is that paper?"

"You have a good eye, Detective Sergeant," I said,

and took some close-ups of Laura Plympton's hand. "You ought to consider a career in criminal investigation."

"Oh yes, very funny."

We very slowly, very carefully worked together to gently spread Laura Plympton's fingers. She must have been murdered early yesterday morning, so rigor had come and gone, leaving her fingers slack in a creepy, rubbery way. In death her bladder and bowels had released, so the smells that rose from her were eye-watering, and buried beneath them were the beginnings of the sweet stink of decomposition.

Owlstone slid the paper out and I lowered Plympton's hand back to its resting place on her breast. I knew that she was dead and far beyond any feeling, but I felt like I wanted to apologize to her for this necessary violation.

We carried the paper to the dresser and carefully unfolded it. It was a quarter of a piece of ordinary computer paper folded several times and then rolled into a cylinder. There were several lines handwritten on it in blue ballpoint:

My Sweet Laura and Precious Zoë,
I know that what I have done is unforgivable.
I have damned my immortal soul for all eternity,
but at least what I have done here in our home
will save you both from greater horrors.
It was the only way to save you both from them.
*They are **everywhere**.*
I could not let them do those things to you.
Not even if I am to burn in hell.
God accept and protect you both.

*My greatest regret is that I will not be able
to join you in paradise.
I will try to make it right if I can, but I know they
are watching.
I don't ask for or expect forgiveness.
They are not kings. They are monsters.
I am only the monster they made me.*

It was unsigned. The paper was stained with bloody
fingerprints and the distinctive pucker marks of dried
water. Tears, without a doubt.

There was a reference to the Kings, but I wasn't sure
what that meant. Was Plympton not part of the Kings?

I am only the monster they made me.

Was that an admission that he had become corrupted
by the Kings? Or had they somehow coerced him into
this?

They are not kings. They are monsters.

No shit.

I looked at Owlstone and saw confusion and compassion warring on her young face. As one we straightened
and turned to look at the bodies on the bed.

"What the hell are we into here, Captain?"

They are everywhere. He had underlined "everywhere" half a dozen times.

"It's Joe," I said, "and in my considered opinion as a
professional investigator, it beats the hell out of me."

Though . . . that was not entirely true. An idea was

beginning to form in one of the darker side corridors in my broken head.

I am only the monster they made me.

My phone rang. It was Church.

"Sit rep?" he demanded.

I told him and started to explain, but he cut me off.

"We have what we need from that site. Leave the rest to the locals. I'm three minutes away. Be downstairs."

"I think I'm on to something here, I don't want to bug out now."

"Would you rather hear about it from the Emergency Broadcast System?"

Shit.

"I'm on my way," I said.

Interlude Thirteen

T-Town, Mount Baker, Washington State
Three and a Half Months Before the London Event

The range master at Terror Town was slim, swarthy, bearded, and had a beaky nose and dark eyes. The name embroidered on his chest was Muhammad. A few sorry souls had made jokes around him with words like "towel head," "camel jockey," and "sand nigger." They misunderstood his stance on racial epithets, because they thought that if he was working this range then Muhammad could not be either a devout Muslim or a true Arab. Of those sorry souls, the ones who were able to walk away from the range under their own steam were encouraged to pack their bags and go find a clue. The rest received the very best of emergency care in the T-Town infirmary.

Circe O'Tree had been there for one of those encounters. The whole thing was over in a second and a man much bigger than Muhammad lay in a fetal position, hands clutching his groin, faced screwed into a purple knot of silent agony. The sight had bothered Circe for weeks. But she could not find any fault with the range master. He never once started a fight; his view, however, was that even small hate crimes should be "appropriately addressed."

Although she worked around violence all day and though she had logged hundreds of hours on the combat ranges and in the self-defense classes, Circe had never before been a witness to actual violence. Even so, threads of violence were sown through her life. Her mother and sister had died violently, her father was in one of the more ferocious departments of government service, and all of her friends were either current or former military or scientists like her, who studied war and conflict.

The relationship between Chief Petty Officer Abdul Muhammad and Dr. Circe O'Tree was complicated, its parameters unspoken. He cut her no slack, but he always gave her a little extra advice and encouragement. He also let her train in the late evenings after the teams had called it a night. Though most of the men at T-Town respected—or perhaps dreaded—Muhammad, they frequently forgot themselves when Circe was on-deck. She was a very beautiful woman with a figure that drew the eyes of normally focused shooters away from their targets. Range scores plummeted when she was on-deck.

And she found the whole thing exceptionally tiresome. She couldn't change her genetics, and dressing down in shapeless clothes was an admission of defeat. After ignoring the testosterone-infused nonsense for months, she began coming later and later to the range. Now it was full dark and the sky above glittered with 10 billion diamonds. The August breeze off of Mount Baker was cool and soothing after hours spent with her computer.

"Your mind is not in the game, Doc," Muhammad growled after she finished her last grouped shots.

Circe cleared and benched the gun. There was no one else on the range, but the proper etiquette had become ingrained. You earned a sharp rebuke only once from Muhammad, and you never forgot it. On her second day at T-Town Circe had stepped past the firing line before all of the other shooters had declared their weapons benched. Muhammad read her the riot act in front of everyone and he was thorough about it. Then he made her stay an extra hour and practice the rules of hand-gun safety, shouting out each step no matter who was firing. The lesson sank in.

She pulled off her ear defenders. "Lot on my mind tonight, Chief."

"You haven't scored this low since your first month."

She looked downrange as the target moved toward her on a pulley. She had fired all fifteen rounds from a Glock 22. She was not a brilliant shooter, but she was a competent and consistent one, usually putting eleven rounds out of each magazine into the kill zone of a suspended target fifteen yards away. At twenty-five yards she lost a bit of her accuracy if firing fast, but in a slow fire drill she was a very good shot.

Muhammad folded his arms and leaned against the wall of the shooting stall.

"Why do you practice with a handgun?"

She almost sighed. This was one of the Chief's ritual questions.

"To save my life and the lives of those in my charge."

"How do you accomplish this?"

"By hitting what I aim at with focus, speed, and commitment."

"Uh-huh. So tell me, Doc, what part of that sounds like 'I got too much on my mind'?"

"Nothing, Chief."

"Very well. Bring your gear."

When he said that it only meant one thing: the combat range.

Circe regretted coming out to the range this late. She had wanted to work off some nervous energy and blow holes in the wild theories that were forming in her mind. Bringing her problems to the range had been foolish.

She gathered up her gear, making sure to do each step of gun safety exactly the right way even though Chief Muhammad did not appear to be watching. She ran to catch up with him and followed him down a long and windy cinder-block corridor. The block walls were filled in with tightly packed dirt to catch ricochets, and the corridors smelled like a graveyard.

They came out into the maze of T-Town's eighteen combat ranges. Each one was designed to allow operatives to train for different kinds of circumstances: city street, subway, airplane, airport, business, government office, house, and others.

Muhammad chose the shortest of the ranges, a mom-and-pop corner store. Circe knew that there were nine Pepper Poppers—metal silhouette targets that could be positioned throughout the range and operated by remote control. They were hinged at the bottom so that they could swing up on fast spring releases or fall back after being shot. At least four of the targets would be hostiles, the rest designated as "possible" non-combatants. The "possible" part was crucial, because in the War on Terror the enemy didn't wear uniforms or team shirts.

"How many mags, Chief?"

Muhammad grinned. He took a magazine from her pack, thumbed four rounds out, and handed it over. "Eleven rounds. Best intel says four hostiles. Could be five. That gives you two per and three for luck."

"I never did this with less than two full magazines."

He shrugged. "Life sucks sometimes. What if a situation turned out to be bigger and badder than you expected? You want to read a rule book at a hostile? Think that'll win the day, Doc?"

"No, Chief."

"Now, you run this range and I don't want to hear from jams, tripping over your shoelaces, or a text message from your friends. You run it like you know *how* to run it and keep your head in the fucking game. You read me, Dr. O'Tree?"

She had never been in the military, but she snapped to attention. "I read you, Chief."

"Then it's time to go to work."

Muhammad put a wooden matchstick between his teeth and walked off the range and into the steel observation bunker. There was a warning buzzer announcing a live fire exercise and the lights in the store came on.

Circe called, "Loading!" She slapped the magazine into the Glock and racked the slide, keeping the barrel pointed into the range, her finger along the trigger guard. Muhammad's words from their very first training session echoed in her mind.

Shake hands with the grip. Snug but comfortable. Get to know the weight. Fit the handle into the vee formed by the thumb and index finger of the shooting hand as high as possible on the backstrap. Your strong hand holds and fires; your weak hand completes the grip and supports.

Muhammad's amplified voice growled from a speaker, "Ready on the firing line!"

Circe could feel her heart hammering, but she took several deep breaths to relax her mind and muscles.

Muhammad spoke from her memories: *Breath control minimizes body movement and that in turn reduces handgun movement.*

"Go!"

Circe kicked in the door and entered fast, sliding to one side and bringing her gun up in a two-handed grip, the sights level with her eyes.

Aim with your dominant eye when shooting a handgun. Even if you're right-handed it does not mean that you are right-eyed dominant. Learn your body and work with it in the most natural way.

A target pivoted toward her. A teenager in a Brooklyn T-Shirt and jeans, but he was pulling a pistol from his belt. Circe shot him in the chest and again in the face.

Tap-Tap!

Squeeze the trigger in a natural and continuous way. Never jerk the trigger.

Another target sprang up from behind a row of canned goods. An old man holding something. A bag of groceries. Both hands visible. No weapon. She spun as she caught sight of movement to her left. A man with an automatic weapon.

Tap-Tap!

Follow through. Apply the shooting fundamentals continuously. Sloppy is dead. Let the process keep you alive.

She saw the shadow of another and was aiming as she turned, checking her target in a split part of a second.

Tap-Tap!

The afterimage of a hand grenade floated in her mind as she stepped and turned and covered high and low, tracking with her eyes. She shuffled sideways to put two rows between her and a grenade blast. There was a bang, and wet confetti filled the air. None of it landed on her.

Then the lights went out and something brushed her. She whirled and faded left, looking for ambient light, seeing a glow splash across the face of a man with a smiling face, but the glow washed down across his chest. Shotgun.

Tap-Tap!

Two targets came up together. Another teenager and a housewife. The teenager wore a sweatshirt with the name of the store. The woman stood behind him, one hand out of sight. The kid's eyes were scared and painted so that he looked nervously back at Circe. It was an almost impossible shot in the dark. She took it.

Tap-Tap!

Four hostiles down. Three rounds left. The lights came on—no, just the emergency lights. Weak and yellow. She turned at movement, saw a woman with a stroller. Lingered for a moment, looking for a trap. No gun, no bomb. Circe moved forward, turning left and right, checking her corners, checking behind her.

There! A figure rose from behind the counter. Big fat guy holding another shotgun. Circe turned, aimed.

Did not fire.

The man looked like an older version of the kid in the sweatshirt. Father? Uncle. The owner, defending his store against the attack. Circe kept the pistol on him.

"Drop your weapon! Do it now—*now!*"

The shopkeeper silhouette dropped back.

And the lights came on.

"Clear and lock!"

Circe stepped out of her shooter's crouch, turning to keep the barrel clear of the entrance. She eased the hammer down, removed the magazine, and ejected the round from the chamber. She held up the locked and empty weapon.

"Clear!"

Muhammad hit the button for the exit door to open and she stepped out, placing her weapon on the courtesy bench. Her ears were ringing and her hand tingled from the heavy recoil.

"Well, well, well," said Muhammad, smiling around the wooden matchstick. "You're not dead, Doc. Congratulations."

"I almost shot that last target."

He shook his head. "You didn't. We don't worry about 'almost' any more than we worry about any other distraction. Combat purifies thinking."

It was one of his most common aphorisms, and she nodded, repeating it softly.

"Now," he said, "it's comforting to know that you *can* bring your game when you need to. Next time you're on my range I want you to remember that. I don't ever want to see bullshit scores like you took back there. You read me?"

"Loud and clear, Chief."

Muhammad smiled and wiggled the matchstick up and down. "Okay, let's agree that your ass has been kicked. Now, Doc . . . what the hell's got you so bent out of shape?"

"It's complicated, but . . ." She hesitated, unsure how to begin.

"With what you do? No kidding." He wore a crooked smile as he shoved his hands into his back pockets. "I believe that it's Miller time. Let's go someplace and talk this out."

"You don't drink."

"Bars serve coffee. I'll watch you drink."

She still hedged. "You'll think I'm crazy."

"And that'll change our relationship how?" He clapped her on the shoulder. "C'mon, Doc. Crazy one buys the first round."

They sat in the T-Town canteen, huddled together in a private corner. She drank white wine; he drank hot tea. She told him everything that she had found online, and she told him all of her speculations.

Chief Petty Officer Abdul Muhammad did not think she was crazy. "I can see it," he said after careful thought. "On both sides of this thing there are enough hotheads ready to pull a trigger or throw a firebomb, and that's as true now as it was during the Crusades and maybe back to Moses and the Pharaoh."

"What do you think about the *Protocols* and all that?"

He sipped his tea. "What, do I think that there are radical Jews out there planning the downfall of the free world?" He shrugged. "Yeah, probably. Just like there are radical Muslims, Buddhists, Lutherans, and Hindus. There's radical everything. That's why there's always a war somewhere. But if you're asking if I think that these Web posts are being made by a vast secret society of Jews, then no. I don't buy that for a moment."

Chapter Twenty-four

Interstate Route 95 South
Philadelphia, Pennsylvania
December 18, 5:37 A.M. EST

Dr. Rudy Sanchez hurried through the terminal, collected his suitcase, and picked up the late-model Ford. His annoyance at having been sent back to the States before even setting foot in England had long since passed, replaced by a growing sense of unease about the man named Nicodemus.

Once he was on the road in Pennsylvania, Rudy called Mr. Church.

"Bug called me a few minutes ago," Rudy explained.

"We had another call from the psychiatrist at Graterford. Have you read the transcript?"

"No, and I can't read it now. Give me the highlights."

Rudy did. When he was finished, Church said, "He
actually mentioned the Kings?"

"His exact words, as Dr. Stankevičius recited them
to me, were: 'Lo! And behold the rise of the Seven
Kings. All shall fall before them!' "

"Interesting," murmured Church. "I'll see that and
raise you one." He told Rudy about the Kings symbol
on Plympton's door and the reference in the note the
man had left in his murdered wife's hand.

"What does it all mean?"

"I would give a lot to be able to answer that question,
Doctor. Maybe you can coax some answers out of Nicodemus."

"I hope so, but I'm not optimistic. Nicodemus is supposed to be in isolation, without TV or newspaper priv-
ileges, and yet he's making references to the London
Hospital and the Seven Kings. He shouldn't be able to
get outside information."

"You question the likelihood of an information leak
in a *prison*?" Church said. "That's almost funny."

"Almost," Rudy agreed sourly. He absently wondered what Mr. Church would look like laughing.
Rudy had never seen the man do anything more than
smile, and even then the emotion looked unwelcome
and unwanted on his features. "Someone at the prison
must be feeding him information, and I doubt they're
doing it just so he can stick pins in the prison therapist."

"While you're there, don't assume trust in anyone, and that includes the prison doctor and the warden."

Rudy sighed. "It's sad that paranoia has become an indispensable quality of good job performance here in the DMS. I'm finding it very hard to trust anyone."

"It's not paranoia if they really *are* out to get you," said Church.

Rudy thought, *Why is it you only have a sense of humor when things are really bad?* But he didn't say it.

"I'd like your full read on Nicodemus," said Church, "as well as any observations you care to share about the staff."

"What do you want me to look for?"

"I'll leave you to determine that, Doctor. I don't want to pollute your perceptions by sharing my speculations. We can compare notes later."

"Okay."

"One more thing, Doctor. I'm bringing in a consultant. Dr. Circe O'Tree. Are you familiar with her?"

"Not personally, but I know her work. I've seen her on TV, read her books. The new one, *The Terrorist Sophist,* should be required reading by everyone in the DMS. She makes some very important points on how terrorists rationalize what they do. She's rather brilliant."

"Yes. She's also being largely wasted working as Hugo Vox's assistant. I think she has more potential than Hugo gives her credit for. Do you have a problem with her consulting on this?"

"God, no. In fact, I welcome her insight."

"Good. She's already agreed and it's our good

fortune that she is currently in London working on another matter."

He disconnected.

Rudy made the turn from I-95 to 476 West. He turned on the news and listened to the latest rehash of the London disaster. Nothing new, so he dialed through Sirius until he found a Mexican ska band, cranked the sound way up, and put the pedal down. As a driver, Rudy was usually careful to the point where Joe called him Tia when he was behind the wheel. He wasn't feeling like an old aunt right now. As Joe was so fond of saying, the clock was ticking.

Chapter Twenty-five

Whitechapel
London, England
December 18, 11:21 A.M. GMT

When Ghost and I came out of the apartment complex the street was crowded with police vehicles, ambulances, and a variety of nondescript government cars that were probably licensed to the various counterterrorism teams I'd met yesterday. Lots of stone-faced guys with wires behind their ears were watching up and down the street while local cops struggled to keep the crowd well back. Everyone looked scraped raw by the unrelenting winds.

I saw a limo idling down the street, well out of the press and angled for a quick departure. The driver gave the headlights a quick flash, so I headed that way, at

times having to be ungentle with the rubberneckers who
thronged the bystreet. By the time I reached it the
driver—in the form of the squat and muscular Sgt. Gus
Dietrich—had gotten out and stood by the rear passenger door. Not sure what Dietrich's job description was
with the DMS. He was gruff, tough, honest, and as de-
pendable as the bulldog that he closely resembled.

"Good to see you, Captain." He offered me a rock-
hard hand.

"Skip the 'Captain' crap, Gus. Good to see you, too.
Wish it was under better circumstances."

"Ha! Let me know when those 'better circumstances' roll around, Joe. I'll take the day off and go
get a massage. In the meantime . . . good luck with this
one. It's going to be a real nut buster."

He opened the door and we climbed inside, happy to
be out of the vicious cold. I slid onto the bench seat and
Dietrich closed the door and ran around to climb behind
the wheel. There were two men on the opposite seat.
One big, one small, neither smiling fuzzy-bunny warmth
at me.

Guy on the left was Mr. Church. He was north of
sixty, but he made it look like a fit forty. Blocky, hard,
with big hands and a face you wouldn't want to see
across a poker table from you. Tinted sunglasses even
in the backseat of the limo. He gave me a fraction of a
nod and there was no expression at all on his face.

The other guy was a gangly, gawky collection of awkward limbs and comprehensive disapproval. Dr. William Hu, chief of scientific research for the DMS. He
had a Mongol face, an Einstein brain, the pop-culture
sensibilities of Joss Whedon, but the compassion of a

ghoul. When I'd first joined the Department of Military Sciences I tried real hard to like him, but that got to be an expensive hobby. He didn't burn up any calories trying to warm up to me, either.

"Captain Ledger," Hu said in exactly the same way you might say "painful rectal itch."

"Dr. Hu," I said, meeting him on the same ground.

We didn't shake hands.

Ghost sniffed the hand Church extended, gave the fingertips a tiny lick, and then sat back. Then Ghost turned and eyed Hu like he was a steak dinner. Hu never attempted to touch Ghost. Hu was an asshole, but he wasn't stupid.

Gus Dietrich put it in gear and the limo pulled away from the curb like we were fleeing the scene of a crime. I grabbed an armrest to keep from falling out of my seat. "Where are we going?"

"Scotland," said Church. "Specifically Fair Isle. Shetland Islands, in the North Sea, very remote, ultrahigh security. A chopper's waiting."

"Why? Has there been another attack?"

"More complicated than that. Short answer is that there is a situation at a viral research station there. A staff member is holding the rest of the employees hostage."

"Why?"

"Unknown."

"He connected to the Kings?"

"To be determined."

"Working alone?"

"Possibly. It's the impression he's conveyed so far. Uses 'I' and 'me' rather than 'we.'"

"Demands?"

"Aside from the usual precautionary requirements—keep our distance, don't try anything, et cetera—he's asked to speak to a representative of Homeland Security."

"Homeland? Does this guy know he's in Scotland?"

"He's American," said Hu. "Baker and Schloss lease half of the island from the Brits."

"Baker and Schloss? The male enhancement company?"

Hu grinned. "Yeah, the pecker pill people. They're a medium-sized pharmaceutical company with a board made up of American, British, German, and French members. Majority stockholders are the Baker family of Martha's Vineyard. Old money. The male enhancement drug put them on the public radar, but they make their real money from government contracts."

"For what? Enhanced soldiers?"

"Viral research," said Church.

"What kind? Germ warfare?"

"Nobody uses that term anymore," Hu said haughtily. "Baker and Schloss has government contracts for tactical-response bio-agents. TRBs."

"Which means what?" I asked.

"Germ warfare," said Church. "The point is that the situation is politically complicated. The title to the land is actually held by the U.S. Government. Baker and Schloss has access to it as part of their research contract."

"Why is it in Scotland?"

Church said nothing.

"What?" I prompted.

Hu snorted. "It's here because it's not allowed to be in the U.S."

I studied their faces. Church was a stone, but Hu was smiling, and he never smiled unless something unpleasant was happening. "I'm going out on a limb here and guess that it's not allowed in the U.K., either."

"No, it's allowed," said Church, "but only under the most exacting circumstances, which translates as 'difficult and expensive.' Those responsible for establishing this facility found it less expensive and more productive to simply move it outside of the scope of domestic regulars and congressional oversight. That itself is problematic in a variety of ugly ways. The nature of the work being done at Fair Isle contravenes half a dozen international agreements."

"Why is it even in operation?" I demanded.

"It's a holdover from a previous administration. And it's one of those things that the layers of government power players fail to tell a new president."

"How—," I began, but he cut me off.

"There are too many secrets to tell any sitting president. At best the President can be briefed in general about the areas of research and given more complete information when the situation requires it. But the career politicians within the infrastructure have a skewed view of both 'need to know' and 'plausible deniability.' They believe they have the right to decide what the President is allowed to know, or not allowed to know."

I knew what he was saying. As much as we don't want to accept the truth, there were layers of government that remained in place no matter which party held power in the White House. Shadow governments, cells and cabals, some of which believed that what they were doing was in the best interest of the American people, though in those rare cases when someone was able to shine a light on them it became pretty clear that money and the power it purchased was the only enduring motive.

"If this got out," Church said, "it could cripple the current administration and it would almost certainly result in some kind of criminal charges for key members of the previous administration."

I started to say something smart-ass, but he headed me off at the pass.

"This isn't a time to collect scalps, Captain. Playing politics has hurt our country too many times. And while I agree that those responsible should be held accountable, that's something best done quietly on our own turf. Spilling this in public would do greater harm than good. The stock market is already taking very bad hits because of the Hospital bombing; this could crash it into a depression. It would also strip the power of the United States in critical negotiations with North Korea, China, and Iran."

"Yeah, stones and glass houses."

He nodded.

I said, "Tell you, though . . . if someone wanted to do just that, this would be a good way to go about it. We have to consider that this might *be* a Seven Kings operation."

"No! Really?" said Hu dryly.

Church adjusted his glasses. "We face three separate problems."

"Let me see if I can guess," I said, and ticked them

off on my fingers. "First, we need to contain the situation and prevent any bugs from getting loose. Second, we need to make sure this doesn't embarrass the ol' U.S. of A."

"Right. And the third?"

"We have to find out why this guy is doing this. You said he wants to talk to someone from Homeland? Not the Brits? Not the press? That's interesting."

"Isn't it, though?" said Church. "He said one thing that I find particularly intriguing. He said that there's still time to stop this.'"

"That doesn't sound like a threat," I said. "Maybe he's not a bad guy. Maybe he's just a scared guy."

"Scared of what?" Hu asked.

"Don't know yet. But you don't take people hostage if you're not scared of something. Not unless you're in it for the money, and this doesn't have that kind of feel."

"Agreed," said Church.

"Or maybe he's part of this thing, whatever it is, and got either cold feet or an attack of conscience."

"And if the Kings are involved we might finally have a doorway into them."

I nodded. "Couple questions, though."

"Go."

"First . . . why me? Where the hell's the rest of the DMS?"

"Everyone healthy enough to report for work has been scrambled and assigned to investigation or protection in the States. As for our teams here, Gog is still on the job in Prague and Magog has gone dark in Afghanistan, though that's expected at this stage of that operation. We can't get either of them here in time and this situation needs a shooter."

I gave him a sour look. "Swell. Joe Ledger, gun for hire."

"If your feelings are bruised, Captain, let me put it more delicately: this situation needs finesse."

"Thanks, but I wasn't about to break out in tears."

Hu made a small grunting sound that I was free to interpret any way I wanted. I considered siccing Ghost on him.

"We do have some local assets, however," said Church. "Barrier is sending Lionheart Team as backup."

"I thought we had to keep the Brits out of this," I said.

"Officially, we have to keep the British *government* out of it," corrected Church. "Brigadier Prebble, head of Barrier's Tactical Field Office in Scotland, is an old friend of mine. He understands our need for discretion and he'll be meeting us in a few minutes."

"Does Benson Childe know about this?"

"Officially, no. Unofficially, I briefed him on the matter and he advised me that Prebble's goodwill is only going to last as far as containment. If there's any kind of biological breach, then Prebble will disown us. As well he should."

"As you would in the same circumstance."

"Of course."

The limo pulled out of traffic and through the gates of a large estate. A military helicopter was parked on the lawn behind the house, the rotors already turning, the engine whine rising to a scream.

Interlude Fourteen

Gault stepped out of the steaming shower and reached for a towel. It wasn't on the rack. Instead Eris moved out of the mist and handed it to him.

Gault snatched the towel from her and pressed it to his naked, scarred face, turning half-away. But Eris moved closer still. She still wore the bikini top, but she had shed the tight pants and wore only the scraps of bright cloth that comprised the bottom of the bikini. Her body was strong and taut, with hard muscles under tanned skin.

"Let me see," she said, touching the hand that pressed the towel to his face.

"No," he said hoarsely.

"Don't be a child, Sebastian," she said in her low and smoky voice. "Neither of us is as pretty as we used to be. Life and time are monsters and they gnaw at us."

She kissed the back of his hand and then tugged lightly at the towel.

"Please don't . . ."

But Gault knew from too many years and too many encounters that Lady Eris could not be told no. She kissed his hand and tugged, and finally he yielded, as he had always yielded to her. She tossed the towel aside and touched his chin, turning his face toward her. Her sea green eyes took in everything, missed nothing. The smile on her parted lips never wavered as each of the bruises and surgical scars was revealed.

"This will heal," she said softly.

"Not all of it."

She touched the crow's-feet at the corners of her eyes, then drifted her fingertips across her throat. "Neither will this. But only fools and mortals worry about these things."

"You aged; I melted," he said as she moved even closer. Her full breasts brushed the naked skin of his stomach. "Surely that's proof of mortality."

"No," she said as she plucked the strings of her bikini. The pieces fell away except for the triangle that had covered her left breast, which was momentarily held in place by the pressure of one taut nipple against the rippled muscles of his abdomen. "No," she said again, "we're not mortals."

She kissed his mouth, his cheek, the corner of his eye, her breath furnace hot against the crooked lines of his scars.

"We're gods," she whispered.

Gault suddenly pulled her to him, crushing her against his chest, her softness pressed to him, his hardness pressed to her, the steam swirling around them both. Her lips and hungry hands were everywhere, touching him, stroking him, guiding him toward wetness.

"Gods," he breathed.

And then they both cried out together as two gods became one.

Interlude Fifteen

T-Town, Mount Baker, Washington State
Three and a Half Months Before the London Event

Circe tried not to fidget as Maj. Grace Courtland, Mr. Church's top field agent and one of Circe's closest friends, read through the Goddess Report.

Grace was slim and fit and was known throughout the counterterrorism community as the Iron Maiden. It wasn't an insult. Grace was a top-of-the-game shooter for the DMS, which made her the best of the best of the best.

"Bloody hell," Grace said as she closed the report.

"Am I crazy or is there something there?"

Grace smiled. "Both, I daresay."

"Am I *wrong?*"

"The FBI sent us a report on this a few weeks ago and they were all over the place with their suspicions, and none of their geniuses came within pissing distance of what you have here. This is brilliant."

"Really?"

"No, I'm lying to you, you daft cow. Of course! Agencies are nodding at the Goddess postings and dismissing them as an aftereffect or a symptom."

"I know! But the dates clearly show that the posts predate the last couple of spikes in hate crimes."

"No doubt, but there are always *other* events that can be held up as causal factors. An Army drone hits a village mosque instead of a Taliban opium warehouse and *bang!*" Grace tapped the report with a forefinger. "But they'll have to take you seriously once they read this."

"They *have* read it. This same report. They see my name on the document and they don't take me seriously."

"Ah." Grace Courtland pursed her lips. "Then the problem is the same one you've been facing since you started mucking about with the Goddess thing, love. There's nowhere to go with it. That's the trouble with the Internet—there are too many ways to create and maintain anonymity. The FBI is all about following bread crumb trails. Here there's no trail to follow, and those wankers are too busy playing with their beef bayonets to try and find a way. That and they're swamped trying to stop the Chinese ghost net from stealing every last effing secret we have." She paused. "Is there any chance the Chinese are involved in this? We've been dealing with wave after wave of their cyberterrorism these last few years."

"Impossible to say."

They sat and thought about it.

"So," Circe said, "you see my problem. Even when I can get someone to agree that there's something going on out there, no one can offer a single suggestion on what to do about it."

"Mm," Grace murmured. "If this was piss easy we'd have solved all the world's problems already. As it is . . . best I can do for you, love, is bring this to Aunt Sallie. She has the cybercrimes portfolio right now."

"But this isn't a cybercrime per se. More like hate mongering, and technically that's allowed under free speech."

"Well, as we don't have a division for cyber fucking-about we'll have to go with what we have." She lifted the report. "Can I keep this copy? I'd like to read it again on the plane."

Circe chewed her lip. "Um . . . Hugo told me to keep this on the down low as far as the DMS is concerned. He said I could talk to you off the record. He'd kill me if he knew you had a copy of that."

Grace smiled and tucked the report into her bag. "If you don't tell him, I won't."

"Thanks!" Circe smiled weakly. "Do you have to get right back?"

Grace smiled. "Not this minute. First . . . I want to tell you about something that you have to swear to God you won't tell anyone else."

Circe crossed her heart and held her hand to God. "What is it?"

"I can't tell you his name. Security reasons, you understand." Grace Courtland leaned forward and put her elbows on the desk. "But . . . I think I've bloody well fallen in love."

Chapter Twenty-six

Over Scottish Airspace
December 18, 2:09 P.M. GMT

We flew to the outskirts of Glasgow and transferred to an unmarked black Barrier helo. The cabin was sound-proofed. Once we were airborne, an officer came out of the cockpit. Medium height, with ramrod posture, a neatly trimmed mustache, and a black beret on which was the medieval castle emblem of Barrier. He gave

Church a "now we're in it" look, and Church nodded. The officer smiled at me and held out a small, hard hand.

"Brigadier Ashton Prebble," he said in a city Scots burr.

"Joe Ledger, sir."

"Yes," he drawled in a way that suggested he already knew who and what I was. "Pleasure to meet you, Captain Ledger. Glad to hear you're back in the game. Timing couldn't be more critical."

I snorted. "Nothing like jumping in with both feet."

Prebble had eyes like blueberries: dark and cold.

Ghost looked him up and down but didn't react in any challenging way to Prebble. I've started trusting the dog's judgment of people. Prebble was "one of us."

"Ashton," Church said, "would you bring Captain Ledger up to speed on where we're going?"

"Of course. We're flying to Fair Isle," said Prebble. The table between us was actually a computer, and he called up an aerial shot of a tiny speck of a place in the North Sea, halfway between Orkney and Shetland. "We've managed to quarantine the island and cut off all telephone, cell, and radio communication. We even shut down the Internet. Nothing's getting off the island and we have gunboats in the waters."

"Has anyone noticed?" I asked.

"They have, but we can play the London Hospital card for all manner of blackouts at the moment. Small mercies."

I glanced at Church. "No offense to the brigadier, but what's on- and off-the-record here?"

"Brigadier Prebble is in the family, Captain."

That was one of Church's catchphrases. It meant that

Prebble was in the select circle of people among whom there were no secrets. Well, none except those Church kept to himself.

Prebble punched buttons that tightened the satellite image of the facility. "Fair Isle is five kilometers long, about three wide. It's almost entirely surrounded by jagged cliffs. Seventy-three civilian residents, not counting the live-in staff at the facility. The civilians live in the southern third of the island, which is where the fertile ground is. They live in crofts along here." He tapped the screen to indicate several small enclosed parcels of arable land, then rolled the curser to shift the image to the central and northern sections. "The northern part is largely rough grazing and rocky moorland. There's a lighthouse on the south end, and a bird sanctuary."

I bent low and studied the aerial image. There was a compound at the northwest tip of the island. A handful of functional buildings surrounded by trees and a fence.

"There are six buildings comprising the Fair Isle Research Endeavor—or FIRE, if you enjoy trite acronyms. According to public charter, the lab is there to study bacteria that affect fish and mollusks. And, before you ask, Captain, there really are some rare and even unique bacteria in those waters that do affect the marine life. It's very good cover, and I believe a portion of the facility is actually dedicated to that purpose. Am I correct, Doctor?"

Hu nodded. "About twenty percent of the work at the lab, and they've actually made some progress, too. Last two years have seen a four percent increase in clam harvests."

"Big whoop," I said. "What about the other eighty percent?"

"Ah," said Prebble as he suppressed a smile. "According to what I'm not supposed to know, there are some very, very nasty bugs being studied there."

"Very nasty," Hu agreed. "Baker and Schloss are working to develop a TRB, specifically an airborne strain of Ebola."

I stared at him in horror. "Why the hell would—?"

"Proactive defense," Church cut in.

"Meaning?"

"Meaning," said Hu, "that someone is inevitably going to develop airborne Ebola. You busted one lab yourself, Captain."

"Yes, and those were nutcases, Doc. What are our guys doing? Working on a cure—?"

"A cure, a treatment, or some prophylactic stratagem," said Hu.

I didn't like it, but I understood it. Ebola is about 97 percent contagious and almost always lethal. Obtaining research samples was necessarily difficult, because if a terrorist organization ever launched a weaponized version of it and we hadn't done our homework we wouldn't live long enough to regret the lack of preparedness. Still sucked, though.

"Bloody marvelous, isn't it?" Prebble said with a tight smile. "And your lot brought the virus here by the gallon. Can't say I'm very happy about it."

"Can't say I am, either," said Church. "After 9/11 there was an overwhelming fear of being perceived by the public as unprepared. It was a bigger concern than actually developing a workable response to a biological attack. That pushed several likely pathogens into active testing immediately rather than waiting until a secure facility could be built somewhere in the U.S. And there may have been a secondary agenda. Some of the people who put this plan together may not have wanted to risk testing on U.S. soil. They felt it was more 'prudent' to exploit the protection of an ally with a strong military in case of an attack by a terrorist group." He glanced at me. "No, Captain, don't look at the logic too closely. It doesn't hold up to any kind of scrutiny."

"Politics," said Prebble, giving that word all the bile it deserved.

"Politics," agreed Church. "By U.S., British, and international law this lab is illegal. It was black book authorized following 9/11, but it was approved too hastily and then given to a private company to manage. If you try to make sense out of that you'll hurt yourself."

"Aye," said Prebble. "I can't stand on a pedestal here, because we made the same mistakes. America wasn't the only country scrambling to retrofit itself for antiterrorism and counterterrorism preparedness."

"You guys are killing my idealism here," I said.

"Let's hope that's all we kill," said Ashton. It wasn't a joke and nobody smiled.

"So," I said, "we seem to be busting our ass to get there, but everything you're telling me is past tense."

Hu said, "This morning, FIRE senior researcher Dr. Charles Grey came into work and brought his wife and son with him. They passed through all the security checkpoints, and he used his keycard to get them all into the bioresearch wing. Totally against all protocols, of course. We reviewed the security tapes, and when one lab tech tried to protest Grey flat out threatened to fire the guy. The tech backed down, more concerned for his job than for protocols." He sneered. "Accidents are always about the human element."

For once I could find no fault with his statement.

Church called up a floor plan on the tabletop computer. "FIRE is built in layers, with a false front around the exterior to make it look like an inexpensive university-level lab. There are offices and staff rooms, and so on, built in the outer ring. They connect at two points through air locks to the main lab complex. Inside there is another and much more sophisticated air lock that accesses what they call the Hot Room. That's where the work on the class-A pathogens is done, and there's a glass-enclosed and pressure-sealed observation tank in the center—the staff calls it the fish tank— and the biological vault is in there. Everyone working in the Hot Room can see the bio-vault, so nobody working there will be surprised when it's opened. There are also warning lights and buzzers of different kinds that go off when the unlocking codes are being entered." Church looked up from the screen. "Dr. Grey called the entire staff into the Hot Room and shortly after that the video surveillance system went out."

"How? Aren't those systems supposed to have redundancies?"

"Yes," Church agreed, "so we can presume that they were deliberately taken off-line."

I thought about that. "Then he can't be doing this alone. No way the security cameras are controlled from the Hot Room or the other labs."

Prebble smiled approvingly. "Good call. No, the fail-safe on the surveillance system has a set of manual controls, and they are in the security office on the other side of the complex. So figure at least one other person. Could be more."

"Is there a shutdown protocol?" I asked. "And is that connected to the door seals?"

Hu said, "There are manual controls for all functions of the outer lab and the Hot Room, but it's only used when the bio-vault is locked and the fish tank sealed. They use it when they're installing new equipment or making repairs to doors and such, and under those conditions the bio-vault with the active samples is sealed and guarded. That system is connected via satellite uplinks to coded routers in a national security satellite. The uplink has been terminated at the source. Same for the hard-lines that connect to the TAT-fourteen transatlantic telecommunications cable. The satellite and cable are functioning normally, but both report a disconnection."

"There's got to be a fail-safe . . . a dead man's switch."

"Sure," said Hu. "But like everything, there is a bypass to it. Bug has pinged it and he's sure that the system has been taken off-line. In fact, the only way to bypass this kind of security is through deliberate and coordinated human action."

"Shit."

"You can't prevent human error," said Hu fussily. "You can only advise against it and encourage adherence to rules."

"It gets worse," said Church. "Because the main lab is not part of any active virus research protocols, it has looser safety features. In fact, it can be manually integrated into the main air-conditioning system for the whole lab facility."

I could feel the blood drain from my face. "What kind of moron would approve that design?"

"The bureaucratic kind," said Church.

"Christ. Can the vents be blocked from outside?"

"Under normal circumstances, yes, but it appears that at some time prior to today Grey or someone working with him disabled the vent overrides. We'll have to review weeks of security tapes and logs to see who worked on it, and that's beside the point. It's damage done. The vent controls have been entirely routed to the Hot Room. All Grey has to do to flood the building is throw a switch."

"What are the options? Can you disable the electrics? Cut the power?"

"Essential services like venting, lights, and air-lock functions have battery backups. It's a safety measure to make sure the automatic seals never lose power."

"What about an electromagnetic pulse? How fast can you drop an E-bomb on the place?"

"This is a hardened facility," said Prebble. "We've examined the option of carpet bombing the facility, but we would need an exact mix of bunker busters and fuel air bombs, and that's tricky. Destroying the building is easy . . . making sure we fry every single microscopic germ is another matter altogether, and our best computer models give us only a probability of ninety-four percent success."

"And since we're talking about airborne Ebola, that might as well be zero," said Hu.

"Yes," agreed Prebble, "and prevailing winds are not

in our favor today. On the other hand, there's a carrier just over the horizon and I've had a quiet word with the captain. He's an old mate of mine. If there's so much as a wee hint that the facility's outer containment is failing, then I make a call and we'll all be having tea with Jesus before you can say 'oh, shite.'"

"You'd drop a nuke?" I asked, appalled. "And only part of my concern is based on the fact that we're flying there. Dropping a nuke on an illegal American bioweapons lab would be . . ." I fished for a word bad enough to describe it and came up short.

"I agree," said Church grimly. "Aside from the physical damage and risk of fallout, neither country would recover from the damage to their credibility on a global scale. It would truly be catastrophic."

"Nevertheless, gentlemen," said Prebble, "should things turn against us I've prepared a set of recommendations for the Prime Minister that includes a nuclear option."

"Let's make sure that things don't turn against us," said Church quietly. "We have several overlapping quarantine protocols in operation, and a Chinook is flying in rolls of industrial-grade quarantine draping. We'll disable all of the external cameras and then drape the building. That should give us an extra step toward first base in the event of a containment breach. Once that's in place we'll roll out our primary response."

"Let me guess," I said. "Me, in a hazmat suit, with a gun."

"Can you recommend something else?"

"Sure. A whole bunch of shooters in hazmats with guns. Seal the outer doors, take out the inner doors with an RPG, burn everything else with flamethrowers, let Dr. Grey be the one having tea and crumpets with the Messiah, and we call it a day." I looked at Church. "But that's not the play you're going to call, is it?"

He said nothing for a moment. This was the kind of moment in which he'd usually reach for a NILLA wafer while the rest of us sorted it out and got into the same mental gear as him. Prebble hadn't supplied any cookies. Church looked almost wistful. He said, "You're the senior DMS field commander on-station, Captain. Do you see that as the best tactical option?"

I sighed. "No."

"And why not?" Church asked, like Socrates guiding a student through a logic puzzle. I hated when he did this.

"Because with that plan we don't get to ask any questions . . . and we need to know why he's doing this."

Church and Prebble nodded.

There was a faint *bing-bing* and then the pilot's voice said, "Touchdown in five, gentlemen."

Interlude Sixteen

T-Town

Mount Baker, Washington State

Three and a Half Months Before the London Event

Hugo Vox stood in the doorway to Circe's office. His face looked haggard, his eyes dark.

"I'm so sorry," he said.

Circe couldn't speak. It felt like a steel hand was clamped around her throat.

Grace . . . ? Her mouth formed the name silently as the first tears fell.

Vox nodded. "Down in the Bahamas. A big DMS action. I don't have the details, but the word is that she died in combat. A lot of people died. The DMS took a lot of losses. It's . . . it's a terrible tragedy. For them . . . and for all of us."

"Grace," Circe murmured, finding a splinter of her voice, but the name stuck in her throat. "God . . ."

"I know you two were close," said Vox.

Circe put her face in her hands. "I just saw her the other *day*!"

"The DMS was facing something really big. Something really, really bad. From what Gus Dietrich told me, Grace may have saved us all. That new guy, Ledger, was able to wrap it up, but Grace Courtland did her part. Yes, ma'am, she did her part indeed. Best of the best, she was."

Circe shook her head, not wanting to hear more. Not now.

Vox turned away, and then paused. He turned back for just a moment and watched Circe's shoulders tremble with the first wave of sobs. He opened his mouth to say something, but he left it unsaid. He sighed and lumbered out.

Interlude Seventeen

McCullough, Crown Island
St. Lawrence River, Ontario, Canada
Four Months Ago

The two silent Korean guards came for Gault and Toys an hour later and led them down the hallway, the end of which was blocked by a gorgeously embroidered brocade tapestry that depicted a scene from the Book of Revelation. Gault bent and slowly translated the Latin stitched along the border.

"'Here is the mind which has wisdom: The seven heads are seven mountains on which the woman sits. There are also seven kings. Five have fallen, one is, and the other has not yet come. And when he comes, he must continue a short time. The beast that was, and is not, is himself also the eighth, and is of the seven, and is going to perdition.'"

"I must have missed that in catechism," murmured Toys.

One of the guards slid the tapestry aside to reveal an elevator door. The guard pressed his palm to a geometry scanner and tapped in a complex entry code. The elevator door opened silently. Toys was impressed with the sophistication of the equipment. The security precautions matched the exacting standards he had always encouraged Gault to use.

The elevator took them deep into the heart of the island. When the doors opened, one guard indicated that they exit, but neither of the two Asians moved to join them. Gault and Toys exchanged a brief wary glance before stepping out into a hallway that had been carved from raw bedrock. There was a set of large and ornately carved teak doors to their right, and as they stepped forward the doors opened toward them without a sound.

They entered a massive chamber. One wall of the chamber was covered floor to ceiling with flat-screen TV monitors; the other walls were hung with tapestries as ancient and elegant as the apocalypse drapery upstairs. The center of the room was dominated by a massive oak table around which there were seven great thronelike chairs and seven expensive leather chairs of the kind Toys had once bought for Gault's private office. On the far side of the table a chair that had a higher back than all the others sat on a dais. It stood empty.

The lights were low except for green-globed lamps positioned for each of the chairs. All but one of the lamps had been angled to spill light toward the center of the table, leaving the person in each chair cast in shadows.

Six of the great chairs were occupied, but the one closest to where Gault and Toys stood was empty. Likewise, six of the leather chairs were occupied. Every face was in shadow, but Toys knew that those faces were turned toward Gault.

"Yes," he heard Gault murmur.

"What?" Toys asked under his breath.

Gault looked at Toys for a long moment, his eyes glassy and distant.

"Sebastian—?" Toys prompted.

Gault did not answer. Instead he took a step deeper into the room.

"Welcome," said a familiar voice, and they turned as

a man in one of the thrones leaned into the spill of light. "Sebastian, Toys . . . it's so good to see you both," said the American in his booming bull voice. It was difficult for Toys to reconcile the gruffness of this man with the elegant majesty of his mother. They were not only un-alike as people, but to Toys it seemed as if they had to be from different species also.

"Welcome!" said the others seated at the table.

Gault nodded silently and, Toys thought, with genuine reverence.

Because of all the grandeur of the room, the moody lighting, the thrones, and the setting, Toys wouldn't have been surprised if the men at the table had been wearing hoods or masks, or at the very least black tie. But the American wore an ordinary three-button Polo shirt and had a pair of sunglasses tucked into the vee. He looked ready for a quick nine of golf rather than a clandestine meeting in an underground chamber beneath a castle.

Gault gestured vaguely to the room. "What is all this?"

The American laughed. "It's pretty much exactly what it looks like, boys. We're a secret society."

"A 'secret society'?" Toys laughed. "Are you taking the mickey?"

"No, I'm serious as a heart attack."

Gault folded his arms and cocked a disbelieving head to one side. "Ri-i-ight. An actual secret society. Like, what? Like the Cabal?"

"They've been smashed flat by the DMS."

"The Trilateral Commission?"

"More effective."

"The Illuminati?"

"Right ballpark."

Toys muttered, "Somewhere Dan Brown just had an erection."

Everyone at the table laughed.

"Seriously . . . who *are* you and what is all this?" demanded Toys.

The American smiled and shrugged. It was a very Gallic shrug even though he was pure New England.

"How would you like me to answer that?"

"I presume 'straightforward' is a nonstarter?"

Another chuckle rippled through the seated figures.

"If we ever decide on a membership pamphlet, it will go something like this," said a man on the right side of the room, and then he spoke in a formal and ominous voice. "We have many names. History knows us as the Sargonai, the heirs and kinsmen of Sargon of Mesopotamia, first emperor in the history of mankind."

The man who spoke wore the robes of a Saudi. Moreover, Toys *knew* him. It was impossible that he was here. In America, in New York of all places, where even the mind-numbed street people would attack him without hesitation.

" 'Sargonai'?" Gault echoed with a smile.

Another leaned forward, a fat man with Slavic features. "It's just a cover name, one of many we've used, but we don't call ourselves that. Not anymore."

"Why not?" drawled Toys. "It's catchy. It would look great on souvenir coffee mugs."

"Hush," barked Gault.

"No," said the Saudi, "let him have his voice. If you are welcome here, then so is your Conscience. As you see, we each have one."

Around the room the people seated in the leather chairs leaned into the light. Four men, two women. Most of them nodded, one waved, and the one seated next to the American saluted with a steaming cup of coffee.

" 'Conscience'?" Gault asked.

The Slav answered that. "It is the policy of the Trust that each of us has a Conscience who is free to speak his or her mind. They may offer advice, provide intelligence, and participate in all of our discussions. All great kings have had such as they, and they've worn a thousand disguises—chamberlain and general, jester and body servant, spouse and lover. Trust is the determining factor; mutual interest and a shared vision are the chemicals that combine to cement their relationship together."

Gault took a step forward and Toys noticed how his friend's eyes had flared with interest at the word "kings." For years Gault had written that word in doodles or used variations on it for passwords. Gault had never explained why.

"You speak of advisors to kings," Gault said. "Is that what you are? *Kings*?"

"Yes," said the American. "We are the Seven Kings of the New World Trust. Sons of Sargon through a thousand generations of men, the fruit of the Tree of Empire. Foretold in the Book of Revelation."

Gault shared a look with Toys.

" 'Seven' Kings?" Gault tilted his chin toward the empty throne.

"Seven we have been; seven we will be again," said another voice. A man at the far side of the table leaned forward. Toys recognized him as an Israeli politician. "Seven is the sacred number of the Goddess."

"Though, admittedly," the American said, "we are one member short at the moment."

"Kings of what?" asked Toys.

The Israeli and the American smiled as if they were waiting for that question.

"We are not kings of countries," said the Israeli. "Each of us embraces a specific path, a specific view, and we claim kingship over everything that falls within the scope of this view." He stood up and in a bold voice declared, "I am the King of War. No gun is fired, no border crossed, no weapons bought or sold but that I am involved. War and the threat of war cultivate commerce and cause innovation to advance by leaps and bounds. War evolves our society and defines our species."

It sounded crazy, the words childishly grandiose, and yet the way in which it was said made the smile die on Toys' mouth. He looked at this man and in a flash of insight believed him. Toys knew that, all phrasing aside, what this man said was the truth.

The Saudi stood. "I am the King of Lies. Truth is the clay in my hands, and information is the most potent force on earth. Nations rise and fall on what is said and what is believed. A whisper in the ear, a story leaked to the press, a piece of information seeded to an intelligence analyst can change the course of world events."

Toys heard Gault catch his breath.

The Russian stood. "I am the King of Famine. The need for food is a universal constant, and no one takes a bite or lets water pass their lips unless I allow it.

Fortunes are made from plenty as they are from want. I am both plenty and want."

Another man stood and spoke in a cultured Italian accent: "I am the King of Gold. Money is the blood of this world. The lack of it destroys people and tears kings from thrones; the excess of it corrupts saints. World economies are mine to bend and twist and crush."

A Frenchman stood. "I am the King of Thieves. My weapons are stocks and banks and loans and the flow of debt between peoples and corporations and governments."

Finally the American stood and spoke in a booming voice: "I am the King of Fear. When a bomb goes off, it has my kiss upon it. Terror stirs the pot of chaos, and in chaos the Seven Kings thrive. I arm the faithful and the fanatical. I allow the disenfranchised a voice. Not to serve their ends, but to serve mine. Ours."

Then all of them together raised their voices and roared out, "We are the Seven Kings. We are chaos!"

They sat, but the echo of their words punched all the walls and pounded Gault and Toys like physical blows. No one spoke until the last echo faded to a whisper.

The American smiled a devil's smile. "And we would like you to join us, Sebastian. We have an opening at our table."

"Opening?" murmured Gault faintly. His eyes were fever bright.

"We would like you to be our new King of Plagues."

"Jesus," hissed Toys, and grabbed Gault's arm, but Gault laid his hand on Toys' wrist and slowly pushed him off.

"The King of Plagues," echoed Gault. He looked at

each man . . . each King. He looked at their thrones and then at the empty throne, and as he did so he touched the bandages that still covered his ruined and remade face.

Toys leaned closed and whispered to him, "Be careful, Sebastian. . . . This is too weird . . . even for us."

But Gault was not listening.

"What do you say, Sebastian?" asked the American. "We need a man of vision, a man who understands the power of self-interest. We need a man who grasps the many wonderful and life-changing potentials that wait in the RNA and proteins of a virus. Someone who is brave enough to use these pathogens like fists." He paused and every eye in the room was on Gault. "Are you that man?"

Gault took an absent step forward, and then another, and a third until he stood at the edge of the table. He rested his fingertips on the cool polished wood and stared for a long minute down at his own distorted reflection.

Then, slowly, he raised his eyes and looked at the assembly of Kings.

"Yes," he said in a voice that was more deadly than smallpox. "Oh . . . yes!"

Toys felt a pain in his heart as if some unseen hand had stabbed him. He looked at the rapt expression on Gault's face, and then he closed his eyes.

No. Oh, Sebastian . . . no.

He did not—*dared* not—say it aloud.

Chapter Twenty-seven

We landed behind a stand of oak trees, scattering goats and gulls. Once the door was open I peered through the window just in time to see another chopper set down, a muscular Merlin HC3 transport chopper. The doors slid open and a dozen Barrier agents in SARATOGA HAMMER chemical warfare suits deployed and ran to formation past the outside edge of the rotor wash.

Prebble, Hu, and Dietrich climbed out of our chopper, but Church shifted to stand between me and the door.

"Hold on," he said. His dark eyes, hidden behind the tinted lenses of his glasses, were like black marbles. "I'm sorry to have cut your vacation short."

"No, you're not," I said.

"No, I'm not," he admitted. "You've been through a lot and I'm throwing you into the fire. Dr. Sanchez tells me that it's too soon, that you need more time to heal. Tell me if I'm making a mistake."

I wanted to laugh. We both knew I'd rather be back in my hotel room in London. Or in the middle of the Sahara. Anywhere but here. Sometimes the absurd nature of what I do hits me. Here I was, a former Baltimore detective still young enough to kick some ass in a pickup b-ball game; a guy with a father who just won a nail-biter of an election to become the new mayor; a brother who was also a cop as well as a husband and a father to my only nephew; a guy who should have been working cases back home and maybe scouting for a wife of my own. With all that, here I was pulling on a combat-modified hazmat suit and gun belt because I was about to enter a building filled with some of the deadliest and more virulent diseases known to modern man, a building held by a lunatic who was threatening to release those diseases. A man I'd almost certainly have to kill and who might be part of a huge secret society trying to tear down the world.

How the hell did that become normal for me? Or for anyone?

Was it too soon? How could I—or anyone in my position—answer that question?

"You didn't make a mistake," I said.

He nodded but didn't move.

"Is there something else?" I asked.

For a moment Church's mouth was a tight and lip-less line of tension, almost a snarl. "I didn't want to tell you this in front of the others. I debated waiting until after you finished with the lab, but I didn't think you'd thank me for that."

"That's ominous as shit, Boss. Spill it."

"There's been another incident."

He told me about the explosions at Area 51. I could feel my stomach turning to icy slush, and there was a roaring in my ears that wasn't the wind.

"Lucky Team, the investigators, the staff at the base," Church said. "Gone. All of them."

"And Echo Team? Top and Bunny—?"

He shook his head. "We lost two. Sergeants Gomez and Henderson. The rest were outside. Scrapes and bruises, but no other casualties. They are, however, the only survivors. Everyone else at the base is dead."

"I-I can't believe it," I stammered.

I didn't know Henderson, but Ricky Gomez had been in active training around the time I took off for Europe. Nice kid from Brooklyn. His brother played single-A ball for the Cyclones. Now Ricky and Henderson and all the others were dust. Just like the four thousand at the London. Ash and bones. I could hear something ripping behind my eyes and a bloody haze clouded my vision. I had to force my voice to sound normal. I used the Cop voice, not the Killer's.

"What do we know?" I demanded.

"Next to nothing. Nellis is sending a team and I've scrambled our people from the casino. We have Jerry Spencer's number two, Bess Tanaka, out there working the scene." Church paused. "So far no one has come forward to claim responsibility."

"Has to be the Kings."

"Probably," he said, "but the unfortunate truth is that they're not our only enemies."

"What's our play?"

"That's being determined now. I've advised the President to keep this out of the media for as long as possible; otherwise the whole base will become a circus. The Internet and cable talk shows are already buzzing with conspiracy theories about the Hospital. This would be gasoline on that fire. We may have to spin a cover story to make it work."

I nodded. "How the fuck does someone take out an entire military base? I mean, seriously—a secret and ultrahigh-security military base?"

"I can only think of one way," Church said, his face turning once more to a mask of cold iron.

I looked at him and then nodded. He was right; there was no other way.

"God damn it." They had to have someone inside.

"I'm sorry I had to dump this on you right before a mission, but I knew you'd want to know."

I nodded.

"Do you want me to pull you from this?"

"Is that a serious question?" I said.

A ghost of a smile crossed his face. "I suppose not."

He offered me his hand.

"Then good hunting, Captain."

We shook, and he stepped aside to allow me to exit the bird.

Chapter Twenty-eight

The State Correctional Institution at Graterford

Graterford, Pennsylvania

December 18, 2:39 P.M. EST

"I'm sorry there isn't more," said Dr. Stankevičius. "Apparently the 'maximum' aspect of the security here at Graterford doesn't extend to my office." As he said it he shot a withering look at the warden.

Rudy Sanchez saw the barb go home. *Certainly no love lost between these two,* he thought.

"The records for this prisoner are sparse at best," Rudy said aloud. "Is there any explanation for the omissions, Warden?"

The warden, a block-faced former state trooper named Wilson, spread his hands. "It's a mystery."

"A mystery," Rudy said quietly, establishing and maintaining direct eye contact.

Wilson shifted in his chair. "Naturally I've initiated a full-scale investigation."

"Naturally. But, tell me, Warden, what does that investigation comprise?"

"Sorry?"

"A full-scale investigation—what exactly will you do to try and locate the missing files?"

"I . . . I mean we will interview the staff, and review the duty logs. . . ." His voice trailed off.

Rudy removed a small notebook and jotted something. Wilson's eyes were fixed on Rudy as he did so, but he didn't let Wilson see what he wrote. The note read: *Get car inspected.*

Wilson immediately launched into a more detailed explanation of what would be done. Computer searches, extra staff brought in to scour the filing cabinets to check for misfiling, a complete search of Nicodemus's cell, follow-ups with all current staff, and interviews with trustees and guards who worked in the medical unit during or after the murder of Jesus Santiago, the young Latino who had been mutilated with the numbers 12/17.

Rudy listened quietly. Then he wrote: *Feed Joe's cat.* And closed his notebook.

Wilson was sweating.

"Thank you, Warden," said Rudy. "I'm sure you are doing everything within *your* powers." He leaned ever so slightly on the word "your." He had no desire to roast anyone over a bureaucratic fire, but at the same time he despised incompetence, particularly in jobs related to health or security. He wasn't fond of it before joining the DMS, and now he knew firsthand how sloppy work could lead to spilled blood.

Rudy turned to Dr. Stankevičius. "Doctor, you indicated to me that you believe Nicodemus to have unusual knowledge of the events taking place in London. Is that correct?"

"Yes."

"Has Nicodemus admitted such knowledge?"

"No, as I mentioned in my report—"

"He mentioned the Seven Kings, is that correct?"

"Yes."

"Just the once?"

"Yes."

Rudy did not mention the graffiti on the wall of the hospital or on the door of the murdered family. Instead he asked, "Has Nicodemus admitted to any of the crimes for which he's been convicted or suspected?"

"No."

"Has he denied involvement?"

"For Jesus Santiago? His response was obscure and evasive. I could not encourage him to say yes or no in simple terms. On the other hand, he flat out denied that he had been talking with Santiago; and the witness to that encounter—a guard—later died of a self-inflicted gunshot wound."

"You don't have any medical records for Nicodemus," Rudy said. "Why is that?"

"There was a fire in the prison medical center," said the warden. "Fire marshal says that it was rats chewing on the wires. They found a charred rat carcass. We lost a couple of years' worth of records."

Bullshit, thought Rudy.

Stankevičius nodded. "Much of our testing equipment and supplies were smoke and water damaged. The fire also damaged the CT scanner."

"And the copies of the medical reports that should be in the file?"

Neither man answered. Rudy sat back and looked at them for several quiet seconds. Both men looked ashamed and nervous.

They're both scared out of their minds. Dios mio! What in hell is going on here?

"I'm sorry, gentlemen, but I'm having a hard time understanding this. This is a maximum-security prison. A model for such prisons, as I understand it. You have a large staff, modern equipment, plenty of resources, and you're telling me that you are unable to compile even a basic medical and psychological profile on a convict who has been incarcerated here for *over fifteen years*? One-room jails in third-world countries can do at least that much. I hesitate to use the word 'obfuscation' here, but—"

"Now wait a minute, Dr. Sanchez," Stankevičius began. "We're not doing this deliberately—"

"No? So, it's just sloppy procedure?"

Stankevičius clamped his mouth shut.

"That's unfair," Wilson said tightly. "We've had a string of bad luck."

Rudy eyed him coolly. "Bad luck is what happens when you buy scratch-off lottery tickets, Warden. As I understand it, it is not a factor in the American penal system, particularly at this level."

Both men stared at him for a second; then their eyes faltered and they looked away. Rudy sighed.

They're too scared to even properly defend their actions. Interesting.

"Very well," said Rudy. "I'd like to see the prisoner now."

The doctor and the warden exchanged a brief, defeated look. Finally the warden got heavily to his feet.

"Of course, Dr. Sanchez."

Interlude Eighteen

The Seven Kings
Four Months Ago

Champagne was served and they all toasted; even the Saudi took a glass, winking to Gault as he did so.

Toys closed on Gault to whisper in his ear, "What the hell are you *doing*? We don't even know what we're getting into here. We just got *out* of a mess. . . . Do you want to walk into another one?"

Gault looked at him, his eyes hard and steady. "I know precisely what I'm doing, Toys. If you're scared, you can leave any time you want."

Toys took a step back as if he'd been slapped. "What are you—?"

The American cleared his throat and waved everyone to their seats. Gault and Toys remained standing, though now they stood a few feet apart. Toys looked both surprised and concerned, but Gault smiled and patted him on the cheek.

"It's all going to be fine," he said quietly. "You'll see."

When everyone was seated, the American pressed a section of the tabletop and it slid open to reveal a computer keyboard. He tapped some keys and the monitors on the wall flickered on to show a series of buildings in different cities.

"First," he said, "let us show you our world. No secrets."

"No secrets," murmured Gault.

"This is the world of the Seven Kings."

On the screens, one after another, buildings erupted into flame. School buses exploded, throwing small fire-wreathed shapes into the street. Jetliners slammed into tall towers, and those towers collapsed, pancaking down and filling the streets with deadly gray clouds. Suicide bombers walked into theaters and train stations. Kings and presidents were caught in indiscretions. Princesses were killed in car wrecks. Drug companies released medications that proved to be more dangerous than the diseases they were designed to combat. Flu epidemics sprang out of nowhere. It rolled on and on. A symphony of destruction that was at once shocking in its scope and elegant in its subtlety.

As each new image played, one of the Kings would tell the story behind it. Misinformation, disinformation, and the placement of carefully selected truths. Fuel thrown onto the fire of religious hatred. Ethnic wars funded by private dollars. Useful assassinations, and even more useful attempted assassinations.

Gault turned to the Kings. "You did all of that? The Towers? All of it?"

"Some of this is our doing," said the King of Gold. "Some of these things are the actions of our enemies. Some were conceived by us but handed over to other groups to carry out. We're often involved well behind the scenes."

The King of Famine said, "We provide ideas, financing, encouragement, and occasionally direct action."

The American nodded to the small man who sat in the seat of his Conscience. "My good friend and Conscience, Rafael Santoro, has overseen many of our most complicated 'events.'"

Santoro bowed slightly. "It is always my pleasure to serve the Seven Kings."

Toys gestured to the screens. "If some of this isn't your actual work," he said, "why show it to us?"

"Well," said the American with a mildly pained expression, "that's *part* of the reason we brought you here. When we said that we will have no secrets from you, we meant it. As much as we would like to truly be the most powerful force on the planet, we aren't."

Toys nodded. "Let me guess—you're in some kind of dustup with the other lot."

"Yes," agreed the American.

"And they're bigger?"

"At the moment."

"And stronger?"

"For now."

"Do they know about you?"

There was an uncomfortable murmur. "Yes," said the

King of War. "They know. They know and they would like to see us all dead."

Toys said, "Do they fight for truth, justice, and the American way?"

"Hardly." The King of Lies laughed. "They are a true shadow government with no higher intentions. They have had a hand in starting virtually every major conflict since the Civil War."

"As opposed to you chaps who are giving out daffodils and free blow jobs," said Toys with disgust.

"Damn it, Toys," snarled Gault, but the Kings surprised them both by laughing.

"I like this boy, Sebastian," said the American. "I always have. Says what he fucking means and doesn't give a rat's ass what anybody thinks."

"Too bloody right," Gault said with asperity.

Toys affected to brush lint from his lapel with a look that said, *I'm rubber; you're glue.*

"Our agenda is not a happy one for the great unwashed masses," admitted the King of Gold. "We are predators and we pretend to be nothing else."

"Then who *are* your enemies?" demanded Gault. He looked as if the very *thought* of enemies offended him on a personal level.

"The Skull and Bones." Several of the Kings said it at the same time, each of them with disgust.

"The actual Skull and Bones?" Toys laughed. "Those wankers at Yale? George Bush and that lot?"

"That lot, yes," said the Saudi. "Though, admittedly, not all of the most celebrated members of that society belong to the Inner Circle and it's the Inner Circle who are the real power. Many of the members do not even believe that an Inner Circle exists. They think it's an urban legend created by detractors of the Skull and Bones. However, it is real, and it is only the Inner Circle which concerns us. That is where the true power is."

Gault said, "Surely the world is big enough for you each to cut a large slice of the global pie. Why the conflict?"

"It isn't of our making," said the King of Famine. "When we first made contact with the Inner Circle we reached out in the hopes of establishing some manner of working partnership. Or at very least an agreement of noninterference."

"How'd that work out for you chaps?" asked Toys.

"Not well. Each attempt to arrange a sit-down with the Inner Circle has resulted in the murder of our agents. Over the last decade the Inner Circle has invested a great deal of time and effort in discovering who we are. A number of our agents have been targeted and killed, many of them tortured for information. We keep a great deal of distance between us and our operatives in the field, so the Inner Circle do not know our names—but they've done considerable damage to our operations. They've also sicced various American and international organizations on us, including INTERPOL, NATO, the CIA, and the DMS. That has made things . . . uncomfortable."

"Why the animosity? Are you both going after the same things?" asked Gault. "Is it simply a competition to grab the most?"

"No. Our interests overlap, but our methods are very much in conflict. And the Inner Circle have become obsessed with controlling all of the power in the Middle

East, which is where we make much of *our* money. They keep starting wars over there."

Toys looked at the King of War. "And you don't?"

"No. We make more money from the threat of war and the arms race than from outright declared war," said the Israelite. "Small wars are okay, but major conflicts stop trade. In cases of decisive victory it can even eradicate whole markets. We profit from the constant escalation, from nations and groups preparing for war, because that means when one upgrades its weapons system its rivals need to do the same."

"Keeping up with the Joneses," said Toys. "With guns."

"Guns, missile systems, jets, tanks, body armor, defense satellites, the works," said the American. "The Inner Circle are directly aggressive. We're chaotic. Aggression causes trade disconnects—and to see that, look at the U.S. and its trade relations in the years following 9/11. They waved such a big stick that they chased everyone else off the playground, and as a result they wound up selling their souls to China. Dumb asses."

"So . . . you *didn't* do the attacks on the Towers?"

"Oh, but we *did*," said the Saudi with a smile. "That was a masterpiece of planning of which we are all very proud. But it was the Inner Circle who derailed our carefully drawn plans by shifting the focus away from Al-Qaeda and onto Saddam. All that nonsense about weapons of mass destruction. Saddam was a murderous fool, but he was no Hitler. He was not even a decent Mussolini. Iran is ten times greater a threat to the United States. Iraq . . . that was purely a grab for oil."

"And to place substantial U.S. military assets in the Middle East," said War. "If we had not stepped in to fund the Shiites and some other interested parties, then the Americans would have flattened Iraq and that would be that."

Gault walked over to the Saudi. "Where do you fit into all of this, then? You are the face of the Al-Qaeda. They are hunted because of you."

The King of Lies smiled. "It was always our intention that the Al-Qaeda take the blame for the Towers. However, we initiated the project and invited them in. They *were* involved, have no doubts, and most of them are as true to their cause as they say. I, however, am not, nor have I ever been. We stoked the Al-Qaeda's hatred of the—*ahem*—Great Satan. Overall, it was one of our greatest successes."

"And we used our people here in the States to amp up anti-Islamic hatred," said the American. "Hate crimes are *mucho* profitable. They impact stocks, they shift populations, they influence elections—and there are profits to be taken at every step of that."

"So you destroyed the Towers to make a buck?" Toys asked.

The King of Gold said, "Most negative world events influence the stock market, mainly because the vast majority of investors are timid sheep who piss themselves if the wind veers. Deliberate negative events, such as terrorist incidents, cause significant and sudden drops in the market. The key is knowing what is coming and, most importantly, *when*. That way you can buy when prices are plummeting. Do it through a hundred intermediaries and you don't leave a trail. We learned that from 9/11. And if the government panics and closes the market, wait it out. It will always reopen and prices will always rise again. Once things stabilize, we begin to sell when prices get to about sixty percent of the pre-panic price. Again, you don't appear to be a strict profiteer. You're just one of the sheep meandering back to the fold after the Big Bad Wolf has been chased off."

"So," said Gault, impressed, "instead of having your people poised to act *should* something happen, you have them ready to maximize the take based on true fore-knowledge."

"Exactly."

"Bloody brilliant."

"Manipulting the United States and its global image has been the key," said the King of Thieves. "America has been a crucial element in Middle East politics since the British withdrew in 1971. Despite all of the hate and criticism leveled against them, intelligent people on all sides of the issue know that they are a positive influence on the stability of the region. If their credibility were so badly damaged that they could no longer adequately play their role, then there would be a regional crisis that would cause oil prices to skyrocket. We saw some of that in 2006 and '7 when Americans were paying over four dollars a gallon to keep their SUVs on the road. Go back in time and you can see other price spikes corresponding to incidents of damaged American credibility and regional instability. The 1973 oil embargo was the first, then the Iranian revolution of 1979 and the Iran-Iraq war the following year. Over and over we see proof of this."

"The current conflict has other useful effects," continued the King of Famine. "Our actions have brought the United States into armed conflict with the Taliban in Afghanistan."

"I thought you were opposed to open war?" said Toys.

War laughed. "Afghanistan isn't an *open* war. It never will be. It's a *guerilla* war. That's fine, because that kind of thing can go on for years and years without any dramatic resolution."

"Which America can't win?" suggested Gault.

"No one can," agreed War. "Not unless you are willing to exterminate the enemy, and America—for all of its faults—is not willing to take that step. Not even the Bonesmen can sell ethnic genocide to the U.S. people. We can bank on that. We *have,* in fact, banked on it."

"Bush is a Bonesman, isn't he?" asked Toys.

"Yes, but he's not Inner Circle," said the American. "Dubya was their public face, and may not have even known it. He's a Texas jokester who couldn't manage a Wal-Mart and the Inner Circle put him in the Oval Office for two terms while they moved behind the scenes."

"What about the current administration?" asked Gault.

"The Inner Circle doesn't have the same kind of control over this president, which is why they are trying to weaken him and discredit his accomplishments. Once he's out, they'll put another one of their mannequins in the White House."

"Don't tell me you voted for the Democrat," Toys said with a grin.

"Actually, we did." The American chuckled. "Though rest assured it had nothing to do with supporting him, his policies, or the do-gooder agenda he's selling. No, we stand behind *anyone* who isn't on the Inner Circle's leash."

"We are trying to meet the Inner Circle on the same ground," said the King of Famine. "They are kingmakers and they have a lot of experience in that regard. We are working toward that end. We want to put one of our puppets in the White House and, ultimately, in Number Ten Downing Street, the Palazzo del Quirinale, the Élysée Palace, and the Kremlin."

"How far along are you?" asked Gault.

Famine shrugged. "We have a program in place now that is designed to increase racial and religious hatred between Islam and Israel, which should embarrass sitting governments and shake some power players out of their seats. Then it will be a horse race between us and the Inner Circle to fill those seats."

"Through religious conflict?" asked Toys, and he was careful to keep his voice neutral.

"None of us have any particular anger toward any religion or ethnic group; however, we agree that hate crimes are good for business. Our business," said Lies. "Our campaign is being driven through systematic disinformation on the Internet, and through bribes and donations to certain extremist groups who lack only funding and a kick in the backside in order to act."

"And by 'act' you mean—?"

"Walking into mosques or temples wearing vests packed with C4. Or leaving bombs in religiously significant areas."

"Christ," said Toys, and Gault cut him an annoyed look.

"There are always people willing to kill in the name

of their God," said Famine. "Because of the open-forum nature of the Internet, laws about free speech, and news media hungry for controversial stories, small and disenfranchised groups have found a voice that can now be heard around the world. It's lovely. With money, Internet postings, and other support, we give them a fist as well as a voice."

"And," said Gault, "because they're vocal factions instead of countries, hate crimes increase, tension increases, but the actual nations don't go to war. And you profit."

The Kings beamed at him.

"This is all so . . . elegant," murmured Gault.

"Elegant, maybe," snorted the American. "But it's riskier than it needs to be."

Gold turned to him. "Not so. Your mother, the Goddess, has done great work."

The American made a disgusted noise.

"You disapprove of this campaign?" Gault asked him.

The American looked around the room before he shrugged. "We may not have secrets here, but we don't always agree on policy. I was the only dissenting voice on this. Mom still hasn't forgiven me."

"What's your objection?"

"It puts my ass on the line. This whole campaign requires me to use resources that are part of what I do *outside* the Kings. If this falls apart, guess whose dick will be in the wringer?"

There was a brief and uncomfortable silence in the room.

"My brother," said the Frenchman quietly, "we've talked about this. There are so many layers of subterfuge between your businesses and the Goddess's plan that they will never dig deep enough to expose you."

"Maybe," snapped the American with bad grace, "but those Inner Circle pricks aren't forgiving and they can bring a lot of guns to bear. They've already aimed the DMS at us. Those sons of whores took out seven cells that we've been grooming for hits here in the States."

"How?" demanded Toys. "How does the Inner Circle know what you're planning?"

There was a heavy silence in the room.

Finally the King of Famine said, "We suspect that the Conscience of our former King of Plagues was leaking information."

Toys glanced at the empty seat. "And where is he now? Seems like you should be turning thumbscrews on the chatty bastard."

"We did," said Gold, and when Toys and Gault looked at him they saw that he wasn't joking. "We can get quite—oh, what's the phrase?"

"We went medieval on him," supplied the King of Fear. "But we got a little overzealous. Well . . . I did, I guess. By the end he was confessing to everything from killing Marilyn Monroe to starting the Chicago Fire. My bad. I thought I could open him up."

"If I may," said Rafael Santoro, placing his palm over his heart, "if there is a next time, please consider allowing me to do what is necessary, yes?"

The American nodded. "Not a problem. I should have waited until you were back in the country rather than having a go at it. Even so, the leak seems to have stopped, though."

The Russian said, "Our goal of instability works even when the Bonesmen are pulling the strings in Washington and, through proxy, the Middle East. We have damaged and will continue to damage governmental credibility, and when America stumbles money spills all over the place."

"And you were there to lap it up?" said Toys with a smile.

"We were there with big fucking buckets!" declared Famine. "The economic crash of 2008? That was ours. It was our riposte to the invasion of Iraq, and we skewered the Bonesmen very nicely."

Gold laughed. "People talk about all the billions that were lost, but money is never 'lost.' It is like energy—it continues to exist in one form or another. Money drained out of banks and automobile manufacturers and it flowed to us through a thousand channels within the global market."

Gault smiled. "This is all brilliant, but . . . is there a place for me in Eris's program?"

"Please," said the King of Thieves quickly, holding up a hand. "In the Chamber of the Kings, she is to be referred to as the Goddess."

Gault bowed. " 'Goddess' it is, and I can't think of a better description for her."

"The first wave of the program is already under way," conceded the King of Famine. "But your late predecessor, the esteemed and much-missed Dr. Kirov, had been working on several key steps of the second phase. They are very much 'your' kind of thing, Brother Plagues."

"Tell me."

He told Gault the plan. The information was staggering in its beauty.

"Kirov had about half of it worked out," said the King of Gold. "And he was preparing for a trip to Egypt when he died. A stroke, by god! A tragic loss and a hard blow, because we don't know how he was going to accomplish several key steps."

"Yeah," observed the American, "it left us with a big fat frigging hole in Mom's evil master plan. Kirov was the point man for this whole operation. Now we have to decide if we can continue with what Kirov had planned, or if we need to cut our losses."

Gault pursed his lips. "I'd like to look at Kirov's research and see his lab. And, of course, I'll need to know *everything* about what you are planning. What you want to do, who you want to kill, and what you hope to accomplish."

"That will take some time. . . ."

Gault smiled a great and icy smile. "Then let's get to it."

Chapter Twenty-nine

Fair Isle Research Endeavor
The Shetland Isles
December 18, 2:41 P.M. GMT

Mr. Church's phone rang and he stayed inside the chopper to take the call. The caller ID said "unknown." The voice said, "Area 51 was the work of the Seven Kings."

"I was wondering when you would be calling," said Church as mildly as if the call were from an old friend. "It's been a while."

He attached a cable to his phone and plugged it into his laptop, initiating a seven-continent multiphasic search that used MindReader to hack satellites and phone company databases.

"Did you miss me?"

"I always enjoy our chats. Do you have something for me?"

"I want to see the Kings destroyed."

The tracking signal began bouncing around from country to country.

"The DMS could accomplish that," Church said, "if you gave us something more concrete to go on."

There was silence on the line. The tracker had so far traced the call through eighteen national exchanges and fourteen service providers.

"Can you at least tell me something about the Seven Kings? What do they want to accomplish?"

There was a sound that might have been a laugh. "They want to break the bones of their enemies and suck out the marrow. That's what they want to do."

"That isn't particularly helpful."

"Yes," said the caller, "it is."

And he disconnected.

The signal vanished without any clue to its origin.

Chapter Thirty

Nicodemus was led into the office. Rudy sat behind Stankevičius's desk. He had borrowed a technique from Mr. Church and had purchased a pair of nonprescription glasses with tinted lenses. Except in direct light his eyes were virtually impossible to see.

"My name is Dr. Sanchez," said Rudy. "Please . . . sit down."

Nicodemus sat. His hands were cuffed to a waist chain and he laid them in his lap. He stared at Rudy with eyes that rarely blinked.

"Please state your full name."

Nicodemus studied him for a long time before answering, "Nicodemus."

"Is that your first name or your last name?"

"It is all that I am."

"Why are you reluctant to tell me your full name?"

"Why do you need it? Only witches and sorcerers conjure with names. Is that what you are?"

"Do you think that's what I am?"

Nicodemus smiled but did not answer.

"Do you know why I wanted to see you, Nicodemus?"

"I know."

"Will you tell me?"

Almost a full minute passed before Nicodemus answered, "It is the nature of prophets to know things that other men do not."

"Are you a prophet?"

"Sometimes voices speak through me."

"Are you aware of the event that occurred in London yesterday?"

"I am aware that souls are in the smoke and that darkness stretched across the sky."

"What else do you know of that event?"

Nicodemus leaned forward. "Are you a God-fearing man, Dr. Sanchez?"

"I am a person of faith."

One corner of the prisoner's mouth curled upward in a small sneer. "Then if you are a Bible-reading man, brother, you will be familiar with the Book of Exodus, chapters seven through twelve."

Rudy had been expecting this. "You're referring to the Ten Plagues of Egypt?"

"You *are* a Bible-reading man! Yes . . . God visited the Ten Plagues on Egypt in order to free the Israelites who had been kept as slaves." He leaned forward very quickly and Rudy noted that the guards gasped and stepped back first rather than lunge forward to restrain the man.

They are just as afraid of this man as Warden Wilson and Dr. Stankevičius, Rudy mused. *What kind of hold does Nicodemus have over everyone?*

Nicodemus's eyes burned with excitement. "Had it been God's will simply to release His people, He could have done so with a legion of angels. But that teaches nothing. Do you know why God sent so many plagues, and why he hardened Pharaoh's heart each time so that the Israelites were not freed?"

"Please tell me." He noted that Nicodemus used the word "God" rather than "Goddess."

"I asked you, Doctor."

"Very well. It seems to be a matter of how one interprets the meaning of the words, bearing in mind that they are translated. I do not believe that the passage is saying that God forced Pharaoh to commit evil, but that God allowed it."

"Why would He allow such a dreadful thing?"

"It is the nature of free will. If we humans have free will, and faith in the face of doubt suggests that we do, then it comes from God. Otherwise no one would be responsible for anything that they do, and that includes acts of charity and kindness as well as acts of evil."

"Then, Doctor, by your own statement you do not believe in the guidance of the Divine in our actions."

"That isn't what I said, and I believe you know that. Guidance is not the same thing as coercion."

He watched Nicodemus's eyes when he said the word "coercion." *Was there a flicker? Did they tighten just a fraction?*

"What about the Devil, Dr. Sanchez? Do you believe that the Devil and his demons can dominate the mind and soul of a person and make them do terrible things?"

"No," said Rudy. "I do not believe that."

"How can you believe in one part of the Bible and not all of it?"

Rudy almost smiled, and he appreciated the trap the little prisoner had laid. Very clever indeed.

"That is a longer discussion than we have time for

now," Rudy said. "Though perhaps we'll have the chance to explore it further. For now, Nicodemus, please tell me why when I ask you about what happened in London yesterday you bring up the Ten Plagues of Egypt? Is there some connection?"

"All things are connected. We float in a pool of time in which all things eddy and swirl."

"Could you be a bit more specific?"

"We are living in biblical times," said Nicodemus. "The Bible isn't a record of what *was;* it is a record of what *is*. The Old Testament, the New Testament . . . they are but chapters in a book that will continue to be written. New pages are being written today. Written into our skins, written on the skies above us, written into our souls. The prophets shout it from street corners and are not heard. False prophets speak it from the television, but even when they tell the truth they are not believed. History is unfolding and the words of the prophets are written on the subway walls and—'

" 'tenement halls.' You're quoting Simon and Garfunkel," said Rudy. "Not exactly Scripture."

Nicodemus chuckled. "Ah, so you *are* awake. I had begun to worry, Doctor. You come here to ask me questions that you already know the answers to, and when I speak you do not appear to listen."

"You are being vague and evasive," Rudy said.

"And you are being disingenuous," countered Nicodemus. "You do know what I am saying."

"No, sir, I do not. But I am willing to listen and to hear." When Nicodemus did not reply, Rudy said, "Please, tell me what you know about what happened in London."

Nicodemus closed his eyes very slowly and then opened them. It was a very reptilian action. "I know nothing about London. The sky is like sackcloth and my eye is blind."

Rudy waited. "Yesterday, when you spoke with Dr. Stankevičius you mentioned a 'goddess.' Tell me about her."

"Not *a* goddess," corrected the little man. "To believe in a goddess presupposes that there are many, and that is an untruth spoken by liars and fools. I spoke of *the* Goddess."

"And yet today you mention God. Doesn't that suggest more than one deity?"

"No," said Nicodemus quickly. "Sometimes my mouth speaks the words it was trained to speak, not those which are in my heart."

"Meaning?"

"God has transformed and *become*."

"Become what?"

"Become all. Male and female. The eternal yin and yang. This is the completion of a cosmic cycle begun before time."

"I see."

"No, Doctor, you do not. You pretend wisdom, but your eyes are blinded by convention and misunderstanding."

"I am willing to learn the truth."

Nicodemus's smile was so strange that Rudy could not easily find an adjective to describe it. The closest he could come was the lurid "goblinesque."

"The Goddess has opened her eye, Doctor, and she

sees all. She has appointed Seven Kings to sit in judgment of all men."

Ah, thought Rudy, *now we get to it.*

"Who are these Seven Kings? Are they real men?"

"They are the Sons of the Goddess and they walk the earth as the Son of man once walked."

"And are they connected with what happened in London yesterday?"

"They are connected to all things. The Seven Kings are everywhere. They look over your shoulder and they see into the hearts of men."

"Nicodemus," said Rudy quietly, "you seem to know so much. Why not put this insight and wisdom to good use? The Seven Kings are doing very bad things. Surely this cannot be the will of heaven."

"Do you pretend to know the mind of the Goddess?"

"No, I do not. But if you do, then *help* us. Tell me something that will allow me to protect the innocent."

Nicodemus chuckled and then repeated the word "innocent" as if he could taste it. His tongue wriggled over his teeth and lips. "I can only repeat what is whispered in my ears."

Rudy sat back. "I do not believe you are telling me the truth, Nicodemus. I believe that you *do* know more than you are saying."

Suddenly, like the flip of a switch, everything on the little man's face changed. In a flash his face lost its sinister cast; the feral intensity in his eyes dimmed like a fire someone had doused with cold water. His mouth worked to speak, but there was no sound. He looked shocked and suddenly stared at Rudy with a deep and terrible desperation.

"Who . . . who . . . ?" he whispered.

"What's wrong?" asked Rudy, rising to his feet.

"Who *am* I?" Nicodemus looked around the office as if seeing the people and the furniture for the very first time. "What . . . where am I? What is this place?"

The guards stepped back in confusion. Even Nicodemus's voice had changed. It was the croaking voice of a weak and sickly old man.

"G-God . . . help me!"

Then Nicodemus stiffened and looked down, but it seemed as if he was looking down into his soul rather than at his body.

"What's happening to me?"

The scream was so immediate and so shockingly loud that Rudy squeezed his eyes shut and clapped his hands over his ears. The guards staggered backward, both of them crying out in fear. The warden and the prison psychiatrist reeled back, feet kicking at the floor to push them deeper into their seats and away from the tearing sound of that voice.

Then silence.

Rudy could barely breathe and he slowly realized that he was holding his breath. Slowly, slowly he exhaled, and for a moment his breath misted in the air as if the room were frigid.

Cautiously, almost fearfully, Rudy opened his eyes. The little prisoner sat calm and erect in the chair. He was smiling. A cruel and secretive smile, a smile brimming with an awful amusement.

He was Nicodemus again. Rudy looked around. The

others in the room wore the expressions of people who had witnessed horror. He had seen expressions like those on the faces of the people at Ground Zero and in Thailand after the tsunami and in Haiti. No one spoke.

Before Rudy could say anything, Nicodemus spoke in a voice that was as soft as a whisper but as grating as teeth on the tines of a fork. "I am looking over water to a dark and pestilential place. From this place a new river of blood will flow, like the Nile flowed with blood when Pharaoh defied the will of God and refused to free the people of Israel. Oh, woe to the enemies of the Goddess. May their bones bend and crack like wheat straw in a hot wind. Stand not in the path of the Goddess's righteousness and wrath."

Rudy licked his lips. "What was that?" he said. "A minute ago—what was that?"

"Why, nothing at all happened a minute ago, and if it did, I was not here to behold it."

"Who *are* you, Nicodemus?"

The little man chuckled. "Maybe I'm that in which you do not believe, Dr. Sanchez." He stared at Rudy and would say nothing else.

Rudy tried several times to elicit further comments, but the prisoner might as well have been a statue. Minutes stretched and snapped and still Nicodemus merely sat there and looked at Rudy.

"Very well," Rudy said at last. He turned to Warden Wilson. "Warden, I think it would be in the best interests of national security for this prisoner to be kept in complete lockdown. He goes nowhere alone, he is allowed no contact of any kind with other convicts, and anything that he says to the guards is to be reported to me or my office right away. Are we agreed on this?" His voice was mild but pitched to accept only agreement and cooperation.

Wilson nodded and then jerked his head to the guards. The prisoner rose without being touched and turned toward the door. But at the doorway he paused and turned back to Rudy.

"I will leave you with one last thing, Doctor, since you are a Bible-reading believer in the Holy Word."

Rudy waited.

"Your friend has stepped into harm's way."

"What do you mean?" Rudy asked.

"When the Sword of the Goddess falls, it is better to stand with the righteous rather than with those who allow the wicked to prosper." He did the slow, reptilian blink once more. "You and yours fight to defend the house of bones and that path is impure and filled with snakes and thorns. The river of blood will sweep your friend away."

Rudy stood. "You accused me of being disingenuous, Nicodemus, and as far as I'm concerned this is a con game. Everyone has friends and a case can easily be made that at any given time one or more of our friends are in some potential danger. Car accidents, plane crashes, take your pick. Scare tactics are cheap theatrics, and frankly, I expected more from you."

Nicodemus smiled. "Well now, sir, I would not want to be compared or confused with carnival barkers and sideshow tricksters. No sir. Yet my comment stands. Your friend is walking in harm's way."

"Which friend?"

The smile became degrees colder. "The killer," he

said. "The one who has lost the *grace* of the Goddess. The one who walks with *ghosts*."

Rudy's mouth went dry. Nicodemus laughed and fell into his intractable silence, and after several minutes he allowed himself to be led away.

"What was that all about?" demanded Wilson in a ghost of a voice.

Rudy's throat was so tight he could not speak to answer.

Interlude Nineteen

T-Town, Mount Baker, Washington State
Two Months Before the London Event

Hugo Vox roared at her, "You did *what*?"

Circe winced. "Grace was a good friend, Hugo, and I thought that she might be able to use MindReader to—"

Vox slammed his open palm down on his desk hard enough to make everything jump. A dollop of coffee splashed onto the blotter. "God *damn* it, Circe, why the fuck did you do that?"

"I thought—"

"You thought? You *thought*! Jesus H. Christ, talking to your pals at the DMS is one thing, but everything—*everything*—official that is going to land on Church's desk gets vetted by me. Every goddamn thing. We live and die on federal goodwill. We piss them off—and breaking protocol is the fastest way to do that—and suddenly they forget where their checkbook is. You *know* that, too."

"I—"

"I don't care what connections you have there. You could bring down ten kinds of shit on my head. What were you thinking, kiddo? You trying to kill me here?"

His booming voice was so loud that it rattled the windows and hit her like shock waves.

"I . . . I'm sorry, Hugo."

He made a disgusted noise and pivoted his chair to face the wall. He seethed in silence for a long time and she let him. She didn't dare say anything else.

Finally he drew in a deep breath and let it out like a hot-air balloon collapsing. Without turning, he said, "I give you a lot of slack, Circe. Because of your dad, and because you do good work, exceptional work, and I've got nothing but praise for it." He turned back to face her. "Except for crap like this. It's not the first time you've jumped protocol, but by god it had better be the last. And I'd say the same thing if you were my own daughter."

"I'm sorry." Tears burned in the corners of her eyes.

"Yeah, well . . . Shit. I don't mind that you spoke with Grace Courtland, but you know goddamn well that it had to be an off-the-record thing. Nothing official, and no copies of a report that I haven't frigging well okayed." He drummed his fingers on the desk blotter. "Okay, here's the deal. The Goddess stuff is over. Give me your final report and then you're off the project effective now."

"But that's not fair, Hugo. I—"

He held up a warning finger. "It is so important to your future that you not finish that sentence, kiddo."

She clamped her mouth shut.

"I've got another project that is career valuable but also off-site. I want you way the hell off the DMS radar for a while. I'm sending you to London. You'll be our liaison for the *Sea of Hope* thing."

"But—"

He cocked his head and glared at her.

"Yes, Hugo," she said contritely.

"This isn't a demotion and no one will see it as such. Hell, it'll probably help you sell more books. But I want you out of T-Town in case your end run brings down any heat. Which it will. So, go pack and, Circe . . . do us both a favor—stay out of my way for a couple of days."

"Yes, Hugo."

She sniffed back her tears and left the office.

Chapter Thirty-one

Fair Isle Research Endeavor
The Shetland Isles
December 18, 2:54 P.M. GMT

"I'm at the door," I said quietly. I was in a hazmat-augmented HAMMER suit with a bunch of *Star Trek* gizmos clipped to my belt. I was miked into the temporary command center set up in the chopper and there was a small camera on my helmet. I passed a sensor gadget over the door frame but got no pings, so I knelt and peered through the glass and along the cracks.

"No visible booby traps. Dalek, what's the call on the lock?" We'd switched to call signs only. Redcap was Prebble; Church was Deacon. Dr. Hu's call sign was Dalek. He was a nerd on several continents.

"The outer door is nothing special, Cowboy," replied Hu. "All of the special locks are inside."

"Nothing visible through the glass," I said. "Proceeding inside."

I took a very careful hold of the metal door handle. No shocks and nothing exploded. I pulled gently and the door yielded, but I stayed on the balls of my feet. If I felt the tension of a wire or heard a click, I was going to set a new land speed record for a scared white guy in a hazmat suit.

The door opened with a wonderfully boring lack of explosions.

I went inside. The reception area was empty and sparsely furnished with a functional desk, a file cabinet, two ugly plastic visitor chairs, and a glass coffee table littered with magazines that were three years old. The walls were covered with posters about bacterial research and its benefits to the fishing industry, a map of the coastal waters, and a complex set of tide tables. I quickly searched the whole room and came up dry. No traps, no surprises.

And that, by itself, was surprising.

There was a set of double doors behind the counter that looked cheap and fragile, but the wood grain was a clever fake and when I ran a finger along the surface I felt the cool hardness of steel. A keycard scanner was mounted in a discreet niche in the wall. All DMS agents have a programmable master keycard, and the key codes to this facility had been uploaded to mine. I swiped the card and was surprised that it worked. I'd expected the codes to have been changed or at least disabled.

I did not, however, take that as a sign that all was well and that the wacky professor was brewing a pot of chamomile for us to share with a plate of ginger snaps. There are a lot of ways to lay a trap.

The door opened with a click. I unclipped a handheld BAMS unit—a bio-aerosol mass spectrometer—from my belt. It was one of Hu's sci-fi gadgets, a few steps up from what they use in airports. The BAMS allowed for real-time detection and identification of biological aerosols. It has a vacuum function that draws in ambient air and hits it with continuous wave lasers to fluoresce individual particles. Key molecules like bacillus spores, dangerous viruses, and certain vegetative cells are identified and assigned color codes. Most of the commercial BAMS units were unreliable because they could only detect dangerous particles in high density, but Church always made sure that Hu had the best toys. Ours wasn't mounted on a cart like the airport model.

I checked several spots in the room and the light stayed green. If there were pathogens loose in here, the concentration was too low for the BAMS unit to detect.

I moved inside.

The door opened into a faux vestibule that was actually a low-level air lock. As I key-swiped the inner door, the one behind me swung shut with a hydraulic hiss. With the BAMS unit in one hand and my Beretta 92F in the other, I moved out of the air lock. The inner room was large and empty. Computer workstations and wheeled chairs, flat-screen monitors in the walls. A Mr. Coffee on a table. Coffee cups.

The scanner was still green, but I had an itch tickling

me between the shoulder blades. It was the kind of feeling you get when you think someone's in the tall grass watching you through the crosshairs of a sniper rifle. I crept across the room, moving on the balls of my feet, checking corners, checking under desks, looking for trip wires, expecting an attack. Doing this sort of stuff for a living does not totally harden you to the stress. Sure, you get cooler, you learn the tricks of ratcheting down the tension on your nerves, but you aren't a tenth as calm as you look. It's one of the reasons we take precautions, like keeping our finger flat along the outside curve of the trigger guard. You keep your finger on the trigger and you either shoot yourself or shoot the first poor son of a bitch who wanders into the moment.

Like the kid who opened the side door to the staff room.

I never heard him, didn't see him, had no clue he was there until he spoke.

"Are you him?"

I instantly spun around and screwed the barrel of the pistol into soft flesh between a pair of large watery green eyes. In the split part of a second it took for me to pivot and slip my finger inside the trigger guard I registered how short and how young he was.

Maybe seven.

Fire engine red hair, cat green eyes in a freckly face that was white with shock as he stared cross-eyed at the gun barrel. In a movie it would have been a comical moment. In the flesh it was horrible on too many levels to count.

"I . . . I . . . ," he stammered, and I stepped back and pulled the gun away, but only just. Kids can kill, too. They can pull triggers and they can wear explosive vests. The only reason he didn't get shot was because his hands were empty.

"Who are you?" I demanded.

He had to try it several times before he could squeeze it out. "M-Mikey," he said. "I'm Mikey Grey."

"Hold your arms out to your sides. Do it now," I ordered, and after a moment's indecision he did it, standing there like a trembling scarecrow as I clipped the BAMS unit to my belt and patted him down. He was wearing jeans and a Spider-Man T-shirt. Sneakers and a SpongeBob wristwatch.

A couple of tears boiled into the corners of his eyes, and despite his best efforts to be brave, his mouth trembled. Seven was no age at all. A baby.

I hated myself for this.

"Is your dad Charles Grey?" I asked, trying to take the edge off my voice and utterly failing. I wasn't prepared for this even though I knew that Grey had brought his family into the lab with him.

"Yes," Mikey said, almost making it a question, unsure of what kind of answer would placate this big, mean stranger with the funny costume and the gun. Then he found another splinter of courage and lifted his chin. "Are you here to hurt my dad?"

"Why would I want to do that, kid?"

"I don't know. 'Cause he said you were."

Christ.

"I'm not here to hurt anyone," I said, and hoped that it wasn't a lie. Of course, this was coming from a guy holding a loaded gun. "But I do have to talk to your dad."

"I'm scared," said the kid. His face was still paper white with fear.

"It'll be okay."

"I'm scared of my dad," he said.

I wanted to peel off my hood and put my sidearm away and give this kid a hug, get him outside this madhouse. I knelt in front of him.

"Why are you scared of your dad, Mikey?"

"He keeps yelling," he said. "Yelling and crying. I don't like it when he cries."

Swell.

"Listen, Mikey . . . can you take me to him?"

"No! You're going to hurt him." He rubbed his eyes with his fists, but the action looked more like he was tired than crying. In the harsh fluorescent lighting his pale skin looked almost green.

"I'm not here to hurt your dad, kid."

He stared up at me, his face filled with doubt; then his eyes shifted away toward the door. "I'm scared to go back in there."

"I'll be right with you, kiddo," I said as I straightened.

The kid sneezed and I instantly jerked back from him and made a grab for the BAMS unit. The light was no longer green. It glowed orange.

Mikey wiped his nose with his sleeve. "I have a cold."

"How long have you had a cold, kid?"

He sniffed. "I don't know. I just got it, I guess."

"Today? Did you wake up with a cold?"

"No." He sniffed again and there was a fine sheen of perspiration on his forehead. "I keep sneezing and I can't find any tissues. I think Mommy used them all."

"Does your mom have a cold, too?"

"She sneezed so much she had a nosebleed."

"Where is she? Where's your mom?"

He looked around for a few seconds, like he was trying to orient himself. "Isn't she here?"

"No. Where is she?"

He sneezed again. I held the BAMS out to try to catch some of the spray.

The light changed from orange to red.

Everything in my gut turned to greasy ice water.

"I . . . don't know," Mikey said distantly. "I think she went to lie down. She had a nosebleed."

Mikey wiped at his nose and stared at the drops of blood on his wrist. He looked at me, confused, wanting and needing an answer. He was swaying slightly, as if there was a strong breeze. Beneath his freckles his color was bad. Definitely green, with dark red splotches blossoming on his cheeks.

I heard a click in my ear and then Church's voice: "Deacon for Cowboy, Deacon for Deacon, copy?"

"Go for Cowboy," I murmured, stepping away from the boy. The kid stood there, clearly unsure of where he was. Blood ran from both nostrils and he didn't appear to notice.

"Cowboy," Church said, "we're receiving the telemetry feeds from the BAMS unit. Be advised that the room is now officially compromised. Repeat, you are in a hot zone. We're getting V-readings."

V for virus. Damn.

I stepped away and touched my earbud. "What kind?"

"Dalek is matching the readings with the facility's database and—"

Another voice cut in. Dr. Hu. "Cowboy, be advised, the kid appears to be infected with a strain of QOBE."

"What the hell's that?"

"It's something they were working on at Fair Isle. Quick Onset *Bundibugyo Ebolavirus.*"

"Say again?"

Church's voice cut back in, "The boy has Ebola."

A cold hand clamped around my heart.

"Then it's in the main air supply. Talk to me about containment, 'cause I'm outside of the Hot Room."

"We've got the exterior vents draped and we're sealing them with foam. Nothing can get out."

"Does that include me?"

"We're airlifting in a hyperbaric decontamination module. We'll soft-dock it to one of the doors. You'll be okay as long as your suit seals are intact." He sounded almost disappointed.

The kid couldn't hear the conversation. He was using his sleeve to blot blood from his nose. At first I thought he was remarkably calm, but when he glanced at me I could see that his eyes were already starting to glaze with fever.

"That's nuts," I whispered. "Ebola has a five-day incubation—"

"Not QOBE," said Hu. "It's a bioweapon engineered to hit and present within minutes to hours. Introduce it into a bunker or secure facility and everyone in there dies. Without living hosts an insertion team in HAMMER suits can infiltrate and gain access to computers and other materials. Infection rate is ninety-eight point eight; mortality rate among infected is one hundred percent."

"Tell me that someone else cooked this up and that we were just working on a cure."

There was silence on the line, and then Hu said, "Grow up, Cowboy."

"We'll talk about that when I get out of here," I said softly, though it occurred to me that Hu probably wouldn't have made that comment if he thought there was a snowball's chance of me getting out.

"What's my time frame here?" I asked.

Church said, "You're fighting the clock. If the boy has just started showing symptoms, say one hour before you're alone in there."

"Deacon," I said, "tell me one thing. Did you know about this?"

"That it was being studied? Yes. That it was off the leash, no."

What remained unsaid was whether he would have sent me in here regardless. I think we both knew the answer to that.

Second day back on the fucking job.

I turned back to the kid. "C'mon, Mikey . . . let's go see your dad."

The kid sniffed again and turned toward the nearest door, but he blinked at it for a moment, his face screwed up with uncertainty.

"What was I doing?" he asked distractedly.

"You're taking me to see your dad." My voice almost cracked.

"Oh . . . okay."

He reached for the knob, turned it the wrong way several times, and then wiped his nose with his wrist. When he reached for the doorknob again there was a

long smear of blood on his wrist. Mikey finally opened
the door and walked through, and I followed, torn between the demands of the mission and the horror I felt
for what I was seeing.

I was watching a child die.

The virus was going to kill him in minutes. An hour
tops. That was all the time this kid had left. There was
no cure, no magic bullet. There was something so enormously obscene about it that I could feel the anger
rising like lava inside me. The Modern Man within
me—the civilized aspect of my fractured persona—was
numb with the shock of this. My inner Cop wanted answers. But it was the third aspect, the Warrior, who
was grinding his teeth in a murderous rage. Even that
part of me, the Killer, was offended by this because
this was something that transcended civilization, transcended law and order: this was the primal and visceral
response to protect the young of the tribe. And here
was one who was in mortal peril, and no laws or
strength of arms could do a single thing. All I could do
was use the last minutes of this child's life to further
my mission.

God . . .

The kid led me through the outer layer of the FIRE
facility—the staff quarters, supply rooms, mess hall,
and other nonessential sections. The doors to each room
stood ajar. No one was there. There were signs of conflict, though: coffee cups that had dropped and shattered
on the floor, briefcases left standing in the middle of a
hallway, discarded purses, and a number of cell phones
that had been tossed to the floor and then smashed under heel. Mikey lingered by a broken BlackBerry that

had a pink gel case. He looked at it for several seconds, chewing his lip and furrowing his brow.

Then he looked up at me. "Mom had a nosebleed," he said. "She had to lie down."

"I know, Mikey. I'm sure she'll be okay," I said, and the lie was like broken glass in my mouth. "Let's go see your dad."

Mikey suddenly smiled brightly. "Daddy's taking us to work today!"

I started to speak, but then the moment passed and the dull, disconnected look returned. Mikey sneezed and continued along the hall.

At the end of the hallway was an air lock, the door of which was blocked by a wheeled desk chair. A sign read: CENTRAL LABORATORY COMPLEX.

"Daddy said to keep the doors open," said Mikey as he squeezed past the chair and entered the air lock on the far side.

"Where is your dad, Mikey?"

"In the Hot Room. Though . . . it's not hot. It's pretty cold in there. Isn't that funny, that they call it a hot room?" He sneezed. "C'mon. . . ."

Everything he said had a dreamy quality to it. Even when he looked at the blood on his hands from his sneeze his expression didn't flicker. It was apparently unreal to him, and I guess that was a blessing. No tears, no screaming, no panic. Even though I was glad the kid wasn't terrified and screaming, his calm was eerie.

I followed him through two more air locks. The front and back doors of those locks whose lock assemblies had been torn apart, the hydraulics bashed out of shape and ripped open.

"Did your dad do that?" I asked.

"I don't know," Mikey said defensively. A fit of sneezing hit him and the kid reeled against the wall and sneezed until blood fairly poured from between his fingers. I crossed to the closest office and found a box of tissues, tore out a fistful, and brought them back to the kid. He mumbled something and used the whole wad to clean his face.

"Mom had a bloody nose, too," he said. Then he seemed to forget about the tissues and they fell from his small fingers.

Tears burned my eyes, but I sniffed them back. I couldn't wipe them away while wearing the suit, and I couldn't risk blurred vision. I bit down on my fury, grinding it between my teeth until my jaw ached.

I followed Mikey through the central labs.

"Daddy's in there," Mikey said, pointing a trembling finger at the far wall, into which was set a much heavier air lock. Huge, thick, solid, and probably impenetrable under any ordinary circumstances. It was the kind of air lock that would have kept even the most virulent pathogen locked in, but I knew that we were past that point. The proof stood beside me, tracing his name on a desktop in his own blood.

This one had not been disabled. But the kicker was what someone had painted on the wall in dark red paint.

The symbol of the Seven Kings.

I bent close to examine it. The HAMMER suit's filters don't allow smells to get in, which was fine with me, because as I looked at the dark graffiti I realized that it wasn't paint. It was blood.

I spoke quietly into my helmet mike: "Cowboy to Deacon, are you seeing this?"

"Copy that," said Church, then added, "I would welcome the opportunity to chat with the person who painted that."

Casual words, but not casually meant.

"Roger that."

I turned to Mikey. "Did your daddy put this here?"

He looked at it for a blank second and then shrugged.

We crossed the room to the door to the Hot Room. The air lock was flanked by double keycard terminals with computer keyboards. The idea was to make sure that no one could enter this kind of lab alone. They used the same thing in missile control rooms. No one can just waltz in and launch the nukes, and the odds of two complete whackos working on the same shift, in the same place, who both wanted to release the Big Bad Wolf were pretty damn slim. These systems allowed for one person to require compliance and agreement from another, and if something was hinky the other person's lack of compliance kept the monster in its box. The terminals were too far apart for one person to operate them both simultaneously. The computer codes had to be entered in unison, as did the key swipes.

Dr. Grey probably used a colleague to gain entry earlier. Why not? Back then nobody knew he was nuts.

Now he sent a kid. His own damn son.

"I have a card thingee," Mikey said. He bent and picked it up from the floor near the air lock. "Daddy told me to leave it here. There's one for you, too. He said we had to type in those numbers and then use the cards. He said to do it together. Like a game. It'll only work if we do it together."

He pointed to the metal door, on which a security day code had been written in what looked like lipstick. Rose pink. A nice color.

"Okay, Mikey," I said in a voice that I barely recognized as my own. "Let's play the game."

Interlude Twenty

The Seven Kings
Four Months Ago

Gault stood by the throne of the King of Plagues. Up close Gault could see that the chair was ornately carved with scenes from Gilles Le Muisit, Hieronymus Bosch, William Blake, and Jean Pucelle's *Psalter of Bonne de Luxembourg*. He trailed his fingers over the carvings of the frantic and helpless doctors, the wretched infected, and the skeletal dead.

"Lovely," he murmured.

"Take it for a test drive, Sebastian," suggested the American, his tone of voice at odds with the grandeur of the moment.

Gault climbed into the seat. It was very comfortable, the leather seat built over padded springs.

Toys stepped up behind him and pushed the heavy chair closer to the table. "Looks good on you," he whispered.

Gault nodded and his eyes were filled with fire. "King of Plagues," he murmured.

Toys looked at Fear. "What now? Does Sebastian swear some kind of oath? Or is it more secret society–ish—you know, with a blood pact and all that?"

The others laughed.

"We thought about that in the beginning," said the Frenchman. "We concocted a dozen rituals and, yes, blood oaths were considered. But in the end we decided on a much stronger ritual."

Gault look up sharply. "What kind of ritual?"

"We gave our word," said the American. "One to the other."

Both Toys and Gault started to laugh and then realized that the American wasn't joking.

"Really?" asked Gault. "That's it? Your *word*?"

The Saudi leaned forward, his face serious and intense. "It all depends to whom your word is given. We each agreed to give and receive our word of trust. We agreed never to lie to one another. To everyone else, to the world, to our closest friends on the other side of that door, yes. We agreed that our word would only matter to the Seven Kings and the Seven Consciences of the New World Trust."

"It's a covenant," said Thieves. "A sacred one."

Toys and Gault exchanged a look that turned into a smile.

Famine cocked an eyebrow. "You find that amusing?"

"Well," said Gault, "it smacks of 'honor among thieves,' doesn't it?"

The Frenchman shrugged. "I assure you that this is not a joke."

"He's right, Sebastian," said the American. "The one

thing we don't joke about is the integrity of our word when given to the others here in this room. It's what bonds us and defines us."

"Very impressive, I'm sure," said Toys. "But what does Sebastian get out of this?"

The grin that bloomed on the American's face was broad and toothy and filled with true delight. "Why, son, you both get every goddamned thing you ever wanted. And I'm not talking about caviar and blow jobs; I'm talking about everything. You think you understand what power is? I'm here to tell you, boys, that you surely do not."

The King of Famine nodded. "When people talk about secret societies they claim that these groups want power, but they don't attempt to decode what the word 'power' truly means. But I will bet you already know."

"Money," answered Gault. "It's always about money. Money buys power—which itself is a catchall term for the ability to do things. Purchase, push, build, destroy, own . . . money is the only path worth walking."

"Root of all evil," said Toys. Several of the Kings nodded at him with approval. "So then . . . what *is* evil?"

"It's how the losers describe the winners," said the American.

Gault nodded and rubbed his palms back and forth along the armrests of the throne. "So," he said, "you really are an ancient society?"

The American gave a dismissive laugh. "Nah. That's the myth we've been constructing. It's what we sell to the rubes. Truth is, we've only been in operation for twenty-five years, give or take. We studied all those conspiracy theories to design our group and build our myth. And we hijack a lot of stuff to make that myth look ancient. It's easy, 'cause if you look hard enough you can find clues to anything, whether it's there or not. That's how all those kooky New Age books about Lemuria and Atlantis and the Alien Reptoids got traction. Take a glyph from some tomb that shows a guy in a weird headdress sitting in a chair, and with the right caption underneath it in a book aimed at the right audience you can convince people that it's a spaceman who visited the Aztecs. Erich von Däniken made a frigging fortune with that, all that *Chariots of the Gods* bullshit. We spent years on that sort of thing, and we used our people to seed it into pop-culture books on ancient societies, historical mysteries, and conspiracy theories. We poured money into programming at local libraries and coffeehouses for the most vocal nut jobs, and we used dummy corporations to set up a lot of the more subversive small presses that publish books about the Illuminati and the Trilateral Commission. All of that stuff. Mind you, some of it's true, of course, and that makes the deception that much more compelling. There's an old carnival barker saying: 'Use nine truths to sell one lie.' That's us."

The Saudi gave a thin smile. "None of us are what the world thinks we are."

Gault turned to him. "Even you? Why pollute your own name, then? Everyone knows your face—"

"Do they?" interrupted the Saudi. "People know what they've been led to believe. You see this face, this beard, these clothes . . . but do you see the dialysis machine that the world press insists I'm dependent upon? Do you know for sure that this beard is real? Or that under this beak of a nose I don't have a smaller one that has been carefully reshaped? Or . . . is the face beneath the makeup the real one and this exterior merely special effects? How do you know that I'm even a Muslim? I could as easily be a Christian or a Jew or a Buddhist or even an agnostic or atheist. You wonder how it is that I am here in this country when every airport security person in the world knows my face. I ask, are you sure that I have ever been out of this country since 9/11? Or that a surgically altered twin is not making videotapes for me in a cave somewhere? Is any of this true? Or real? I am, after all, the King of Lies."

"Your people would tear you to pieces if they got so much as a whiff of this," Gault said.

The Saudi shook his head. "My 'people' are all here in this room."

Gault leaned back and folded his arms. With narrowed eyes and pursed lips he studied the Kings. "Well, well," he said softly.

Toys gestured to the empty throne on the dais. "Who's that for?"

"Ah," said the King of Gold, "that is for the Goddess. It was the Goddess who gave birth to the Seven Kings. It was her idea."

"It was a family idea," corrected the American. "*We* cooked it up together and *we* brought in the first of the other Kings."

The Frenchman turned and bowed. "Indeed, my friend, and I meant no insult. Everyone here honors your contributions."

"So . . . what is my role?" interrupted Gault. "You say that I'm to be the new 'King of Plagues.' It sounds wonderful and flattering, but in practical terms, what does it mean? If your goal is to destabilize rather than destroy, then you surely don't want a global pandemic."

"God, no!" laughed the Frenchman. "We want a scalpel, not a sword."

Toys looked at Gault, saw how those words cut delicately into him. *A scalpel, not a sword.* How beautifully phrased to appeal to Gault's vanity. How sweetly it matched his hungers, his passions. *They know him too damn well.*

Gault nodded slowly.

"Then let us seal this in sacred honor," said the King of Famine.

They all stood and placed their hands over their hearts. Sebastian Gault and Toys exchanged a brief look and then did the same. The room quieted and one of the Consciences must have touched a rheostat, because the lights dimmed to a soft glow that extended no farther than the table.

"Sebastian Gault," asked the American, the King of Fear, "do you pledge your life to the Seven Kings of the New World Trust?"

Without a second's hesitation, Gault said, "Yes, I do."

"Will you keep the secrets of the Seven Kings of the New World Trust?" asked the Israeli, the King of War.

"I will."

"Will you share your truths with the Seven Kings of the New World Trust?" asked the Saudi, the King of Lies.

"I will."

"Will you share your secrets openly with the Seven Kings of the New World Trust?" asked the Russian, the King of Famine.

"Yes, I will."

"Will you trust your fortune to the Seven Kings of the New World Trust?" asked the Italian, the King of Gold.

"I will. Freely and completely."

"Will you forswear all other allegiances in favor of the Seven Kings of the New World Trust?" asked the Frenchman, the King of Thieves.

"All but one," said Gault. "I have long ago placed my life and trust in the keeping of my friend Alexander Chismer. Toys. As long as he is part of this deal, then I agree with my whole heart."

Toys looked up at Gault's face, surprised at his words. Surprised and more touched than he would have ever admitted.

"Toys is your Conscience," said the Saudi. "You speak for him with this oath, and he is oath bound to us as are you."

Everyone turned to Toys, who was shaken by everything that he was hearing, and his voice was charged with emotion: "I will always be with Sebastian."

There were appreciative nods all around.

The King of Fear said, "Sebastian Gault, do you pledge your life to the Seven Kings of the New World Trust?"

"I do," said Gault, and as he said it he felt tears burning in the corners of his eyes.

"Then," said the Saudi, "welcome to our brotherhood. All hail the King of Plagues!"

In the small room the applause was thunderous.

Chapter Thirty-two

Mikey and I entered the codes and swiped the keys. If he thought there was anything odd about what he was doing or if he wondered why he was doing it, he said nothing. His eyes were almost completely glazed, though, and the bleeding was worse.

"I'm sleepy," he said. He leaned against the wall inside the air lock, and as the big door swung shut behind us he slid down and sat on the floor. He looked at me for a moment and I searched for some flicker of awareness, some spark, but there was only the vacuity created by the disease that was consuming him. He lay down on his side, curled his arm like a pillow, and rested his head. His eyelids drifted shut, long lashes brushing round cheeks, and he went to sleep. Blood pooled on the floor around him.

There was nothing I could do. Not a goddamned thing.

I wanted to scream, to pound my fists on the walls. But all I could do was continue, to go on, go deeper into this madness.

God help the first person I caught up with who was part of this thing.

I pressed the controls on the other side of the air lock. A simpler one-man system. The locks clicked, the air pumps hissed, the disinfectant spray blasted me, and the light went from red to green. Funny. Green is supposed to mean that it's safe to proceed. I cut a last look back at the boy. Safe.

Inside my head the Warrior screamed for blood.

The inner door opened and I stepped into a surreal world. The room was large, much bigger than I expected, and there was a massive steel vault in the center of the floor, surrounded by very thick curved glass of the kind used in commercial aquariums. Inside this "fish tank" standing in a loose line around the vault were twenty-eight people in hazmat suits. Each faceplate was covered with strips of white surgical tape except for a narrow eye slit. The suits were pressure inflated so that they all looked like that Stay Puft Marshmallow Man, and the suit material was opaque, so except for height it was impossible to tell the men from the women, and even that wasn't certain. They were identical. All traces of race, age, and gender were smoothed to a homogenous and alien sameness.

No one held a gun.

"Step out of the air lock." The voice came through the lab's PA system. It was a man's voice. American accent. However, if someone in the fish tank was doing the talking I couldn't tell.

"I'm good right here," I said.

"Step out of the air lock or I'll shoot one of these people."

"Not a chance."

"You don't believe me?" He sounded way too calm, given the situation. I guess I did, too.

"Sure I do, but I'm not going to give you a new target."

"Having an attack of the jitters?"

"No, I'm having an attack of common sense."

He actually laughed at that. But the laugh was sharp and twisted like he had barbed wire in his throat.

"Are you Dr. Grey?"

A pause. "Yes."

"You haven't asked about your son."

Another pause. Longer this time. "Is he dead yet?"

"You knew he was sick?"

"Yes."

"Did you infect him?"

Seconds ticked by.

"Yes," he said, and now I could hear the strain in his voice. It was like bending close to a piece of steel and seeing the tiny stress fractures.

"Why?" I asked, my voice as calm as I could make it.

"I did it to save him."

"Well, nice fucking job, Einstein. That poor kid just bled out in the air lock."

The PA system was bad, full of distortion, but I could hear his ragged sobs.

"I did it to save him!" he cried.

"From what?"

No answer.

"Listen . . . Dr. Grey," I said, "let's stop dicking around here. You've gone to a lot of trouble to do all this, and to get me here. If you have a list of demands, or you want to make some kind of statement, then I'll listen. But you have to make a show of good faith."

"Faith?"

"You have to let some of these people go. Give up a

few hostages. Show me that you're at least willing to be reasonable."

"No," he said in a voice that sounded as vague and distracted as his son's had been. "No . . . I think we're well past the point of being reasonable."

"No, we're not. There's still time to—"

"There is no time. Time ends here, ends now."

"Bullshit. If that was the case, then why send for someone from Homeland? Why go to such elaborate lengths? If you have some political or social statement to make, then this is not the way to be heard."

The people in the room shifted nervously. I stayed crouched down behind the heavy door, trying to find my target. Still nothing. Or was there? At the far end of the fish tank, one of the figures had shifted position, but she did it very cautiously. It was a small figure, almost certainly a woman, and she slowly raised her arm so that her forearm lay across her midsection. Her hand was curled into a loose fist, but as I watched, she uncurled her index finger. It took a second for me to process it, but then I realized that she was pointing to a spot outside the tank. I deliberately turned away, sweeping my eyes and gun in a wide arc as if covering the room, but when I swept back toward her she was still pointing. She even twitched her hand a little to emphasize her meaning.

"This isn't about politics," said Grey. He muttered something else after that, but it was too low for me to hear. A remark to himself. I think he said, "At least I don't think it is."

I surreptitiously cut my eyes in the direction the woman indicated and saw a row of gray filing cabinets lining the far side of the Hot Room. There were several of them and from where I stood I couldn't see what was beyond them, but if someone was on the other side, they'd be able to see the fish tank and my reflection in the glass. It couldn't have been a large space, and there wasn't enough cover for someone to stand behind it. But . . . was someone sitting on the floor? Yeah . . . there was enough cover for that.

Gotcha.

"Then what's it about, Doc? Give me something so I can help you."

"I don't need help!" His voice was thicker. More tears, or had he been exposed to the pathogen as well? The big clock in my head went *tick-tock*.

"Then tell me what you do need."

"I need you to step out of the air lock. I swear I won't hurt you. But I need to see you. I need to look into your eyes."

"And why would that be?"

"Because I need to know if I can trust you."

"Trust is a funny request from someone who just killed his kid."

"I could have vented the Ebola into the atmosphere," he said. "I didn't have to warn anyone. I didn't have to bring you here. I could have made this much worse."

Worse than murdering your own kid? I wondered, but he was right. If a strain of fast-acting airborne Ebola reached England or the Continent . . .

"If you want to earn my trust, Doc, why not let some of the hostages go?"

"*No!*" he snapped with abrupt ferocity. "No, they stay."

"And you want me to become a hostage, too?"

"No," he said, and maybe it was the distortion of the PA system, but he sounded genuinely surprised. "No, don't you get it? This isn't about you! I don't want to hurt you. I don't even know you."

"But you do know these people. Aren't they your friends? Your colleagues and co-workers?"

"Exactly!" he said as if he'd just made a point.

He sneezed. I heard it through the PA system and I heard it in the room. He was definitely over behind the filing cabinets.

"I don't have much time," he said. "God . . . Mikey."

"Where is your wife, Dr. Grey?"

He didn't answer.

"Is she dead, too?"

"Yes," he said after a long pause.

"Help me understand this. You take your co-workers hostage and yet you kill your own family?"

"I won't explain over the com system."

Seems that my options dwindled down to just one.

"Okay," I said. "I'm going to stand up and step out of the air lock. If this is an ambush, believe me when I tell you that I'm better at this than you are. If I see a gun in your hand I will shoot you dead."

"I won't shoot you."

"Same rules apply if I see a trigger device. You're not winning friends here."

"No," he said, "I expect not. Monsters don't have friends."

That was a comforting statement.

"Coming out," I called, and I let my gun lead the way as I straightened and eased out of the air lock. The hostages all took an involuntary step back as I fanned the pistol barrel across them. I had the file cabinets in my peripheral vision, and I was ready to bust a cap in absolutely anything that moved.

Suddenly I heard a ripping sound to my right and knew for certain now that he was there. There were no shots, no further sounds.

I had my pistol in a two-handed shooter's grip and I moved low and fast, checking every corner, and when I reached the wall of filing cabinets I took a breath and then whirled around.

Dr. Charles Grey sat on the floor. He held a beaker of some evil-looking liquid in his left hand. His pistol lay next to his right thigh. The hood of his hazmat suit was gone, torn open and partly off, which explained the tearing sound I'd heard. His face was puffed and red from crying, but he wasn't sick. Not yet. He'd been waiting for me to arrive before subjecting himself to the Ebola pathogen.

He looked up at me with eyes that were filled with a devastating sadness. The microphone fell from his hand.

"Help me," he said softly. "Please, for the love of God help me. . . . I don't want to kill the world."

Interlude Twenty-one

The Seven Kings
Four Months Ago

After the oath was given and accepted, there was a party. The Kings and their Consciences left the chamber and went up into the castle, where tables had been set, food laid out, and a thousand candles lighted. There were scores of people—members of the upper-echelon staff, rock stars, politicians, famous artists.

The American took Gault and Toys aside before they entered the ballroom.

"Careful what you say in here."

"These people don't know?" asked Gault.

"Nah. They think this is a party, and most of these lunkheads are professional party people. They jet-set around the world to wherever the party is. Drinking, snorting, and fucking their way through the glitterati landscape. No cameras are allowed and the stuff that happens here never makes it to the press."

"Yes," murmured Toys with a smile, "we've swum in these waters for years."

The American laughed. "Good point. Then you know the rules."

"The only rule is silence," said Toys.

"Fucking A." The American clapped them both on the shoulders and then dove into the eddying waters of flesh and excess.

Gault made to follow, but Toys touched his arm. "Sebastian . . . are you sure about this?"

"About what? Getting drunk and getting laid?"

"I'm being serious here."

"Why?" asked Gault. "Why are you even hesitating? I could tell when we were in there that you didn't like it. Why? This is what we have both wanted *forever*. All this power has been handed to us."

"When you're done coming in your pants, how about stepping back for a perspective check? Don't you think this is all too much too soon? And too free?"

A look of disappointment flickered over Gault's face.

"I understand that you're still off-balance from what happened with Amirah and the Seif Al Din, Toys. Granted our luck turned bad with that." He touched the bandages that covered part of his handsome face. "Don't think that I've forgotten, or could ever forget. But sometimes fortune does smile on people. We've landed on our feet here. We've landed hip deep in gold dust. We're among friends."

"They're not my friends," said Toys defensively.

"Sure they are. They're my friends and what's mine is yours. Now stop being a pussy and let's go get what we deserve!"

Toys started to protest, but Gault clapped him hard on the shoulder—much harder than had the American—and pulled him into the noise and movement of the party.

Chapter Thirty-three

The Blue Bell Inn
Skippack Pike, Blue Bell, Pennsylvania
December 18, 3:07 P.M. EST

Rudy stopped at the Blue Bell Inn and asked for a table as far away from other diners as possible. The place was warm and cheery with Christmas decorations and twinkling lights. Rudy barely registered them. He was shown to a corner deuce where he ordered coffee and waited for the server to go away. Then he removed his cell, activated the scrambler, and called Mr. Church.

For once Church actually answered the phone. "Doctor," he said tersely, "is this important? Otherwise—"

"It's very important."

"Then give it to me fast. We're in the middle of something here."

Rudy did, though a couple of times he felt as if he were wandering down shadowy side corridors of speculation. Church listened without interruption, but when Rudy was finished he said, "Verify that he mentioned the Ten Plagues of Egypt."

"Yes."

"And a river of blood?"

"Yes."

"And he mentioned Grace and Ghost?"

"He used those words in a sentence. It might be pure coincidence, but I doubt it."

Church grunted.

"Mr. Church," Rudy said, "I want to be frank with you."

"By all means."

"This man frightened me."

"In what way? Because he appears to have insider knowledge?"

"Not precisely. It's more that he appears to have . . ."

"Say the word, Doctor."

"Okay. He appears to have unnatural knowledge." Rudy licked his dry lips. "What is happening over there? How come I can't get through on Joe's phone?"

"Captain Ledger is participating in an active operation."

"Is he in danger?"

Church did not answer.

"What did Nicodemus mean by 'river of blood'?"

After a moment, Church said, "I'll call when I have information that I can share."

Church disconnected, and Rudy sat alone.

"Dios mio," he breathed.

Interlude Twenty-two

The Seven Kings
Four Months Ago

"So . . . you make your fortunes by chaos?" Gault asked as he and the American strolled through the fragrant gardens on the island. Toys trailed along a few feet behind them, and watchful guards were posted in camouflaged observation posts. Gault carried a glass of whiskey and soda; the American had a balloon of brandy. The American took slow drags on a cigar. Behind them the castle was lighted up like a Disney palace. Music and laughter from the party were muted by the dense trees.

" 'Chaos' is a good catchall word," said the American. "By its own nature it resists specific definition. 'Destabilization' is maybe a little more precise. Any time the status quo takes a hit we make a buck."

"And yet your day job—if it's not too vulgar to call it that—is all about stabilization."

"Yeah, well, life's a fucking comedy act isn't it?" They strolled in companionable silence for a bit. "With my day-job stuff . . . you *do* see how that allows for the other stuff to work, right?"

"Absolutely."

"So, you can see why I'm not too crazy about Mom screwing with it."

"Of course," said Gault neutrally.

"I'd rather we stuck with events like 9/11 and the London subway bombings. That stuff hits the market like a tsunami, and we turn a buck while staying far, far away from the action."

"You prefer to play it safe?"

"Fucking right. The risks should all be on paper or in predictions of percentage points. We shouldn't be risking our own goddamn necks."

"That's less . . . exciting."

The American snorted. "Don't lecture me on what's exciting, Sebastian. You're a nice kid, but you laid your balls on the chopping block when you got involved with Lady Frankenstein over in Afghanistan. And you *didn't* profit from it. You're on the lam and you lost how much money?"

Gault said nothing.

"Mom's more like you," continued the American. "She grooves on the danger. She was against the bank thing we did a few years ago."

"You robbed a bank?"

"Ha! We robbed every bank on the Continent. We spent fifteen years orchestrating the recession that slammed everyone at the end of '08. That was mine, right from the beginning. No risks, and we made insane amounts of money."

"From an economic downturn?"

"That's just it, Sebastian: the Seven Kings don't see what's been happening as an economic downturn. It's simply a turn; it's a sudden and radical change. Look, imagine that the economy is like an hourglass. Turn it on its head and the sand flows in a safe and predictable way. But if that same glass had holes in its sides, then during the process of turning it around some sand would inevitably fall out."

"And when the glass is turned, you're standing under those holes ready to catch the spill?"

"Sure. Here's the crazy thing: most of the actual methods we use to scoop up the sand are legal. We have legions of people working for us holding the buckets. Investors, brokers, trust attorneys. For example, back at the end of 2009 our hedge-firm guys raked in billions in profits. Record one-year takes. Since we helped to destabilize certain banks, we knew who was likely to fall and who would remain standing. While most investors were running for the exits or swallowing bottles of sleeping pills, we used our people to scoop up beaten-down bank shares. We bought Bank of America stock when it had dropped below a dollar a share, and then sat tight as the bailout shored up the holes we'd kicked in the sides of the ship. A bunch of ultraconservative boneheads didn't follow suit because they thought that the government was about to nationalize the big banks. There were times no one else was even bidding." He took a deep lungful and blew pale blue smoke over the heads of a thousand roses. "During the resurgence, one of our guys scooped up about twelve billion after fees in the second quarter of '09 and did even better in each quarter of 2010. That was just one of our guys."

"No one noticed?"

"Sure they noticed, but they don't draw the right conclusion based on what they saw. It's like that old joke about six blind guys trying to describe an elephant. One touches its ears and thinks the elephant looks like a fan, another one touches its tail and thinks it's a snake, and another one touches its tusk and says it must be like a spear, yada, yada."

"*Three* blind men," Gault corrected.

"Six," the American said without rancor. "The American poet John Godfrey Saxe translated that story from an old Indian legend cooked up by a Jainist philosopher. Some lazy ass shortened it to three men."

Gault grunted as he sipped his whiskey.

The American gave him a foxy wink. "I know you think I'm a fucking moron 'cause I talk like I'm a blue-collar chowderhead from South Baaaston."

"Only sometimes."

"Only sometimes," agreed the American.

"Point taken," Gault said. "My apologies."

"Fuck it. The Seven Kings don't apologize to each other. Or to anyone. We also don't take offense. In fact, it's useful to try and never take anything personal. You're above that shit now; you live in a Big Picture world now, Sebastian. It takes some adjustment to think of yourself in those terms."

"As a king?"

The American nodded.

"It may take some getting used to," Gault murmured, "but I expect I'm going to like it."

"Oh, you will."

They walked on, pausing as a fat peacock strutted across their path, taking his time and pretending not to notice the two tall men.

"Faggot bird," the American muttered. "Eris loves

them. I'd like to turn my dogs on 'em. That'd be wicked fun."

"Hedge funds," Gault prompted.

"Well, yeah, hedge funds. When a lot of businesses tanked, we cleaned up buying properties for pennies on the dollar, and did better buying billions in beaten-down commercial mortgage-backed securities. For a while the fluctuations in the bond market pretty much gave us a license to print money."

"What if the market doesn't recover?"

"We won't be aboard any ship that's actually sinking, and if we have to take a loss here and there to maintain respectable credibility, then we're taking a chunk of the back end. The stuff our accounting department does is science fiction."

"How do you keep yourself safe from the IRS and the FBI?"

The King of Fear chuckled. "Most people run from the feds because they know you can't fight 'em and you can't beat 'em in court. We don't have that problem."

"Why not?"

"This is what I mean by 'Big Picture,' Sebastian. Small minds try to figure out how to dodge the bullet the system shoots at them. Big minds try to fight the system by wrapping themselves in layers of legality."

"And that's what you do?"

"No. We're Big Picture, but we're Big Picture *as viewed by Kings*. What we do is plan ahead. Years and years ahead. Anyone involved in the actual crisis is going to get looked at very closely, right? What we do is plan far in advance and then we seed people into the system. We're everywhere, Sebastian. We're in all levels of government, all corners of Wall Street and other national financial districts. We're in Congress and the White House. We're deeply positioned in the IRS, FBI, SEC, EPA, FTC, . . . and everywhere else. We have significant players in the Republican and Democratic parties. And we have people peppered through the press. We're on both sides of every argument, every congressional bill, every peace accord, every global summit. Chaos isn't about taking sides. Kingship is about ruling *all* of it."

They stopped by the cliff and looked out over the wind-troubled waters of the St. Lawrence River.

"Who does your dirty work? Hits and bombings and such?"

"We recruit from existing extremist cells. We fund them and protect them, and then we tap them to be our street troops. We call them the Chosen, and they're sold different versions of a bill of goods about rewards in heaven. Or whatever else they'd sell their souls for. Money, pussy, whatever works. You'd be surprised how many of these soldiers of God will sell their own mothers for a few hundred K and a California blonde with plastic tits. Kind of ruins your faith in suicidal fundamentalism."

Gault laughed and the American blew smoke rings at the moon.

"Couple, three years ago," continued the American, "my man Santoro came up with an idea to build a more elite combat team. The Kingsmen."

"Catchy."

"It inspires a sense of pride and entitlement. I put Santoro in touch with some ex-Delta and SEAL guys and they built a training program that is world-class and wicked hard. Couple of guys out of every group die or get crippled. We let the other cadets shoot the cripples. Sounds harsh, I know, but it also makes them hard as fucking nails. Real fire eaters."

"How are these Kingsmen used?"

"Black ops, wet works. That sort of thing. We had one tussle with the DMS. Our team lost, but it was an overwhelming-odds situation, and the DMS thought they were facing some rogue cell of ultrajihadists."

"The DMS teams are the toughest I've ever seen," Gault warned.

"Yeah, well . . . we'll get a chance to test that."

"These Kingsmen . . . what's their incentive?"

"Numbered accounts in the low seven figures. Plus they watchdog each other, and that keeps them all straight. Lots of trust between them. Real pride. No way they'd screw each other over. They have a real sense of pride, and they are totally devoted to Mom. Eris has built her mystique to the point that some of these guys really think she is a goddess. She's convinced them that she is a direct descendant of Sargon the Great of Akkad, so the Kingsmen believe they can trace their warrior lineage to the first emperor in human history. That's quite a legacy. Santoro is their general, role model, and chief badass."

"He seems like a capable chap."

"He's a fucking nut bag. Don't get me wrong, I love the guy like a son, but he is eight beers short of a six-pack. Santoro absolutely believes Mom's a goddess. That's not a joke. Guy gets a spiritual boner every time her name is mentioned, and once—just once—one of the Kingsmen saw Eris walk by and didn't yet know who she was, so he made a crack about wanting to tap that, and Santoro was right there. Jesus fucking Christ, you never saw anything so fast and nasty. Santoro told the guy to pull his knife, and mind you, this guy was ex–Force Recon and he was a badass mamba-jamba and twice Santoro's size. But my boy cut him four kinds of bad: long, deep, wide, and often. He humiliated him and carved pieces off the guy and then did things to him while he was down and dying that I don't like to think about. Had the guy begging for forgiveness from the Goddess with half a tongue and his guts in his lap. Talk about an object lesson. There had to be forty, fifty of the Kingsmen—full team members and cadets—watching that. By the time he was done, Santoro was painted red from head to toe and he looked like some kind of demon. The other Kingsmen knelt—actually fucking *knelt*—in front of him, and then Santoro led them in a prayer to the Goddess. That, my friend, is how legends are made."

Gault stared at the American. "Bloody hell."

The King of Fear chuckled. "Life's weird for us, but you get used to it."

They began walking again.

A little while later Gault said, "If you disapprove of Eris's plan are you outside of it? Or do all the Kings work together on everything?"

The American puffed his cigar before answering, "It's one for all and all for one. For the most part. I have a couple of my own gigs running, but this thing—what we're calling the Ten Plagues Initiative—is what everyone else wants to do, so I'm doing my part. But there are threads that could lead back to me. Granted, it would take some pretty damn creative logic jumps to connect the dots, but even so that's more of a trail than I like to leave. The DMS are not as stupid as my darling mother thinks." He cut Gault a look. "You know that firsthand."

Gault touched the bandages. "Yes. But . . . tell me, is this the first time the other Kings voted against you?"

The American smiled. "Yeah. Kind of caught me off-guard, too."

"Is this going to be a problem?"

"Nah," said the American. "I got it handled."

TOYS TOOK MICROSIPS from a glass of wine as he trailed along behind Gault and the American. Neither man had so far bothered to direct a single comment to him. Nor did they lower their voices to prevent him from hearing the conversation. He supposed that it was all meant to be a sign of trust, an unspoken acknowledgment that he was privy to all of their secrets.

But it didn't feel that way to Toys.

He sipped his wine and digested everything he heard, and kept his thoughts to himself. In the darkened woods the peacocks screamed like damned souls.

Chapter Thirty-four

Fair Isle Research Endeavor
The Hot Room
December 18, 3:10 P.M. GMT

"Are you him?" It was the same question his son had asked me. "I told them to send someone from Homeland Security."

"Then I'm him," I said.

"Where's Mikey?"

"You know where he is, asshole."

Tears ran down his cheeks. "Was it fast?"

"What do you think?"

"God." He licked his lips. "It's important that you understand. I need to make you believe me when I say that I loved my son."

"Save it for Saint Peter. He likes a good bullshit story," I snapped. "Right now I need to know why you're doing *all* of this."

He wiped his streaming eyes and nose with a forearm. I reached out with a foot and pushed the pistol out of his reach.

Grey flinched and clutched the beaker to his chest as if that might protect him from my anger.

"Why don't you put that beaker down?"

"You'll kill me if I do."

"I'm already talking to a dead man." I showed him the BAMS unit. "Ebola's all over this place. Besides, after what happened to your kid, I'm not sure I'd do you the favor of giving you a quick way out. You should feel what he felt."

"Yes." His eyes were bleak but steady. "I should. I gave Mikey a little morphine first. But . . . not for me."

"If you're looking for admiration for your sacrifice, too bad. Now . . . put the beaker down."

"No. I need something to make you stay with me until I get it all out."

I tapped the chest of my HAMMER suit. "Sorry, but scary as that Ebola shit is, I'm covered."

He shook his head. "That suit has polycarbonate

components. This is filled with a rapid-action strain of pseudomonas bacteria. It eats oil. They use it for cleaning up oil spills, but this strain was designed for bioweapons use. It would dissolve the seals in your suit before you reached the first air lock."

"Well, kiss my ass," I said. "You've really thought this through, Doc. You earn the merit badge for Mad Scientist of the Week. It'll look great in your obituary."

I was calculating how fast vapors would spread if he dropped the beaker compared to how fast I could get my ass the hell out of here.

"I'm sorry."

"Sorry doesn't buy much sympathy these days. This is your play, Doc, so . . . talk."

He did.

I expected it to be about politics. But that wasn't it at all. Instead Dr. Charles Grey told me a horror story. There were no ghosts or vampires in it, but it was scary as hell.

He and his family lived in a cottage on the other side of the island. A few weeks ago, while Mikey and his mom were preparing a Thanksgiving dinner for the American staff at FIRE, Grey walked into his study, felt a sudden burn on the back of his neck, and then woke up five minutes later tied to a chair with a hood over his head. There was at least one man in the room with him. A frightening, invisible figure who spoke politely but told of dreadful things that would be done to Grey's wife and son if the doctor did not do exactly what the man wanted. The man stood behind Grey and pulled off the hood. Then he reached past Grey and began placing photographs on the table in front of him. Photos of women who bore a strong physical resemblance to his wife. And little boys who looked like Mikey.

"The pictures they showed me . . . the things that were done to those other children. And to the women. Inhuman things. It was unbearable to think that someone could do that to another human being. To innocent children. To women. Then . . . he placed pictures of Mikey and Alicia next to the others. He had pictures of my wife shopping, of her in the bathtub, of us making love. The thought that they had stolen our privacy, that they were somehow watching us all this time . . ."

"Your boy, too?"

"Yes. Pictures of Mikey sleeping. One of him using the toilet at school. God!" He gagged and I didn't know if it was the first touch of the Ebola or the sheer horror of what he was remembering.

"Why didn't you go to the police?" I demanded.

"They warned me not to. He showed me a picture of a little boy . . . I mean I think it was a boy. Had been a little boy. The man said that this was the result of someone else notifying the authorities. He said that if I told anyone, even my wife, then this would happen to my son. To Mikey. Even if they had to wait a month, or a year, or ten years. One day my son would vanish and if we ever found him at all there would be only pieces left to bury. He said if that happened, I would receive an e-mail with a video file showing everything that had been done to Mikey, and that the last thing the boy would be told before he died was that this was all my fault. He made me believe that there were worse things than death. Even the way Mikey died—" A sob tore its way out of his chest. "Even the way he died wouldn't be a millionth as bad as what they would have done to him. And if I *did* this and let my family live, I'd go to jail and *they* would still be out there. How could I trust that they would leave my family alone? They might . . . they might . . ." He shook his head.

"There's witness protection—," I said, but he cut me off.

"Witness against whom? I never saw his face. He wore a black mask. All I could tell was that he was a male and had a Spanish accent."

The Spaniard. The mysterious figure who was the liaison between the Chosen, the Kingsmen, and the Seven Kings. Son of a bitch.

Grey glared at me. "So . . . do you want to tell me that the police, or even the military, would protect me from someone I couldn't identify? Besides," he said, his mouth a taut and bitter line, "he said that they had people in the police, in the military, in the government. He said that they had people everywhere."

"And you believed him?"

"Wouldn't you?"

I thought, *Yeah, I probably would.*

"And," Grey went on, "he said that he would occasionally reach out to me through other means to prove what he said. He wasn't lying. I found notes in my locked car. Voice mails in five different voices on my phone. Notes on my desk." He swallowed. "Even a folded note in my lab coat here in the Hot Room. They *were* everywhere. I thought about running, but if they are everywhere, where could I run?"

Grey sobbed so hard that he almost dropped the beaker. My heart was in my throat. When he wiped his nose it left twin red smears on the forearm of his hazmat suit.

"I gave them both morphine. This strain of Ebola works very fast. I thought it would hurt less than a gun. I . . . I'm not good with guns."

"Why not overdose them with morphine?"

Fresh tears welled in his eyes. The tears were pink with blood. "I didn't think you would believe me unless you had no choice. Seeing Mikey would convince you."

I wanted to take my gun and pistol-whip the shit out of him. I wasn't a doctor and even I could have figured fifty ways to do it better than he'd done it.

"What about the rest of the staff?" I said. "Why hold them hostage?"

"I told you . . . I found notes on my desk, in my lab coat. And then the security cameras and ventilation cut out. They have someone else here. I don't know who, so I made everyone put on hazmat suits and go into the fish tank. I locked it from the outside." He coughed and there was blood on his lips.

"Are the people in the fish tank infected?"

"No, but it's in the air with them. If you trust your people, then maybe you can interrogate them. Get one of *them* to talk. I didn't release the virus until the tank door was sealed. I put a bicycle lock on the crash bar and broke the key off in the lock. You'll have to cut it to get them out."

"I'm still a step behind you here, Doc. If you're going to hand everyone over to us, why not turn yourself and your family in? This isn't some candy-ass drug buy. This is international-incident stuff. This is terrorism. We'd be able to protect you; I guarantee it."

Dr. Grey looked at me with eyes that wept tears of blood. "He said that they are everywhere. The police, INTERPOL, *everywhere*."

"And yet you asked for someone from Homeland."

"What else could I do? I had to make this big enough so that it would be harder for them to cover it up."

"How do you know I'm not one of them?"

"I looked out the window. I saw the helicopters land. Not all of you can be involved. I mean . . . if you are, then my family is better off out of a world like that. And if you're *not* involved . . ."

He looked to me for encouragement, and I gave him a small nod.

". . . then please *do* something."

"You haven't told me much, Doc. How is this connected with the bombing at the London?"

Grey stared bug-eyed at me. "Is it? Oh my God! Are you sure?"

"The Seven Kings put their mark on both places right before things went to hell. You're involved in this thing; you tell me."

He gave me a frank and uncomprehending stare. "Who are the Seven Kings?"

"Their symbol is painted in blood on the wall outside of the Hot Room."

"I . . . saw that outside when I sent Mikey to . . . to . . ." He shook his head. "I don't know what it means."

"The guy who roughed you up, the Spaniard. Did he say anything about why they were doing this? Or about what they wanted?"

He laughed and then abruptly turned his head and spit blood onto the cold floor. "He never said why. He only told me what he wanted me to do. He said, 'Go to your job, remove the Ebola from the vault, and spill it on the floor of the Hot Room.' "

"Nothing else?"

"Just that. Since the fail-safes were supposed to kick in as soon as there was a biological accident, I thought that all they wanted was an incident. Maybe kill some of the staff and expose America's involvement in secret bioweapons testing. It's the only thing that made any sense. Then the vent controls went down and the fail-safes never kicked in."

"And he never mentioned the Seven Kings?" I asked. "Or even just 'Kings'?"

"No, just the Goddess, and I—"

"Goddess? Tell me exactly what he said."

"Both times he attacked me he mentioned the Goddess. When he promised not to hurt my family if I did what he wanted, he swore by the Goddess. And yesterday, when he attacked me in my garage, he said that 'nothing is impossible if the Goddess wills it to be.' He held a knife up to my eye and made me swear that I believe in the Goddess. I . . . got it wrong first, I said that I believed in God, and he got so mad I thought he would kill me right there. He kept ranting about faith and how the Goddess was his shield and he was her sword. Crazy stuff like that. Then he gave me his knife and told me to kill him. He said that his faith would protect him."

"What did you do?"

"What could I do? He said that if I didn't try to kill him he would go upstairs and turn Mikey into one of his *angels*. God. That's what he called the poor women and children in those photos. Angels. He called his victims 'angels.' "

Grey described how he had tried to kill the Spaniard and how the man had disarmed and beaten him without effort. "He was so fast. I . . . I never saw him move. God, please! I couldn't let him do that—I couldn't let him turn Mikey into an angel."

His sobs were as deep and as broken as any I'd ever witnessed. This man, this Spaniard, had killed Dr. Grey long before today. He'd broken Grey's spirit and his mind and cut away the fabric of hope and trust that bound his life together. It was horrible to witness and it provoked in me an atavistic dread of the Spaniard, and of the Seven Kings and the Goddess they worshiped. A dread . . . and a killing rage that burned like boiled acid under my skin. I wanted to face this man, and I knew that I didn't want to do so from the cold and antiseptic distance of a gun. I wanted to be up close and very personal with the Spaniard. Knife to knife, or—far better yet—hand to hand.

Grey coughed and the sound dragged me back from the edge of a red darkness and into the broken moment. I looked at Grey and thought about Plympton. The selection of these men had to have other elements. I mean . . . hell, I had a family that I loved—my dad, my brother and his wife and kid, couple of aunts—but I wouldn't slaughter four thousand people in a hospital to protect them. I'd find some other way to keep them safe while I looked into it. So, okay, I'm a cop and a federal agent, and psychologically speaking I have a headful of bees and spiders, but I could not believe that there were levers strong enough to turn me into a mass murderer.

What was it about Grey and Plympton that made them different?

"I'm going to find out who did this," I said. "I am going to find them and I can guarantee you, Dr. Grey, I will show them what 'terror' really means."

He closed his eyes. "I wish I could believe you."

I said nothing to that. He was starting to drift. Bloody sweat was leaking from his pores.

"Is there anything else you can tell me?" I said softly.

He nodded weakly. "I wrote an account of it. Of everything. It's on my laptop, in the documents section. My password is *grásta*.' With an accent over the first *a*. It's hidden in a folder called 'Christmas List.'"

"What's *grásta* mean?"

"My family's Irish. That's Gaelic," he said. "For 'mercy.'"

I stood and stretched out my left hand. "Give me the beaker."

He smiled and looked at the swirling brown mixture with the red veins. "It's not what I said it was," he said. "It's just coffee and Tabasco sauce."

He handed it to me. I still took it carefully and set it on the desk.

"Mercy," I said.

"Grásta. But I don't deserve it." He buried his face in his hands. I could hear him saying the names of his wife and son over and over again.

Mercy.

I'm no saint. Furthest thing from it. But I can at least grant a little mercy.

I raised my gun and put the laser sight on him.

Interlude Twenty-three

Aboard the *Delta of Venus*
The St. Lawrence River
Four Months Ago

Sebastian Gault lay with his head on Eris's naked breast as the stars wheeled overhead. The boat rocked gently under them, dark water slapping against the hull. Far away on Crown Island, cicadas and crickets made the darkness pulse with life. Fireflies were pinpricks of light as they flitted among the tall grasses on the banks of the St. Lawrence River.

"I'm glad you accepted our offer, lovely boy," Eris murmured.

"You knew I would," said Gault. "It feels a little surreal, though. Kings and thrones."

She laughed, deep and throaty. "It *is* surreal. We're remaking the world into what we want it to be."

"I hadn't expected you to be the driving force for this thing."

"Oh . . . you know, 'behind every great man is a—"

"totally psycho power-hungry bitch?"

"Exactly."

"And sonny boy is fine with that?"

"He's less devoted to the Goddess than his fellow Kings, but he'll do his part."

"What about the others? Are they all still in your corner?"

"They are," she said as she ran her fingernails down his chest and over his hard stomach. "I have a special relationship with each of the Kings."

"God, please don't tell me that you and your son are—"

"No." She laughed. "Just the other Kings. I'm corrupt, lovely boy, but not tacky."

"Thank god for small mercies."

"Thank 'Goddess,'" she corrected.

"Ah, yes."

They lay together and watched as several meteors burned their way through the blackness. Minutes drifted past them on the current of the night.

"Sebastian . . . ?"

"Mm?"

"You loved her, didn't you?"

"Who?"

"Amirah. Your pretty little Iraqi mad scientist. You really loved her, didn't you?"

He closed his eyes, shutting out even the simple beauty of the star field above. "Love is a quicksand pit."

"You're being evasive."

"Did I love her? Yes. Deeply, and despite the fact that she was married to another man, and despite the fact that I had several times planned to kill her, and despite the fact that she betrayed me and tried to kill me, I loved her to the end." He made a low, feral sound and a shudder passed through his whole body. "I still do, and I wish I could take a scalpel and carve that emotion out of my body. I'm not joking, Eris. . . . If I could actually cut it out, I would."

"Is that what your plan is? The course of action you proposed to the Kings—is that the scalpel you want to use?"

He sat up and looked down at her. It was so dark that she was merely a paleness woven into the fabric of shadows.

"What's that supposed to mean?"

Eris propped herself on one elbow. "Oh, don't take offense, Sebastian. You can't possibly be dense enough to believe that you're not damaged goods. We all are or we wouldn't be the people we've become. You are one of the greatest pharmaceutical researchers on the planet, a self-made rags-to-riches billionaire, and yet you've spent most of your adult life covertly funding terrorist organizations and creating exotic diseases just so you could be the first to bring treatments to market. You're a thoroughly corrupt mass murderer. You paid to have a certifiably insane molecular biologist design a pathogen that could easily—easily—have caused a global pandemic of apocalyptic proportions. If it wasn't for Joe Ledger and the DMS, this whole world would look like a sequel to *Night of the Living Dead*. And now you have been brought into a secret society, a group that has asked you to help them destabilize the economies of the global superpowers by any means necessary. You are all those things, lovely boy, and yet when you spoke to-night about what you would be willing to do as part of the Seven Kings there wasn't a flicker of greed in your voice. There wasn't ego or megalomania. What I heard was a person in pain who wanted to stop hurting."

"How do you know what I said or how I said it, damn it? You weren't even there."

She laughed. "I'm *always* there, Sebastian."

Gault said nothing.

"And you, lovely boy, are still being evasive. Surely you have the balls to admit the nature of your motivations. Or should I go looking for them?" Her fingers brushed his upper thigh and he batted them irritably away.

"What do you want from me?" he snapped.

"Only the truth," she said. "That's the only thing that matters between us. Between the Seven Kings, their Consciences, and their Goddess. No lies, no secrets."

The wheel of night turned and turned above them before Gault could bring himself to speak, and when he did there were ghosts in his voice.

"I . . . died," he said. "When Amirah betrayed me, when it all crashed down . . . I died. I could feel it inside. It was like a poison had taken hold of me. You know how they say your life flashes before your eyes? It does. I saw everything that I had done; I saw all the versions of myself. The child, the lad, the young entrepreneur, the man. I saw myself expand into a captain of industry. I saw the specific moments of my own corruption. My first dirty deal. I saw the faces of the people who were dead because I wanted them dead. I saw the friends betrayed and cast aside. And I saw Amirah's face—beautiful before her betrayal and beautiful and monstrous after. I saw the monster that lived within me. I felt the humanity in me die, Eris. I felt it go and . . ."

His fingers closed around hers and she squeezed back.

". . . and I was glad. *God,* I was so glad to be rid of it. It was a tumor, a canker." His voice was a reptilian hiss.

"Sebastian . . . my lovely boy . . ." Eris bent toward

him, finding his face in the dark. She kissed his eyes, his cheeks, his lips, and as he spoke his cold words were breathed into her hot mouth.

"All that remains is the monster," he said.

Eris took him in her arms and held him. Tears flowed like hot mercury from her eyes and splashed on his shoulder.

"This is so beautiful, my sweet," she said. "This is what Caesar knew when he realized that he was more than man. This is what the pharaohs knew, and the first emperor of China. To be a King—a true king—is to be greater than a man." She showered his face with a thousand quick kisses. "You've ascended. You've *become*. Anything and anyone to whom you were attached before this moment is gone. You don't *need* them anymore. You are a King, a true king of this world, and you will be a god in the next."

They clung together in the darkness of their own passion.

BELOWDECKS, IN A cabin that was spacious, luxurious, private, but not as soundproof as its designers intended, Toys, the Conscience to the King of Plagues, sat on a bunk, his knees drawn up, arms wrapped around his shins, fingers interlaced, head leaning against the hull. The cabin was as dark and desolate as his heart.

He had listened to the sounds of Sebastian and Eris making love, and it had amused him, even aroused him. Then he had listened to their whispered conversation.

All that remains is the monster.

Toys stared at the darkness in his cabin, but what he saw was a deeper and greater darkness within. He looked at his own hands. They were bloodstained, too; he knew that. Since he had become Gault's personal assistant and closest confidant, he had charred his own soul with unnumbered crimes. His Catholic guilt had been nicely off-line for years now, surfacing only long enough to compel him to light a candle two or three times a year for all of the lives he had helped to destroy. His comfort and solace had been that over the last two thousand years the Catholic Church itself had done far worse, even without counting the excesses of the Inquisition.

But this . . .

Somehow this felt beyond that, maybe beyond redemption.

And the irony was that the catalyst to these dark thoughts had been the word, the label that the Kings used for people such as him.

"Conscience."

Was there ever a crueler word?

The boat rocked gently, creaking as boats will. Far away a buoy clanged to mark the channel passage. His interlaced fingers pressed together so tightly that pain pulsed in every joint and sent fire flashes along his arms. The pain was the only thing that kept him from screaming.

All that remains is the monster.

"God," he whispered as the first tears fell from his eyes.

Chapter Thirty-five

I stood in front of the fish tank, my pistol down at my side. The marshmallow people inside stared at me through the surgical tape slits. I couldn't see their eyes, but they could see mine.

I used my free hand to press the button for the intercom.

"Listen to me," I said. "You know what Dr. Grey did. You know he's dead."

A few of them nodded. Most stood as still as statues.

"He had an accomplice. Someone sabotaged the security systems and bypassed the vent controls. The plan was to release the airborne Ebola to the atmosphere. That means that one of you in there is in on this."

They cut sharp looks at each other, many of them taking involuntary steps back from whoever was nearest, and often colliding. There was a buzz of voices.

I leaned into the wall mike.

"Shut the fuck up."

They froze and stared at me.

"I'm talking now to the person who sabotaged the systems. If you are not a terrorist . . . if you were coerced into this, then you have one chance. Identify yourself and provide any help and information you can and I promise that any threats made against you or your family will be dealt with. If someone threatened to harm members of your family, let us know now so that we can send teams to take them into protective custody. This is bigger than local police; this is bigger than any one government organization. This is connected with what happened yesterday at the London. That means this is international terrorism of the worst kind. There are no limits to what we will do to protect you and your family if—and only if—you step forward and cooperate with us right now."

I stepped back. They looked at each other. Probably friends reaching out voicelessly to each other, hoping to see innocence in familiar eyes and be judged innocent in turn. Or maybe looking for traces of guilt.

"All lines of communication to this island have been cut," I said. "That means that no word of what's happening here will get out. If you've been told that harm will come to your loved ones unless the pathogen is released or the news hits the airwaves, then you need to speak up now. We can have teams anywhere in less than fifteen minutes. And all teams will be monitored, so even if there is a spy in the network he won't be able to act before he can be stopped."

No one said anything.

I edged closer and tapped the glass with my gun.

"I'm having a really bad day, folks . . . so believe me when I tell you that if you don't come forward and we find out who you are—and we will find out—then your day is going to make mine look like a Disney flick. Tick-tock."

Nothing.

"Okay. That's your call. Bear in mind, this isn't U.S. soil and this facility does not officially exist. Anyone involved in this is hereby designated as an enemy combatant. You are about to disappear into the system and you will never resurface. There will be no one left to speak for your family."

I started to turn away.

"Wait!"

The crowd inside the fish tank stepped back from one figure. It was a large man near the back.

"Please!" he said urgently. "They said they'd kill my mother and my sisters. They . . . they showed me pictures of what they'd do. Can you help them?"

I stepped close to the glass. "What's your name?"

"Chip Scofield, building maintenance. God, please tell me you can help them. They said that if the rivers didn't run red with blood, then the blood of my family would run like a river." His voice was rising to a hysterical pitch. "Oh, God—get them out!"

"Calm down, Chip. You're doing the right thing. Can you tell me anything about them? Can you tell me anything about the Seven Kings?"

"Yeah. The Spanish guy who—"

Suddenly two shots rang out and Scofield was slammed forward against the glass with such force that blood shot all the way to the ceiling and splashed the glass for a dozen yards to either side. I heard him grunt in surprise with his last truncated breath. Everyone screamed and lunged away from a slender figure who stood with her back to the far wall.

It was the woman who had pointed the way to Dr. Grey, and she held a .32 automatic in her gloved hand.

She fired two more shots. Right at me. The glass of the fish tank spiderwebbed, but I was already diving for the floor. Another two shots and the whole front of the tank exploded outward, throwing huge chunks of reinforced glass into the Hot Room. As I rolled sideways there was a fifth shot. I came up into a shooter's crouch, my gun out in front of me in a two-handed grip, but when I put the laser sight on the spot where the woman had been standing it illuminated the center of a fresh splash of dark red. The woman slid slowly down the wall, her hand falling away from where she had placed the barrel beneath her chin. The wall behind where she had stood was splashed with blood, brains, and bits of bone.

The screams from the other staff were shrill and unrelenting.

I held my ground, fanning the gun back and forth, looking for another target, but I knew it was over. I'd had a single chance at this, and now it was gone.

Interlude Twenty-four

The Seven Kings
Four Months Ago

Gault and Toys returned to their separate apartments before dawn, but almost immediately Gault rapped on Toys' door and came sweeping in, glowing with energy.

"This is bloody marvelous!" he said.

"Marvelous," Toys agreed without inflection. "Drink?"

"Martini," Gault said, and Toys mixed them. "God, I can't wait to read Kirov's notes and see what they've been doing. A terror campaign based on the Ten Plagues? It's brilliant."

"You're praising a terror campaign, Sebastian." Toys jiggled the pitcher. "Maybe you need a double."

Gault laughed and accepted a glass. "Let's drink a toast."

Toys gave an unenthusiastic grunt.

"What's with you? You seemed pretty effing eager back in the Chamber."

"Did I? Mm. Maybe I was caught up in the moment," Toys said. "I thought you were, too."

Gault snorted. "This isn't just a 'moment,' Toys. This is our life now. Why is that so hard to grasp?"

"Sebastian, we've been on the run for months. You were betrayed and nearly killed. After all these weeks of surgery and pain, you should be careful. Take things slow."

"Oh, sod that. This situation is tailor-made for me."

Toys noticed that Gault had changed his reference from "us" to "me." It confirmed his fears. "Tailor-made? Really? Sebastian, we narrowly—*narrowly*—avoided being killed during your last 'can't fail' master plan." He paused and took a breath. "Look, we have money, and we still have youth and strength. We don't need this. Let's face it, we are not cut out to be evil geniuses. We never were. Let's take the money and bloody well run."

"Not a chance. We already ran. Now we've arrived."

"Christ." Toys flapped an arm. "And of course the fact that there's a woman involved has *nothing* to do with your wanting to stay. You already have that look in your eyes."

"What look?" Gault's voice was suddenly cool.

"You know what I mean."

"No, why don't you tell me?"

Toys sighed. "Don't start a fight, Sebastian. It's just that when there's a woman involved you—"

"I what?" interrupted Gault sharply. He slapped down his martini glass hard enough to slosh the contents onto the wet bar and crossed the room to stand uncomfortably close to Toys. "I *what,* Toys? Are you saying that if I become interested in a woman I lose control? Or perspective?"

"I didn't say that."

"Then what *are* you saying? You're comparing the Goddess to Amirah and—"

"Whoa, Sebastian, let's have a little effing perspective. We're not in the Chamber now and Eris is not a goddess."

"Perspective?" Gault murmured. He edged closer still, so that his breath was hot on Toys' face. "Yes, let's both have a perspective check. When things went wrong in Afghanistan I had a moment of weakness. I won't deny it, Toys, and I needed you. I really did."

"Yes," Toys said in a hoarse whisper.

"But . . . what happened when I called out for your help? Do you remember?"

"Sebastian, I—"

"*Do you fucking remember?*" Gault snarled.

Toys tried to meet Gault's fierce glare, but he felt his own eyes growing moist and weak. He turned his face away.

"You slapped me, Toys. I was in pain, I was desperate and your response was to attack me."

"It wasn't an attack, Sebastian, and you damn well know it. You were sinking and I needed to snap you out of it." Toys suddenly threw his drink against the wall and wheeled on Gault, his own anger finally rising. "If I hadn't, then that fucking whore Amirah would have released a doomsday plague. *A doomsday plague.* How can you of all people not grasp what that means? If you want a perspective check, then embrace that for a moment. Christ, you're lucky I didn't put a bullet into you right there and then, because I bloody warned you about her. I warned you over and over that she couldn't be trusted, and each time you ignored me."

"She was my—"

"What? Your 'lover'? Get a sodding grip, Sebastian! She was playing you. She played you all the way and then she turned into a goddamn zombie and tried to *eat* you. I mean . . . how thick are you that you can't see that you were wrong?" He jabbed Gault in the chest with the tip of his finger. Gault flinched but held his ground. "Or have you become so bitter and arrogant that you can't admit that you made a misstep? You want to get mad at me for hitting you? Go ahead!"

"I'm warning you, Toys—"

"No! You don't warn me." Toys jabbed his finger again, much harder this time. "If we're going to be part of this bullshit, then while you go and play King I'll be the Conscience I'm *supposed* to be. If there are no lies and no secrets in this absurd secret bloody society, then let that start right here and now. I love you, Sebastian. Like a brother. More than a brother, but I will not take your shit. Not now, and not ever. And I will not let you make another mistake."

Gault looked down at the finger that was still pressed into his chest right above his heart. He slowly, gently reached up and pushed it away.

"Listen to me, Toys," he said softly. "Don't think I'm unaware and ungrateful for what you've done for me over the years. You've been closer to me than family. You are my family. I've never had secrets from you. But don't forget who you were before I found you. A minimum-wage laborer in one of my plants. I was the one who saw something special in you, the potential. I paid for your education; I put you in that posh flat; I let you buy whatever you wanted."

"And I earned those things a thousand times over."

Gault gave a single stubborn shake of his head. "When I found you, you were *nothing*."

"Maybe," hissed Toys, "but a few months ago this 'nothing' kept you from destroying 'everything,' so don't be all high-and-mighty with me."

Gault's mouth opened and closed. He turned and began striding away, but within a few steps he slowed and stopped. His rigid shoulders slumped, and in a gentler voice he said, "The world has changed, Toys. It started when Amirah betrayed me. I feel . . . I feel like the fires that burned my flesh also burned away something else." He turned. "It burned away my weakness, my doubt. I can look back at the Seif Al Din project and I can see where I went wrong, just as I can see how I would do it all differently. Life usually doesn't give you a chance to start over, to do it the right way . . . and yet here we are. Not only is this a second chance; it's a chance at something greater, grander, than anything we imagined. All of those wild, mad dreams we had, they're nothing compared to this. We passed through fire, Toys—you and me—and we emerged as changed beings. Purified. No longer ordinary men. The universe has opened the door to greatness. Don't you understand? To greatness."

The moment held and stretched.

Toys wiped tears from his eyes. "Is this what you want, Sebastian?" he asked quietly. "Look me in the eye and tell me, brother to brother, that this—the Seven Kings, the path to domination, all this death and destruction—is what you truly want."

Gault crossed the room and placed his hands on Toys' cheeks, framing his face. He bent and kissed Toys on the forehead. Gault's eyes burned like candles.

"Yes," he said. "This isn't just what I want, Toys. This is what I will *have*."

Toys searched Gault's face, looked deep into his friend's eyes. He shivered. If eyes were the windows of the soul, then . . .

God save my soul, he thought.

"Okay," he said softly. "Okay."

Interlude Twenty-five

The Seven Kings
Four Months Ago

The American sipped his whiskey as he watched the replay of the argument between Toys and Sebastian Gault. It was the fourth time he had viewed it. During each viewing he focused on a different aspect of the spat. This last time he had zoomed in to watch the expressions on Toys' face. He found them very interesting.

He swirled the whiskey, enjoying the tinkle of ice cubes.

"Okay," said Toys. "Okay."

The American played that back with the sound up, listening for subtleties of intent and meaning in the young Englishman's voice.

The King of Fear smiled.

Chapter Thirty-six

Fair Isle Research Endeavor
The Shetland Isles
December 18, 3:47 P.M. GMT

I stood naked in a decontamination chamber while antibacterial and antiviral agents blasted me from every possible angle. I scrubbed my skin until I glowed in the dark. Afterward they made me stand in a full-scale BAMS unit for five minutes.

"You're clean," Hu announced, though he sounded almost disappointed.

Everything I'd been wearing, including my sidearm, was sealed in a steel drum filled with some kind of acid. Even the fumes from the acid were vented through filters and stored in tanks. I was okay with the procedure. If this strain of Ebola ever got out it would make 28 Days Later look like a Pixar comedy.

I just wished that there was some way for all these gadgets and chemicals to scrub the filth off my soul.

I dressed in an extra set of Barrier BDUs and a pair of sneakers that were half a size too small. All I had left of my personal belongings was my anorak and my dog. Ghost came and sniffed me suspiciously a few times, confused by my lack of scent, but I rubbed the back of my wrist to coax some of the natural oils to the surface and when he took another sniff he licked my hand. I knelt down and hugged the furry monster for a while. If it was too tight, Ghost didn't seem to mind. He wagged his tail and whined a little, sensing the hurt that I felt. Dogs are truly the best of companions. You don't need to explain. They know as much as they need to know, and they are loyal no matter what sins you've committed.

As I got to my feet I looked at FIRE. It was draped in sheets of heavy gray cloth and men in hazmat suits were spraying the cloth with noxious-smelling foam. Above us, a dozen choppers armed with Hellfire missiles kept watch. Somewhere over the horizon Prebble's chums in the Royal Navy were poised to turn this whole island into a memory of charred dust if the right word was given.

Church was waiting for me near our chopper. The winter sun was setting and a bank of clouds was rising from the horizon line like a curtain being cranked into place.

Church handed me a cup of coffee. "It's instant," he said, "but it's hot."

I sipped it and winced. It tasted like the stuff they'd been spraying me with.

"First," he said, "a complete team from Nellis is on-scene at Area 51. The five remaining members of your team are fine and have been treated for minor wounds." When I said nothing, he went on. "Jerry Spencer has taken over the Plympton crime scene."

"He have anything to say?"

Church almost smiled. "He isn't happy that you messed with the evidence."

"I'll cry about it later."

"Other than that, he told me that he would call me if he had anything and asked that I stop bothering him while he was working. His natural warmth and charm are apparently unaffected by the scope of this disaster."

I nodded toward FIRE. "What about Scofield's mother and sisters?"

"Both sisters are already in protective custody in Newark and San Francisco. His mother is in a nursing home in Delray Beach. I sent Riptide Team out of Miami to guard her. We're running background checks on every employee and patient at the nursing home. As soon as we can get a trusted gerontologist on-site we'll move her to a secure facility."

"And the shooter? The woman?"

"Nina Snow, assistant professor of infectious diseases from Johns Hopkins. Top marks, clean record. Considering how she ended things, it's possible she was under similar coercion. She's single and we're working to locate family. Bug is coordinating the background checks."

"That's a lot of resources."

"Yes. And if this continues to escalate we may be forced to rely on other agencies, and that opens us up to all sorts of potential complications." He paused. "Tell me again what Scofield said to you. About the river of blood."

I closed my eyes and found the words. " 'They said that if the rivers didn't run red with blood, then the blood of my family would run like a river.' "

"Yes. That troubles me."

"All of it troubles me. The phrasing doesn't match the rest of what he said. He was clearly quoting, or attempting to quote, something that was said to him. It has a distinctly biblical structure to it. Rivers running red with blood. You're going to need a different kind of specialist to sort that out. Not my kind of job . . . I'm just a shooter."

Church glanced briefly at a flight of gulls flapping across the iron gray sky. "Walk with me, Captain."

We walked toward the cliffs in the red glow of the dying sun. I hunched into my coat and kept taking sips from the coffee, mostly to let the steam warm my face. If Church felt the cold, or cared about it, it didn't show. I'm not sure if I found his iron stoicism admirable or loathsome. It made him seem inhuman. He said nothing for five minutes, letting me sort through my shit.

Finally, he said, "That was hard."

I said nothing.

"I contacted Dr. Sanchez and brought him up to speed. He thinks I'm a monster."

I grunted, and he cut me a brief look.

"Do you need an apology for this?"

"Would you give me one if I did?"

"It's unlikely."

"Then, no."

"Do you feel used, Captain?"

"Sure."

"Do you think that it was unfair of me to put you into this?"

I stopped and waited for him to stop and face me. "Let's cut the shit, Church. They don't hire nice guys to do what we do, but I'm not interested in putting a Dr. Phil spin on this. Do I hate that I had to do it? Sure, who wouldn't? Do I wish it had been someone else in there?

Fuck yeah; I'd rather be with Megan Fox on a topless beach in the South of France. But I'm not. I'm here, and I was the right man for the job. Sucks to be the truth, but there it is."

He studied me for a slow five-count, then nodded and turned. I fell into step beside him.

"One last question," he said.

"Sure."

"When you were in there . . . was that the Killer or the Cop?"

I had never told him that I had disparate personalities floating around in my head, but I knew that prior to hijacking me into the DMS he had his people hack my psych records. Rudy still wanted to skin him for it. I didn't like it any more than Rudy did, but given the nature of the extreme threats we face, I could understand it. To a degree.

"The Cop."

He nodded. "Glad to hear it."

I sighed and rubbed my eyes. The coffee tasted like vulture piss, but I drank it anyway.

After a moment, he said, "Tell me what we know now that we didn't know before we got here."

"We know the Seven Kings are behind this and the London Hospital. I'll be mighty damned surprised if they didn't do Area 51 as well."

He nodded.

I said, "We know that the Kings' point man, the Spaniard, was here in Scotland as late as this morning. If I had to guess, he oversaw the Hospital thing by turning dials on Plympton and maybe some others at the Hospital and then he came here to get this in motion.

This took time, so he must have made multiple trips to London and here. We might get lucky with airline records and whatever boat service brings people out here."

"Yes. I've got Bug on that already. What else?"

"We know that he works on a pattern."

"Tell me."

"He picks people who not only have families but who are absolutely devoted to them. People willing to kill others to prevent harm from coming to their own. I know I'd kill to protect my brother, his wife, and their kid, but I wouldn't blow up a hospital to do it. No, that's got to be a specific kind of person. Snow seems to be the exception, so we can't discount the possibility that she was more 'agent' than 'victim.' The question is how the Kings are identifying people who are vulnerable to this kind of coercion."

"Employee records can be hacked," Church suggested. "*We* do it all the time."

"Sure, but would that kind of thing be inside an employee's records? I mean, imagine asking that question on a performance review: 'Would you release a virus capable of creating a global pandemic to keep your kids safe?' Pretty sure we would have gotten wind of that."

He nodded.

"So, maybe these guys are accessing psych records. We need to look for commonalities there, see if they've used the same therapist, or therapists in the same network. There has to be a link to how they're getting this kind of info."

"I asked Dr. Sanchez to coordinate with Bug on the proper search arguments. What else?"

"They like backup plans. They had three people here.

Grey, Scofield, and Snow. Probably the same thing at the Hospital. Unfortunately, that screws the math even more when it comes to employee psych profiles. Three people of that kind in the same place. I might be able to buy that at the London, but not in a place like FIRE. Too small. That's weird unless somehow they were seeded here. We need to look at transfer records, too."

"Hugo Vox can help with that. He's the top security screener in the country, and he owns a number of employment agencies for this kind of work. He may be able to determine how the Kings are working the employee profiles."

"Good. Set it up. One more thing we know."

Church cocked an expectant eyebrow.

"We know they plan well in advance, which means we are way behind the curve here. God knows how many other events like these are cocked and locked."

"Yes."

We walked in silence for another minute. "What's my next step?" I asked. "I'd like to head back to London and—"

"No. Childe tells me that word's gotten around that you killed two London cops and put another in intensive care. A formal statement has been issued by the commissioner that these three were part of the terrorist cell responsible for the bombing, but—"

"But some cops aren't going to buy that. Shit."

"I don't think there's anything more you can do here, Captain. You've done very good work. You're booked on a flight to the States."

"Area 51?"

"No. You'll land in Philadelphia and meet up with

Dr. Sanchez. He called me while you were in the lab. I think we can say with certainty that Nicodemus is involved."

Church told me what had happened during Rudy's visit to Graterford. It didn't make me want to dance and sing.

"This guy is pretending to be—what? A prophet?"

"Unknown, though from the description Dr. Sanchez gave, Nicodemus is either pretending to be demonically possessed or suffering from an unusual form of multiple personality disorder. So far Nicodemus's references are distortions of biblical references. Old and New Testament, as well as the Apocrypha."

"Lots of psychos read the Bible, especially in prison. He could be pulling stuff out of his ass to jerk our chains."

"And he mentioned the Goddess."

"Which ties to the Spaniard," I said, and he nodded.

"And Nicodemus mentioned the 'Elders,' but there wasn't enough context to infer a meaning. Most likely it's a reference to the *Protocols of the Elders of Zion*. There were Internet references to that via some posts by the Goddess."

I asked what that was and Church explained about the early-twentieth-century propaganda.

"World's full of nuts. How's that tie into this stuff?"

"Unknown. Could be part of a plan to foment religious violence, or it could be simple misdirection. We still need to understand where these clues are supposed to take us." Church paused. "And there were a few other things he said."

He told me the rest, about what Nicodemus had said as he was being led out.

"He actually said that?" I demanded. "Nicodemus referred to a friend of Rudy's who had 'lost the *grace* of the Goddess'? 'One who walks with *ghosts*'?"

"Yes," drawled Church. "Interesting, isn't it?"

"Son of a bitch."

"Dr. Sanchez was badly shaken by those comments. However, the remark that I find most significant is the one about the river of blood that was supposed to sweep you away. It ties into what Scofield said, but it was clearly directed at you."

"Yeah. That's a real ass-biter."

"What do you think of it?"

I cut a look at Church. "If you are asking if I think this Nicodemus character is getting messages from the spirit world, then no, I don't. I wasn't swept away by a river of blood. We stopped this from happening. To me it says that he knew that I was going to be here and something about me personally. Grace's death, the name of my dog. Shit that could be found out. But he didn't know that things were going to spin our way on this."

Church smiled. It was a rare thing for him to do and it wasn't at all a friendly or happy smile. The Angel of Death might smile like that. "Nicodemus said that to Dr. Sanchez before I even picked you up at the Plympton crime scene. How would anyone know that I was going to assign this mission to you?"

The wind howled past me for a long time. Ghost whimpered slightly, but I couldn't tell whether it was from the cold or his canine senses had caught the specters on the wind that we humans could not see.

We started walking again.

"I also received a call from our informant," he said.

"Deep Throat? What did he say?"

Church told me. "On the surface the conversation appears to flow normally, but I'm sure there was a code in there. A clue. One line stands out: *'They want to break the bones of their enemies and suck out the marrow.'* I told him that it didn't seem helpful and he insisted that it was. So we need to add the words 'break,' 'bones,' and 'marrow' to our key words and see what happens."

I nodded. "We'll sort it out. We still have a lot of resources we can throw at this. No matter what it takes, we'll find them."

He half-turned and studied me. "What makes you think so?"

"We have to," I said. I was aware of how that sounded.

Church let a little time pass before he replied.

"I don't want to preach cynicism, Captain," Church said, "but if you stay in this game for any considerable length of time you may experience an enlightenment that is akin to what the national consciousness of America went through between the end of World War Two and the end of the Vietnam War."

"What, a loss of innocence? I just shot someone, Boss, so I think—"

"No. The epiphany was that there are some wars you can't win. There are some wars, in fact, that are so big and yet so subtle that all you can hope to do is catch glimpses of them as they move through your life."

I looked at him.

He shrugged. "This has that feel to it."

"What . . . Are you saying you don't think we'll catch them?"

"We don't even know who they are, Captain. We're

miles from certain knowledge of any kind. Even the things we've learned today could be carefully seeded misdirection. This is the nature of the War on Terror. Sometimes there is no face, no name, no target for us to point a gun at. It can be disheartening and daunting, and the frustration of it has forced a lot of players out of the game."

"But not you," I said.

"Not me."

"Why not?"

Church didn't answer that. Instead he said, "The darkness is all around us. Very few people have the courage to light a candle against it."

"I'm not that kind of idealist."

"Nor am I. We are of a kind, Captain, and neither of us is holding a candle against the darkness. Like the unknown and unseen enemy we fight, people like you and me, we *are* the darkness. In some ways we are more like the things we're fighting than the people we're protecting. Granted our motives are better—from our perspective—but we wait in the shadows for our unseen enemy to make a move against those innocents with the candles. And by that light we take aim."

"Is that all we are?" I asked. "Hunters in the dark?"

"Isn't it enough for you?"

"I don't know. I don't want that to be all that I am."

Church nodded.

We stared out to sea, watching as the thickening clouds were underlit by the setting sun. The colors were intense. Dark reds and hot oranges. It looked like the whole world was on fire.

Part Three
Ten Plagues

The governments of the present day have to deal not merely with other governments, with emperors, kings and ministers, but also with the secret societies which have everywhere their unscrupulous agents, and can at the last moment upset all the governments' plans.

—BENJAMIN DISRAELI

Chapter Thirty-seven

Prebble's team gave me a lift to Heathrow. It was a silent trip except for some murmured condolences for the losses suffered by the DMS. We were all in mourning. The final death toll from the Hospital had been released.

Four thousand one hundred sixteen people.

That was eleven hundred more than had died in the fall of the Towers. Add to that the body count from Area 51: 79 people on the research and development team, 26 support staff, 8 from the Nellis Air Force Base Military Intelligence Team, 6 members of Lucky Team, 9 men and women from Area 51's on-site security team, and the 2 members of Echo—130 all told. Add Plympton's wife and daughter, Charles Grey and his family, and two dead in the fish tank and the total was 4,253 dead in less than two days.

Those numbers were full of broken glass and splinters. You couldn't touch them without bleeding.

I sat in one of the padded seats on the chopper with Ghost's head on my lap and stared inward into some of the empty darkness in my head.

I wished that Grace was with me.

God Almighty, Grace . . . why aren't you here?

I closed my eyes and tried not to scream. Inside my head the Warrior was ramming the point of his knife into the ground over and over again, teeth bared in a feral snarl of unrelenting bloodlust. The Modern Man was hiding somewhere; he just couldn't deal. I wanted the Cop to emerge, to assert his cool control, but for the moment he was silent, and ugly winds blew across the darkness of my inner landscape.

I dozed for a while, but my dreams were nasty and I woke to the sound of my phone buzzing. I flipped it open.

"Do not tell me there's been another attack," I said by way of hello.

"No," said Mr. Church, "but here's a twist for you."

"Hit me."

"Jerry Spencer and his team found the body of Trevor Plympton in the subbasement of the hospital."

"Killed by the blast?"

"Hardly. The debris kept him fairly intact, but it is clear that he had been systematically and comprehensively tortured."

"Ah, Jesus. . . . Were they able to fix the time of death?"

"Best guess is two to six hours after the deaths of his family. Well before the bombs went off."

He let me process that for a moment.

"That is a twist," I said, "but it tells us something. It straightens the logic."

"Tell me."

"If Plympton had been coerced into bringing the bombs to work and setting them up for fear that something bad would happen to his family, he might have snapped. He might have killed his wife and kid and then gone to work to maybe stop the bomb."

"Why kill his family?" Church asked.

"Because he was about to betray the extortionists."

"Why not go to the authorities?"

"Plympton told us why in his note."

" 'They are *everywhere*,' " Church quoted.

"Yes, and he believed that to the point of killing his wife and daughter in order to protect them from worse treatment at the hands of the Seven Kings."

"So, who killed Plympton?"

"Good question. We know from Fair Isle that the Kings had several agents in place. They clearly used the same setup here. So we're back to what we talked about on Fair Isle, that the Kings have a way of identifying certain psychological profiles within their target facilities."

There was silence at both ends of the line as we each thought about all the things that were wrong with that.

"It smacks of too much inside knowledge," said Church.

"Way too much."

"Let me work on that end of things," he said. "In the meantime, I've arranged for a specialist to liaise with you. Dr. Circe O'Tree. She's an analyst who specializes in the social, religious, and historical justifications for terrorism. She'll join you on the flight to the States."

"Good. We can use the help. But . . . where do I know that name from?"

"I doubt you watch *Oprah,* so I'll venture that you saw her latest book in the stores. *The Terrorist Sophist.*"

"That's it. Looked interesting," I said. "Should have picked it up."

"Pick it up in the airport," he suggested. "It's useful stuff. Dr. O'Tree works for Hugo Vox out at Terror Town, though she's been in London for the last two months working in security logistics for the *Sea of Hope*. Her track record for intuitive leaps and Big Picture perspective checks is remarkable. I tried to recruit her for the DMS, but she declined."

"Why?"

When he didn't answer, I said, "She sounds like a sharp cookie. I'll try not to embarrass the home team."

"That would be nice," Church said dryly. "Last thing before you go. We have the first lab reports from the Hospital fire. They've found residue consistent with a large quantity of automobile tires. They were apparently stored on the top floor of the Hospital in several rooms that had been roped off, ostensibly for plumbing repairs. Hospital officials have no explanation for that, and they believe that the tires had to have been brought in very recently. We can presume that Plympton and/or others working for the Kings brought them in within the last twenty-four hours before the fire."

"Why? To increase the toxicity of the smoke or special effects?"

"That's Spencer's take. There are a number of ways in which a pall of darkness can be spun into a political or religious statement. And it may tie in with what Dr. Sanchez learned at Graterford. That's a good topic to run by Dr. O'Tree."

He disconnected.

I CHEWED ON that for the rest of the flight to Heathrow. Gus Dietrich had arranged for an aide to be there with my suitcases. I ducked into a bathroom and changed out of the BDUs and into a light traveling suit.

Ghost, looking like a tortured martyr, went into the cargo hold in a big box. Even when I gave him his favorite toy—a well-chewed stuffed cat with DR. HU stitched on its chest—from the looks Ghost threw me you'd have thought I'd just whipped him with a chain.

Did I feel guilty as I kicked off my shoes and stretched out my legs in first class? Could I imagine his piteous whines as I sipped my first glass of Jameson?

Yeah, but I dealt with it manfully. I finished the drink in two wheezing gulps, ordered a second and took a slug, then rested the glass on my thigh. My eyes started drifting closed and I didn't fight it.

"Captain Ledger—?"

I fought the urge to heave out a frustrated sigh as I cranked open one eye. "Yes?"

A woman set a briefcase down on the adjoining seat. She was very likely the most beautiful woman I had ever seen in real life.

"Mr. Church told me that you'd be aboard this flight," she said. "I'm Dr. Circe O'Tree."

I stared up at her and for a moment I forgot all about death and destruction. I also forgot that I'd buckled my seat belt, so when I tried to stand and shake her hand I jerked to a halt and spilled my whiskey all over my crotch.

Smooth.

Chapter Thirty-eight

We both looked at the dark stain spreading on the front of my trousers.

"Well," I said, "I guess there's no way I'm going to make a bigger jackass of myself than that, so we can go on the assumption that everything else will be less of a disappointment."

Circe O'Tree arched an eyebrow. "Oh, I don't know. We have a long flight ahead of us."

Damn.

She was average height, but beyond that all other uses of the word "average" went right out the window. Circe had a heart-shaped face framed by intensely black hair that fell in wild curls to her shoulders. She had full lips, high cheekbones that a model would have sold her own offspring for, and a set of heart-stopping curves. The brown of her eyes was so dark that the irises looked black. I figured her for Black Irish with a dash of Greek. She wore a tailored tweed skirt and jacket over a sheer white blouse. She wasn't dressed to show off, and there wasn't a hint of flirtation in her smile, so this was all on me. I could blame it on being caught off-guard. Sure, that sounds good.

"Mind if I sit?" she asked.

"Please," I said, fumbling for what few manners I had left.

She sat and laid her briefcase on her thighs and tried not to smile at the whiskey spill. When the cabin attendant saw the mess and—God help me—tried to dab at it with a cloth, Circe turned aside and bit her thumb to keep from laughing.

I yanked out the tails of my shirt to hide the damage. The attendant, red faced and flustered, brought fresh drinks, a new whiskey for me and a Coke Zero for Circe.

"So," I said, "want to start this over again? 'Cause really I'm not as much of an imbecile as evidence might suggest."

"I try not to hold first impressions against people."

"Thank god for that. Can we try those introductions again? You are—?"

"Do you want the full name or the one that fits my driver's license?"

"Give me the whole enchilada. I've got time."

"Circe Diana Ekklesia Magdalena O'Tree."

"Yikes."

"I have a complicated family history."

"No kidding."

" 'Circe's' easier." She held out a hand. She wore rings on most of her fingers and a silver band of Celtic knots around her thumb. Her grip was strong, the way a woman's is, without affected delicacy or an attempt to prove herself by trying to crush my bones. I noticed that there was a line of callus running from her index finger to her thumb. Shooters get calluses like that. Her trigger finger was the only one without a ring. File that away.

"Captain Joseph Edwin Ledger," I said. "Joe to my friends."

"Nice to meet you, Joe."

"You hold any rank?" I asked.

She shook her dark hair. "Just the degrees. M.D., couple of Ph.D.'s, bunch of master's. I was a world-class nerd."

"What fields?"

"It's a mix. Archaeology, anthropology, physics, psychology, and medicine with a specialty in infectious diseases."

I whistled. "Weird mix."

"Less weird than it appears. I've always known that I wanted to work in the threat assessment field. Counterterrorism and antiterrorism. The physics and medicine help me understand the specific nature of the WMDs we might face; the archaeology and anthropology give me a lot of cultural perspective. And the psychology allows me to crawl inside the heads of freedom fighters and political extremists."

"Makes sense, but you must have started collecting degrees in grade school."

Her smile abruptly dropped about twenty degrees. "Are you going to tell me that I look too young to be so smart?"

"Uh . . . no. My comment was meant to convey appreciation of your accomplishments, not to condescend."

Circe said nothing. Insecure and a bit touchy. File that away, too.

"Church said you were in London for the *Sea of Hope* thing. I just got the skinny on that yesterday."

"And—?"

"And what?"

"Most of you people seem to think that it's an extraordinary waste of security resources and probably an overall waste of time."

" 'You people'? What the hell's that supposed to mean?"

"Military types. Covert-ops types."

"Ah. You mean *male* types. Sorry, Doc, but I wasn't going in that direction. If you want to hear what I actually think, try asking it without the challenge."

She sat back and appraised me for a moment, but it was hard to tell what conclusions she was drawing. She said, "Okay, so what do you think of Generation Hope?"

"No bullshit?"

"No bullshit."

"I think it's long past due, and I'm encouraged to know that the project was conceived by the *next* generation. The current generation in power—on both sides of the aisle—spend too much time with their heads up their asses playing partisan politics and not enough time planning for the future. I don't like the grasshopper viewpoint when it comes to issues that affect the whole world. That said, I think the *Sea of Hope* is about the best target I could think of for a terrorist attack, so providing top-of-the-line security for it makes a lot of sense."

Another long moment while she fixed those dark, calculating eyes on me.

"Okay," she said. "Points for that."

"Gosh, thanks."

Circe gave me a charming smile. "We're not going to get along well, are we?"

I laughed. "Actually, I kind of hope we are. I'll behave if you will."

She shrugged. "It's worth a try."

That bought us a few seconds of awkward silence. I waited for her to fill it. She didn't, so I caved and asked, "You've worked with Church before?"

Something flickered in and out of her eyes and she brushed a nonexistent piece of debris from the leather cover of her briefcase. "Once or twice."

"He speaks highly of you," I said.

"Does he?" she said distractedly. Her eyes drifted down to her hands for a moment, and I couldn't tell if she was being evasive because her history with Church was awkward or because she was intimidated by the thought of him. She wouldn't be the first person in a power position who got moody and introspective when Church's name was mentioned. There was something about Church that made you assess everything from how clean your fingernails were to how many sins were left unconfessed on your soul. After a few seconds she raised her eyes and looked at me.

"It might be useful if you brought me up to speed on what you've learned," she said. "Mr. Church said that you're already forming some useful theories . . . ?"

"Don't yet know how useful they are," I said, "but here goes."

I told her everything that had happened since Church called me yesterday. The jet was far out over the Atlantic by the time I finished. While I spoke she took a lot of notes on her laptop.

The story hit her pretty hard and her eyes were wet. "Fair Isle. That encounter with the little boy—"

"Mikey," I said.

"Mikey. That must have been very difficult."

"Harder for him than me."

"No," she said, "I don't think so. He's past it now; he's out of it. You have to carry it around with you."

"It's part of the job, Doc."

She shifted to study me, eyes narrowing again. "Why are you doing that?"

"Doing what?"

"Blowing it off as if it's nothing? You watched a little boy die a horrible death today. You had to use him in order to do your job. Are you going to sit there and tell me that it's just another day at work? What, you did that and now you can clock out and watch the in-flight movie?"

I sighed. "What should I do? Break down and cry?"

"It would be a little more human."

"Sure . . . and I'll probably get around to that. I'm not that kind of macho. But at the same time, how would it get me through the rest of today? People I know have died today. I killed two people yesterday and someone else today. I want to hunt down the people responsible for what's going on and kill them. Would disintegrating into tears get me through any of that?"

"You live a difficult life, Captain."

"So does a nurse in a charity ward. It's all relative, and the name is 'Joe.'"

"And the loss of your men?" she said. "You must be devastated."

"Sure. Granted, I've been away and didn't really know them, but they wore the uniform, so anyone in the field is going to feel the loss."

She nodded. "Funny, most professional soldiers who said something like that would come off sounding like a bad actor in a cheap action film. You don't."

"Thanks. I think."

"It's more typical of the kind of person Mr. Church tends to hire for his teams. He needs tough men and women, and granted there will always be a bit of the tough-guy catchphrases being tossed around, but most of the people I've met have a deeper level." She cut me a sideways look. "And no, Captain Ledger, that is not in any way a flirtatious remark."

"I never for a minute thought—"

"Yes, you did," she said, but she said it pleasantly. Or so I thought. "Of course you did."

"No, really, I—"

She held up a hand. "Okay, let's throw some cards on the table so we can move forward without stepping on eggshells. Fair enough?"

"Yes?" I said dubiously.

"I work at T-Town, which is about ninety-nine percent men, and all of them either are alpha personalities or think they are. That said, what we have here is the standard dynamic for sexual tension. I'm moderately good-looking, I have big boobs, and I get hit on by everyone from the pastor of my church to baristas at Starbucks, and by every single guy at T-Town except for my boss and the range master. I don't blame them and I don't judge them. It's part of the procreative drive hard-wired into us, and we haven't evolved as a species far enough to exert any genuine control over the biological imperative. You, on the other hand, are a very good-looking man of prime breeding age. Old enough to have interesting lines and scars—and stories to go with them—and young enough to be a catch. You probably get laid as often as you want to, and you can probably count on the fingers of one hand the number of times women have said no to you. Maybe—and please correct me if I've strayed too far into speculation—being an agent of a secret government organization has led you to buy into the superspy sex stud propaganda perpetuated by James Bond films."

"My name is Powers," I said. "Austin Powers."

She ignored me and plowed ahead. "We're in the middle of a crisis. We may have to work closely together for several days, or even several weeks. Close-quarters travel, emotions running high, all that. If it's all the same to you, I'd rather not spend the next few days living inside a trite office romance cliché. That includes everything from mild flirtation to sexual innuendo and double entendre and the whole ball of wax."

She sipped her Coke. The ball landed in my court with a thump.

I leaned back and smiled.

"What?" she asked.

"I can't tell you how refreshing it is to hear this."

She was flustered by that for almost a full second.

"You agree?" she said guardedly.

"Agree? While you were talking I was doing a little mental preflight check and, yeah, I had every typical male reaction in the book. Eyes, boobs, legs, the works. And you're not 'moderately good-looking'; you're a fucking knockout and you know it. Or you should know it if you have a mirror. So yeah, I get that attraction is part of the proliferation of the species. And from a purely observational point of view I'm guilty as charged. No question," I said. "And no apologies."

She raised an eyebrow.

"I'm as male and horny as the next guy. Maybe the next four guys, and sure, that's the alpha-wolf drive-to-breed gene firing on all cylinders. Good call. On the other hand, you pointed out that I'm a professional of the kind Mr. Church hires. Not only don't I think with my biceps or trigger finger; I don't think with my dick."

Circe considered that, nodded.

"One more thing," I said. "Despite the hardwired urges, I'm also not on the market. I'm letting my heart take a long vacation. It might even retire to a cave."

"Broken heart?" she probed. "Someone dump you?"

I almost let her off the hook, but I actually respected her for her candor. "No," I said. "The woman—the extraordinary woman—with whom I was in love died."

Circe's lips parted, but she said nothing.

"She died on the job. If it wasn't for her, you and I couldn't be here having this conversation because the whole damn world would have gone to hell and, yes, in a handbasket."

I could almost hear something go *clunk* in her head as a couple of disparate pieces of information fell sharply into place.

"Oh my God," she said softly. "Grace Courtland? *You* were the one she was in love with?"

I nodded.

"Did Church tell you?" I asked.

"No," she said. "Grace did."

That hit me like a punch between the eyes. "Grace told you about us?"

"No . . . not really. She told me that she was starting

to fall in love with someone. Someone . . . in the DMS. I . . . I thought she meant Mr. Church."

I laughed. I couldn't help it; a single bark of shocked laughter burst out. "Church?"

"That's funny?"

"Funny weird, not funny ha-ha."

We sat in silence for a moment. I sipped my whiskey and hoped for a nice midair collision.

"As initial encounters go," I said, "this is a doozy."

"Where does it leave us? Except literally and metaphorically out to sea?"

"If we're adults, it means that we can start with a clean slate, a fair mutual understanding, and a shared agenda."

She smiled. "I like that."

We shook on it.

"Now," I said. "It's your turn."

She gave me a half smile, kind of a "you asked for it, buster" look, and then told me all about the Goddess.

Interlude Twenty-six

The Seven Kings
Three and a Half Months Ago

Toys tried to catch Gault's eye, but he was deep in conversation with the King of Lies. They were laughing. In the two weeks since they'd come to the castle, Toys and Gault had grown wary of each other. Gault had thrown himself into the world of the Kings and the Goddess with his whole heart. Toys walked more circumspectly around the fringes, playing the role of Conscience for protective cover but generally feeling trapped.

You, my friend, he said to himself, *are in a right pickle.*

Suddenly the room went silent and all eyes turned as the door to the chamber opened and Eris came in. She wore a white dress, long and tailored, and although the cut was simple and the design plain, on her it looked like a regal gown. Everyone stood. Each King, each Conscience, got to his feet, and as Eris walked across the room they all bowed.

Not wanting to stand out, Toys bowed as well. As he did so he imagined how good it would feel to slip a knife into her kidney. *Do goddesses bleed like ordinary mortals?* he speculated darkly.

Eris ascended the throne on the raised dais, then waved everyone else to their seats. They sat like obedient dogs, Toys thought. All except the American, who took his time.

In this lighting, in this setting, Eris looked ageless and beautiful and more regal than anyone else Toys had ever met in the flesh. And he'd met most of the crowned heads of Europe. Everyone beamed at her in a way that Toys thought looked truly . . . worshipful. That was the only word that fit.

It troubled him.

The King of Famine got to his feet. "Goddess . . . we are complete again. We are Seven."

"Seven is the sacred number." She looked at Gault. "Do you know why?"

He shook his head like a man in a dream. "Tell me. . . ."

A wicked smile played over Eris's lips. Toys thought that it was half virgin, half whore, and thoroughly corrupt.

Eris raised her arms as if in invocation. "The world was made during seven days of Creation, and it will end when the Seven Seals spoken of in the Book of Revelation are opened. The number seven is key to every religion, every path to spirit. Look into the sky and behold the seven-starred constellation of Saptarishi Mandalam representing the Seven Sages."

"Seven upon seven mysteries!" intoned the group.

"The Virgin Mary experienced seven joys."

"And endured seven sorrows," the Kings replied.

Toys saw that Gault's lips were moving. He could not know this information—Gault was a lapsed Presbyterian—but it was clear that he wanted to participate, even to the point of trying to speak a litany to which he had never before been privy. Toys was sure that Gault was unaware that he was doing it, and that alone was frightening, because Gault was always aware. His perception was the thing that had always defined him. Now, in the space of seconds, he had descended into ritual behavior. Cult behavior.

Toys wanted to grab him, slap his face, and drag him out of this madhouse.

"There are seven heavens in Islam and seven fires in their hell," said Eris.

"Heaven and hell," said the crowd. "Linked by seven doors."

"The Jews know this truth," said Eris. "God told the Israelites that they would displace seven peoples when they entered the land of Israel."

"Hail the power of Seven!"

Eris spoke of seven dimensions and sets of seven gods and demons in a dozen religions. She named seven dates as the key moments on which history turned, and the seven secret families who brought Europe out of the Dark Ages. She spoke of sevens in astronomy and physics, geography and philosophy. Her voice rose to a screech as she spoke of seven as a core number in sacred mathematics, naming it as the fourth prime number, a Mersenne prime, a double Mersenne, a Newman-Shanks-Williams prime, a Woodall prime, a factorial prime. . . .

Toys could feel the pull of the magic she wove, and it took every ounce of his will, and every splinter of his hate, to keep from being swept away by it all.

Everyone else was completely caught up in it, their faces aglow with fanatical light. None more so than Santoro, who looked like he was having a long, slow, and very powerful orgasm as he stared at the Goddess.

The only other person in the room who did not look like he had been transported by the Goddess was her son, and when Toys looked across the room he saw the American looking directly back at him. And he was smiling. It was a small thing, a tiny curl of the lip that betrayed a subtlety at odds with his bombastic personality. As Toys watched, the American flicked a look at Eris, then rolled his eyes in a "can you believe this bullshit?" expression, then smiled again at Toys.

No one else noticed. The others were with Eris in a completely different place.

Toys risked the smallest of reciprocal smiles, and the American gave the tiniest of nods. Then the King of

Fear turned his face away and pretended that he, too, was enraptured by the Goddess.

Eris turned to Gault and whispered, "Now, my newest son and King, tell me a secret known to the King of Plagues. Tell me a secret of Seven."

Everyone turned toward Gault and Toys almost reached out to touch him but could not make his hand move. The moment—every bizarre part of it—was unreal and alien.

Gault licked his lips and blinked, but his eyes remained glazed.

"Whisper truth to us," coaxed Eris.

And Gault said, "There are seven types of viruses in the Baltimore classification. Double-stranded DNA viruses; single-stranded DNA viruses; double-stranded RNA viruses; single-stranded RNA viruses, positive sense; single-stranded RNA viruses, negative sense; positive-sense single-stranded RNA viruses that replicate through a DNA intermediate; and double-stranded DNA viruses that replicate though a single-stranded RNA intermediate."

When he began speaking his voice had the flat intonation of a student repeating information from a textbook, but with each new type of virus he named his voice became more thoroughly charged with emotion. With passion.

"Jesus," whispered Toys, but nobody heard him as the Kings and the Consciences and the Goddess broke into cheers and applause. And even though it felt like lifting bricks instead of hands, Toys made himself clap, too.

"And," said Eris, raising her hands to heaven, "there are Seven Kings. Speak, that the world may know!"

The American reached for his wineglass and raised it. In his booming bass voice he cried aloud, "I am the King of Fear!"

The Israeli did the same; but crying, "I am the King of War!"

And the Russian: "I am the King of Famine!"

The Saudi: "I am the King of Lies!"

The Italian: "I am the King of Gold!"

The Frenchman raised his glass. "I am the King of Thieves!"

All eyes turned to Sebastian Gault. The glaze in his eyes changed as Toys watched. It no longer spoke to a mindless vacuity but to an intellect that was as deep as pain and as precise as torture. Gault lifted his glass and stared for the briefest of moments at the contents; the wine was as dark as welling blood. He looked from it to the Goddess on her throne.

"I am the King of Plagues!" He yelled it. Fierce and wild, full of pride and hubris and hatred.

Eris smiled. "The world belongs to me and I sanctify and bless you, my seven glorious Kings. Let those who oppose our will perish in torment. This I say before you all!"

"The Goddess!" they all screamed.

Then the Kings drank, and the Consciences drank with them. Even Toys, against his own will, fumbled for his wineglass and sloshed some bloodred wine into his mouth, though it burned like acid in his throat.

Chapter Thirty-nine

Circe told me about the Goddess and the hate crimes inspired by her online postings.

"Okay," I said, "that lines up with what we've gotten from Plympton's note, Dr. Grey, and that fruitcake Nicodemus. You're the expert on symbolism and we're ass deep in it—so what the hell are we looking at? And, just a heads-up, if you say that you don't know I'm pretty much going to throw myself out of the plane."

"Don't kill yourself just yet. Between what you have and what I have, we may actually have something here."

"But—? You say that, but you have 'but' written all over your face . . . and, yes, I am fully aware of how that sounds, so please pretend I didn't say it."

Circe smiled. She had a good smile and so far I hadn't seen very many of them. "*But,*" she said, leaning on it intentionally, "the scope of it is so . . . big."

"Mr. Church said something today. He told me that sometimes a war is so big and yet so subtle that all you can hope to do is catch glimpses of it as it moves through your life. I don't like to accept that, but I'm beginning to think he's right."

She nodded. "That's the nature of a terrorist organization. They're more like an online virtual community. They don't physically exist in any one place. There are some here, some there, . . . and most of them don't even know each other. Not on a *real* level." She chewed her lip and considered. "Let's look at this one piece at a time."

"Hit me," I said.

"The Hospital fire. After looking through all of the employee lists, all of the programs and services, the research highlights, et cetera . . . , there are two things that stand out. The first is the scope. It's big. So big you could call it 'epic.' No one will be unaware of it, and that kind of scope adds weight and authority to any subsequent message by the perpetrators."

"Right. A terrorist who blows up a hot-dog cart isn't taken as seriously as one who knocks down the Twin Towers."

"Exactly. Second point is that we are finding out information about the Kings. I would *like* to think that our side is simply so smart that we've been able to compile information very quickly, but—"

"But," I cut in, "information is being handed to us. Deep Throat, Nicodemus, the confessions of Plympton, Scofield, and Grey . . ."

She nodded. "And the Goddess posts."

"So, we're being fed this stuff? Why?"

"It speaks to the interpretation of the events. It shows us, the good guys, the size and scope of our enemy's plan. Another way to interpret an 'epic' scale is 'biblical.'"

"They want us to see this as something off-the-scale?"

"Sure. It reinforces their mystique."

"How does that help them?"

"If they are not tied to a specific religion like Islam or Christianity, or a political ideology like democracy or communism, then their message won't carry the same weight."

"I get it," I said. "By building the mystique of a secret society acting out the orders of a goddess but by using elements of existing religions, they make us see them as ancient, powerful, and mysterious."

"It's window dressing," she conceded, "but it works."

I nodded. It really was working.

"Moreover," Circe continued, "they are also raising the bar. 9/11 gouged a scar into everyone's psyche. The only way to one-up that was to go bigger. Blowing up Windsor Castle or Parliament would have been big, but a hospital has more emotional punch. It sends a very clear message: There is no one safe from the Seven Kings. No religion, no race or national background, no age, no gender. The Kings are willing to kill babies and old people. They are saying that they are not afraid of anything. They are saying: 'We are above you and your laws. We are, in fact, your *Kings*.' The presence of a goddess suggests that the action of the Kings is mandated by a higher power. Based on what Nicodemus said, the Goddess transcended the older 'version' of God by embracing more aspects and combing them to become who she now is. 'Become' is the key word. We see that a lot in cases of transformative megalomania and sociopathy. A person 'becomes' something higher through ritual acts that include sacrifice."

"*Silence of the Lambs* and *Red Dragon*," I said. "Serial killers do that."

"Killing is proof of dominance over ordinary life as well as the pathway to ascendency."

"Nice. What about the black smoke?"

"Yes. That makes no sense except as a symbol. I saw it from my hotel room. It was extremely thick, and the TV reporters kept saying that it looked like night over the Hospital. If we didn't have Nicodemus's comments to go on, then we might have been fumbling around with metaphors. He mentioned the Ten Plagues of Egypt. He fed us the connection."

"Look, I mostly ducked out of Sunday school to play baseball, so can you give me the Cliffs Notes version of the whole Ten Plagues thing?"

She smiled. "Moses and his brother, Aaron, confronted Pharaoh to ask that the Israelites be allowed to leave Egypt. He refused, so Moses appealed to God, Who in turn taught Moses some magic. Stuff like transforming his staff into a serpent and causing or curing leprosy. Unfortunately, the Egyptian court magicians were able to duplicate most of the same tricks."

"So the Ten Plagues was a pissing contest?"

"I'm not sure biblical scholars would agree with that interpretation. It was supposed to prove the power of the One God over the many gods of Egypt."

"Politics," I said, and she nodded. "So, Plague of Darkness. What's the skinny?"

Circe tilted her head back for a moment, accessing memories, then recited: "That's Exodus, chapter ten, verses twenty-one and twenty-two: 'And the Lord said unto Moses, Stretch out thine hand toward heaven, that there may be darkness over the land of Egypt, even darkness which may be felt. And Moses stretched forth his hand toward heaven; and there was a thick darkness in all the land of Egypt three days.'"

"The black smoke from the burning tires didn't cover the whole land and it didn't last for three days."

"Right, but keep an open mind. Most scholars believe that much of the Bible is metaphor."

"Okay. And you said something about the Nile turning to blood."

" 'And the Lord spake unto Moses, Say unto Aaron, Take thy rod, and stretch out thine hand upon the waters of Egypt, upon their streams, upon their rivers, and upon their ponds, and upon all their pools of water, that they may become blood; and that there may be blood throughout all the land of Egypt, both in vessels of wood, and in vessels of stone.' Exodus, chapter seven, verse twelve."

"That talks about the water itself turning to blood."

Metaphor," she said, holding up a scholarly finger. "Metaphor. If an airborne strain of Ebola escaped and reached mainland England, people would start bleeding out by the tens of thousands. Blood would flow like a river, or as close as you would want to get."

"Damn," I said. "What are the other plagues?"

"They vary in type and severity. If the Kings are using weaponized versions of them, we're not seeing them unfold in the same order. The third and fourth were plagues of gnats and flies. The fifth was a terrible disease that targeted the Egyptians' livestock. Cattle, oxen, goats, sheep, camels, and horses. The sixth was a plague of boils on the skins of Egyptians. During the seventh plague fiery hail fell from the sky and thunder shook the land. The eighth plague was locusts and the ninth plague was total darkness, so that's the London Hospital. The tenth was—"

"Whoa, whoa!" I said. "Did you say *locusts*?"

She looked alarmed. "Yes, why?"

"Christ!" I leaned close. "Area 51. Son of a bitch!"

"What do you mean? They use a bomb to destroy—"

"Metaphor, Doc," I said. "The R and D team out at Area 51 was working on a brand-new stealth fighter-bomber. The craft's designation was *Locust* FB-119."

"Locust . . . ?" Circe's dark eyes widened. "Oh my God. . . ."

Interlude Twenty-seven

The Seven Kings

Three and a Half Months Ago

In the days following the "Ritual of Seven" Toys kept to himself. When asked, he said that he was meditating on the mysteries of the Goddess. The others actually accepted that as a valid answer, which both amused and appalled Toys.

The only person on the island that he could bear to be around was the American. All interaction between them had so far been wordless eye contact during Kings meetings. However, on the way to a planning meeting Toys found himself in the elevator with the King of Fear.

The American smiled like a grizzly. "How are you settling in?"

"It's a bit much at times."

"That's not what I meant."

"I know what you meant."

The American studied Toys for a few seconds, and the genius mind behind the oaf was clearly there in his eyes. "If I were a betting man," said Fear, "I'd put the whole wad on the fact that your King doesn't really

know the first thing about what goes on in here." He
tapped Toys with a thick finger. Not on Toys' head, but
over his heart.

Toys didn't dare respond to that. He smiled as the elevator descended into the heart of the island. Then, apparently apropos of nothing, the American said, "You
know, some people don't think that Judas was a traitor."

Toys blinked at him in surprise. "What—?"

"Some people think he tried to keep Jesus from fucking up a good thing."

The elevator stopped and the doors opened silently.

Before the King of Fear got off, he turned and said,
"Some people need to be saved from themselves. Even
Kings and goddesses." He chuckled. "Funny old world."

Interlude Twenty-eight

Jenkintown, Pennsylvania
December 19, 9:01 A.M. EST

Whenever her cell phone rang Amber Taylor's heart
spasmed as if she'd been stabbed in the chest. She
wished she could have set a special ringtone for him,
but there was no way to know which number he would
use. Once the man called from Amber's home. Another
time was from her daughter's cell. When Amber later
asked the girl if she had lent her phone to someone
else—a stranger or someone she knew—the girl said
no, it had been in her school locker all day. That had
been one of the worst moments since this whole nightmare began. True to the man's threats, he and his people seemed to have total access to Amber's life. Nothing

and nowhere was safe. That's what he had told her that first time.

Nothing and nowhere.

"You and those you love are only safe as long as we allow it."

"We." Such a horrible word, filled with dreadful and unlimited potential. Who were "we"? How many of them were there? Would the police even be able to make arrests? Based on what evidence?

You and those you love are only safe as long as we allow it.

Amber Taylor feared her own cell phone. She feared his call. Any call. *If* she dared, she would have thrown the phone into a culvert, let it sink into the muck and filth where it belonged. But she knew that she could never do that. He would never allow it, and the punishments for any infraction of his rules had been clearly outlined to her. The memory of those terrible photographs was always right there behind her eyelids, cued up on her mind's internal audiovisual projector.

Her cell rang just as she closed the door to her three-year-old BMW and Amber jumped so badly she missed the ignition keyhole and dropped her keys. Amber dug frantically into her purse and found the phone on the third ring. She checked the screen display. *Wolpert*. She sighed in relief and sagged back against the seat. Cathy Wolpert was her best friend and neighbor.

Smiling in anticipation of a manageable crisis—probably something else about the wedding plans for Cathy's daughter—Amber flipped open the phone.

"Hi, Cathy—"

"Hello, Mrs. Taylor," said the man with the Spanish accent.

His voice was quiet, polite, but it grabbed her by the throat and throttled the air out of her world.

"Oh, God!"

"Not quite," said the man. "But close."

"Are my children all right? God . . . you didn't touch them—?"

"Shhh," he soothed. "Shhh now. Emily and Mark are fine. I can see Emily right now. Such a pretty little face in that tiny school bus. Her new braces are quite nice. She wears them well."

"Don't—"

"Isn't it nice that she doesn't try to hide them behind her hand when she talks? Not even when she smiles. She's very self-possessed for her age, don't you think?"

"Please," Amber begged. Her voice was already raw, as if she'd been screaming. "Please don't hurt my babies."

"Why would I? You haven't done anything that requires that they be hurt, have you?"

"No!"

"So why would I let anything happen to them? Unless you demand that I act, then none of us will touch a hair on her head. Or Mark's head. That is our agreement, yes?"

"Yes." Tears boiled from the corners of Amber's eyes and fell like acid down her cheeks. "Why are you doing this?"

The man laughed. It was the first time she had heard

him laugh, and the sound of it made her cringe. The laugh was unspeakably ugly. Deep and filled with a knowledge and delight so dark that it threatened to burn the light out of the clear morning sky.

"Mrs. Taylor," he said, "do you know why I am calling you today?"

"Y-yes."

"You knew that this day would come. I told you that I would make this call."

"Yes," she whispered hoarsely. "When?"

"Today," he said. "Right now."

"But . . . my children . . . I have to—"

"No, Mrs. Taylor, you only have one thing to do. We are watching your children. We are waiting for you to do what you have promised to do."

"I need to know that my babies are safe!"

"That's up to you. If you do this, then I swear to the Goddess and by all of her works that I will not harm them. When this is over for you, it will be over for them. They will live to grow up and grow old and put flowers on your grave."

"Please don't make me do this. . . ."

"Or," he said softly, "you could spend your remaining years putting flowers on *their* graves. That is . . . if you could ever find where they were buried."

Amber tried to shout at him, but her voice broke into splinters of fear and grief and tears.

He hung up, but Amber heard him whisper something as the connection was broken. A single word.

"Delicious . . ."

Chapter Forty

Top Sims found his team waiting for him clustered around a big black Tactical Vehicle in the main garage. The TacV looked like an oversized SUV, with a bulked-up back bay filled with weapons and equipment. Each of the team—DeeDee, Khalid, and John Smith—affected a posture of cool disinterest. A passerby would have thought they were waiting for a train. Only Bunny stood apart, hands in his pockets, head down, staring at the concrete between his feet.

The team nodded to Top, who returned the nod and headed over to talk with Mike Harnick, the chief mechanic at the Warehouse. Harnick was leaning on the hood writing on a clipboard and he looked up and smiled as Top approached.

"How we doing, Mike?"

"Black Bess is good to go. The extra armor adds weight, so I put a sixty-gallon tank on it."

"What's that extra weight do to the speed?"

Harnick shrugged and patted the hood. "She'll get to about eighty and that's it, but she'll drive straight through a wall, and nothing short of an RPG is going to dent her."

Top clapped him on the shoulder and then walked over to where Bunny stood.

"How you doing, Farmboy?" Top asked.

Bunny shrugged.

Top stepped closer. "We lost people before."

"In fights, Top. Not like this." Bunny shook his head. "When I was in-country in Afghanistan and Iraq we lost a lot of guys. During the surge, hunting the Taliban in the hills. I collected a lot of dog tags and folded a lot of flags. But this . . . it's like someone just swatted them off the planet. They never saw it coming, never even had the chance to go down swinging."

"It's the way cowards fight, kid," said Top. "They don't have the numbers and they don't have the balls to come at us in a straight fight, so they plant bombs. They don't care who dies. It ain't war. There are no rules, no ethics, no mercy, no honor. That's who we're fighting these days."

Bunny turned to him, and Top could see that the young man's eyes were puffed and red. Top would never mock him for those tears, and neither would anyone in the Warehouse. But Top knew those tears burned.

"That's the point," Bunny said harshly. "They're blowing up buildings all over the world and they won't stand up and fight. Fuck, man, I don't know who to hate."

Top nodded. He felt it, too. The anger, the rage, was there in his chest, a self-perpetuating and self-consuming ball of heat that had nowhere to go.

"I need to get into this fight, Top," Bunny said. "I need to get into it or I'm going to have to walk away from it."

"Well, guess what, Farmboy? We just got orders to drive up to Philly and rendezvous with Cap'n Ledger."

Bunny gave him a sharp look. "The captain's back?"

"Yeah, and he's already chasing this like a hound

dog. Got into some shit in England. Cap'n put three of 'em down."

Bunny straightened. "Does that mean we know something?"

"Don't know what we know, but when were you ever around Cap'n Ledger when the bad guys weren't trying to take a shot? Ain't a good place to stand if you want to be safe, but if you want to go hunting in Indian Country, then saddle up."

Bunny sniffed and let out a breath, blowing out his cheeks and stretching his big arms until his shoulders popped. "Okay, then. If he's in it, then I'm *definitely* in it."

Top slapped him hard on the shoulder as they walked over to the SUV.

Khalid stood by the rear passenger door and had overheard the conversation. "We're all in it now, big man," he said. "They drew first blood."

John Smith leaned against the rear fender, a plastic coffee stirrer between his teeth. He nodded.

"Then it's their ass," said DeeDee. "Let's bring the pain."

She held out her fist and took the bump from Bunny and then the others.

They piled in with DeeDee driving and Top riding shotgun. The TacV was armored and stocked like a rolling arsenal. It also had Sirius radio uplink and DeeDee dialed it over to Classic Blues. The song that was playing as they rolled out of the Warehouse was Robert Johnson's "Hellhound on My Trail."

They took that as a sign. Or maybe a credo, because they were the Hellhounds.

Interlude Twenty-nine

Toys touched Gault's arm just as they were about to enter the Chamber of the Kings. "Sebastian," he said, "please consider what you're about."

Gault smiled, but it lacked warmth. "Oh my God, will you *stop* with this bullshit? You've been whining about this for weeks now."

"It's my job to give you a perspective check, don't forget."

"It's not your job to advocate small thinking."

"Oh, please, that's not—"

"Besides, since when did you become squeamish?"

Toys stepped back and folded his arms. "Squeamish? Is that what you think?"

"Pick a better word, then. 'Timid'?"

Toys felt the blood drain from his face. "Oh . . . be careful now, Sebastian," he said softly.

Gault stepped toward him so that their faces were inches apart. "I'm going to tell you for the last time, Toys . . . stop pushing me. Learn your fucking place."

With that he turned and swept into the chamber.

Inside, the other Kings were on their thrones, their Consciences by their sides. The screens on the walls showed charts and maps or ran with lines of carefully gathered intelligence. Eris sat on her throne, a magazine-thin laptop on her thighs. She had half-glasses perched on her nose and Toys thought that for the first time she looked closer to her age.

Here's hoping you have a stroke and die, you blood-sucking hag, he thought.

When Toys and Gault were in their seats, the King of Lies stood. The Saudi was dressed in a European suit, his beard trimmed short, and he wore no *ghutra* on his head. It made him look like a different man, and Toys wondered if the longer beard was indeed part of a disguise.

"Thank you all for coming on such short notice. I trust you've all had a chance to read through the preliminary report prepared by Plagues? Yes?" He looked around, saw general nods, and continued. "Gold has reviewed the financial requests and informs us that the overall cost for this operation is three percent higher than anticipated, but I think we can all agree that it will be worth the investment of those additional millions."

More nods.

"The next phase is twofold. The logistical phase will be jointly managed by Fear and Gold, for all of the obvious reasons. The Goddess and I will continue to oversee the disinformation program. Goddess?"

Eris raised a hand to acknowledge the applause. Toys glanced at Gault and saw that he was fairly glowing with pride and lust. The fool. Toys cut a look at the American and saw that his hands barely touched as he pretended to applaud.

Lies then introduced Gault, who stood to a renewed wave of applause. He bowed to Eris and then stood silent for a moment, his dark eyes drifting from face to face around the table, waiting as the chamber gradually fell into an expectant silence.

"I've reviewed all of Kirov's work," began Gault,

"and although I hold my predecessor in great esteem, there were some serious flaws in his theories. The short version is that some of the science is simply not going to work. We can push the boundaries of science, but we cannot break them. Not yet, anyway. I know this comes as a blow, because for years now the frontiers of paleo-microbiology have been crumbling as scientists like Professor Kirov hammered away at them with innovative ideas and radical research. But it is the nature of science that some experiments do not succeed even when most of the evidence seems to lead toward success."

No one applauded that comment. A scowling King of War said, "Kirov assured us that this *would* work. He was ready to take a team to Egypt to harvest the bacteria or virus or whatever it was from the tomb of the Pharaoh's son. Our whole campaign was built around his recovering and reactivating that disease. Now you're telling us that it was all a waste of time? We've invested considerable time and funds into this venture."

"With respect, Brother War," said Gault with a placating smile, "that is Kirov's problem. He may have been overenthusiastic when crafting that plan, since much of what he promised was based on speculation, not on research."

Toys found himself crossing his fingers under the table. If Gault had hit a dead end, then there was some chance that he was not going to destroy himself with another harebrained plan.

"Kirov's theory was that the Death of the Firstborn was a communicable pathogen. That much he had already proven to be incorrect. His secondary approach

was to then create a new pathogen or mutate an existing virus to target only firstborn children and use that
against the children of the Inner Circle. It's bold, it's
ballsy, but it's equally flawed. There is nothing gene-
tically unique about firstborn that would open a selec-
tive door to a designed pathogen. Granted, crafting such
a disease would have been beautiful, and though it
would have contributed to the desired goal of overlay-
ing science with religious mystery, it simply cannot be
done. To labor on it is an exercise in futility, and a costly
one at that."

"Then we are going to come up short on our campaign," said the American, smiling faintly and cutting
a look at the Goddess. "We're screwed."

"No, my brothers," Gault said with a smile, "we are
not. If science has taught us anything it's that a way will
open. When one form of treatment fails, we often learn
enough from its failure in order to design a more effective protocol. Observation and compensation are
key to scientific advancement."

Eris smiled. "Tell them," she purred.

Gault leaned his palms on the table. "The answer lies
within the phenomenon of pain. Our desire is to *hurt* the
Inner Circle. Hurt them so deeply, so profoundly, that
they will be crippled. Unable and unwilling to make
another move against us. That is the true task."

The Kings and Consciences turned slowly to look at
one another, and there were many thoughtful nods.

"Kirov had the right idea, but not the right plan. I
have a better plan," Gault continued. "One that allows
us to use everything we've already done. The disinformation campaigns through social media and the

Internet, the manipulation of extremist cells, and the whole culture of modern terrorism. But it adds an element of coercion that has only been touched upon before."

Toys noticed that Santoro sat up straight at the word "coercion" and his lips wriggled into an unpleasant and hungry smile.

"My esteemed brother the King of Fear has the resources to bring this program to fruition. With his vast network of contacts, and with the tactical genius of Rafael Santoro, I believe we can get *my* program up and running in under a month, which would allow us to complete it according to the same timetable as Kirov's plan."

There was a moment of stunned silence, followed by questions from everyone at once.

Toys used the commotion to lock eyes with the King of Fear. The American looked briefly furious, but he covered it by slapping on another hearty smile. However, he must have felt Toys' eyes upon him, because he turned and gave him a very brief but definite wink.

"And now, my brothers," said Sebastian Gault, "here is how we will do it."

Chapter Forty-one

In Flight
December 19, 9:03 A.M. EST

I called Church. "You're gonna love this, Boss," I said, and told him about the plagues, including the almost certain connection to the Locust bomber.

He said, "It's a short list of people who knew about

that project. I'll talk to the President. Is there anything else?"

"Yes. I'd like you to make a video."

"Is this going to be one of your attempts at humor?"

"No. This is serious, and it might help us head another Kings event off at the pass."

"Tell me."

I did. He listened and then disconnected without comment. It's always a Hallmark moment with him. You always feel like your call is the centerpiece of his day.

As I tucked my phone away, Circe said, "You think there will be more Kings attacks?"

"Don't you?"

"Sadly, yes. But it may not be in what could be called an 'ordinary way.'"

"Meaning?"

"Apart from the calls to violence, a lot of the Goddess posts are hints that her cult is part of an ancient belief system that is only now revealing itself. By incorporating references to other goddesses, she's essentially borrowing their history. Hijacking it and claiming it as part of her legacy. If the Goddess is part of the Seven Kings organization, and I think we both agree on that, then the Kings might not actually have to commit seven more acts of terrorism. They can find some that have already happened and retroactively claim that they were responsible. I mean, it wouldn't take much to suggest that 9/11 was the rain of fire and ash plague."

"Maybe. Time frame is off."

"Maybe not. Take the Plague of Frogs. Unless the Kings already have a target in mind that has a frog connotation, like the Locust thing with the bomber, they could claim that the frog extinction is their doing."

"Wait! What? When did frogs become extinct?"

"What planet are you living on?" she said with exasperation. "Toads and frogs are dying out in huge numbers. It's well documented. There have been TV specials. Of course, the science tells us that it's because of pressure from the expansion of agriculture, forestry, pollution, disease, and climate change."

"How would that have major PR punch for the Kings? I mean, I don't want to see Kermit take a dirt nap, but . . . these are just some frogs, right? How's that work in a biblical way?"

She muttered something under her breath that sounded suspiciously like "*Neanderthal.*" Aloud she said, "The die-off of amphibians could be a sign of possible future damage to other parts of the ecosystem, because frogs and toads are especially vulnerable and thus are the first to disappear. Also, a mass disappearance of amphibians would create broken links in the food chain, and that would definitely have an adverse impact on other organisms. If the Kings were to hijack this, it would elevate the public perception of them as unstoppable and possibly supernaturally powerful."

"Okay," I said, "I see it. From a propaganda point of view it only matters that the Kings take credit. Anyone who says they aren't involved has the job of trying to prove a negative, which is self-defeating. I mean, what could the Al-Qaeda do to dispute it? Have a TV debate? Besides, the DMS has already taken out Seven Kings cells that had Al-Qaeda ties. Your 9/11 hypothesis might even be real."

"God," she whispered, and her dark eyes went wide.

"At the risk of sounding terribly macho, Doc, I want to find them and shoot them. A lot."

She nodded. "I'll load the gun."

Then something occurred to me. "Hey, didn't you say that you gave a copy of your Goddess report to Grace?"

"Yes."

"It's funny, because she never mentioned it to me, and neither did Church. When did you give it to her?"

"At the end of August." Circe looked down at her hands. "I tried to call her the next day, but she was already involved in something. I never found out what it was. Then a couple of days later I heard that she died."

Damn. Bull's-eye, right in the heart.

I closed my eyes. The whole mess with the Dragon Factory and the Jakobys started on the twenty-eighth. Grace died on August 31. Because of her the world didn't die on September 1. The ache in my chest was so fresh, so raw, that I wanted to scream. I could see every line, every curve, of Grace's beautiful face. I could smell the scent of her, taste her lips, feel the solid, lithe warmth of her in my arms.

I felt something warm on my forearm and for a single crazy moment I thought that somehow Grace had reached out of those shadows to reassure me. But when I opened my eyes I saw that it was Circe O'Tree's hand on my arm.

"I'm sorry, Joe," she said.

I took a breath and shook my head. Circe moved her hand away, a little embarrassed.

"I don't think your report was ignored," I said, my

voice a bit thick. "I don't think Grace ever had a chance to pass it along."

Circe looked depressed. "God, I would hate to think that we could have somehow prevented this. The Hospital and the rest."

"Let's not Monday-morning quarterback it. We're doing good work here. We'll get this stuff into Mind-Reader and who knows? We might actually be somewhere."

Circe nodded but didn't comment.

I snapped my fingers. "Wait . . . you said there were *ten* plagues. River of blood, darkness, frogs, ghats, flies, pestilence, boils, rain of fire, and locusts. That's only nine. What's the last one?"

All the blood drained from her face. "The last one is the worst of all. It's the one that finally broke Pharaoh's resolve and made him free the captive Israelites."

"What was it?" I asked, but I thought I already knew, and the knowledge scared the shit out of me.

She recited the passage in a hollow voice. "This is what the Lord says: 'About midnight I will go throughout Egypt. Every firstborn son in Egypt will die, from the firstborn son of Pharaoh, who sits on the throne, to the firstborn son of the slave girl, who is at her hand mill, and all the firstborn of the cattle as well. There will be loud wailing throughout Egypt—worse than there has ever been or ever will be again.'"

She paused and watched my face as the horror sank in.

"The tenth plague is the death of the firstborn children of the entire country."

Interlude Thirty

Crown Island
Six Weeks Ago

On the morning of the first of November, Toys walked down to a deck that overlooked a particularly lovely stretch of the island's rocky coastline. He sat in a deck chair, alone with thoughts that had become increasingly troubled and convoluted.

Toys heard a soft footfall and turned to see that Rafael Santoro stood alarmingly close. Few people were able to sneak up on Toys. Peripheral awareness was something he prided himself on, and he was immediately irritated.

Santoro held two steaming cups in his hands. "May I join you?"

Four or five variations of "go fuck yourself" wriggled on Toys' lips, but he held his tongue and ticked his head toward the other lounge chair. Santoro handed him a cup and lowered himself onto the chair.

The view was spectacular. The sun had risen above the rippling waters of the St. Lawrence River, red and orange fire igniting from a million sharp wave tips. The rocky edge of the island was marshy, with tall bulrushes through which blue herons picked their way with the delicacy of monks.

Toys cut a covert glance at Santoro, but the little man seemed not to notice. He sipped his tea and appeared to be fascinated by the dragonflies flitting among the reeds. The Spaniard had an interesting face, like one of the medieval saints on the tapestries in the dining hall: high cheekbones, hooded eyes, full lips, and a light in his eyes that suggested a complex inner life. The man's appearance was so strangely at odds with what Toys knew about him: torture, extortion, terrorism, mass killings, and personal murders so numerous that they were recounted in summary form.

The Spaniard sipped his tea. "Tell me, my friend," he said softly. "How are you enjoying life as the Conscience to the King of Plagues?"

"So, tell me," Toys said after a few minutes, "what do I do as 'Conscience'?"

"That depends on you, and on your King."

Toys snorted. "I'm still adjusting to the concept of Sebastian as a king."

"You find it amusing?"

"Amusing? Not in the least," he said, and that was truer than his tone conveyed. "Though this whole setup seems a bit dodgy. It's more like a movie than real life."

"But it is life," observed Santoro. "The world does not turn by itself. It requires that kings step up to lead."

"Very profound."

"It's true. The Seven Kings have always existed. I speak in the abstract. Before the Kings there were others. Always others. It is a necessary evil, yes?"

"'Evil' is an interesting word choice."

Santoro smiled thinly. "It is evil, by the standards of the sheep." He gestured with his mug to the unseen lands beyond the sunrise. "But evil is a concept constructed by man, and therefore it is subject to laws and interpretations. If we were subject to the same laws we would have to own guilt for what we do, but we do not

acknowledge the laws of any land. We maintain the conqueror's point of view, which is self-justifying."

"How so?"

"Tell me: who was more evil, Alexander the Great or
Adolf Hitler?"

"Hitler."

"Ah, but you say that without considering it. Hitler
is regarded as evil because he slaughtered millions of
people and tried to conquer Europe. By the standards
of those who defeated him, he was evil. Alexander
tried to conquer the entire world, a process that resulted
in a higher percentage of deaths than during Hitler's
war."

"Hitler tried to exterminate whole races of people."

"Alexander issued challenges to cities and nations. If
they surrendered to him, he let them live, and even pre-
served their cultures. But if they opposed him, he
slaughtered them wholesale. He killed the men and sold
the women and children into slavery. How is one more
moral than the other? Do you want to debate degrees of
acceptable genocide?"

"As a matter of fact," Toys said, "I don't."

Santoro nodded and they watched the sun climb
higher. In the glow of the new sun his saintly face was
beatific. It troubled Toys and he turned away.

Santoro asked, "Do you feel it's wrong?"

"Right and wrong is another discussion I don't want
to have."

"That is as it should be, yes?"

Toys looked at him in surprise. "How so?"

"Well, my friend, if we are to accept that we are con-
querors in the purest and oldest sense of that word, and

if that means that what we do is governed by rules we set which, by their nature, are outside of the laws of any land, then right and wrong are concepts without substance. They don't apply to us because they are specific to individual cultures and we are not."

Toys sighed, feeling himself drawn into the discussion despite his better judgment. "What about basic human rights?"

"Ask the Chinese that question."

"Pardon?"

"Human rights, as we understand them today, are based upon Western ideals of democracy. These Western values are themselves profoundly bound up with strong individualism, profiteering, and capitalistic competitiveness. The Confucian system does not subscribe to any of those values. There is not a single statement on human rights to be found within the Confucian discourse. Confucianism advocates duties and responsibilities and makes no case at all for individual rights. They believe that they act according to Heaven's Mandate, in which the ruling body does whatever is necessary for the greater good, even if that means the sacrifice of individuals of the lower classes. Do you follow?"

"Yes. So . . . you're saying that human rights are as subjective as any other set of rules?"

"Absolutely, and the subjectivity in question is the perspective of the most powerful. That is why when I kill for the Seven Kings I am not committing murder, nor am I participating in acts of terrorism. Those are subjective concepts, and our worldview is grand. It is our mandate from heaven. As a result, we are above all of that, yes?"

"Just because we say we are?"

"Yes. And because we have the power to enforce our own and particular set of rules."

Toys looked for the hidden meanings in Santoro's words, but the man was nearly impossible to read. On one hand, he appeared devious and multifaceted, and on the other, his intent seemed dreadfully straightforward. Toys decided to test the waters.

"What about the people who surround kings?"

"Which kings?"

"Oh," Toys said casually, "take Jesus. King of the Jews. If laws don't apply to kings, what's the trickle-down effect? Do the laws of right and wrong apply, say, to Peter?"

"For betraying Christ?" Santoro gave an elaborate shrug. "He was weak, but he believed, and he recanted his weakness to the point of martyrdom."

"And Judas?" He pitched it offhandedly, but Santoro's face darkened.

"That was a betrayal because of personal fear—Judas betrayed Christ into torture and death. His was an unforgivable affront that cannot be redeemed. In my pride and sinfulness I have prayed that I could meet such a man and teach his cowardly flesh to sing songs of worship and praise." As he said this he touched his wrist, and Toys knew that there was a knife hidden beneath the sleeve.

Santoro smiled and for the first time Toys could see the killer behind the saint. He looked into Santoro's eyes and saw—nothing. No life, no spark of humanity, no genuine passion. There was absolutely nothing there. It was like looking into the eyes of a monster. A zombie. Or a demon.

Toys nodded as if agreeing to the sentiment, but inside he shivered. He found it curious that there was such a gap in beliefs between Santoro and the American. He'd suspected as much, hence his reference to Judas, but the Spaniard's reaction was unexpectedly intense.

Not a confidant, then. Note to bloody self.

"What if Judas genuinely believed that Jesus was making a misstep?" he prodded. "I've heard a bunch of different theories. One is that Judas may have thought that Jesus was becoming a danger to his own cause and that Judas went through proper channels of the church—the Sanhedrin—to try and head him off at the pass before he got into worse trouble."

Santoro said nothing. He listened, eyes narrowed, mouth pursed.

"Another theory is that Judas was a bit more 'Old Testament' than Jesus and he had him arrested in the hopes that once Jesus was in peril he would be forced to reveal all of his glory and power and kick Roman ass."

The birds sang for a long time before Santoro answered. He studied Toys, but Toys was too practiced a hand at dissembling to allow anything that he felt to show on his face. He sipped his tea and waited.

Finally, Santoro said, "You ask troubling questions."

"You asked me about Hitler."

Santoro nodded, taking Toys' point. "The question supposes that Jesus was fallible."

"Are either of us that inflexible that we think that he wasn't? Or couldn't have been? After all, Jesus doubted. He lost his cool and trashed the moneylenders outside of the temple. Let's face it—the whole *point* of his being here was to be human. To show that if he, locked in flesh and filled with the full roster of human emotions, can have faith and ultimately do the right thing, then so can we. That all falls down if he was infallible."

Santoro nodded again. "Please do not be offended by this," he said softly, "but you are smarter than you look."

Toys gave him a charming smile. "Now why would I be offended at that?"

"I meant it as a compliment. You are deeper than you appear. People are often fooled by you, yes?"

Toys shrugged.

Then Santoro tried to blindside him. "Do you have doubts about what the King of Plagues is doing?"

Toys was expecting it and he kept his expression and body language casual, as if this were just another part of the same discussion.

"Sebastian is as fallible as any other man. I love and respect him, and I would kill *anyone* to keep harm from touching him. You understand that?"

"Of course." Santoro's eyes glittered.

"But I'm supposed to be his Conscience. His advisor. It's not that I doubt Sebastian," he lied. "It's more that I need to make sure *I'm* doing my job in the way that best serves him and the Kings."

"And the Goddess," amended Santoro.

"Of course," said Toys smoothly. "Sebastian loves her very much."

"As do we all."

"So . . . where does 'conscience' play into all this?"

Santoro relaxed slightly. "Conscience is what we choose to make it. The devil on your left shoulder and the angel on your right are slaves to *your* will."

"Ah," said Toys, as if he understood what that meant. And, with a sinking heart, he did. He stood and tossed the rest of the tea into the river. "This gives me a lot to think about, Rafael. Thanks. . . . I appreciate it."

And may you have an aneurism next time you're jerking off to a picture of the Goddess, you great freak.

Santoro inclined his head and sipped his tea.

Toys thrust his hands into his pockets, hunched his shoulders in what he hoped would convey a posture of thoughtful introspection, and headed along the path toward the castle.

As he walked, however, he weighed Santoro's words against the weight of the conflict within his heart. *The devil on your left shoulder and the angel on your right are slaves to* your *will.*

The cries of the gulls overhead sounded like the screams of drowning children.

If we were subject to the same laws we would have to own guilt for what we do, but we do not acknowledge the laws of any land. We maintain the conqueror's point of view, which is self-justifying.

"Yes," Toys murmured aloud. "Too bloody right we do."

Chapter Forty-two

Amber Taylor sat like a robot in her office. Her hands were folded in her lap, her fingers like sticks of wet ice. Inside her chest her heart was beating too loudly and without rhythm.

His voice, *his* words, still echoed in her mind. *Do it,* he'd said. *Do it today or . . . or . . .*

Today.

She was supposed to die today.

She was supposed to kill today.

She would never see her babies again.

She would have to trust that *they* would keep their word and leave her family alone. He promised they would. If she did what they said. If she became a murderer.

He had made her swear. On the lives of her children. On the lives of her babies.

Amber slid open her top desk drawer and stared down at the horrible weapon of destruction that lay there among the pens and paper clips and pushpins.

A ring of keys.

They lay there, pretending innocence, looking like nothing. Keys to the lab, to the vault. The keys were right there. No one would think twice if she picked them up, walked out of her office, walked down the line of cubicles to the elevator. Took it to the basement. Opened the door to the lab. And the one to the vault.

The rest was a security code, and that was in her head.

Simple actions. Each one easy. Each one unobtrusive. So easy.

After that . . .

God.

Nothing existed beyond that thought except horror. Amber Taylor closed her eyes and prayed. She had not been to church since her husband died. Not even to take the kids. Religion and God were as dead to her as Charlie.

And then . . .

Something happened that had she possessed any faith she might have thought was divine intervention. But Amber lacked that belief, that optimism.

And yet.

There was a sound. Five beeps from the PA system and then a voice: "This is a security alert. This is a security alert. All employees are required to turn on your intranet. There is a critical news bulletin from Homeland Security. All employees are required to watch this bulletin. It will be broadcast in real time in sixty seconds. This is not a training exercise."

The message repeated.

Amber blinked several times, unsure of what she was hearing. On the third repeat it logged in: *Homeland Security.*

Her hands lifted by reflex, her icy fingers making the necessary keystrokes, logging on, pulling up the intranet.

The screen changed. First black and then the red, white, and blue eagle shield of the U.S. Department of

Homeland Security. Then the shield dissolved into a man seated in what looked like an airplane seat. He was big, blocky, in his sixties, but he looked strong. Dangerous. Amber could recognize dangerous. He wore tinted glasses, but she knew that if she could see his eyes they would be fierce.

"Good afternoon, ladies and gentlemen. My name is Dr. Bishop, director of special medical services for the United States Department of Homeland Security. You are all probably aware of the tragic event that occurred in London two days ago. The world press has called this an act of terrorism, and so it is. But it is far more than that. The security at the London Royal Hospital was compromised by two or more of the employees at that facility. Those employees did not, however, do this out of choice. They were coerced. A group of terrorists made threats against the families of these people. These threats were as terrible as they were insidious. As a result, good people were forced to do terrible things."

Amber's hands contracted to fists.

"And while this recent act of terrorism did not occur on United States soil, the investigative divisions within Homeland Security believe that there is a strong possibility that some Americans may be victims of the same kind of coercion. Coercion that could lead to further heinous acts.

"I am speaking now to employees in hundreds of private companies and government facilities. If you are watching this video you are employed in a critical area of viral research, energy, health sciences, or defense. If you have been approached by people who have asked you, or attempted to force you, to do something that could lead to harm to others and damage the safety of your community, I urge you to act. If you have been threatened, or if your loved ones have been threatened, you must make the correct and courageous choice. You must contact the authorities. I know you have been told that to speak out will bring harm to your family. I know that you are afraid. Probably terrified. However, you cannot believe or trust these people. They will *not* keep their word. They will attempt to harm those you love even if you do what they want. Do not destroy your own life, the lives of your friends and colleagues, and, most important, the lives of your family by believing the threats of cowards and criminals.

"There is a toll-free telephone number and an e-mail address at the bottom of this screen. Use them today. Use them right now to contact me and my team. We are ready to act *immediately*. We will protect you and your family. And with your help, we will stop these criminals before they can hurt other families."

There was more. At least Amber thought so, but her mind refused to process it. She sat there in her chair, alone in her office, at the monitor that was flanked by framed pictures of Emily and Mark. All she saw, however, was the telephone number.

Tears burned in her eyes.

The keys were still in the drawer. The world still turned.

"God . . . ," she whispered.

Chapter Forty-three

We landed under a sky so bright and sunny that it seemed like it was intended as mockery with all that was going on. As Circe and I hustled out of the gate we were met by one of the junior DMS agents from the Baltimore office, a red-haired kid named Riordan, waiting for us at the departure gate. He nodded to me, but he was looking at Circe. I glanced covertly around. Everyone was looking at Circe. Her face was neutral and I wondered if the attention was an ego boost or a total pain in the ass.

"You supposed to be our driver?" I asked.

He shook his head. "No, sir. Delivery boy. Mr. Church said that you wouldn't want a driver."

"Nope."

He held out a set of keys. My own keys. "Your Explorer is parked outside. My partner is getting your bags and arranging for your dog to be transported to the curb."

He said all this to me but was still looking at Circe.

"*Get her bags, too,*" I said, leaning on the tone of voice enough to snap him out of his love daze. After Circe described her bag and the kid went away, she looked at me and laughed.

"What?" I asked.

"Alpha wolf bullies young pup."

"Oh . . . stick a sock in it, Doc."

She was still laughing as we stepped out into the

December wind. Fifteen minutes later we were on I-95 and heading north.

Interlude Thirty-one

Valley of the Kings, Egypt
One Month Ago

REUTERS NEW STORY

CAIRO, Egypt—Yesterday, tomb raiders broke into the recently discovered burial crypt of a previously unknown mummy who many top archaeologists believe may have been the firstborn son of Pharaoh Amenhotep II. In what seems like a bizarre modern twist on Indiana Jones, Amenhotep II is believed to have been the Pharaoh during the time of Moses. If so, then biblical scholars feel confident that this son was killed by the Plague of the Firstborn, the tenth plague directed against Egypt by God, and the one that resulted in the Israelites being set free.

Archaeologist Zahi Hawass, head of Egypt's governmental Department of Antiquities, was quoted as saying, "This was a pristine tomb. Unopened. To have broken the seals and looted it is a great loss to science."

According to Cairo police officials, the mummy's wrappings had been cut and long sections of skin had been removed with what appeared to be medical precision. Officials have declined to speculate on the nature and purpose of this desecration.

Chapter Forty-four

Amber Taylor left work without notifying anyone. She stole someone else's red winter coat from the staff room. She put on sunglasses and wound a scarf around her face, pulled the hood up, and slipped out through the delivery dock. She walked quickly to the parking lot, got into her car, and drove as fast as she could to her children's school. She was careful to obey all traffic laws, however. She did not want to get stopped by the police. Not yet, and not now. During the short drive to the school she obsessively checked the mirrors for any sign of a car following her. She saw nothing, but she knew that did not prove a thing. Except for that day the Spaniard came to her to ruin everything and to show her the pictures of the things he called angels, she had never seen anyone. And yet she knew they were watching. They were probably watching right now.

Her stomach felt like it was filled with rusted nails. She popped the glove compartment and took out the large bottle of TUMS EX that she always carried. It was the fifth bottle she had gone through, the extra-large container. She ate six of them while she picked her way through traffic to the school.

When she pulled into the school parking lot the kids were playing in the big concrete yard. A game of tag in one corner, ball in another. Emily stood talking to three of her friends and Mark sat on the steps nearby reading a comic book. Spider-Man. Mark loved comic books.

Emily was already reading chapter books, and with her mind she would graduate soon to Young Adult novels.

God, Amber thought, *let that happen. Let my babies grow up. Help me keep the monsters away.*

She pulled to a stop as close to the school-yard gate as possible and left the engine running as she did a slow surveillance of the area, turning in the seat, craning her neck, looking at every person, every face. None of them looked like it could belong to the face of the man with the Spanish accent. No one looked like they could be one of *them.* Everyone looked ordinary.

She sniffed back tears, then tapped the horn.

Emily looked up first and smiled. She waved. Amber got out of her car and hurried into the school yard.

"Come on, honey; we have to go."

"You got a new coat!" said Emily.

"Yes. Say goodbye to your friends. Mark! Come on, honey. Grab your things." She hustled them to the car, belted them in, got in, and locked the doors. Then she left the parking lot, turned left, and drove like hell toward home.

As she drove, she made a single phone call to a number that was burned into her mind.

Chapter Forty-five

Jenkintown, Pennsylvania
December 19, 1:19 P.M. EST

We got off of I-95 and started picking our way across northeast Philadelphia.

Ghost sat in the backseat and laid his head on the

storage bin that separated the front bucket seats. He was still mad at me for putting him in the jet's cargo hold and probably wouldn't warm up until I bribed him with food. So, I went through a McDonald's drive-through and got a couple of Filet-O-Fish sandwiches and an order of fries and gave them to Ghost.

"Is that good for him?"

"He likes fast food."

"Two sandwiches and fries? What, no Coke?"

"Hey," I said, "he's only a dog."

She stared at me as if I was a lunatic. Fair call. Then she turned and watched Ghost wolf down the fried squares of fish, mayonnaise, buns, and all, and then he settled down and ate the fries more slowly.

"I've never seen a dog eat French fries one at a time."

"He'll share if you ask nice."

Ghost looked up as if he understood that comment and regarded it as heresy. He placed one paw over his fries and gave Circe a steely stare.

"Bon appétit!" she said, and turned back. "I'm more of a cat person."

I was both. I had a marmalade tabby named Cobbler back at the Warehouse, but it didn't seem to be the right time to bring him up. So we drove in silence for a while.

My phone rang. Church.

"Change of plans," he said curtly. "You won't be picking up Dr. Sanchez. He'll come to meet you in Jenkintown. Echo Team is also inbound to the same destination."

"Christ, don't tell me there was another attack," I growled. Circe turned sharply at those words.

"Not yet," he said. "Your video message idea seems

to have borne fruit. A woman named Amber Taylor has barricaded herself and her children inside her house. She called the number we gave during the broadcast. She says that a man with a Spanish accent told her that he would kill her children if she did not do what he said."

"Son of a bitch. What did he want her to do?"

"To release fleas into the Philadelphia subway system."

"Fleas infected with—?"

"Take a guess."

"Oh, shit."

He gave me the address. I immediately shifted into the fast lane and put the hammer down. Ford Explorers aren't exactly sports cars, but mine had been given the DMS version of the Police Interceptor package adapted for an SUV. I stamped down on the gas and the Explorer shot forward, the needle climbing to a hundred and then past it.

"Joe, what's wrong?" demanded Circe, bracing her feet and gripping the support handle bolted to the frame.

"You know history," I said through gritted teeth. "If you were looking at a worst-case scenario of a disease transmitted by fleas, what would it be?"

"Yersinia pestis," she said without hesitation, and then the implications of my question and her response caught up to her. Out of the corner of my eye I could see the color drain from her face.

Yersinia pestis. A bacterium that can take three primary forms when spread from flea to humans. *Pneumonic, septicemic,* and *bubonic.*

Plague.

Chapter Forty-six

I drove past the Taylor house without a pause, circled the block, and drove past again. I checked out each of the cars parked on the street and didn't see anyone sitting in them. All of the plates were local. No pedestrians.

Amber Taylor lived on West Avenue, just off of Route 611. A blue BMW sat out front. Right color, make, and plates.

"Are we going to wait for your team?"

"No," I said. "I want to talk to this woman ASAP. If the Spaniard leaned on her, then we may have our first solid lead. We can't risk waiting . . . but it's your call if you want to stay here or—"

"I'm going in," Circe said in a tone that brooked no argument.

"Fine, Doc, but remember that this is a criminal investigation."

"Yes, yes, and you're the alpha. Get a grip, Joe; this isn't my first time in the field."

She said it with a lot of conviction, but I thought she was lying. I was pretty sure that this *was* her first time out of the world of "what if." Even so, I kept my mouth shut on all the ways I wanted to reply to that. I took my Homeland ID case out of the glove box and looped the lanyard around my neck. We got out and I checked the street again. Nothing moved except the breeze through the December trees. I let Ghost out of the back. There was a case in the back marked with a rubber stamp of a blue old-style British police telephone box. In the TV show *Doctor Who* it was called a TARDIS, a kind of time and space ship. In the real world it was the box of special ultra-high-tech doodads provided by Dr. Hu and his team. I opened it and stuffed a few gizmos into my pocket.

I petted Ghost, who had caught my nervous tension and was fidgeting. I pointed to the Taylor house. "Watch. Call-call-call." With that command he would watch the street and then bark like a crazy dog if anyone came within a dozen yards of the front door. The DMS trainer, Zan Rosin, had brought Ghost to a superb level of efficiency, and I worked with him every day to perfect the command and response between us. Ghost had a peculiar habit, though. When I gave him an order he opened and closed his mouth with a wet *glup*. His way of saying, "Hooah."

Circe and I cut across the brown lawn and mounted the three steps to the stone porch. All of the houses on the street were decorated for Christmas. I noticed that Taylor's was, too, but the work was sloppy. Lights strung crookedly, window decorations put up in haste. Circe noticed it, too.

"Nerves," she said quietly. "Probably trying to fake it for the kids."

I knocked on the door and waited. Nothing happened, so I tapped again.

"Joe," Circe said without moving her lips, "the curtain moved, someone's—"

"I know. Smile and look helpful."

"Who are you?" a voice demanded from behind the door.

"Federal agents, Mrs. Taylor. Department of Homeland Security."

"Prove it!"

I held up my ID so anyone looking through the peephole could see it. Then I removed my wallet and showed my driver's license to prove the name matched. There was a picture in the adjoining glassine compartment. Grace.

"How do I know you're who you say you are?"

"Do you still have the number you called?"

A pause. "Yes."

"Call them. Ask for a description of the agent they sent. My name is Joseph Edwin Ledger. My partner here is Dr. Circe O'Tree. Have whoever you talk to describe us."

"Okay. But if you try to force the door I'll—"

She cut herself off before finishing the sentence. She didn't know what she would do. I don't think she had a gun or she would have threatened us with it. Scared people often do.

We waited. I could hear her speaking to someone, but her voice was muffled. All I could make out was "yes," repeated several times.

"Okay, they gave me two questions to ask you."

"Hit me."

"What is your cat's name?"

"Cobbler. And my dog, who is watching the house right now, is Ghost."

"That wasn't the other question. The man said to ask you what he called you when you first met."

"He said I was a world-class smart-ass. He's right, too. I hold several international records."

I actually heard a short laugh from behind the door.

"Okay . . . I'm going to open the door."

We waited and I could imagine the woman taking a steadying breath, trying to muster the optimism to trust the moment. She had her kids in there. If Santoro had done to her what he had done to Dr. Grey, the images of her children as victims of the Spaniard's knife—as his *angels*—would be overwhelming.

The lock clicked. I traded a look with Circe. She looked as wired as I felt.

The door opened an inch and we saw a single terrified eye. Bright blue and filled with a kind of profound dread that should never be in any human's eyes, let alone a parent's.

"We're here to help," said Circe softly.

A tear welled in the corner of that bright blue eye.

"Don't let them hurt my babies," she begged.

I smiled—and I don't know if it was the Cop or the Warrior who shaped that smile—and said, "Not a chance."

Interlude Thirty-two

Crown Island

One Month Ago

"It's done."

The Goddess smiled into the phone. "Ah, lovely boy, I never had a doubt. Was it difficult?"

"Toys whined about it," Gault said, "but it was *more* than worth it. We'll be in Cairo in two hours and back there before this hits the news services."

"Hurry home to me, Sebastian," Eris purred. "I want you here. In my arms. Inside of me."

"If I could sprout wings, my love," he murmured, "I'd already be in the air. Oops, the cab is here. Got to go. I'll call you when I land in Toronto. Have fun on the Internet."

"Oh, I will. By this time next month the Inner Circle will be rending their garments and beating their chests."

"Don't forget gnashing their teeth and wailing. The gnashing and wailing is such a kick."

They were both laughing as they disconnected.

Interlude Thirty-three

Regent Beverly Wilshire
Beverly Hills, California
One Month Ago

Charles Osgood Harrington III disliked speaking on the phone. Most of his calls were taken by various assistants and secretaries. His cell phone had a private number given to a very select handful of people. Even his son didn't have it. Which Harrington considered a good business move since his son, Charles Osgood Harrington IV—known as C-Four to everyone from the police to the national media—was a good-for-nothing waste of time.

So when his cell phone rang Harrington assumed that it was one of that small circle from whom he was always happy to take a call.

"Charlie," said a breathless voice.

"Carl?"

H. Carlton Milhaus was a very old and very dear friend, and an associate in a number of business deals in the Middle East.

"Jesus, Charlie . . . have you read your e-mail? The *club* e-mail."

"No."

"Log on, for Christ's sake. We all got it. Call me later. I think we need to meet."

Milhaus would not explain, so Harrington switched on his computer and when it was ready he used an ultrasecure log-on to access the e-mail account shared by the twenty-one members of his private club.

Harrington spotted the e-mail at once. The sender was listed as *Private*. The subject read: *To the House of Bones*.

Harrington licked his lips and opened the e-mail. It read:

> *The tomb of the Pharaoh's son has been open.*
> *The firstborn son of Pharaoh fell to the wrath of*
>   *Heaven.*
> *To defy Heaven's will is to feel divine wrath.*
> *Woe to the firstborn sons of the House of Bones.*
> *The Angel of Death rises again.*
> *The Angel of Death left its seed in the flesh of the*
>   *Pharaoh's son.*
> *Science, the new magic, will raise the Tenth Death*
>   *from the Dust.*

"My *god*!" Harrington gasped. He reached for his cell and called Carlton Milhaus. Forty minutes later Harrington was aboard his private helicopter, hurtling through the skies toward a meeting with the other twenty members of the Inner Circle of the Skull and Bones Society.

Chapter Forty-seven

Jenkintown, Pennsylvania
December 19, 1:49 P.M. EST

Amber Taylor was thirty-five but looked older. Living under the terrible stress of the Spaniard's threats had aged her, chopped sharp edges into her face and made her look like a refugee from a war-torn country. In a very real sense, I suppose she was.

"Where are your children?" Circe asked as soon as we were inside.

"In the basement playroom," Taylor said quickly, but as she said it she took a reflexive step to stand between us and the door to the cellar. "They're watching a video. They . . . don't know."

I glanced around. We stood in a short entry hall. There was a tall faux Ming vase from which a hockey stick, a pool cue, and a baseball bat sprouted. She caught my look. "In case," she said.

The woman had grit.

Circe guided Taylor into the living room. "Mrs. Taylor," she said quickly, "we are going to help you. Captain Ledger has his team coming. They'll be here any minute. They are military Special Forces and they can protect you and your children from anyone."

Taylor did not look immediately relieved.

"He said that they would know if I left work, or . . .

picked up the kids. Or anything. He said that they were *always* watching. He showed me pictures. From here. From inside the house—"

"Don't worry about that anymore. I set up a jammer. They're not seeing a thing."

"He'll *know* that I did something." The fear in her voice was like a poison fog that clung to the air around her. I hoped like hell the Spaniard would show up. There were a few things I'd like to discuss with him. And then I wanted to rip his fucking lungs out.

"'He'?" Circe asked. "Do you mean the man who threatened you?"

"Yes."

"What can you tell us about him?"

She described what we already knew. A compactly built man wearing dark clothes and a mask, and who spoke with a Spanish accent. The rest of her story echoed the same horrors we got from Grey. Threats, the knife. The photos of the *angels*.

"How many pictures did he show you?"

"I . . . I don't . . ." She stopped, dabbing at her eyes while she thought about it. "Maybe twelve of each. Women, and children. Six boys, six girls. I . . . think they were boys and girls. It was hard to . . . to . . ." She shook her head.

Circe looked at me with eyes that were fierce and bright and wet. I could imagine the sickness and rage that she felt. Inside my own head I could feel the Warrior start to howl. Even the civilized Modern Man part of me wanted blood.

"Tell me about what they wanted you to do."

"It was the fleas. . . ."

Her company was part of a group of companies working on a government-funded project to develop a lasting treatment for *Yersinia pestis*. Although the plague was rare these days, there were still cases of it, and there was always the risk of terrorists weaponizing a strain. It was the same argument that justified the testing of Ebola at FIRE.

It was hard to accept it and hard to knock it down, because weaponized bubonic plague would truly be a terrible weapon and one that would be easy enough to distribute. Releasing infected fleas into widespread and uncontrolled animal populations, particularly rats, would do it. Antibiotics could be used to fight the disease, but an outbreak would create panic and would be hard to stop once started. Especially if the rats that were infested with the plague fleas were introduced in areas with large homeless and poverty-level populations. Her company was testing the latest strains of the bacteria on rat subspecies found in the subway systems of Philadelphia and New York. There were enough infected fleas at Strauss & Strauss to begin a medium-scale epidemic.

"That's what they wanted me to do. Go into the lab and take canisters of fleas and then drop one in each of ten stations on the Broad Street Line and ten on the Market-Frankford Line."

"There would be a fairly long lag time between that and an outbreak," said Circe. "How would they know if you had done what they asked?"

"They said to release fleas in the staff room. Into coats and gloves, scarves, boots."

"But you did not do that," prompted Circe.

Taylor shook her head. "I . . . almost did."

"What stopped you?"

"There was a video. From a doctor working with Homeland."

"Dr. Bishop?" I suggested, and she nodded. Score one for Church.

"*They* said that once I did that they would know right away."

"Did what? Release the fleas at work?"

"Yes."

"Which means that there was someone else at your office?"

"Yes. I got messages sometimes. Little reminders." She described finding notes with words like "watching" and "everywhere" and some with the kids' names on them. It was a lot like what Dr. Grey had experienced.

Fresh tears broke from Taylor's eyes. "He said that no matter how long it would take, they would come after my babies. Can you really keep them safe?"

She was so convinced that her own life was over that she only asked about her kids. It was admirable, but it was also interesting in that from a detached point of view it was clear that her own life meant nothing compared to her kids' lives. I know that parents will die for their kids, but I believed I was seeing a hint of the precise kind of mental-emotional configuration that had to exist in people targeted by the Spaniard.

I heard Ghost bark once. Short and sharp.

Not a danger warning. I smiled. I knew what that meant.

There was a knock on the door.

I said, "The cavalry has arrived."

Chapter Forty-eight

"Deacon?"

"Hugo," said Church. "Do you have something for me?"

"Maybe. I just got off the phone with Marty Hanler. I've been trying to get him to join the think tank, maybe kick the group in the ass a bit, 'cause without him the only things they've come up with are 'jack' and 'shit.'"

"He won't leave Margie for that long. Between the surgery and the chemo—"

"I know. But with all that's going on I thought it was worth a shot. Anyway, he told me something disturbing and I recommended that he call you."

"What is it?"

Vox told him.

"That's disturbing," agreed Church. "Very disturbing."

"What are you going to do about it?"

"Captain Ledger is in the area. I'll have him meet and debrief Marty."

"Ledger's back in the game?"

"Yes."

"Glad to hear it. That boy's a demon."

Church did not comment on that. Instead he said, "Circe is with him."

Vox whistled. "That's an interesting pair."

Church made no comment and ended the call.

Chapter Forty-nine

The two people at the door did not look like soldiers or terrorists. They wore long coats and felt hats. Each one of them carried a valise and wore a bright smile.

"Have you heard the word of God today?" asked the shorter of the two, a blonde woman with ice blue eyes.

"Have you been saved?" asked the other, a black man with scars on his face. He handed me a copy of *The Watchtower.*

"Well, hallelujah," I said, and stepped back to let DeeDee and Top enter the Taylor household. I checked the street and saw that it was empty. No sign of Echo Team's vehicle.

As I closed the door, Top said, "We're parked two blocks over; engine's running for when you give the word. We have the TacV."

"Deployment?"

"John Smith's on the roof of a house down the street. Khalid's spotting for him. Bunny's at the wheel waiting on your word."

Circe and Amber Taylor had come into the entrance foyer.

"Mrs. Taylor, this is DeeDee Whitman and Bradley Sims. They are part of my team and they will be escorting you and your children to a secure location."

"Just the two of them? He said that they—"

"We have the whole team with us, ma'am," said Top. He had a deep voice and a fatherly tone. "And at need we can bring a world of trouble down on anyone who tries to hurt you or yours. Count on it."

She looked into his eyes, searching him, reading him. She must have found something to believe in, because she suddenly threw her arms around his barrel chest and hugged him fiercely. He stroked her hair as she sobbed.

Top inspires that kind of confidence in people. I don't.

DeeDee stepped aside and touched her ear jack. "Scream Queen to Dancing Duck, how's the weather?" She listened. "Okay . . . copy that."

"What have you got?" I asked quietly.

"Zips in the wires, Boss," she said. "A white van just drove past Bunny and turned onto this street." She knelt and fished something out of her valise. It wasn't a religious tract. She handed me a tiny earbud and a booster unit. I clipped the booster to my belt and screwed the bug in my ear. "Team on one, Command on two."

She also handed me three extra magazines and I stuffed them into my pockets. DeeDee had an M4 slung under her coat.

I tapped the bud once. "Echo, Echo, Cowboy on deck. Call signs here on out."

I heard Bunny say, "Welcome to the jungle, Boss."

"Sit rep."

"One white van, two in the front, unknown in the back."

"Got it," said Khalid. Smith wouldn't comment. He hardly ever speaks. "We have two hostiles on foot in the back alley. Hold on. Make that four hostiles. Two heading northeast. Two coming from the west. Van has stopped. Counting hostiles. Looks like the driver and one other only."

"Six?" complained Bunny. "That ain't even a fight."

"Keep it tight, Green Giant," scolded Top.

"We need someone with a pulse," I said. "I'm in the mood for a conversation."

"Hooah," they said.

I turned to Circe and Taylor. "Go get the kids. DeeDee, go with them. Quick and quiet. Do it now. Just coats and gloves. Don't stop for anything else."

I tapped the earbud and called Khalid. "Dancing Duck, did they leave anyone at the van?"

"Negative, Cowboy. Driver and the other are walking along the street. They're passing your Explorer. Wait; hold on. Shit. The driver put his palm on the hood to feel for engine heat. They're drawing guns."

"Chatterbox," I said.

"Got 'em."

I hurried to the window and looked out just in time to see both of the men stagger backward and fall into the hedges that lined the street near where I'd parked. Less than a second, two perfect head shots. No sound at all. I couldn't tell where the shots had come from, but Smith was the hammer of God up to 350 yards.

I turned at the sound of commotion and saw DeeDee herding Taylor and her kids out the cellar door.

"What's happening? What's going on?" the kids demanded. Then they saw Top and me standing in the foyer. Top had shed his disguise. Under the topcoat he wore black fatigues, body armor, and belts from which were slung the kinds of weapons most people only see on TV or in movies.

"W-what—?"

I started to say something, but Top Sims brushed past

me. He knelt on one knee. "Look, kids. There's something happening and we're here to protect you and your mom. I'm a kind of policeman. We all are. We're going to take you and your mom to a safe place."

"But . . . but . . ."

"There are a couple of bad men in the neighborhood. We need to take care of that, and we will. That's what we do. But I need you guys to be brave and strong and help us get your mom to a safe place. Can you do that?"

Their eyes were the size of hubcaps and their mouths were little round "ohs," but they both nodded. Top gave them a warmer smile than anything his enemies would believe him capable of.

"Okay, now this man here is the boss. You can call him Cowboy. That's his—"

"That's his call sign!" declared young Mark.

Top grinned and patted Mark's arm. "Well, look at you! I'll bet you know all about cops and bad guys."

"Are there terrorists out there?" Mark asked, his eyes huge with excitement.

"They are bad men," Top assured him, not using the word "terror." "But we got that covered, 'cause there are more of my friends outside. We're all going to get into a big truck and drive away to a nice safe place."

I turned away and smiled. Top was a dad; I didn't have any kids. Right then, I'd have gone with him to an ice-cream shop or a ball game.

"Cowboy, Cowboy," said Khalid, "be advised. Company in sixty. Looks like back and west side. Two and two."

I tapped the earbud. "Chatterbox . . . Sergeant Rock's coming out with friendlies. Keep 'em safe."

" 'K,' " he said.

"Green Giant," I growled to Bunny, "we're waiting on you. Bring Black Bess to the front door. Quick and noisy."

"Rock and roll," he answered.

To Top I said, "Get the kids into the car. Scream Queen, you're with me."

In the distance I could hear the rumble of a heavy engine as the big DMS TacV thundered down the street toward us. Ghost started barking like mad and I knew that he sniffed the hostiles.

"Now!" I yelled, and jerked the door open. Ghost stood at the edge of the porch, craning his neck around toward the back, barking with heavy monster barks. Bunny screeched to a halt and leaped out. The kids—and even Circe—goggled a little at the size of the driver, but he waved them on and opened the back door, fanning a big IMI Desert Eagle over their heads as they ran.

From inside the house I could hear glass breaking as the hostiles smashed their way in through the back door and side window. With the barks and yells and engine noise, they had to know that a rescue attempt was in progress, so they weren't going for stealth. They opened fire at once, filling the house with hot rounds as they crowded inside, trying to flush us out toward the two men from the van. They apparently didn't know that they were two head shots past the point where that plan was going to work.

I flattened out against the living room wall behind the couch with Ghost on the floor beside me. I told him to be quiet and ready. He looked ready to tackle Godzilla.

DeeDee climbed to the fifth step on the staircase and crouched low.

The hostiles were working in pairs. Two out front, the others a room and a half behind them. Nice combat spacing. We could kill them all, but we couldn't capture them all.

The first two men rushed through the TV room and into the living room, heading straight for the open front door. We let them pass; then DeeDee and I wheeled around the edges of the wall and opened up on the other two. It was a classic ambush and they didn't have a chance. We put three shots in each and then spun off of that, closing to zero distance with the other shooters, who were skidding to a stop, scrambling to turn, realizing that they'd been mousetrapped.

DeeDee reached her target half a second before I did, so I got a peripheral view of how she handled him. She used the stock of her rifle to slap his AK-47 wide; then instead of checking her swing and bringing the stock back for a head shot, she continued the circular swing of the weapon and caught him in the face with the barrel. The guy's nose and upper teeth exploded, but before he could scream DeeDee kneed him in the groin; as he bent forward she knee-kicked him in his broken nose.

The second guy was about my size and he knew that he was too close to use a long weapon, so he tried to slam me across the chest with the length of it. I checked my forward momentum so that his thrust stopped a half inch short. I didn't have a long gun and didn't need one. Ghost shot past me and under his gun and hit the shooter teeth first in the crotch. He screamed and tried to club the dog, but Ghost was trained to fight armed men. He released the first bite and jumped up inside the circle of the man's arms, biting fast and hard, tearing muscle and tendon and cracking bone so fast it looked like the shooter had thrust his arms into a leaf shredder.

"Off!" I called, and that fast Ghost jumped sideways. He crouched and growled, fur up along his spine, mouth bloody, eyes fierce.

The shooter went down in a messy heap and curled into a fetal ball, wrapping his head with his ruined arms. I kicked his gun out of reach.

Outside, the TacV roared away.

I stepped back to offer cover while DeeDee slapped Speedcuffs on the two shooters. One was unconscious, the other screaming.

"Juice him," I ordered, and DeeDee pulled a syringe from her kit and jabbed it into the screaming man's arm. It wasn't painkiller. His eyes rolled up and he passed out, sagging to the floor with a thump. Then she applied a fast field dressing to the critical wounds.

I tapped my earbud.

"Cowboy to Echo. House party is over. Got two sleepy guests."

"Copy that," said Khalid. "Area is secure."

"Green Giant, talk to me."

"Class trip is away," said Bunny. "I got six police units inbound to your twenty."

"Outstanding," I said.

Khalid showed up at the door and I tossed him my keys. He brought the Explorer over and we loaded the prisoners, moving with haste and only marginal care. We needed them alive. Comfort wasn't an issue.

By the time the cops converged on the house, we were in the wind, following Black Bess north along Route 611.

Interlude Thirty-four

The Seven Kings
December 19, 2:00 P.M. EST

Sebastian Gault set down his phone and stared at it for a long moment. Then with a growl of sudden anger he swept everything off his desk—phone, laptop, whiskey glass. It all crashed to the floor.

A moment later he was crouched over the debris, brushing ice cubes and broken glass off his phone. He dried it on the front of his shirt and then sat on the edge of the desk and opened the phone. It still worked. He punched a number.

"Yes," said a soft voice.

"I just heard from Fear."

"As have I," said Santoro.

"Do you have a team in the area?"

"There is one very close; I can pull them off of that job and put them on this. A matter of minutes; however, taking action would be ill advised, yes? Things are not—"

"Don't tell me what things are *not*, god damn it. I want you to do something right fucking now! And I want it splashed across the wire services. I want everything else wiped off the sodding news by it. Do you understand me?"

Gault's voice had risen to a banshee shriek.

The ensuing silence was so complete that Gault

wondered if Santoro had hung up on him. If that little Spanish prick had, he'd skin him alive.

"Is this also the will of the Goddess?" Santoro asked mildly.

"Yes."

Another moment of silence.

"Very well," said the killer, and he disconnected.

Chapter Fifty

Willow Grove, Pennsylvania
December 19, 2:38 P.M. EST

We rolled into the Willow Grove Naval Air Station. There were two DMS choppers already on the ground— a burly Chinook and an Apache gunship. Shooters from Broadway Team from the Hangar in Brooklyn had the perimeter secured. I shook hands with Lt. Artie Mensch, Broadway's topkick.

"Busy morning, Joe?" he said, offering his hand.

"Same weird shit, different weird day."

We watched as Top and Khalid guided Amber Taylor and her kids into the Apache. Bunny and John Smith rolled the gurneys with two prisoners over to the Chinook.

Mensch nodded. "We're taking the prisoners straight to the Hangar. They're prepping the surgical suite now. Aunt Sallie's going to want to talk with these boys." He cut me a look. "You haven't met her yet, have you?"

"No. Looking forward to it, though."

He laughed. " 'Looking forward' to meeting Aunt Sallie. That's funny."

"What's the joke?"

"You'll know when you meet her."

He clapped me on the shoulder, whistled to his team, and within a few seconds the helos were sky-high and tilting into the wind to head north.

I saw Circe O'Tree standing beside Black Bess. She looked small and lost, so I headed over to her.

"You did good work today," I said. "Mrs. Taylor needed someone like you."

"Someone like me?"

"Smart, steady—"

"And female?" Circe asked challengingly.

"I wasn't going there," I said. "You're a doctor and a shrink. That woman needed that every bit as much as she needed my team of shooters."

Circe studied me for a moment. "Sorry."

"Don't worry about it."

Circe nodded and pulled her winter coat more tightly around her shoulders. She shivered even though the wind wasn't blowing. She stared at the choppers that were disappearing into the gray December sky. Her face was pale and her eyes had a jumpy quality.

I took a shot. "First time you ever saw someone killed?"

She nodded.

"Hitting you like a baseball bat upside the head, I expect."

Another nod.

"You want to talk about it?"

She looked at me and shook her head.

"Would food and a whole lot of alcohol help?"

"Yes," she said flatly, then turned and walked toward my Explorer.

She passed Top without comment. He watched her pass, pursed his lips, and came over to me.

"First time?" he asked.

"First time," I agreed.

"She's out from Terror Town, right? I read a couple of her books. Thought everyone out there was a vet of some kind."

"She is now."

He grunted. "So . . . what's our next play, Cap'n?"

As if in answer to his question, my cell buzzed. I flipped it open.

"Sit rep," snapped Church.

I told him. "We even have two prisoners en route to the Hangar. They'll need a few million Band-Aids, but they have a pulse."

"That makes a nice change," he said. "For you."

"Ha-ha."

"Please extend my appreciation to Echo Team. Excellent work. Have your team refresh and reload there at Willow Grove. I'll clear the paperwork. They'll catch up to you."

"Why? Where will I be?"

"Southampton. You know where that is?"

"Sure."

"There's a Starbucks at Street Road and Route 232. You are to meet my friend Martin Hanler. Do you remember him?"

"Yeah, he flew me out to Colorado during the Jakoby thing. Why am I meeting him?"

"He just called me to say that blowing up the London Hospital was his idea."

Part Four
Conspiracy Theories

For you see, the world is governed by
very different personages from what is imagined
by those who are not behind the scenes.

—BENJAMIN DISRAELI

Part Four

Conspiracy Theories

Chapter Fifty-one

Circe and I pulled into the Starbucks in Southampton, where Routes 232 and 132 meet. I started to get out, but Circe opened her briefcase on her lap and removed her laptop. I sat back. "Aren't you coming in?"

She looked at the store and made a face. "Marty and I never quite hit it off."

"You know him?"

"Since I was a kid. If you don't mind, I'll stay here and go over my notes. We have so much information . . . there has to be some answers buried in all of this. Besides . . . Marty will probably be more candid without me there, anyway. You're one of the boys."

I smiled. "Okay. I'll give you the highlights of this when I'm done."

"Can't wait."

I clicked my tongue and Ghost bounded out of the backseat, but before I could reach for the door handle a car beep made us turn. A rental sedan pulled into the lot and Ghost was wagging his tail so hard he nearly knocked me over. Rudy Sanchez parked and got out, smiling at us despite everything else that was going on.

Rudy is short and carries a couple extra pounds, but he's tougher than he looks and he has the most intelligent face I've ever seen. He's also the only person on earth who I trust completely and without reserve. I got out and we shook hands, and then he pulled me into his version of a bear hug. We slapped each other's backs as Ghost yipped and danced around us. He loses all traces of self-respect around Rudy. Rudy bent and vigorously rubbed Ghost's head and received a comprehensive face licking.

"Hello, you furry monster. You keeping Joe out of cathouses?"

Then Rudy looked past me and saw Circe step out of the Explorer. "Dios mio!"

"Keep it in your pants, Rude. That's Dr. Circe—"

"O'Tree," he finished, grinning hard enough to injure himself. "I know. I saw her on *Oprah*. My, my, but the good Lord was in a generous mood when he made her."

Circe walked over to meet us. Before I could make introductions, she said, "Dr. Sanchez?"

"Dr. O'Tree."

"It's 'Circe,'" she said, smiling brightly and extending her hand.

"Rudy," he said exactly the same way someone would say "your slave." Even Ghost seemed to roll his eyes. "I've read your books. Fascinating work. Insightful."

"Thank you," she said graciously. "And call me Circe."

"Mr. Church said that you'd be part of our team on this. I'd like to share my interview notes with you."

"The Nicodemus interview?"

"Yes."

"I'd love to see them," she said, "and I have some things I'd like to run past you."

I said, "You two want to stay out here and copy each other's homework while I go inside?"

Rudy looked at me with a charming smile. "Yes, thanks. Buzz off."

They tuned me out and were deep in conversation as they headed to my Explorer. I glanced down at Ghost. "I do believe we have been snubbed, my shaggy friend."

He had no comment, so we went inside.

As I reached for the door handle I shivered unexpectedly and looked suddenly back at Rudy and Circe. It was a weird feeling that was based on nothing I could name, but I felt as if there was a shadow cast over them both. I lingered for a moment, letting my ears and eyes pick apart the surroundings. Was something wrong? Out of place?

No. There was nothing. A goose had walked over my grave, as my grandmother would say. Gradually the shadow in my mind receded.

Ghost looked at them and gave a single, short *whuf.*

Interlude Thirty-five

New York City
December 19, 5:36 P.M. EST

Toys touched his fingers to the glass, feeling the cool caress of the December wind. Behind him, Gault and the American sat on opposite sides of the big man's

desk, heads bent together in a discussion on logistics for
the newest phase of the Ten Plagues Initiative. On the
wall a silent flat-screen TV showed a shot from an aerial view of the scene of a gunfight in Jenkintown, Pennsylvania. The legend across the bottom of the screen
read: *Terrorism?*

Below the window where Toys stood, New York was
sprawled in gaudy splendor beneath a gibbous moon.
Millions of lights. Millions of beating hearts. Toys' own
heart felt like a piece of broken crockery in his chest.
As cold as the night and as removed from real humanity as he was up here on the fiftieth floor of the building
that the American owned. One of the big man's many
holdings. Here, Los Angeles, Denver, Atlanta. The man
was immeasurably wealthy. Toys smiled thinly as he
mused that he, too, was now wealthy. He had millions
of dollars of his own money in numbered accounts. A
gift from the American.

So you don't have to keep sucking on Gault's tit. That
was how the American had phrased it.

I could leave, Toys thought. *I could walk out the door,
get into a cab, and vanish.*

How long, he wondered, before Gault would even realize that he was gone? Then how long would it take
Gault, using the vast resources of the Kings, to find him?
A week at the most. And what would Gault do? Have
him brought back in chains? Forgive him? Kill him?

Toys could not pick which option was most likely. He
sighed and leaned his forehead against the glass. Gault
had become the King of Plagues in every sense. He was
fully invested with the Kings. He was one of *them*, heart
and soul.

Which left Toys . . . where?

He had no idea.

The last four months had given him new definitions for both "heartache" and "hell." Although Toys managed to fake interest in the Ten Plagues Initiative, he knew that it didn't fool Gault. Not completely, anyway. The only comfort, and it was a cold and dubious comfort, was that Gault did not grasp the nature of Toys' disapproval. He thought it was cowardice.

Cowardice.

Jesus. Toys wanted to take a knife and rip Gault's guts out every time he thought about that. Twice in the last month he had come into Gault's room in the middle of the night and stood over his bed, watching Gault sleep, holding a knife in his sweating palm.

Cowardice?

How could Gault have wandered so far from himself that he could not recognize love?

Not for the first time, Toys wondered if Eris really was some kind of sorceress.

He and Gault barely spoke unless it was about incidental things. A second round of martinis, travel plans. Nothing of consequence.

Gault's time was taken up playing the role of the King of Plagues. He had entered the world of the Kings with a will, and even though bombings were not under his purview, Gault had actively participated in the planning of the London event. He had also selected Fair Isle. Toys was secretly pleased that the Ebola release had fallen flat.

Rivers of blood my ass, he mused.

And the woman, Amber Taylor, had dodged away as well. *Bloody good for her.*

He knew that although the failures could not be laid at Gault's feet, they were nonetheless failures connected to his overall plan. The failures were embarrassing to the Goddess as well, and that really pleased Toys.

Now they were poised for the next round. More killings. More death. And still they hadn't reached the real centerpiece of Gault's plan.

Toys wondered if they would all drown in a river of blood of their own making.

We deserve it.

The phone rang and the American answered, spoke quietly for a moment, and then hung up.

"I need to deal with something," said the King of Fear as he lumbered toward the door. "You boys make yourself comfortable."

He closed the door behind him.

Toys stood by the big picture window and looked out at the New York skyline. This was the fifth of the American's offices he had visited in the last few months, and he marveled at the fact that despite the differences in locale, each office was decorated identically, down to the bottles in the wet bar, the brand of expensive furniture, and even the art on the walls. He knew that this all made some kind of statement about the man, but he wasn't sure what that statement's message was. On the surface it seemed to suggest a mind that possessed a single fixed image of the world, but Toys knew that this was not the case. He wondered if it was more misdirection on the American's part. A statement intended to cement a certain limited view of who he was into people's minds.

Behind him, Gault sipped a Scotch and soda, the ice cubes tinkling against his lips.

Toys turned. "There's still time," he said.

"Don't start," muttered Gault quietly. "I'm not in the mood to have this discussion again."

"We haven't *had* this discussion yet. Every time I try to bring it up, you growl at me or storm out of the room. I'm supposed to be your Conscience—"

Gault snorted, which shut Toys up as effectively as a slap across the face.

Toys rubbed his eyes. He felt old and used up. "Oh, bloody hell," he said sharply. "I'm going to say it anyway."

"I wish you wouldn't," warned Gault.

Toys crossed the room and stood in front of Gault.

Gault took a sip, sighed, then said, "Okay. Have your say. Get it out of your system. I suppose I owe you that much."

Ha, Toys mused sourly. *If you paid what you owed me, Sebastian, we'd be thousands of miles away from here and running fast.*

Aloud he said, "When we escaped the meltdown in Afghanistan you were too badly injured to walk. I carried you out of there, Sebastian. Carried. On my back."

"You want a sodding medal? Fine, I'll buy you one."

"Hush." Toys said it softly, and something in his tone made Gault close his mouth on another barb. He gestured with his glass for Toys to continue. "When we escaped and we got onto the medical transport, that was the most frightening time of my life. Not because I thought that they would catch us. No . . . I was afraid that with everything crashing down I would lose you."

Gault blinked in what looked to Toys like genuine surprise. "You didn't lose me," he said softly.

"Yes, I did. Not then, but since then. In bits and pieces. I lost some of you before, to Amirah. I know you loved her, but you have to admit that I did see through her deception all along. If you had listened to me, things would never have gotten out of hand. I know that I've said that before and every time I do you and I have a row about it, but it's true. I was right about her."

Gault shrugged and his tone grew harder. "Okay, you were right about her. Bully for you."

"Given that," Toys persisted, "why can't you take a moment and step back from all of this? The Kings, the Ten Plagues, the *Goddess*—all of it. Step back and at least consider whether I might be right again."

"About Eris?"

"Yes. In a lot of ways she's as mad as Amirah was."

"So?"

"I think she *believes* that she is a goddess."

"Again . . . so?"

"She isn't," Toys said viciously. "She's a woman who knows that despite good genes and some natural longevity, this is the last blast for her as a sexual icon. Once her beauty really starts to fade, the other Kings will lose interest. Remember that 'glamour' is another word for an illusion or spell. That's what she's cast. Because she acts the part of the Great Beauty of the Ages, she is taken as such. It's affectation, and she's charismatic enough to pull it off. She's also probably scared out of her mind because she has to see, day by day, that she is nearing that line when, once it is crossed, she will become *ordinary*. A woman. Not a goddess. An old woman."

"You're jealous of her," sneered Gault.

"No. Even I'm not that damaged . . . and don't think that you can do me any harm by attacking my sexuality. I'm not conflicted about who I am, Sebastian. I know who I am. Just as I know who you are."

"And what am I, O wise and mighty Conscience?"

"You're a fool," Toys said acidly. "If you were merely naïve and oblivious I could forgive it, but you're the smartest man I've ever known. Ever. So, this refusal to see Eris for who she is, and to refuse to see this Ten Plagues madness for what it is, that's deliberate and stubborn foolishness."

"You're treading on thin ice, Toys, and your time is almost up."

"When you conceived the Seif Al Din project I objected to it, as you may remember. Not because I'm capable of taking the moral high ground—we both know I'm too thoroughly corrupt for that—but because it wasn't a good balance of reward and risk. A mistake could have led to a global pandemic, and very nearly did. If it wasn't for Joe Ledger and the DMS, your mistake would have been the very last one in history."

"Joe Ledger is a dead man," sneered Gault. "He slipped us in London, but I'm going to have his guts for garters."

"Will you listen to yourself? You're obsessed with him as if he's the cause of your problems."

"He is."

"He isn't. You're not a supervillain and he's not your arch nemesis. This isn't a sodding comic book."

"Don't be insulting."

Toys sighed and flapped his arms. "Now, here we are again, standing at the brink of another needlessly risky venture. What are the rewards? You want to cripple the Inner Circle? Really? Since when did they mean *anything* to you? Four months ago you'd never heard of them. But then Eris fucked the last bits of common sense out of your head and suddenly you are willing to launch a program that will not only cause countless deaths but could very easily spark conflicts that will tear nations apart. Why? What do you think you'll accomplish with that?"

Gault said nothing. He sipped his drink and watched Toys with hooded eyes.

"Shall I tell you then?" asked Toys.

"Oh, by all means. Show me how smart *you* are."

"This isn't about being smart, Sebastian, so don't try to turn it into a contest to see whose brain weighs more. I *know* you're smarter than me. You're smarter than almost everyone. You're just not as smart as you think you are." Toys stepped closer. "You want to rise above your human weaknesses, Sebastian. Just as Eris wants to rise above the truth that she must inevitably age, you want to rise about the truth that you can be hurt. You're both playacting at being gods because you can't *stand* the thought that you are human. Flawed, limited humans."

Gault finished the last of his drink and set the glass down on the American's desk. "Go to hell," he said softly, then shook his head. "No . . . *rot* in hell."

He turned toward the door and Toys laid his hand gently on Gault's arm.

"Please, Sebastian . . . I'm begging you. Don't *do* this."

Sebastian Gault hit Toys in the face. A single wickedly fast punch that caught Toys in the mouth, bursting his lips against his teeth. Toys staggered back, clamping his hands to his bleeding mouth, shocked into a horrified and broken silence. Blood welled from between his fingers and dripped onto his shirtfront.

Gault looked down at his own fist as if surprised that it had just done that. "Rot in hell," he said again. Quietly, without emphasis, his voice as dead as his eyes.

He turned and left the room.

Toys sank slowly to his knees, blood running in lines down his chin and splashing on the floor. He caved in around his pain. Not the pain of torn lips and mashed gums, but the red howling ache in his chest.

He squeezed his eyes shut, and wept.

Interlude Thirty-six

Regent Beverly Wilshire
Beverly Hills, California
December 19, 5:37 P.M. EST

Charles Osgood Harrington IV—known as C-Four since he was thrown out of college—was a total pain in the ass. Everyone knew that and agreed on it. The media loved to hate him and ran paparazzi pictures of him almost daily, usually peeing in a sacred fountain in Italy or in a perp walk after a DUI, or those infamous pictures of him during his first and second stays in county correctional facilities or work-release camps.

C-Four's father's lawyers hated him because he was so irredeemably arrogant and unrepentant in court that he instantly alienated judges and juries. The members of the various boards on which his father, Charles Osgood Harrington III—Three to his cronies and the press— was the chair. The stockholders hated him because each time his personal life detonated onto the headlines the shares in the family companies—Harrington Aeronautics, Harrington-Cheney Petrochemicals, Harrington and Milhaus Fuel Oil Company, and the fourteen others—tumbled. The administration of Yale hated that they were coerced into pushing him through with a degree even though he rarely attended a class and was never sober, but the Harrington family and their friends wrote checks larger than the outrage of the board of regents. Even C-Four's friends only stayed with him because they thought he was richer than God and liked to show it off by spreading cash around. On a whim he flew the cast of *Gossip Girl* to a clothing-optional island. Another time he bought a hotel just to throw a party, and once he purchased a Mercedes dealership on a bet and then lost it in a run of poker hands that same night.

When his name came up on programs like *Dr. Phil* and *Ellen,* kind-hearted but misinformed guest stars speculated that C-Four suffered from emotional damage that was the result of having been too famous even from birth. They discussed how the rich and privileged bear a terrible burden because they can't be real and said that C-Four's escapades were no different from the early excesses of Paris Hilton and Lindsay Lohan, both of whom had been romantically linked with him at one time or another, at least according to the tabloids.

Three only had one son. His daughter, Victoria, had married a civil-rights lawyer from Boston and was now only tolerated at Christmas. The keys to the kingdom would be passed to C-Four.

Father and son sat in leather chairs by a penthouse window in the Regent Beverly Wilshire. A tall Christmas tree sparkled and glowed behind them. Neither of them had decorated the tree and neither cared who had. Three had barely registered that there was a ten-foot tree in the room. C-Four had draped unused condoms on it like tinsel.

"I would prefer you not go," said Three.

His son waggled the engraved and gold-embossed card. "Are you fucking kidding me, Dad?"

"Watch your language."

C-Four snorted. "Oh, right, 'cause you don't want me to spoil my image."

"No, I just don't appreciate you talking like you're from the gutter."

"Fuck that."

Three fumed into the amber depths of his Scotch.

"This gig is going to be too cool to miss." He reached for the return envelope, which had fallen to the floor. He fished a pen from his pocket, scrawled a brief note, stuffed the card into the envelope, and licked the glue. When he was done, he held it up between fore and index fingers. "You should be happy they even invited me."

"If I had known about it in time I would have made sure you weren't invited. It isn't appropriate that you should go. No one at Yale remembers any 'good old times' with you. At best you were a figure of fun, and I suspect you received that invitation out of pity."

"Thanks, Pop. Always nice to know that you care." C-Four shook his head and finished the last of his drink. "Besides, this isn't one of those über-mysterious Inner Circle things. And it's not for you and your crew of vultures and thieves. For once it's my generation instead of the corrupt old farts you hang out with."

" 'Corrupt'?"

"Sorry, Dad, was that the wrong choice of words? Would 'insanely manipulative' be better?"

"Charlie . . ."

"Don't even try to call me that. And don't pretend that I don't know what you and your Inner Circle Bonesmen are all about. Christ, everyone with Net access knows about the shit you assholes pull." C-Four held up the sealed return envelope. "Besides . . . this is going to be the party of the century."

C-Four got up and walked over to the wet bar, mixed a complicated drink, drank half of it standing there, and then strolled to the Christmas tree.

"In what way?" demanded Three.

C-Four took another pull on the drink. "I doubt you'd . . ." His voice trailed away and he stood frowning at the tree.

"You doubt I'd what?" snapped his father.

"Hm? What?" C-Four looked at his father with a confused smile on his face. He touched his cheeks. "What?"

"You said you doubted that I'd—what?"

C-Four's confused smile flickered like a lightbulb whose filament was burning too thin. He shifted uncertainly and Three could see that there was something wrong with his son's face. It looked weirdly uneven. Knobbed. Almost . . . *blistered*. "I . . ."

"Charlie, what's wrong?"

His son tore at his collar, exposing his throat. All along his upper chest and neck dozens of red spots were appearing, rising from pinpricks and swelling into boils even as the young man stood swaying.

"Good God!" yelled Three. "What the hell did you do to yourself?" C-Four's fingers twitched and the glass tumbled from his hands. It hit the thick Persian carpet, bounced, and splashed ice and alcohol over his bare feet. But the young man did not seem to notice. He stood there with a half smile, brows knit, head cocked into an attitude of listening as if he was pondering some great internal mystery. Boils blossomed across his face and on his hands. When he touched the ones on his face, they burst with sprays of red mist.

"Careful, dammit . . . ," his father said, starting in his chair. Then he froze in place as C-Four raised dreamy eyes toward him.

"I feel really . . ."

And blood exploded from his mouth and nose.

"Charlie!"

Charles Osgood Harrington III erupted from his chair as his son's knees suddenly buckled and he dropped. C-Four landed on his knees and fell sideways against the tree. The whole mass of it—tree, tinsel, ornaments, condoms, and fairy lights—canted sideways with the young man on top of it. Blood geysered from C-Four's mouth and the boils on his skin burst. His father was thirty feet away and he crossed the room in a shot.

But C-Four was already dead.

Chapter Fifty-two

Hanler saw me and stood as I approached. He offered me his hand and gave me a single-pump shake that was dry and rock hard. Marty Hanler was in his mid-sixties, with receding gray hair and a deepwater tan. He had bright blue eyes that looked merry but were as focused as a sniper's eyes. He peered past me out the window.

"Is that Circe? Wow . . . she's really . . . filled out."

When he straightened he caught sight of my face. My expression flipped some kind of switch inside his head, because immediately the caveman receded and the writer stepped forward. He cleared his throat and looked at Ghost. "That's a good-looking shepherd. Is he friendly?"

"Occasionally."

"Can I pet him?"

"Can you type without fingers?"

He stuck his hands in his pockets.

We ordered coffee and sat in the back and there was some nice cover noise in the form of a mixed tape of pop stars singing Christmas songs. Ghost lay down between our chairs, within petting reach, but Hanler didn't rise to the bait.

I'd met Hanler through Mr. Church, but I've known about him since college. His espionage thrillers always hit the number one spot on the bestseller lists. So far, four of them had been made into movies. Matt Damon starred in the last one. I owned the DVD, but I didn't say that to Hanler.

"Mr. Church said that you had something for me."

" 'Church,' " he said, smiling with teeth so bright I felt like I was getting a tan. "I'm still not used to calling him that. He'll always be 'Deacon' to me."

"Is that his real name?" I said, pitching it to sound offhand, but Hanler flicked his shooter's eyes at me.

"Good try." He laughed. "Ask him."

I grinned. "Which means that you don't know, either."

He shrugged and sipped his coffee. "Okay, I called the Deacon because I think someone took an idea I had and maybe put it into practice in the most terrible possible way." He cut me an amused look. "Settle down, Dick Tracy. . . . I'm not here to confess. I said I may have come up with the scenario, but I'm not part of a global criminal conspiracy."

"Hit me."

"It's a plot for a novel. The Hospital thing."

"When was the novel published?"

"That's the weird part. I've been knocking the idea around for a while. It's something I thought I'd do if I ever started a new series. My Rick Stenner books are all set in the U.S. except the flashback one, *Black Ops,* which is set during the invasion of Baghdad. But I've been wanting to spin off the Xander Murphy character for a while now. He was a supporting character in *White Gold,* and the readers really took to him. Kind of low-rent James Bond type that—"

"I know," I said. "Jude Law played him in the movie."

"Right, right . . . so you know. Okay, well, I figured

that if my writing schedule ever opened up a bit, or if the Stenner books got stale, I'd do some Murphy books. It would be a switch to—"

"Slow down. . . . You're saying that the Hospital scenario is from a book you *plan* to write but haven't actually *done* anything with?"

"Right."

"There are no early drafts?"

"There are no drafts at all. Never got that far."

"Notes? Plot outlines, anything like that?"

"Nope. The idea's still up here." He tapped his skull. "That's one of the reasons I'm so concerned. I mean, if it was something that I'd already published—"

"Then we'd have six billion suspects."

"I don't sell quite that many books."

"Anyone can read your stuff in a library," I said.

"Good point. On the other hand, if it was something I'd written but which hadn't yet been released, that would narrow it down to the staff at my agent's office, my lawyer, my family, and my publisher. Still a lot of people, but a narrower field."

"So, who have you told about this plot?"

"I belong to a couple of writers' organizations and we have conventions every year. The pros do a couple of panels for the fans, and then we decamp to the closest bar and spend the rest of the weekend networking or bullshitting. You know, gossip, industry news, that sort of thing. After a couple of rounds we start one-upping each other about what would make the absolute best kick-ass novel and how we're the guy to write it."

"And that's where the Hospital idea came in?"

"Yeah. This was a convention called ThrillerFest. I was at the bar in the Hyatt with a whole bunch of other writers. We were all hammered and we were doing the one-up thing with the perfect thriller plot. I told them about the Hospital bombing."

I said, "Tell me why you picked that hospital."

"You probably can't tell from my accent, but I was born in London. Grew up in Whitechapel, about two blocks from the hospital. We emigrated when I was seventeen and I lost my accent in college theater courses. My first job, though, was as an assistant orderly at the London. Mostly I pushed a laundry cart around, but I was in every part of that hospital every day. I could draw a diagram of it from memory, or at least a diagram of the old building. So, when I needed a landmark for my imaginary terrorists to blow up, I picked that one."

"Write what you know," I suggested.

"Exactly."

"So, who stole your idea?"

He grunted. "I'm pretty sure Osama bin Laden wasn't doing shots with us that night."

"When was this?"

"Couple of years ago. July 2009."

"Who was there?"

"In the bar? Christ, *everyone*. Place was packed. People were coming and going. I can't tell you for sure who was in our conversational circle when I talked about that scenario. We were all pretty well hit in the ass. It was late, though. Midnight at least, which means that the party was in full swing."

"Give me some names."

"Well . . . David Morrell was there for some of it. He asked me later if I ever wrote the book."

"Morrell?"

"Guy who created Rambo? Who else? Let's see. . . . Gayle Lynds was there. Sandra Brown, Doug Clegg, Steve Berry, Vince Flynn, Eric Van Lustbader, Ken Isaacson, John Gilstrap . . ."

He rattled off a long list of names. I recognized some of them from Hugo Vox's Terror Town think tank. I wrote down all of the names. By the time Hanler was finished rooting around in the rubble of that drunken memory we'd compiled a list of twenty-eight names. Of those eleven were definites. Four of them were hazy maybes. The rest had all been at the table, but he didn't know when or for how long.

"Anyone else there?"

"Maybe, but I was seeing pink lobsters by the time I rolled out of there. I should have been arrested for the way I drove the elevator to my floor."

We sat in silence for a few moments, drinking our coffee, thinking it through.

"Your plot," I said, "did it involve bringing in oil or rubber in large quantities? Or pallets of tires?"

He gave me a shrewd look and for a moment I could see the brains behind the bestseller bluster. "You're talking about the black clouds? Yeah, I saw that on TV and thought it was odd."

"Not part of your story?"

"No."

"Any religious themes in your plot?"

"Just the usual stuff. Fundamentalist Shiites. Not very original, I'm afraid, and I'd probably have changed it in the writing. The genre's moving away from using Muslims as the go-to bad guys."

I said nothing.

Hanler sipped his coffee and stared up at the ceiling. "It would be kind of weird if a writer was involved in this sort of thing," he said. "We cook up the worst possible catastrophes. Brilliant crimes, terrorist campaigns, mass murders. We get inside the heads of serial killers and extremists. Good thing we're the good guys."

"If all of you are," I said.

"Yeah, there's that. Sorry this wasn't more useful. And I hope like hell that I didn't waste your time."

Me, too, I almost said aloud.

We stood and shook hands. Hanler eyed me for a moment. "Look, Joe, if it turns out that it was one of the people at ThrillerFest or someone from the T-Town group, someone who used my idea . . ."

"Yeah?"

"Put the son of a bitch down like a rabid dog."

"Why? For stealing your idea?"

"No," he said without humor. "Because it means that I'm partly responsible, however far removed, for the deaths of four thousand people. I have trouble sleeping at night as it is. I think knowing that for sure . . . Christ, I think that might kill me." He sighed and smiled a weary smile. "Come on; let me buy you one for the road. And something for Circe and your pal."

And that fast everything went all to hell.

There was a series of firecracker pops somewhere outside and the whole front set of windows of the Starbucks exploded inward.

Chapter Fifty-three

Starbucks
Southampton, Pennsylvania
December 19, 5:43 P.M. EST

A barrage of heavy-caliber bullets tore into the coffee-house, tearing apart the counter, shattering the big urns of hot coffee, sending stacks of paper cups flying, and ripping apart the spot where I'd been standing a split second before.

The heavy front glass was thick enough to have deflected the first rounds; otherwise I'd be dead. Instead I hooked an arm around Hanler and a young woman wearing a Grinch sweatshirt. I felt two hard jerks at the flaps of my sports coat and knew that a couple of rounds had missed me by inches. We hit the deck just as the first screams rose, louder than the gunfire. Then a second window blew and suddenly I was screaming myself as glass splinters rained down on my head. I shielded my eyes with my arm.

"Down! Down! Get down!" I roared.

I pivoted and looked out from under my bent arm. Most of the customers were already in motion, dodging and ducking, leaping over counters and pitching themselves behind the overstuffed chairs. But a few stood there with slack mouths and eyes like deer on a highway . . . and the bullets tore them to rags. A college jock with a Rutgers ski cap flew backward into a display of stocking stuffers, his white parka blooming with red flowers. As he fell his outflung arms knocked down an old man and a teenage girl, sending them sprawling and saving their lives by accident as the heavy-caliber rounds swarmed the air.

Even through the thunder of gunfire I could hear Ghost barking like crazy, but I couldn't tell if he was hurt.

"Hanler! Crawl behind the counter! Hanler!" I yelled, but Marty Hanler didn't reply, and he didn't move. He lay facedown on the floor and blood spread from beneath him in a growing crimson pool. Damn.

"He's over there!"

The yell came from the shattered window and a split second later a line of bullets pocked the floor near my head. I used my right foot to shove the screaming young woman out of the way as I rolled in the other direction. I tore open my sports coat, found the knurled grips of my Beretta, racked the slide as I rolled to a kneeling position, and brought the weapon up in a two-handed grip. The first of the shooters stepped through the window. He wore heavy body armor and had a scarf wrapped around his nose and mouth and wore ski goggles. He held a Colt AR-15 Tactical Carbine, firing at anything that moved.

I gave him a double tap.

The first round punched into his sternum—it didn't penetrate his vest, but it froze him into the moment—and I put the next round through his right eye. The impact snapped his head back and probably broke his neck, and it painted the two men behind with blood and brains. I shot the second one in the mouth as he tried to yell.

The third shooter swept the room with an AR-15 that had an oversized hundred-round drum magazine. Bullets chopped the floor and turned tables into clouds of splinters.

And . . . oh Christ—Rudy and Circe! *They were still outside*.

If they were still alive.

Rudy didn't carry a gun, but he had common sense, good survival instincts, and a cell phone. I hoped he was hiding under my car calling for backup.

The counter above me disintegrated into a storm cloud of splinters and I threw myself forward and down, one arm hooked over my face to protect my eyes as I went onto my side and fired blind. I put half a magazine through the flying debris and the chatter from the assault rifle abruptly stopped.

"He's over behind the counter!" a man yelled from the other side of the store.

Suddenly three other long guns opened up from the far end of the store, blasting the side window and running lines of destruction along the floor. People screamed as bullets found them, punching through heavy winter coats, tearing chunks out of legs and arms, and splashing the floor with red.

This was going from bad to absolute frigging disaster. Adrenaline was pumping through me by the quart, but at the moment it was triggering more of the flight impulse than the desire to fight all these guys. I was scared out of my mind; I'll admit it to anyone.

"Grenade, *grenade*!"

I didn't know if someone was calling for a frag or telling his comrades that he was throwing one, but I did not want to wait around to find out. I came up firing and put the rest of the mag downrange, forcing them back for a second. The grenade dropped from dead fingers and fell outside the store.

There was a huge *whump!* and a dozen car alarms began to blare.

Any hope I had that the blast had taken out the rest of the shooters was blown to hell as they opened up again. And I prayed that Rudy and Circe were nowhere near that grenade when it blew.

I had only one spare magazine and I swapped it out as I flung myself to the left, hitting the base of the front wall. Broken glass covered the floor, and as I slid out of the line of fire the jagged shards tore through my trousers and bit into my left thigh like a swarm of piranha.

The third shooter—the one I hit while firing blind—was down but not dead. He lay partly inside the coffee shop and was slowly trying to crawl back out. Blood dripped from a thigh wound and another on his right forearm. The strap of the AR-15 was wound around his injured arm.

I stretched for a long reach just as the other shooters opened up again. My scrabbling fingers caught the strap and I jerked it toward me, hauling gun and gunman into the store. The shooter tried to make a fight of it, but I wasn't in the mood. I jerked harder and as he flipped over onto his back I chopped down on his windpipe with the butt of the Beretta.

There was movement to my left and I saw Ghost crouching behind the ruined counter, his teeth bared, his white pelt dottled with blood. His muscles bunched as he prepared to make a run at the gunmen.

"Down!" I snapped. It was forty feet to the side window, and fast as Ghost was, he'd never get them before they got him. The dog gave me a fierce, despairing look. He wanted to be in this fight. He probably smelled my blood and the ancient instinct to protect the pack leader was coming close to overriding his training.

Behind me a man growled, "C'mon, Turk; get this motherfucker!"

Then one of the gunmen kicked the rest of the glass out of the window and stepped through. There were at least a dozen people in the coffeehouse, and most or all of them were hurt. A lot of them were dead, too. I cut a look at Hanler, but he lay in the center of a lake of blood and wasn't moving. I didn't think he was ever going to.

Son of a bitch.

I took the AR-15 and from the weight I could tell that the drum mag was more than half-gone. How many rounds left? Twenty? Thirty? The dead man's coat was open and I flipped back the flap, saw a second mag hanging from his belt, and made a grab for it.

The shooter caught the movement and suddenly the dead man's body seemed to rise from the floor as rounds punched into his meat and muscle, jerking the corpse into a horrible parody of convulsive life.

Lying flat on my back, head toward them, I raised the rifle with both hands and emptied the first magazine at that end of the store. It sounds easy, but the recoil slammed into my upraised arms and threatened to tear them out of the shoulder sockets.

The gun clicked empty way too soon; I'd guessed wrong about how many rounds were left. There couldn't have been more than a dozen rounds left, but it bought me a second's worth of grace, which was all I needed to swap out the magazines.

I drew a breath, then let out the loudest war cry I could. Who knows what I said or if I said anything at all? Just noise. Loud and feral, the primitive and inarticulate cry of the Warrior within as I rolled onto my stomach and came up into a low crouching run, firing from the hip, blasting on full auto as I dodged from wall to wall. I don't know how I didn't get shot. Battlefields are like that. Sometimes you have the best armor and the best cover and a ricochet pings off a wall and punches your ticket, and sometimes you feel painted with magic as you run through hellfire without a scratch. Bunny calls it having a *Die Hard* moment. Top says that it's Madman Mojo. I don't have a name for it, but I made it to the counter alive. I hip-checked Ghost and sent him on a nail-skittering sideways slide into the wall. He yelped in pain, but he was still on his feet and out of the line of fire.

Then the tone of the fight changed. Only one gun continued to pour fire my way; the others were shooting at something outside.

Rudy and Circe?

It sounded like a dozen guns in play out there.

I dove for cover, and my heart sank in my chest. There were more of them, and no matter how much of a *Die Hard* moment I was having, I couldn't win against an army. In the movies a hero can win against unlimited odds. This wasn't the movies. I was already slowing down and I was going to run out of ammunition very soon. And then I was going to die.

There was a scream and a crash and I looked up as one of the shooters came backward through the window, arms flung wide, chest and face exploding like fireworks.

Then I heard it.

"Echo! Echo! Echo!"

A deep, bass rumble of a shout.

Top!

The shooters at the far end turned toward the shouts, and I rose up and hosed them. But one of them spun and fired a full mag at me. I felt the wind of the first rounds as I dropped back out of sight.

There were more screams, and no more rounds came my way.

I ducked and crabbed sideways and looked down the store and saw that one shooter was gone, punched back out through the window and sprawled like a starfish on the hood of a parked Hyundai. A second man had dropped his weapon and was trying to stop his life from leaking out of a hole in the side of his neck.

The third shooter held his ground and was slapping a fresh magazine into place. I'd been waiting for that moment, and I rose up from hiding and ran at him. Ghost was right on my heels, racing along with the silent speed that a fighting dog has when blood is in the air and it's time for the kill. The AR-15 was a burning monster that bucked and jerked in my hands as I put twenty rounds into the shooter. Vest be damned. I drilled a hole through his chest you could drive a truck through, and what was left of him pinwheeled out through the window.

Two more shooters ran past the window, heading toward the front, but I heard a fusillade of mixed-caliber reports and both men staggered back, turning and juddering as Echo Team chopped them apart. There was more movement outside and I saw Top Sims and Bunny duck down behind a car and trade fire with yet another pair of shooters. How many of the bastards did they send? I mean, I'm flattered and all that they think I'm that tough, but an entire army seemed a bit excessive.

I reached the window. The man with the neck wound wasn't hurt near as bad as I thought and he pivoted and used a bloody hand to draw his sidearm. There was a flash of white, a fierce growl, and a sharp crunch, and then the gun arm collapsed into red junk as Ghost took him. He screamed, but Ghost growled like a monster out of myth.

"Keep!" I ordered Ghost, and the big shepherd stopped short of killing the man but didn't let go of the mangled arm.

I crouched and did a fast look around the corner of the window. There were four shooters on my right, all of them firing over the hoods of parked cars. It was weird. You see scenes like this in Iraq and Afghanistan, not in suburban Pennsylvania. I'm sure there was a lesson in there about cultural arrogance, but I was too busy to sort out the nuances at the moment. I dropped the AR-15 and took the sidearm from the guy Ghost was babysitting. The guy didn't seem to mind. He was busy trying not to scream.

I sighted down on the closest shooter. Top caught my eye and shook me off. I withheld my shot and then saw why. Khalid Shaheed had worked his way around to the far side and was three steps from a flanking position. One of the shooters must have spotted him and started to turn, so I blew out the windshield of the car he was hiding behind. He made the mistake of being surprised and looking up.

Khalid put a round through the guy's ear.

The other shooters faltered, caught in a cross fire.

Top bellowed at them in his leather-throated sergeant's voice, "Drop your weapons and step out from behind the vehicles! Do it *now*!"

It was a simple choice. It was their only remaining choice. An idiot could have recognized it as the only way out of the moment.

But the dumb sons of bitches went for it. They opened up on Khalid and on Top. The return fire came from Top and Bunny, from Khalid, from me, and from DeeDee, who appeared out of nowhere and took up a shooting position right outside the window. It was a four-way shit storm, and it was over in seconds. Nobody was going home from that party.

DeeDee looked up with a dazzling blue-eyed smile. "Howdy, Boss. Did you get me a vanilla latte with foam?"

I actually laughed and then I heard tires squeal. I jumped out of the window and sprinted for the front of the building with DeeDee on my six. A white van roared past us and headed for the far exit. The side door was open and I saw two men with scarves standing braced in the opening. They both had assault rifles and I was starting to pivot, reaching to push DeeDee out of the way, when there were two sharp cracks and the men pitched backward into the van. I whipped my head around and saw John Smith lying chest down over the hood of Black Bess, his sniper rifle smoking.

The van was still going, the driver hell-bent on getting his ass out of the parking lot. We all opened up on the vehicle, battering it with rounds, but the driver had the pedal on the floor and we didn't have a good angle on him.

"Rudy!" I bellowed as I broke into a dead run.

"Here!" came a strangled croak from the other side of the building. I spun and cut across the lot to try to cut the van off. As I cleared the corner I saw Rudy on his knees, right hand clamped over his left arm, his face white as paste as blood poured from between his fingers.

What I saw behind him twisted my brain around.

Circe O'Tree stood over Rudy, legs wide in a solid shooter's stance, holding a smoking Glock .40 in a two-handed grip, the barrel pointed right at me.

I almost shot her.

However, she wasn't aiming at me. She was aiming past me, and I whirled and dodged sideways as she fired. Her first three bullets exploded the van's windshield and the next two hit the driver in the face. The van suddenly swerved as the driver pitched sideways, his dead hands dragging the wheel hard over. The van missed Circe by ten feet and Rudy by less than a yard. It plowed into the back of my Explorer and crushed it like a beer can.

For one crystalline moment the entire scene was dead silent, as if we were all frozen into a photograph from a book on war. This could have been Somalia or Beirut or Baghdad or any of the other places on our troubled earth where hatred takes the form of lethal rage. We, the victors, stood amid gunsmoke and the pink haze of blood that had been turned to mist, amazed that we were alive, doubting both our salvation and our right to have survived while others—perhaps more innocent and deserving than ourselves—lay dead or dying.

Chapter Fifty-four

Then the moment crumbled to dust as sirens burned the air and hearing returned to our gunshot-deafened ears so that we heard the screams of those still clinging to life.

"Top!" I yelled.

"Clear!" he called as he and Bunny came out from their points of cover and swarmed the dead, kicking away their weapons, checking for pulses behind the appearance of death.

I turned and ran toward Rudy, but Circe was there, pushing him down. She had a knife in her hand—God only knows where it came from—and she was cutting his sleeve away, yelling at him to hold pressure there, there, dammit, changing from the person who had just killed into the doctor who had dedicated her life to doing no harm. Tears glittered like diamonds at the corners of her eyes.

"Dr. O'Tree," Rudy said in a voice slurred by shock and pain, "it's a pleasure to—"

"Shut up," she snapped.

"Okay."

As Circe worked, her gaze kept flicking up and past me. I followed her line of sight and saw the six small holes clustered in the center of the driver's windshield of the van. The figure inside was slumped sideways, eyes wide and fixed and nothing much else remaining of his face.

DeeDee knelt beside Circe with an open field surgical kit. She popped a surette of morphine and jabbed it in Rudy's arm. He said something in Spanish that sounded like "I love you," and passed out.

I tried to help them, but they waved me off.

"Inside! The people!" Circe cried in a voice that was as fragile as cracked porcelain.

The sirens were getting louder. Help was coming. Thank god.

I ran to the front of the destroyed Starbucks just as the first police cars came screeching into the parking lot.

I stepped into a scene from hell. The ceiling lights had all been blown out. People were screaming. Those who could still scream. I looked in through the shattered window. Too many of the sprawled figures lay still and silent, their voices silenced forever. The place looked like it had been spray painted with red, but it wasn't the cheerful holiday red of Christmas.

There were no other shooters. The woman in the Grinch shirt was on her hands and knees, splinters of glass glittering in her hair like stardust. She looked around at the carnage. Then she looked down at the figure that lay beside her.

Marty Hanler.

She screamed. I couldn't blame her.

"Federal agent!" I yelled. "Police and ambulances are on their way. Everyone stay down!"

Top and the others swarmed past me to provide first aid.

Ghost stood above the last of the shooters. The only one still alive. I had to step over the dead and dying to get to him.

"Off," I said quietly, and Ghost released the ruin of an arm. "Watch."

The man was white from blood loss, but he was far from dead, the wound in his neck was bad but not fatal, his arm was probably a total loss unless he got to a top-notch microsurgeon in the next hour or so, but even with all that he would live. When he looked up into my eyes I could see the precise moment when he realized that surviving this was not going to be any kind of mercy.

Not for him.

Interlude Thirty-seven

The Seven Kings
December 19, 5:51 P.M. EST

When the American came back to his office he found Toys sitting on the floor, his shirt covered in drying blood, dark stains on the carpet. Toys held his head in his hands as if it would crack and fall apart if he didn't press the broken pieces together.

"Holy shit," said the American. "What happened?"

Toys sniffed, shook his head. "I tried to tell him," he mumbled. "I tried to explain the danger he was creating for himself."

"Ah," said the American. "Yeah, I could have told you that was a waste of time. He hit you, huh?"

Toys sobbed into his hands.

The American took a clean towel from the wet bar

and poured ice cubes into it and handed it to Toys. Then he took a bottle of Don Julio tequila, pulled out the stopper, and dropped it on the bar. He placed his back against the wall and slid down to the floor so that he sat next to Toys. He nudged Toys with his knee and handed him the bottle. Toys shook his head.

"Take a fucking drink," growled the American.

Toys sighed, took the bottle, and drank a careful mouthful through torn lips. Coughed, gagged, drank another. He handed the bottle back and the American took a pull. For the next ten minutes neither said a word. They passed the bottle back and forth and let the minutes harden the cement that held their thoughts together.

"He's going to get himself killed," Toys said.

"Probably."

"It's your mother's fault."

"It's both their faults. They were made for each other."

They each took a pull.

"I think I've been fired as his Conscience." Toys tried to laugh about that, but his lips hurt too much.

"You'll always have a place with the Kings, Toys," said the American.

Toys looked at him. "Why? I'm Sebastian's luggage. What am I to you?"

"Don't sell yourself short, kiddo. You have clarity of mind. You can see the Big Picture without getting seduced by the shiny little details."

"You mean I'm a cynic."

"I prefer 'realist,' but yeah."

Toys held out his hand for the bottle, took a pull.

They drank in silence for a long time. Then the American said, "I don't have anyone to talk to."

Toys looked at him in surprise. "What? You have—"

"Santoro? He's a psychopath. I use him the way I'd use a gun. Point and shoot. But if it came down to where he had to decide between me and Mom, you know how he'd jump."

"Is it going to come down to that?"

The American nodded. "Yep. You know it is."

Toys sighed. "Sebastian, too. A Goddess, a King, and the Angel of Death. Very nice. You could build a heavy metal album on that."

The American laughed. "Guess you've figured out that the whole 'no secrets' thing between the Seven Kings is a frigging joke. Always has been. Some of them take it seriously, and I pretend to . . . but I always hedge my bets. I don't trust easily. With the Kings, I've made a fortune. I'm damn near richer than God, but I don't really enjoy it. I fuck around with money because what else do I have?"

" 'When Alexander saw the breadth of his domain, he wept for there were no more worlds to conquer.' "

The American grunted. "A misquote from Plutarch, but it hits the bull's-eye. My point is, though, that I can't trust the Kings. I can't trust Santoro. And I *never* trusted my mother. I'm glad I wasn't actually raised by her. She was a rich debutante when she had me, but she gave me up and my dad raised me. He was a blue-collar guy. When he struck it rich, they got married, but by then I was in college. I didn't know how corrupt she was until I was twenty-two or -three, and I didn't know how crazy she was until I was thirty. She was already working on this Goddess thing when I created the Seven Kings."

"That long ago?"

"Sure. She's brilliant, but she's totally fucking nuts. Gault is perfect for her. Brilliant but nuts."

"Sebastian is broken."

"A lot of people are." The American nodded and took a pull from the bottle. "Sebastian and Mom are pushing this Ten Plagues Initiative forward despite everything I've tried to do to stop it."

"Like . . . ?"

The American turned to him and smiled. "Before I answer that, you answer me this: if you had to pick one quality that defines everything the Kings stand for, what would it be?"

"Chaos—?"

"C'mon, kiddo . . . you know as well as I do that's just the company line. What're the real characteristics?"

Toys thought about it. "Misdirection. Lies, misinformation, disinformation. All of that."

"See, you are a smart young fellow. Misdirection. The Israel-Islam thing? Misdirection. The terrorist attacks—9/11, the India attacks, bombing of the USS *Cole*? Misdirection. The whole Ten Plagues Initiative is mostly misdirection. Most of it is a pure profit machine, like we've been saying. But some of it—a lot of it—is to keep eyes looking in the wrong direction even among us. You can't believe hardly anything we say, even when we're telling the truth."

"Okay. So, how does that answer my question? How does it explain how you've been trying to stop Eris?

Mostly it looks like you've been helping her. . . ." His voice trailed off and he smiled as much as his mashed lips would allow. He cocked an eyebrow. "When Dr. Kirov died it nearly derailed the Ten Plagues Initiative."

The American grinned approvingly. "Didn't it, though."

Toys smiled as much as his damaged lips would allow. "Kirov's death was pretty convenient."

"Uh-huh. It should have stopped the Initiative in its tracks. But . . . Mom talked the Kings into bullying me about calling Gault."

"You didn't want to bring him in?"

"Hell no." He handed over the bottle. "Can you guess why?"

"Because . . . he would do what he *has* done. He'd figure a way to make the Ten Plagues Initiative work."

"And ain't that just a kick in the fucking ass?" The American patted Toys' knee. "Now . . . keep thinking that through."

They sat side by side on the floor while Toys worked it out. Toys asked, "When did Eris first ask about Sebastian?"

"Six months ago. Right around the time Dr. Kirov had his first stroke. A ministroke. Son of a bitch bounced back faster than I expected."

"Six months. That's . . . right around the time that the DMS started hitting cells being trained to support the Initiative."

"Uh-huh."

"We know that someone has been making anonymous calls to Mr. Church to tip him off."

"Yep."

"In order to reveal the location of those cells, the caller has to have a source within the Kings organization."

"That's what the Kings believe. There have been all sorts of internal witch hunts to find the blabbermouth. Turns out, it was Kirov's Conscience."

Toys looked at the big man, but the man's smile never wavered.

"Inconvenient that the man died before someone as persuasive as Santoro could make him talk," Toys suggested.

"Yeah, what interesting timing that was."

Toys took a final sip of the tequila and set the bottle down. "A Big Picture kind of person might look at that and wonder if Kirov's Conscience was ever truly dirty."

"They might."

"And that person might also wonder if there is truly a war between the Seven Kings and the Inner Circle."

"Indeed."

"And that person might wonder if the entire thing was misdirection from the jump. Maybe to *start* a war."

"And how would that benefit the Kings?"

"It destabilizes those in power."

The American grinned like a happy bear. "How's the mouth doing?"

"I can barely feel it."

"Does it hurt too much to talk on the phone?"

"No."

The American got clumsily to his feet. As he did so his cell phone fell from his pocket and landed next to the bottle. He pretended not to notice it.

Toys looked at the phone and then up at the towering bearlike anomaly of a man. This King of Fear.

"Remember what I said to you a while back? About how Judas got a bad rap when he was really probably trying to save Jesus? In fact, here's a bit of interesting biblical trivia. In Luke 24:33 and Mark 16:14 it clearly states that when Jesus rose from the dead he met with 'the eleven.' Most people assume that the missing disciple was Judas, who was supposed to have killed himself out of remorse for his act of betrayal. But in John 20:24 we learn that the missing disciple was Thomas. So . . . that means that the other eleven *included* Judas. And in 1 Corinthians 15:5 the Apostle Paul says that Matthias wasn't voted in as the replacement twelfth Apostle until forty days after the Resurrection. So . . . Judas was still there. In fact, in Acts 1:25 we learn that Judas 'turned aside to go to his own place.' People don't read the whole Bible. They don't get the Big Picture. Judas's death was a fake, and considering that God *ordained* his betrayal, and Jesus *predicted* it, Judas was acting according to the will of God. He wasn't a traitor—he was a company man who did the right goddamn thing, even though it was the hard goddamn thing to do. He was a Big Picture guy. Just like me and you." He smiled down at Toys. "Lock up when you leave, kiddo."

He turned and lumbered out.

Toys stared at the empty doorway for a long time, and then he set down the ice and picked up the phone. It was an exotic model with a kind of scrambler attachment he'd never seen before.

Chapter Fifty-five

Every cop in five towns and some from Philadelphia descended on that parking lot. The streets were closed off, the airspace declared a no-fly zone except for SWAT choppers.

The cops wanted to bag my team, but that wasn't going to happen. We had the right credentials, and by the time the first ambulance rolled in Echo Team was already at work on the survivors. Khalid was an actual M.D., so he and Circe sectioned the coffee shop and triaged the wounded. Bunny, Top, and John Smith went to work patching bleeders, immobilizing injured backs and necks, removing the most immediately threatening glass splinters, and treating people for shock. Then waves of EMTs arrived, as well as a couple of carloads of nurses and doctors from the nearby hospital. As the professionals claimed the scene, we backed off.

I called the DMS but was unable to get Church on the phone, so I told the duty officer the pertinent details and said that we needed someone on the horn to the local chief of police and probably the governor.

Top caught up with me. "Khalid's got the prisoner stabilized. Want to go have a little chitchat?"

"Yes, I do."

My nerves were still jangling and I had the jitters and sick stomach that often follows violence and an adrenaline surge. If I had the time I'd throw up, then buy a pint of Ben and Jerry's and curl up in my room and watch Comedy Central until I passed out. Fat chance of that. My thigh hurt like hell, and blood from the cuts had pooled in my shoe, so I sloshed as I walked.

I went over to the corner where the wounded shooter was being prepped for transport. Khalid had removed the man's scarf, goggles, and hat to reveal a face that was as American as apple pie. Well, as American as pizza and cannolis. His skin was a greasy gray, and pain had etched deep lines on either side of his mouth. His eyes followed me with glassy uncertainty. An IV bag was plugged into his arm and he was wrapped in bandages. His uninjured hand was cuffed to the stretcher on which he lay.

Ghost sat a yard away looking like he was unhappy to have had his fun interrupted. His white pelt was streaked with blood, but he didn't appear to be seriously hurt. I stood over the shooter and looked down at him.

"What's his status?"

Khalid rocked back on his heels. "He's lost a lot of blood, but we've stabilized him for transport."

"Put him in the back of the TacV. Do not transport him until I say so. I need to ask him some questions, but we need privacy. Is he able to talk?"

The shooter answered that one himself. He glared up at me and said, "Fuck you."

I smiled at him.

Chapter Fifty-six

While the shooter was being loaded, I popped the lock on my Explorer, found a plastic container of Wet Ones, and did a quick job of cleaning and examining Ghost. He had some minor cuts from flying debris and a splinter thick as a coffee stirrer gouged into his back. I told him to sit and be still and I pulled it out. Ghost whined and even bared a tooth at me, but it was all show. He braved it out, and luckily the splinter had gone in at an angle so it stuck mostly in the rubbery top skin, missing the real meat and muscle below. The cut didn't even bleed much. I put a pad on it and wound some surgical gauze around his barrel chest.

"You'll live, fella."

Ghost used his "I'm dying, please be kind" face on me, so I gave him a couple of Snausages and emptied a bottle of spring water into his plastic bowl. My hands were shaking so badly I spilled half of it.

Ghost licked my hand and looked into my eyes for a moment before he bent and began lapping up the water. Yeah, the best of friends, no doubt.

My phone rang and I sat on the ground to take the call. Church.

"Ten shooters. Nine dead, one in DMS custody, and—"

He cut me off. "How is Circe? Is she injured?"

"No. In fact, she took out one of the shooters."

There was a long silence. "She killed him?"

"Yes. But listen, there's more. Your friend Marty Hanler . . . he's gone, Boss. He went down in the initial attack. He never saw it coming, and I doubt he felt anything."

Church was silent.

How did a guy like him process that kind of news? I've buried a lot of loved ones over the years and I've had to eat a lot of my own pain, but I also have had friends, like Rudy, my dad and my brother, and for a while Grace to help me deal.

Who did Church have?

All he said was, "That is unfortunate."

Then he changed his tone, shifting into a "business as usual" mode that I found disconcerting.

He said, "Talk to that prisoner. Find out what he knows."

"I can't do that with a lot of civilians around."

"Then do it in the air. I'm sending a Chinook from Willow Grove. Rendezvous with it in Tamanend Park. It's two miles up Route 232."

"Copy that."

"Is the prisoner stable enough for interrogation?"

"Probably, but he's a pro. He's not going to talk—"

"Captain," Church snapped, "I'm not asking for an estimate on how difficult it is for you to do your job. People are dying and he has information we need. Surely some solutions will occur to you."

He hung up.

Ouch.

* * *

I WAS JUST about to climb into the back of the DMS TacV when Circe came out of the ruined Starbucks, wiping her hands with a wad of paper napkins. Her hair was in disarray and there were bloodstains on her clothes. Ghost wagged his tail at her. Guess he forgave her for being a cat person.

"How are you?" I asked. It was one of those insanely lame questions we ask when nothing more sensible occurs to us.

She shrugged, then shook her head. "I don't know."

"You did good work back there," I said.

Saying that caused a visible change in her. One moment she was a doctor who had spent the last twenty minutes struggling to save lives—she had been surrounded by death and blood, but to a degree she was in a known world and in the center of her own power—then my words jarred her back to the moment before she had entered the coffeehouse. She looked down at the powder burns on her hand. Circe had the calluses of someone who spent regular hours on a pistol range, and she'd handled her gun with professional skill and accuracy. Even so, her face went paler still and her mouth twisted into sickness.

"I don't understand this," she said. "Why did they do this?"

"That's what I intend to find out."

"I mean . . . why hit us? We're not even close to anything yet."

Her chest hitched as if she was fighting a sob. Or struggling to swallow bile that had boiled up into her throat.

"Where'd you get the gun?" I asked.

Jonathan Maberry

"It's mine."

"You had it on the plane?"

"Yes. I'm cleared to carry because of my work with *Sea of Hope*. I have to be ready to fly anywhere at a moment's notice. Hugo Vox and Mr. Church cleared it for me."

"You learn how to shoot at T-Town?"

She nodded and brushed a tear from her eye.

"Is this the first time you shot someone?" I asked gently.

She nodded again. "I've fired I don't know how many rounds at the combat ranges . . . but . . . but . . ."

Suddenly her color changed from white to green. She abruptly spun away from me, ran to the side of the building, and threw up in a trash can. I tried to comfort her, but she gave a violent shake of her head and I backed off.

Ghost gave me a "smooth move" look and whined a little as Circe continued to cough up her fear and disgust and—if she was as human as the rest of us—self-loathing.

I understood that. No matter how much you hate someone, no matter how justified you are in pulling the trigger, at the end of the day there are only three possible emotional reactions to killing another human being. You either like it, in which case you shouldn't ever be allowed to touch a gun again. Or you feel nothing, in which case the words "cry for help" should be tattooed on your forehead and they should lead you away to a nice, comfy therapist's couch. Or you feel like you just committed an unforgivable sin. After the moment is over, as you stand there feeling the adrenaline ooze out of your pores and the cordite stink of discharged rounds mixes with the coppery smell of blood, you feel the enormity of it. You took a life.

Circe had shooter's calluses. She had to have prepared for this moment.

That preparation saved lives, but you absolutely cannot fully prepare a person for the reality of having ended a human life. But the fact that it appalled Circe was proof of a heart and mind that was not already inured to basic humanity or corrupted by a disregard for the sanctity of all life.

I wanted to tell Circe this, but this wasn't the time. She wouldn't be able to hear it now. Right now she needed to survive the reality of the event, and that would add a layer of callus on her soul.

Damn.

"I got this," said a voice, and I turned to see DeeDee. She closed on Circe and put a sisterly hand on her shoulder. A lot has been said about "brothers in arms." In the twenty-first century we're going to have to broaden that view to include sisters in arms. I backed off and then turned toward the TacV, where my suspect waited.

Interlude Thirty-eight

The Milhaus Estate
Martha's Vineyard, Massachusetts
December 19, 6:04 P.M. EST

On Martha's Vineyard, police cars and an ambulance were tearing along the winding back roads toward the mansion of H. Carlton Milhaus, CEO of Milhaus and

Berk Publishing. The company published, among other periodicals, *The Fiscal Conservative* and *Right Smart*. Milhaus's eldest daughter, Sandra, was using the estate for a combination holiday party for the company's executives and fund-raiser for the Republic senator from Massachusetts.

As the emergency vehicles roared through the gates, the officers could see that every light in the house was on. Despite the cold, people in cocktail dresses and dinner jackets were standing outside on the patio and lawn. Many of them had hands to their throats or faces, and all of them had shocked eyes.

The first-in officers knew that everything they said, everything they did, here among these people would be scrutinized. A single misstep, a carelessly chosen word, could crush their careers. They'd seen it happen over and over again to their peers. Their former peers.

The first responders entered with as much haste as caution would allow. The EMTs were a dozen steps behind.

They stepped into a world of elegance and sophistication, of holiday cheer and conspicuous wealth, of shocked white faces and bright red blood.

Sandra Milhaus lay faceup, her feet on the second and third steps of the grand staircase, her arms flung wide with an inartistic abandon, her green silk gown twisted around her pale legs. Her eyes were open, as was her mouth. Her coiffed blond curls lay in the center of a pool of blood that, by perverse chance, spread around her like a halo and reflected the Christmas lights on the walls and banister. That she was dead was obvious, even from a dozen feet away.

The officers cut each other a quick glance, knowing they had just stepped out of a potential "incident" at the party of one of the richest families on the Vineyard and stepped into a crime scene that would be front-page news, even with all that was going on in London. When they were still five feet away they froze.

Sandra Milhaus was not merely dead. Every inch of exposed skin was covered with lumps like boils. Some of them had clearly burst and leaked blood or clear fluid that was tinged with pink. The others were pale knobs, the color lost from the settling of blood in her body after her heart had stopped.

They stood on either side of her, careful not to step in the blood.

"Who can tell me what happened?" asked Jimmy Redwood, the male officer. "Was she allergic to anything?"

There were a hundred people clustered around. On the stairs and balcony above, in the open doorway of the grand ballroom to their right and the dining room to their left. The officers recognized many of the faces from the news.

Redwood's partner, Debbie Tobias, turned to the nearest person, an older woman. "Ma'am, do you know if she ate something she wasn't supposed to?"

The woman shook her head and didn't—or perhaps couldn't—answer.

"Please," said Tobias, pitching her voice for authority but not intimidation, "was she sick before the party?"

The EMTs came hustling in, carrying their heavy equipment boxes.

"What have we got, Jimmy?" the lead paramedic asked Redwood.

"I don't know, Barney. Looks like allergic reaction."

The EMT closed on the body. And stopped.

They looked at each other.

This wasn't anaphylaxis.

"Oh, shit," said Barney.

His partner, Paresh, cut a worried look at the crowd and then pulled Tobias closer. He whispered urgently in her ear, "Get everyone out of here, but keep them contained."

Barney was already on the phone, calling in the visible symptoms. Neither he nor his partner made any attempt to touch Sandra Milhaus.

Tobias looked up at Paresh. "What is it?"

But the EMT shook his head. "I don't know. But for God's sake get these people contained, Debbie. *Now!*"

Interlude Thirty-nine

Feasterville, Pennsylvania
December 19, 6:05 P.M. EST

Rafael Santoro did not want to make this call. In all the years during which he had served the Goddess and the Seven Kings he had only had to make such a call twice. This was the third time he would have to report not one failure but two.

The King of Plagues answered, his voice mildly distorted by his scrambler.

Instead of a greeting, Gault said, "I'm watching CNN. I'm hearing a lot about an attack on a house in Jenkintown that ended with four dead and two taken. I'm also hearing about a bunch of trigger-happy wankers who shot up an effing Starbucks. I'm hearing about civilian casualties. I'm hearing about a dead sodding writer. Can you guess what I'm not hearing about? I'm not hearing about Amber-fucking-Taylor and her children being spooned into body bags. I'm not hearing about a dead federal agent named Joe-effing-Ledger. Want to fucking tell me why not?"

Santoro took a calming breath. He was deeply ashamed. "I have no excuses."

"Who'd you send? The frigging Mousketeers?"

"I used local assets on both jobs."

"Kingsmen?"

"Chosen. Trey Foster and his team out of Philadelphia were given the Taylor pickup. I used Sarducci and his team for Starbucks. That is the Jersey crew I've used for three situations for the Kings over the last year."

"Did they screw those up, too?" Gault's voice was loud and full of acid.

"No," said Santoro calmly. "Both teams have done good work for us in the past."

"God damn it, Rafael."

"They were unprepared for the arrival of DMS field teams at both locations."

"What?" Gault screamed the question so loud Santoro winced and held the phone away from his ear. When the King of Plagues was done shouting, Santoro explained what had happened.

"Such calamities are the price when action is taken without planning, yes? Had I been given more time,

I would have scouted the area, set watchers on the perimeter, and listened for activity on our information stream. However . . ." He let the rest hang.

"Describe them to me," snapped Gault, and when Santoro finished he said, "That's sodding Echo Team. They're Ledger's team, but what the bloody hell are they doing in Southampton?"

Gault shouted more and Santoro endured it, sighing quietly as he drove. As much as he loved and honored the new consort of the Goddess and even though he would gladly die for this man, as he would for any of the Kings, Sebastian Gault could be a tiresome bore. And he was loud. Santoro, however, was never loud. Loud was crass—except for the loud shrieks and cries of his *angels* in their moment of transformation.

"How bad is this?" asked Gault.

"Nine of the Jersey team are dead, as are four of the Philadelphia team. Three operatives are in DMS custody."

"Can you get to them?"

"Impossible."

"What do they know?"

"Nothing of any value. Even under torture they have nothing useful to reveal."

Which was only partly true. They knew Santoro's name and that he worked for the Seven Kings, but Santoro did not think that this provided enough of a threat to risk having the King of Plagues lose his temper again.

"What would you like me to do?"

Gault sighed. "There's nothing you can do. Let the DMS have them." He sighed again, deeply and for a long time. Santoro could almost feel Gault's blood pressure dropping. "Besides . . . and to be fair, I did ask for this to be splashed across the news feeds. It was. I was hoping that it would reinforce the threatening presence of the Kings . . . not make us look like imbeciles."

Santoro did not comment.

"Very well," said Gault. "We're going to write this off. Perhaps the Goddess can find a way to spin this in our favor. In the meantime, put a couple of people you can trust on Ledger, and if the opportunity comes up kill the bloody bastard."

"With pleasure."

"Meanwhile, we have bigger fish to fry. The Inner Circle should be getting some very bad news right about now. You did good work setting that up," Gault said grudgingly. "The Goddess is well pleased."

"It is always my pleasure to serve the Goddess," said Santoro.

He disconnected and drove randomly through the towns that adjoined Southampton. It hurt him that both of his victims had slipped the punch. Perhaps, if he was lucky and the grace of the Goddess touched his destiny, he would have another opportunity to kill those two. This time, however, he would do the job himself. Not once in his entire life had Santoro failed when he, rather than a team, was the instrument of death. Not once.

Chapter Fifty-seven

We crowded into the back of Black Bess. Top, Bunny, Ghost, and me. The others established a perimeter outside and nobody got past them.

I sat on the bunk opposite the prisoner. Ghost sat on the floor, his head rising above the level of the gurney, his dark eyes filled with predatory intensity. The shooter looked from me, to Ghost, to Top and Bunny and back again. It was evident he didn't like what he saw in our faces. No reason he should. The TacV was wired for digital recording, and Top gave me a wink to indicate that it was running.

"Here's the way it sits, dickhead," I said to the shooter. "You're in the shit up to your eyeballs. There are eight dead civilians and nineteen wounded. We're with Homeland and you've been designated as an enemy combatant and a terrorist, so the Patriot Act just got shoved up your ass. That means you have no rights. You don't get a lawyer, you don't get to make a phone call, and you are about to vanish from the face of the earth."

"Kiss my nut sac," he said with a sneer. Even with the morphine it was a pretty good hard-guy act. But he was playing to a tough crowd.

I continued to smile. Bunny, his bulk filling the entire back of the truck, squatted on his heels and chewed gum. Top sat on a metal equipment case just above the shooter's head, and his face was one that I wouldn't have wanted to look into if I was this deep in my own crap.

"You're going to be on suicide watch, so you won't be sneaking out of this." I kept my tone normal, my voice quiet and reasonable. Giving him information, not making threats. Letting him think he had bargaining room. "You'll disappear into the system. You'll get the very best medical care. You might even keep that hand. We'll want you healthy because the stronger you are, the longer you'll last in interrogation. Understand me, friend, you won't hold out . . . you'll just last longer. We will get every bit of information you have. No question about it."

He grinned at me with bloody teeth. "Take your best shot, asshole."

His accent was New Jersey. Local boy.

"Print him," I said, and Bunny produced a small electronic device.

The shooter clutched his good hand into a fist.

Bunny popped his gum. "I can take prints off severed fingers, too, genius."

Jersey Boy kept his fist clenched. He was playing this role to the end.

"Take 'em from the other hand," said Top, nodding to the swollen tips of fingers that stuck out of the layers of gauze around Jersey Boy's torn and shattered forearm.

Bunny left the fingers attached but he used the injured hand to take the prints. It got very loud in the TacV. Ghost broke into a stream of agitated barks, and I let him go for a while, then quieted him with a control word. He settled down, but he continued to stare at the shooter as if he was an unfinished lunch.

Jersey Boy lapsed into a breathless, panting silence. Greasy sweat glistened on his face.

Bunny checked each contact scan and then pressed the upload button that sent the high-res digital files to the satellite. MindReader would have them in ten seconds and we'd have a match in a couple of hours.

"You got one chance to make the rest of this process a lot less painful," I said. "Talk to me now. Freely, openly, without coercion. You help us and I promise you that we will reward that cooperation."

Jersey Boy shook his head. I had to give the guy points for balls—he had a real pair of clankers. No frigging brains at all, though, because I believe he actually thought he was going to tough it out.

Top must have been reading my thoughts. "Boy's too stupid to know when someone's handing him a lifeline."

"That ain't a lifeline, Tupac," the shooter said. "You want to put me in jail for the rest of my life, go ahead. Put me in Gitmo if you want. Don't matter a goddamn thing. My man Santoro will have me back on the street inside a month."

"You think so?"

He raised his head and glared at me. "I know so. Do whatever you want. You dickwipes just stepped into a world of hurt bigger than anything you ever heard of. The Seven Kings are going to rip your world apart, Ledger. You and the rest of the DMS. You, that psychopath Church, that cunt O'Tree, these ass clowns here—all of you are already dead and you just don't know it yet."

Top grunted in real surprise. "Well, well," he said, "ain't that interesting as shit?"

Bunny blew a big pink bubble, popped it, and continued to chew. His poker face was still in place, but from the way the muscles at the corners of his jaw bunched and flexed I knew that he was probably as rattled as I was.

The shooter had said the name Santoro. That was a nice name. A Spanish name. Very interesting.

"The 'Seven Kings,' huh?" I said. "Why don't you tell us all about them?"

"Why don't you suck my—"

Without saying a word, Bunny reached out and grabbed Jersey Boy's shattered wrist, gave it a light squeeze. It wouldn't have dented a soda can, but the shooter screamed loud enough to hurt my ears.

Outside I heard the sergeant supervisor yelling indignantly, demanding to be let in. DeeDee's voice cut him off in mid-protest. I couldn't hear what she was saying, but it redirected his outrage from me to her.

When Bunny released Jersey Boy's wrist the bandages were soaked through with blood and the man's face was gray. Without taking my eyes off him, I said, "Top, tell the blues that we're commandeering this prisoner on the grounds of national security. Have the rest of the team follow. Bunny, you're driving."

"Where we going, Boss?" Bunny asked as he clambered past me into the driver's seat.

"Somewhere . . . quiet," I said, and gave him directions to Tamanend Park.

"You're digging your own grave, Ledger," said the shooter. "We're going to kill everyone you ever knew or loved. Your family, your friends, your neighbors, and your dog. You just signed their death warrants."

I rose and leaned over the prisoner and bent my face to within an inch of his. I said nothing. No words could convey the outrage, naked fury, and bottomless contempt I felt, so instead I smiled at him. It wasn't the Cop or the Modern Man smiling. This was the blood grin of the Warrior who crouched inside my head and knew that he was about to be let out to play.

The shooter must not have liked that smile, because after a few seconds the contemptuous grin he wore dimmed and then faded completely. And he looked very appropriately afraid.

Interlude Forty

Aboard the *Delta of Venus*
The St. Lawrence River
December 19, 6:17 P.M. EST

Sebastian Gault sat on the edge of the sofa, bent forward with his elbows on his thighs, watching as Eris worked her magic on the computer. The boat rocked gently with the cross-waves of the choppy St. Lawrence River as the captain steered it away from Crown Island.

All day she had been seeding the Net with vague comments about the wrath of the Goddess striking down the firstborn of the wicked. That sort of thing. She crafted original posts and sent them to her team, who kept the social media engines revving hour after hour. Online speculation as to who these firstborn were was spreading like wildfire. In the wake of the London bombing and what was now being called a terrorist attack in Southampton, Pennsylvania, these posts were having a measurable effect on the world market. The President had ordered Wall Street shut down for another day, but other markets around the world were staggering.

Gault got up and strolled over to the wet bar to make drinks. "I wish there was a way you could aim your virtual hate arrows at the real world."

"At Joe Ledger," she said with a laugh.

"Yes. I want *his* balls nailed to my trophy wall."

"You're even talking like a King now. How delightful, lovely boy."

Gault laughed and sat down to watch her magic turn to dark sorcery.

Chapter Fifty-eight

The Crime Scene
Southampton, Pennsylvania
December 19, 6:09 P.M. EST

I stepped outside the TacV and called Church.

"Santoro?" He tasted the name. "Could be our Spaniard. I'll have Bug run that. You get anything else from him?"

"Not as much as I will get."

"He needs to have a pulse when he gets to the Hangar, Captain."

"Don't sweat that, Boss. He'll be alive and kicking. Can't say he'll be enjoying life, but that's the breaks."

"Tragic. What else do you need?"

"We have to roll, which means I'm going to lose control of this scene. If the shooters met with Santoro, then there is a chance, however small, that we can pick up some DNA or hair and fibers from their gear and vehicles. I need you to talk to someone who will in turn call Southampton PD and impress upon them the importance of not touching a goddamn thing."

"Not a problem. Jerry Spencer touched down at Philly International eight minutes ago. I had Fran Kirsch drive up from the Warehouse with a full team and all the gear Jerry will need."

Fran was a forensic photographer and Jerry's right hand. She had all of the warmth and personality he lacked. She also had a degree in psychology, which helped with profiling while collecting and analyzing the evidence.

"Good. You get anything more out of the two survivors from Jenkintown?"

"No. They're both Chosen—too low-level to be of any use."

"Damn."

"I want you and Dr. Sanchez up here at the Hangar ASAP. Bring Dr. O'Tree as well." He paused. "How is she handling this?"

I was surprised he cared enough to ask. "She's pretty rattled. First time she's dropped someone. It leaves a mark."

"Yes," he said, and I could hear the whisper of ghosts in his voice.

THE PARK WAS a few miles away. We loaded Rudy and the shooter into the waiting Chinook. I detailed

DeeDee and John Smith to drive Black Bess to Brooklyn. The rest of us piled into the bird. Once we were airborne I told Ghost to lie down and stay; then I checked on Rudy. Since he'd been shot, Circe seemed to have claimed the role of mother hen. She got him situated in as much comfort as the transport helicopter would allow and heaped blankets on him to prevent shock. She hooked an IV bag to a clip on the wall.

I saw that his eyes were open and he was looking around trying to make sense of where he was.

"Hey, Rude," I said, squatting in front of him, "how you doing, buddy? Are you comfortable? Anything I can—"

"Vete a la verga, pendejo," he snarled with as much venom as morphine would allow.

"All righty then, I can see you need your rest." I turned to Circe. "Say, Doc, can you give him another dose of morphine?"

"He's already had enough."

"No, he hasn't."

Circe gave me a withering look and tucked the blankets in under Rudy's chin.

I MADE MY way aft to where Khalid was watching over the prisoner.

"Joe . . ."

I turned to see Circe hurrying after me. She looked fierce and angry.

"Doc, are you going to tell me to go fuck myself, too?"

"Is that what he said?"

"Pretty much."

"He's never been shot before."

"I know, and I'm sorry that he's joined the club."

"Look," she said. "I know you're going to interrogate the prisoner and—"

"Doc, if you're winding up to give me a speech about human rights and civil liberties, then save—"

"No," she said, cutting me off. "I just spent the last forty minutes doing patch jobs on men, women, and children. Children, Joe. Every person in that place was wounded. Eight are dead. Four will lose limbs and at least one fifteen-year-old girl is going to be a quadriplegic and—"

"I was there, Doc. What's your point?"

She stepped close and looked up at me with eyes that were as black and merciless as the twin holes of a double-barreled shotgun. She jabbed the hard nail of a stiffened index finger into my chest and in a fierce voice she said, "If that son of a bitch in there knows something that might stop this from happening, then you go and *fucking get it.*"

I've seldom heard anyone put as much venom in a single sentence. I stepped back, reassessing everything about this woman. For just a second her tone of voice and ferocity of personality reminded me of Mr. Church. No wonder he respected her. I smiled.

"This isn't something to smile about, Captain. I didn't say to enjoy it. Just get it done."

"Hooah, Doc."

She held her ground for a moment, her eyes full of challenge and aggression; then she whirled and stomped back through the cabin and sat down next to Rudy. I saw her take his hand. She did not look at me again.

After a moment I turned and went aft. Jersey Boy watched me come, and he glared a "do your worst" look at me.

"He's a jumped-up street punk," murmured Khalid. "He may not know much."

"We'll see."

As it turns out, he knew a lot. Not as much as I wanted to know, but more than we already knew. And more than he wanted to give.

Interlude Forty-one

New York City
December 19, 7:26 P.M. EST

Toys sat in the American's office, the bottle of tequila nearly empty and resting against his crotch. He was in the big man's chair, watching the iron gray clouds scrape their way across the winter sky and thinking some of the darkest thoughts he owned. The first time his cell phone rang he ignored it. And the second. Finally, when it began ringing for the third time in five minutes he snatched it up, expecting it to be Gault, expecting this to be the call that would end with his oldest friend telling him to sod off . . . but it was not Gault.

Toys punched the button. "Hello?"

"How's the mouth?" asked the American.

"Less dreadful."

"Any tequila left?"

"Not much."

"Finish the bottle if you want. Good for whatever ails you."

"This is why you've been calling?"

"Hardly. I wanted you to know that Mommy Dearest and her boy toy have launched phase two of the Initiative. The bodies are already dropping."

Toys sighed. "Guess there's no turning back now."

"Nope. On the upside, Joe Ledger is still sucking air."

"What?"

"Yeah, the crew Santoro hired screwed the pooch. It's on the news. The rest of the Kings aren't going to love Gault for this. It makes us look clumsy."

"How'd Ledger escape? I thought Santoro was sending a whole team. Did you do something?"

"Me? No. Ledger slipped the punch all by himself. Well, he had his crew of goons. Echo Team. And . . . you'll dig this . . . Circe O'Tree was there. She apparently capped one of Santoro's shooters."

Toys started to laugh, but it hurt his mouth. "Maybe Eris will finally have that stroke I keep hoping for," he said.

"Hey now . . . that's my mother," said the American, but he was laughing, too.

Their laughter faded into a thoughtful silence. Finally, Toys said, "Isn't there any way to stop the second phase?"

The American grunted. "Not a chance. It's already too late."

"Damn."

"You worry too much, kiddo, and you're looking at the wrong end of the timetable. Who gives a flying fuck if some of the Bonesmen spawn bite it? You need to decide if you want to let Gault's showpiece play itself out."

"He closed me out of that whole thing. What can *I* do?"

The American was quiet for a moment. "Maybe something will occur to you," he said at last, and then he hung up.

Toys set the phone down on the desk. He placed it next to the other phone, the one the American had dropped. Toys leaned forward on his elbows and considered that other phone for a long time.

Something did, in fact, occur to him.

Chapter Fifty-nine

In Flight
December 19, 7:43 P.M. EST

For most of the flight I sat alone, processing what I'd learned from the shooter—whose name was Sarducci—and seeing if any of these new pieces fit the weird puzzle that was the Seven Kings. The fact of there being so many crucial employees in secure facilities kept shouting in the darkness of my thoughts, but I couldn't yet understand what it was trying to tell me. Abstract thinking is like that. You gather facts and then throw them into a bag with guesses and bits of the unknown, and either a picture leaps out or it doesn't. I kept shaking the bag and reaching in for a new fistful of Scrabble pieces.

When my phone rang I expected it to be Church, but the caller ID was blank, which was weird, because I have a DMS account. Nobody's supposed to be an "unknown caller" to us.

"Yeah," I said neutrally.

There was nothing. No . . . I could hear someone breathing.

"Bad time for an obscene phone call, sport," I said.

"Joe Ledger?"

A male voice. Soft, a trace of an accent.

"I'll see if he's in. Who's calling?"

"Don't be clever," he said. "We don't have that kind of time."

I was sure it was a voice I hadn't heard before. He was trying to speak with an American accent, but it was a fake. I was sure of it. I pressed the three-digit code to initiate a trace.

"It's your dime," I said.

"You're looking for the Seven Kings."

Ah. "Who are you?"

"Don't be daft," he said. "And don't bother to trace this call. It's routed through a dozen networks on five continents."

"Are you the person who's been calling Mr. Church?"

"No. But—"

"Are you calling to screw around or—?"

"No, I'm calling to collect my thirty pieces of silver," he said. He sighed and I waited. "I am not going to tell you who the Kings are or where to find them. Not all of them. I am not going to reveal all of their plans or give you the intelligence necessary to bring down the entire operation. That really would be a betrayal."

Even with the scrambler I could hear the turmoil in his voice. It made him sound hysterical and even a little drunk. Either way, it was clear that this was someone who absolutely did not want to make this call.

"I am, however, going to offer you a deal."

"I'm listening."

"This isn't for me," he said, "and I want your word."

"I can't give any word unless I know what I'm swearing to."

He paused and he was probably chewing his nails.

"I am going to say a name. It's all I can give you, but you should be able to put two and two together to figure where to be to stop what the Seven Kings are really doing. You'll save a lot of lives. You'll be a hero."

"I'm not looking to be a hero, sport. If you have information that can save lives, then let me have it."

"I want your word. That's the price."

"My word on what?"

"That you won't kill him."

"Kill who? The person whose name you're going to give me?"

"Yes. Swear to me that you won't kill him and I'll tell you."

"How can I guarantee that?"

"You're smart, Ledger. You'll figure out a way. Do I have your word?"

I hesitated.

"Or," he said, "I could hang up right now and you can watch the world burn. You think that what's on the telly is the *real* news? Believe me, mate, this is the warm-up act. I want you to do something about it."

"You have a lot of faith in me."

"I should. I already have scars because of you," he snarled.

"Whoa, slow down. Do I *know* you?"

His snarl turned into a laugh. "No . . . I doubt you

even know my name. But you know *his*. You're almost as much to blame as *she* is. Him and that slut Amirah."

And that fast someone sucked all the air out of the chopper's cabin.

Amirah.

Holy Mother of God.

I knew the name he was going to give me. I knew it and I prayed like hell that I was wrong.

"Okay," I said quietly, hardly trusting my voice not to crack, "tell me."

"Give me your word."

What could I do? I could lie, and it probably would be a lie. He would have to know that. So, what value did my word have to this man? On the other hand, what did I have to lose?

"Very well," I said. "I give you my word that if I can take him alive and unharmed, I will."

"Swear it."

I did. I actually did.

There was a muffled sound. It wasn't a laugh; I was sure of it. I think it was a sob.

He said, "There are Seven Kings. Gold, Fear, Lies, Plagues, Famine, War, and Thieves." He took a breath. "Sebastian Gault is the King of Plagues. If he isn't stopped, he'll wipe them all out. And I know—I *know*—that he won't stop there. She'll keep pushing him and pushing him, filling his head with dreams of godhood until he creates another doomsday plague. I know he'll do it . . . unless you stop him."

I closed my eyes. God.

Sebastian Gault.

The man who tried to release the Seif Al Din pathogen. The man who came close—so very close—to destroying everything. It was because of him that I was sought out and recruited into the DMS. The last guy to hold my job had been killed. Slaughtered along with his entire team.

Sebastian Gault. If I had a personal bogeyman, then he was it.

After we stopped the release of Gault's pathogen, a worldwide manhunt was launched. As large and as aggressive as the search for Osama bin Laden—and so far, just as futile. We'd begun to suspect that Gault was dead, his body burned in the same geothermal meltdown that had destroyed the lab where Seif Al Din was created. But now . . . Gault *and* the Seven Kings.

I felt as if I was falling through space. I pressed my back against the cold metal skin of the Chinook.

"Gault is responsible for the Hospital . . . for Area 51? Gault's part of the Seven Kings?"

"Only for a few months. We were brought into this after . . . after . . ."

"After the Seif Al Din. A lot of people thought Gault died in Afghanistan."

The man laughed. A small, sad sound. "Maybe he should have. Maybe we both should have."

And that's when I knew who the caller was.

"You said that what's happening now was part of something else, something bigger?"

"Yes. Gault and the bitch. They've taken this whole thing away from the Kings and they're going to bury us all with it."

"Who is the woman? What's her name?"

I knew that it couldn't be Amirah, Gault's former

partner and the designer of the Seif Al Din pathogen. I knew for sure that she was dead. I'd pulled the trigger.

"No," he said. "You don't get that."

"Then give me something else," I said. "Give me Santoro."

"Christ! How do you even know that name?"

"Give him to me."

"Why?"

"If you know him, then you know why. Give me him and I'll move heaven and earth to protect Gault."

He was quiet for a moment. My cell had been running the trace for almost two minutes now and it hadn't beeped the signal that alerted me to a successful hit. Must be the same technology Deep Throat used.

"Find Gault and you'll find Santoro. That psycho prick will be in the thick of it. He wouldn't miss an opportunity to see that much pain. Now, I'm sorry, I have to g—"

I took a risk. "Toys!"

I expected a scream or a yell of denial or a theatrical attempt to pretend ignorance. Instead he gave a small laugh. The risk had paid off. Gault's best friend, valet, personal assistant, and maybe more. Alexander Chismer.

Toys.

"See?" Toys said shakily. "I said you were smart. That's why they tried to kill you today. I'll give you one more thing and you have to remember it; otherwise all of this goes to shit."

"Tell me."

"*They* are everywhere. The Kings, their agents, Santoro's people. They're everywhere. Even some of the people you work with and some of the people you're going to try and rescue. Some belong to the Kings, and some will do anything to keep Santoro out of their lives. You understand what I mean? You can't trust anyone. Or anything. Nothing is what it seems. It never is with the Kings. That's it, that's all I can tell you. Now figure out the rest."

But he did not disconnect. I waited through several heavy seconds.

This time I knew the sound I heard was a sob. Toys said, "If you succeed, Ledger . . . do me one more favor."

"If I can."

"If you save all the lives that are on the line . . . see if you can spare a little pity. Go to church and light a candle."

"For Gault?"

"No," he said. "For my soul."

Chapter Sixty

Over Pennsylvania Airspace
December 19, 7:46 P.M. EST

I stared at my cell phone for a full minute.

"God Almighty," I said aloud. Ghost heard the tone of my voice and came over to me and licked my face, looking into my eyes to see if the pack was in some kind of trouble. It surely, surely was.

And yet . . .

Toys.

It happens that way more often than people think. Cops spend 90 percent of a case gathering evidence, analyzing it, doing interviews, running computer searches, and building a profile of the possible culprit, and then they get a phone call from out of left field that tells them who, what, when, and where. Ten times more criminal cases have been solved by anonymous tipsters, people hoping for rewards or confidential informants.

Who in hell would ever expect Toys to be mine? Or to be the one who hammered a crack into the hardest case the DMS ever tackled.

I was sweating badly and I dragged a forearm across my eyes.

They *are everywhere. . . . Even some of the people you work with and some of the people you're going to try and rescue.*

I looked around the cabin of the Chinook and inside my head the Warrior was drawing his knife and squinting through the gloom.

Who did I trust? I'd been away for months, and Santoro had more than shown that he could turn ordinary and trustworthy people into killers.

I thumbed open my sports coat. The handle of the Beretta was comfortably close.

Rudy?

He lay in a narcotic doze while Circe sat beside him, tapping away on her laptop. If Rudy was under Santoro's thumb, I think I'd lose it. Rudy was my best friend. Closer to me than my own brother. He was the only person on earth I trusted completely. No . . . no, it couldn't be Rudy.

Circe?

Who was she really? She worked for Hugo Vox at

Terror Town. She was in position to know the security secrets of a lot of crucial operations, and that included probably access to security information on facilities like the London Hospital, Fair Isle, maybe even Area 51. After all, Church and Vox both trusted her. An unscrupulous person could exploit that trust. Sure, she looked beautiful and innocent and forthright, but she could also be a good actress. I'd met spies and moles before. They aren't picked for that kind of work if you could just look at them and say, *Yep, that there's a spy.*

And she was pretty handy with a gun. On the other hand, she didn't pop a cap in my favorite head, so props for showing good judgment. Unless that was part of a plan to win my confidence and insinuate herself into the DMS.

Across the cabin, Circe brushed dark curls from her face; then she looked at Rudy and placed a hand very tenderly on his chest and kept it there for almost a minute while he slept. I didn't want it to be her.

A few feet away, Top and Bunny were seated side by side. Bunny was dozing; Top was strip-cleaning his M4. He caught me looking and gave me a slow nod. I nodded back.

Bunny and Top had been with me since I joined Echo Team. We'd saved each other's lives a dozen times over. They were brothers to me.

On the other hand, Bunny had four sisters and lots of nieces and nephews. He had parents. That gave the Kings a lot of dials they could turn. Same with Top. His daughter, Monique, lost both her legs in Baghdad two Christmases ago. A Taliban mine blew up under her

Bradley. Top was divorced; his ex-wife was a nurse. I knew Top still cared for her, maybe even still loved her, and he certainly loved his daughter. If Santoro threatened them, especially Top's wheelchair-bound daughter, was there anything he *wouldn't* do to protect them?

That was a hard call. I'd like to think that both men would come to me, or to Church, with it. Of course . . . I'd been away, out of touch and out of reach.

What would I do if one of them had been turned by the Kings?

I'd try to save them if I could. Them and theirs. And if I couldn't? If they came at me? Shit. I knew what I would do, and I could hear the Warrior grunt his dark approval.

That left Khalid, DeeDee, and John Smith. I knew them, but I didn't really *know* them. We had less history. Smith was a closed book that nobody could read. Maybe Church, maybe Rudy. No one else.

DeeDee? She had no family, no close friends. If she was a rotten apple, it would be more likely in the role of a spy rather than a coerced victim.

Khalid? The doctor and scholar who was also a first-class shooter. I liked him and I knew that I trusted him. But it occurred to me that I didn't know much about his family. He had a brother here in the States, but the rest of his family lived in the Middle East. Iran, Egypt, and some in Saudi Arabia.

I realized that I was not adding Church to my list. If he was a bad guy, then we were all totally fucked. I'm pretty dangerous, but he scares me. He scares everyone. You simply cannot imagine him losing a fight, and I

doubt he ever has. He's brilliant, cold, vicious, detail ori-
ented, and largely a mystery. If it came down to a fight
between us, I didn't like my odds.

I flipped open my phone and called him. He picked
up on the third ring.

I told him everything Toys had said.

Church listened without comment and the silence
continued after I was done.

Finally, he said, "What's your ETA?"

"Thirty minutes."

"Talk to no one about this," he said. "No one."

I began to ask him a question, but Church hung up
on me.

I settled back against the wall, my jacket open and
the butt of my Beretta within easy reach, and stared into
the middle distance all the way to Brooklyn.

Chapter Sixty-one

The Hangar
Floyd Bennett Field, Brooklyn
December 19, 7:57 P.M. EST

Mr. Church's phone rang as he entered his office. He
looked at the screen display. He frowned and let it ring
twice more before he flipped it open.

"Deacon? You there?" said the gruff voice. "You got
a minute?"

"Half a minute, Hugo. What do you need?"

"I've been hearing some scary stuff. Is Circe okay?"

"You heard about Starbucks? Yes, she wasn't hurt."

"Did I hear right that she popped someone?"

"Yes."

"Her first time. Poor kid. I was kind of hoping she'd skip that milestone."

"Life's hard for a lot of people, Hugo."

"I know. . . . I heard about Marty, too."

Church said nothing.

"He deserved better than getting gunned down like a dog," Vox continued. "Ledger's a lucky bastard."

"He might disagree. People keep trying to kill him."

"He keeps not getting killed, though, Deac'. From what I heard about Starbucks, he's the luckiest son of a bitch on two legs."

Church said nothing.

"Did Ledger get any useful intel from the surviving shooter?"

"No," said Church. "The man is critically wounded and we don't expect him to recover. It's unlikely we'll get anything out of him."

There was a pause at the other end. "Really? I heard that he was talking and—"

"You've been misinformed, Hugo. We're getting nowhere with this. Now, I hate to break this off, but I have a meeting. I'll be in touch when I have something fresh."

Mr. Church disconnected and placed his phone on the desk. He walked around and sat in the leather chair. There was an open pack of vanilla wafers in the top drawer. He removed them, selected a cookie, and ate it slowly while staring at the silent phone.

Chapter Sixty-two

We came in low past the Gil Hodges Bridge and landed in a fenced-off compound near the Rockaway Inlet, just outside of Hangar Row in Floyd Bennett Field. There were six black unmarked DMS choppers lined up. Two AH-64D Apache Longbows, a monster of a Chinook like the one we were in, and three UH-60 Black Hawks. There were rows of Humvees and TacVs. Everywhere we looked there were armed guards. Everyone looked tense.

DeeDee and John Smith hadn't arrived with Black Bess, but knowing the way DeeDee drove, they wouldn't be far behind.

Sgt. Gus Dietrich met us on the helipad. He held out a hand. "Glad to see you boys in one piece. Well, mostly. Sorry to hear about Rudy taking a hit."

"Could have been worse," said Bunny.

"It could always be worse," agreed Dietrich.

Nurses and orderlies arrived with two-wheeled gurneys. Circe O'Tree took charge of the wounded as if it was her right, and the nurses did not argue the point. I found that odd but didn't comment on it.

The prisoner was hustled off with a pair of armed agents flanking his gurney. If he thought his day had been crappy so far, he was on his way to see Mr. Church, so it wasn't like things were going to be sunshine and puppies.

Dietrich led Echo Team and me through the main entrance.

This was the first time I had visited the headquarters of the Department of Military Sciences. It was at least twice the size of the Baltimore Warehouse, which was pretty big in its own right, and even bigger than Department Zero, the massive office in L.A. It housed over six hundred scientists, soldiers, and support staff.

"Mr. Church landed ten minutes ago," Dietrich said as he punched the code to open a side door. "Top, why don't you take your team in for some chow? Ask anyone and they'll show you where it is."

Top nodded and peeled off with the others to follow the gurneys. Dietrich turned back to me. "The Big Guy's expecting you."

Dietrich led me into the Hangar's operations command center. Ghost trotted along at my heels, eyes wide, nose and ears gathering data. The massive main room was circled with glass-enclosed labs and workrooms, and overhead was a latticework of steel walkways. There were more armed guards inside and a lot of people moving like busy ants in a nest. There were tiers of stainless-steel catwalks and elevated computer stations. Metal gleamed; colored lights flashed. It was Christmas in Bill Gates's head.

"Wow," I said. "Nice to see my tax dollars at work."

I saw Church, his head bowed in conversation with a short black woman with a round face, granny glasses halfway down her nose, and long dreadlocks. The person he was talking too made me do a double take. I tapped Dietrich on the shoulder.

"Okay . . . why is Whoopi Goldberg here and why is she talking with Mr. Church?"

Dietrich laughed and didn't reply. I felt like I was going crazy. The woman looked exactly like the actress. She wore a blouse with an orange Sudanese print, a necklace of chunky colored stones, and rings on every finger except her trigger finger. She smiled as we approached, but there was no trace of humor in the polished black ice of her eyes.

Church beckoned us closer.

"Captain Ledger," he said, "I want you to meet the DMS Chief of Operations—Aunt Sallie."

I was convinced that this was some kind of bizarre practical joke. "Um . . . hello?" I said, but as I extended my hand the woman spoke and the illusion was shattered as if she'd struck glass with a hammer.

"Feel free to wipe that shit-eating grin off your face, Captain," she said in an accent that was pure back-alley Brooklyn. "I'm *not* her, so let's just bury that nonsense right now."

I am seldom at a loss for words, but the best I could manage was a mumbled, "Ma'am," as I took her hand. She had a grip like a vise and she gave me one hard pump while she looked me up and down. Her gaze had the same invasive and impersonal precision as an X-ray.

Ghost sniffed her and then quickly backed up several paces and lay down.

Aunt Sallie studied me. "So, you're the hotshot shooter from Baltimore."

"I'll have to put that on my business card."

"The one who let Marty Hanler get killed."

I did a slow three-count before I trusted my voice to reply.

"It's a pleasure to meet you, too."

"Are we going to have to make sure you have full-squad backup every time something gets a little rough?"

"Feel free to kiss my ass," I said pleasantly.

"You got your full and complete share of mouth, don't you?"

Beside me I heard Dietrich murmur, "Oh boy."

Aunt Sallie turned to Church. "Give us a minute?"

Without waiting for a reply, she took me by the elbow and led me twenty paces away. The placement of her fingers on the nerve clusters was very precise. It hurt and she knew it hurt, but I didn't let so much as a flicker show on my face. She knew that, too.

When we were out of earshot she said, "Okay, Ledger, here's the deal. Marty Hanler was a good friend of Church's, and more important, he was a good friend of mine. We'd been through fire together. You let someone put him on their trophy wall, and that means you lost all points on my scorecard. Mr. Church may think you piss rainbows and shit little gold coins, but as far as I'm concerned you're a reckless field agent and a psychological basket of worms."

"We were ambushed by ten shooters with automatic weapons in a professional cross-fire attack. Let's see *you* do better."

"I *have* done better, and even at my age I can run your ass all over a live-fire combat range."

"Do you want to blame me for the four thousand dead at the London just because I was in England? How about

Hurricane Katrina? I went to Mardi Gras once. Do I look good for that?"

"Don't try to be smart, Ledger; you don't have the tools for it."

"You're a charming lady. So happy to make your acquaintance."

She let that pass. "Before Church hired you, all you did was some penny ante police bullshit and an Army tour during which all you did was jerk off. Before the DMS you had zero field time."

"And since then, ma'am, I—"

"Call me Aunt Sallie or Auntie," she snapped. "Call me ma'am again and I'll kneecap you. Don't think that's a joke."

"Whatever. If I'm supposed to be impressed by all this, I'm not. You don't like how I handle things? Too fucking bad. Church scouted me, so if you have any problems with my qualifications then you can take 'em and shove 'em where the sun don't shine. But let's be real clear on one point, *Auntie:* I don't give a rat's hairy ass what you think of me. Honestly. I really don't. I don't know you well enough to dislike you, but I could put some effort into that."

"Nice speech. Here's the bottom line: I read your psych profiles and I think you're a danger to our cause. Sure, you racked up some wins, but a lot of good people seem to die around you, and that marks you with a permanent red flag in my book."

"You finished?"

"For now."

"Fuck you," I said.

She smiled, then turned and walked back to Church and the others. I took a breath and followed.

"You two kiss and make up?" Church asked.

"Sure. I promised him a blow job later if he buys me dinner."

"Looking forward to it," I said.

Church said nothing. He carefully unwrapped a stick of gum and put it in his mouth, then folded the silver wrapper into a neat little square. We all watched him do it and I saw Dietrich's eyes flick from Church, to Aunt Sallie, then to me, and then he stared past me into the middle distance. He was having a very hard time keeping a straight face.

Finally Church said, "Captain Ledger, I would like you, Dr. O'Tree, Dr. Hu, and Aunt Sallie to join me for a brainstorming session. Let's convene in fifteen minutes. It's been a long, bad day for everyone, but we need to be sharp for this."

Auntie nodded and headed off to set things up, throwing me a short and pointedly dismissive look as she went.

Dietrich turned to follow, but I leaned in to whisper to him.

"Is she always like this?"

"Nah, you caught her on a good day. She's usually pretty cranky."

Church said, "Captain, you might use that time to clean up."

I nodded. My clothes were dark with dried blood and I still hadn't looked at the damage to my thigh, which hurt like a son of a bitch. I turned to go, but Church touched my arm.

"Hold on," he said quietly. We walked out of earshot

of the rest of the staff. After the reaming from Auntie I thought I was going to get fried by him, too, but instead he offered his hand. "You did good work today, Captain."

"Doesn't feel like it," I said honestly.

"Anyone can be ambushed. It's the nature of war."

"That doesn't make me feel any better."

"No," he agreed. He adjusted his glasses. "However, if the call you received is good intel then it's probably a game changer."

"You know, Boss," I said, "I listened to the tapes of your conversation with Deep Throat, and Toys isn't the guy who has been calling you."

"Same anti-trace technology, though."

"Yeah, which brings up its own set of questions. If Toys and Gault are part of the Kings organization, then can we continue to believe that Deep Throat is *not* also part of the Kings?"

Church nodded. "I've been giving that considerable thought, Captain, and I tend to agree with you. Either he's a mole who shares his phone with another mole or we're not seeing a conflict between organizations. I think this is an internal matter."

"Which explains why Deep Throat was so cagey about giving you much information."

"Yes. If two groups within the Kings are pursuing different agendas, or—more likely—if two operations within their organization have come into conflict with one another, then using the DMS to injure the other party can be viewed as a clever strategic move."

"It's pretty damn devious."

He spread his hands. "Secret society."

"Yeah, okay, but what does that mean? Are Deep

Throat and Toys calling from different ends of the playground? Or are they working together?"

"Impossible to tell at this point. What would your guess be?"

"My gut tells me that they're on the same side."

He nodded.

"But," I added, "considering that we *know* that every move in the Seven Kings playbook is built around deception and misdirection, I'm not sure we can trust any guess."

"I don't intend to."

"Toys said that the Kings had agents among the people I trust, and among the people we have to rescue."

"Feeling paranoid?"

"Yep."

"Welcome to my world. I've long considered paranoia to be a job requirement."

"Is there anyone in our ranks we should be looking at?"

"I'm looking at everyone."

"Isn't there anyone you trust completely?"

Church gave me his tiny fraction of a smile. "Everyone I trust is in this building," he said.

"But not everyone in this building has your trust."

"No."

"Where do I stand?" I asked.

"Where do I?"

Before I could answer, he patted me on the arm.

"Get cleaned up and we'll talk more at the conference."

Church turned and walked away.

Chapter Sixty-three

We gathered in a large conference room with a table into which were built computer workstations. There were plasma screens on all the walls and a multipanel central computer screen for teleconferencing. Everything was tomorrow's idea of state of the art. Aunt Sallie, Church, Dietrich, and Dr. Hu were there. Bug peered at everyone from one of the view screens. The last to arrive was Circe O'Tree, and she pushed a wheelchair in which sat a disgruntled and deeply embarrassed Rudy Sanchez.

I smiled at him, but he held up a stern finger. "One word, Cowboy, and I will find a way to kick your ass."

"Just wanted to say that I'm glad you're feeling up to this. Can't be easy."

He gave me an evil look. "Really? I find getting shot to be so invigorating."

Circe left his wheelchair with me and ran over to give Aunt Sallie a hug. For me it was a real WTF moment. And not just because I couldn't imagine anyone *liking* Aunt Sallie. It just seemed like such a surreal occurrence.

When Circe stepped back from Aunt Sallie, she saw that Church was there. Circe froze and her face went blank. No hugs there, just a formal handshake and a few words privately exchanged.

Curiouser and curiouser.

Church signaled for everyone to take their seats. I

helped Rudy out of the wheelchair and into a seat next to mine at the table. Circe came and sat on Rudy's other side.

"How are you?" I asked.

"I'll live," she said. "Where's your dog?"

"In my room eating his way through most of a large cow. At least that's what I think the kitchen staff delivered. Might be an elephant. Ghost was in monkey heaven."

"Glad someone's in a good mood. I'm not, and I'm having a hard time processing all of this."

"Doc . . . before this whole thing gets started, I wanted to say that I respect and appreciate everything you did today. You put your ass on the line twice. You may have saved my life and you definitely saved Rudy's. That van would have run him over if you hadn't fired on it."

"I already thanked her, Cowboy," Rudy said, but I ignored him.

Circe's eyes glistened. "Does that mean I get to curse, get a tattoo, and say 'hooah'?"

There was just the hint of a smile as she said it.

I grinned. "Yes, you do."

"Hooah," she said with dry irony.

"Hooah."

We traded a fist bump.

"Dios mio," Rudy breathed.

"Are you children done playing?" snapped Aunt Sallie from across the table. Circe and I whipped our hands back like we were caught going into a cookie jar.

On the central display, a dozen screens came to life showing the faces of directors of the various DMS field offices, most of whom I knew by sight or reputation. Church took his chair, but before he spoke he raised a small remote and pointed it at the door. There was a hiss of hydraulics and the clang of heavy locks.

"We are in full lockdown," he announced. "I am hereby initiating a Class One security protocol. You are all hereby bound by Executive Order A-9166/DMS. All participating stations are to activate protocol Deacon Alpha Ten. Verify."

One by one the DMS field commanders gave their verification. This was only the second time since I'd been with the DMS that we had gone to our highest security status. I understood why, but from the confused and concerned looks on the faces of everyone else they didn't. Even Aunt Sallie frowned at Church.

"What's going on, Deacon?" she asked, eyes narrowed. "We get something hot?"

"Red-hot," Church murmured to her, but to everyone else he said, "I will say this, and I want each of you to understand why I'm saying it. It is possible that the Seven Kings have infiltrated the DMS. If this is so, then we *will* discover the name or names of whoever is on their leash. If any of you are under coercion from the Kings, now is the time to let me know. This is a closed conference. The secret will be safe and we will act immediately to protect you and your family. If you have been the victim of coercion, then I offer a complete amnesty as long as you tell me now. That offer expires in thirty seconds."

We waited out those thirty seconds. Church's face was as hard as granite. I could see several people begin to sweat. There was a plate of vanilla wafers on the table in front of him. Church selected one, bit off a piece, and munched it thoughtfully. His eyes were invisible behind the tinted lenses of his glasses. Everyone waited. Except for the crunch of Church's strong white teeth on the cookie there was no sound.

"Time's up," said Church. "I direct each team leader to spread the word to their staff members. Same offer. Come to me directly and I will protect them. Failure to do so would be . . . unfortunate."

Considering the circumstances, the statement was almost bizarrely dry and formal. Except that we all knew what lay beneath the calm surface of Church's words. No one spoke. We watched him finish his NILLA wafer and wash it down with a sip of water. I cut a look at Rudy, who raised his eyebrows at me.

"Very well," said Church. It was impossible to read his expression. It was somewhere between one of those giant rock faces on Easter Island and Darth Vader. "I'm going to play a recording of a phone conversation that occurred less than an hour ago. The call was made to Captain Ledger's phone using the same anti-trace technology used by the confidential informant who has tipped us off to the Kings. I'll play it twice. Listen without comment first, and then the floor is open to speculation afterward."

He used the same remote to start the playback.

He need not have cautioned everyone to silence. Every mouth was slack with shock; every set of eyes stared in absolute horror.

Finally it was Rudy who broke the silence.

"Madre de Dios!" he said. "Gault?"

"Sebastian Gault," agreed Church gravely. "The King of Plagues."

Dr. Hu smiled like a kid on Christmas morning. "That's soooo cool." Everyone stared at him, but he gave an unapologetic shrug. "Hey, without guys like him this job would be booooring. That guy rocks."

"Can I kill him?" I asked Church.

"Maybe later," Church said. He sounded so convincing that Hu's smile faltered. To the group Church said, "I want to review all of the pertinent information. You're on point for this, Captain. Bring everyone up to speed."

"Okay," I said, "here's the short course. We know for sure that the Seven Kings are behind this entire crisis. We know that Sebastian Gault has the designation within the Kings organization as the 'King of Plagues.' We know that there are also Kings of Fear, Famine, Gold, War, Lies, and Thieves. Beyond that, we don't know anything else about the nature of their organization, including whether they are an ancient or modern secret society. We know that they use campaigns of disinformation and information manipulation, and in a minute I'd like Dr. O'Tree to talk more about that."

She nodded.

I continued, "One of the methods used by the Kings is coercion, most or all of it perpetrated by a man named Santoro, who we've been calling 'the Spaniard.'"

"Hold on a minute," interrupted Hu. "Extortion? Not blackmail?"

"No," I replied. "Blackmail is messy and it leaves a trail. MindReader would have tripped over that in at least one or two of our background searches. We've been constantly updating the search arguments for the victims, and we've hacked everything from their e-mails to their tax records. People are never completely pristine about their own wrongdoing; otherwise no one could blackmail them. Besides, it's hard as hell to blackmail someone into murder and suicide. Death pretty much cancels the leverage, so some of the vics would have fessed up. No . . . each of the victims had a family, right? What better leverage is there than a direct threat to loved ones? The victims are told that if they don't do it, then something far worse is going to happen. With that kind of pressure, people will definitely kill . . . or die."

Church said, "The threat would have to be made in a way that leaves no doubt as to whether the extortionist would follow through."

"Absolutely," I agreed. "They would need to really mind-fuck their victims."

"It's hard to imagine that working," Hu said.

"Really?" I said. "If someone told you to murder a co-worker or they'll kill your whole family, you wouldn't pop a cap in one of your lab assistants?"

"No way. My folks are in China, and my brother is a total asshole."

"Okay, imagine if you had a soul instead of a big empty place in your chest."

Hu actually smiled at this. "Sure. But how do you make a leap to that scenario?"

"Let me read the note I found at Plympton's apartment." I dipped into the shared case files and sent it to the main screens. I read the note aloud and then re-read a few key lines. " 'I know that what I have done is unforgivable. . . . But at least what I have done here in our home will save you both from greater horrors.' That's significant."

"I agree," said Rudy. "And it's reinforced by the last line: 'I am only the monster they made me.' This is a man driven to extremes. He's guilty, certainly, but only after the fact. He's not apologizing for anything done prior to what he clearly considered a mercy killing."

Hu thought about it for a moment and gave a grudging nod.

I said, "We see similar things in the case of Dr. Grey and the staff at Fair Isle. And we know for sure from the deposition of Amber Taylor. The extortionist has to bring a lot to the game, though. He'd have to already know something about how staffing and procedures work at facilities of this kind. You can't just Google that. On the flight from Pennsylvania I had the opportunity to interrogate the surviving shooter from the Starbucks hit. His name is Danny Sarducci."

I uploaded his military ID photo and Sarducci looked every bit the punk he was.

"Twenty-nine, from Trenton, New Jersey. Lot of stuff in his jacket. Four arrests for armed robbery as a juvenile. A judge let him join the Army instead of going to jail, which means the Army taught him how to fight and use better weapons. He was brought up on charges of sex with a minor in Afghanistan. The girl's family didn't call it rape, though from his commanding officer's report that's what it was. After Sarducci was kicked out, he was picked up by Blue Diamond Security."

"Ugh," said Dietrich. "*Those* assholes."

Blue Diamond had made the papers as often as Blackwater and had been the first mercenary group thrown out of Iraq for a laundry list of offenses.

"Yeah, those assholes," I agreed. "Sarducci went off the radar six years ago. Now jump to this morning and he was crew chief of a team of well-equipped shooters assigned to kill Mrs. Ledger's favorite son."

Aunt Sallie and Hu both snorted at that.

"Sarducci gave us the names of the other shooters, and they all have similar backgrounds. Low-level muscle who went off the public radar a few years ago. Half of them have military backgrounds, but it was mostly one tour and out. One deserter who ran to keep from getting recycled by 'stop-loss.' I asked Bug to hack Blue Diamond's records."

"I got nothing, Joe," said Bug. "They've been using a closed system. No hardlines, no Wi-Fi. Paranoid as shit. They probably know about MindReader and are taking no chances. Everything is intranet, which means we'd have to go and physically tap into their wires."

"Maybe we should," I said.

"That would be a bitch of a job," said Aunt Sallie. "They're based in Honduras and their compound is more fortress than military base. It would be easier to destroy it than infiltrate it."

"Works for me," muttered Dietrich.

"Who hired Sarducci?" asked Frost from the Denver office.

"Santoro. Sarducci described him as an adult Hispanic male, about forty. Slim but very fit. Looks like a wrestler. Fast hands and extremely good with a knife, which jibes with Dr. Grey's experience. I gave the physical description to Bug and he's running it through MindReader."

Bug frowned. "Don't get your hopes up, Joe. That description fits about forty million Hispanic males, but we're cross-referencing with key words."

"Sarducci knew that Santoro was part of the Seven Kings," I said, "but he didn't actually know what the Kings were beyond some rah-rah rhetoric. He said that Santoro talked about the Kings all the time. How they were going to reshape the world. How they were the personification of Chaos on earth—not his kind of phrasing, of course, so he was probably quoting Santoro. He said they pay well and in cash. Sarducci and his crew did several jobs for them, and Bug's cross-referencing the names and dates."

Dietrich asked, "Did he give you anything else? Like why he wanted to kill Marty Hanler?"

"They weren't after Hanler," I said. "They were after me. And, I think, Circe."

Circe's eyes flared. "What?"

I tapped a key to replay one of Sarducci's comments. "The Seven Kings are going to rip your world apart, Ledger. You and the rest of the DMS. You, that psychopath Church, that cunt O'Tree, these ass clowns here—all of you are already dead and you just don't know it yet."

"Sorry for the vulgarity, Doc. His words, definitely not mine."

Church leaned forward and looked hard at me. "Sarducci threatened Circe?"

"Yes."

It's weird, his expression did not really change, but somehow his blank face suddenly conveyed a degree of menace that I have seldom before experienced. The others in the room must have sensed it, too. Everyone turned to look at Church.

He sat back and brushed cookie crumbs from his sleeve.

"Interesting," he said softly. "Please continue."

His eyes were fixed on Circe, who colored and turned away.

"Sarducci was very forthcoming with threats."

"Anyone else make his greatest-hits list?" asked Dietrich.

I ticked my chin toward Aunt Sallie. "Not by name, but he used a few vulgar gender-specific racial epithets. This bozo is not a fan of Affirmative Action or women in the workplace."

Aunt Sallie smiled thinly. "Nice to be noticed here at the back of the bus."

"I got nothing else useful from him. He's a lowlife piece of crap and I hope we find a hole and drop him into it."

"Count on it," murmured Aunt Sallie. She wrote something on a slip of paper and slid it across to Church, who read it and gave her the tiniest of nods.

"By the end he was rerunning the same stuff. The DMS is going to fall; we don't stand a chance; the Seven Kings will rule; we're all going to die; rivers of blood will sweep us away. That sort of thing."

"More rivers of blood," Dietrich said. "The fuck is it with these guys and rivers of blood?"

"Maybe they really had their hearts set on the Fair

Isle cluster fuck going south on us," said Auntie. She gave me a look that seemed to say that with me at the helm she was surprised it didn't.

I manfully restrained myself from throwing my coffee cup at her. "There was one other thing Sarducci said," I continued. "It came out kind of sudden and it was clear that he didn't want to say it. He went off on a tangential rant to try and hide it."

"What was it?" asked Church.

"He said that Santoro had a worse hard-on for the DMS than the Kings had for the Inner C."

"The Inner C?" Dietrich frowned. "Is that a gang name?"

"No," said Church. "And that is very interesting, Captain. It ties into something my informant told me when he called yesterday. He said that the Kings '*want to break the bones of their enemies and suck out the marrow.*' '*Bones*' is the operative word."

"Wait!" said Circe suddenly. "I have something on that, too." She gave everyone a quick recap of the Goddess posts she had been tracking for months. She scrolled through her data and then put a Twitter post on the screen. "One of her posts mentioned bones."

Woe to the firstborn sons of the House of Bones.

"It was in the posts after vandals broke into a tomb in Egypt," Circe said, and explained about the tomb of the lost *firstborn* son of Amenhotep II, seventh pharaoh of the eighteenth Dynasty of Egypt. She leaned on the word "firstborn."

"Cool," said Hu.

"Okay, bones and bones," said Dietrich, "how does that relate to the 'Inner C'?"

"Son of a bitch," breathed Aunt Sallie. "The goddamn Bonesmen."

Chapter Sixty-four

The Hangar

Floyd Bennett Field, Brooklyn

December 19, 8:41 P.M. EST

"Bonesmen?" asked Circe. "As in the Skull and Bones?"

Aunt Sallie gave her an approving nod. "Right, and the Inner C has to be the Inner Circle."

"I thought they were a myth," said Dietrich; then he answered his own comment, "Right, and we're the DM-fricking-S, so they're probably real." He sighed and shook his head. "One of these days we're going to find out that UFOs, Godzilla, and vampires are real, too. Sometimes I hate this job."

Aunt Sallie shared a private smile with Church, and we were welcome to make anything we wanted out of that. It made me wonder if something that Dietrich said hit a nerve. With my luck it would be *Godzilla*.

"Have we had any dealings with the Inner Circle?" asked Rudy.

Aunt Sallie nodded. "Mr. Church and I have been looking into them since before the DMS was founded. We've been considering making them a 'project,' but they're sly cocksuckers and gathering evidence on them is a lot like trying to punch through smoke."

"We may have to take that look," said Church quietly.

Circe said, "If we are to interpret this correctly, the Inner Circle are enemies of the Seven Kings."

Church didn't comment and he gave me a tiny shake of his head, so I kept my mouth shut about what he and I had discussed before the meeting.

"Looks that way," Hu said, looking very pleased. "A clash of secret empires. This is *sweet*."

"This can't end happily," said Circe. "What are we into here? Is this a three-way fight, or are we getting caught in the cross fire?"

"Points for using combat slang," I said.

"Bite me," she muttered; then to the group she said, "Actually, a clash makes a lot of sense. It explains the tip-off information. And it makes sense that the Inner Circle would reach out to the DMS."

"Does it?" Church murmured.

"Sure," agreed Aunt Sallie, "to use us to do the dirty work instead of having to endanger any of their own assets."

Dietrich nodded. "Smart."

"Isn't it a little obvious, though?" asked Rudy. "I mean . . . if these are separate groups and if they are as secret as they're supposed to be, then how do they know so much about each other? How can the Inner Circle know so much about the terrorist cells working with the Kings that they can feed reliable tips to Mr. Church?"

"A double agent," suggested Circe.

"Or they managed to plant someone inside the Kings," Auntie ventured.

"No," decided Circe. "It's too pat. If the Inner Circle wanted the Kings torn down, then they could just as easily pass that information along within channels. The

Bonesmen are supposed to be wired into every level of government. Going outside their own network is an unnecessary risk."

"Right," agreed Rudy. "A letter with no return address would accomplish the same thing."

"Doc's right," Dietrich agreed. "It's either showing off, or it's clumsy—"

"Or it's misdirection," finished Circe. "Don't forget the Goddess and her posts. It's all about misdirection."

"Sorry to interrupt, guys, but you got to see this," said Bug. He hit some buttons and suddenly we were looking at Wolf Blitzer. The feed cut in mid-sentence. "—rocked the foundations of power as four scions of powerful American families died under what can only be called 'suspicious circumstances.' Sources at the Centers for Disease Control in Atlanta have not yet declared this to be an outbreak, and so far no one else who was in the company of the four victims has become sick. Even so, each site has been quarantined and—"

Aunt Sallie snapped her fingers at Bug. "Shit! Pull up a list of known members of the Skull and Bones."

"On it." The list flashed onto a second screen. Bug scrolled through the names, highlighting them as he went. Harrington, Milhaus . . . one, two, three, four. "Oh, man . . . they're all on the list."

"They're Inner Circle," Auntie said. "Those four are power players, and two of them for sure are Inner Circle. My guess is that all of them are."

"Dios mio," breathed Rudy. He put his hand on Circe's arm. "You know what we're seeing here?"

We all knew, but Circe put it in words: "The deaths of the firstborn."

Rudy actually crossed himself.

"There's been a fifth death," interrupted Bug. "Just came in. Jessica St. Stevens, daughter of—"

"Congressman Pierce St. Stevens," said Church. "I know him. Close friend of Dick Cheney. Jess is his only child. She's estranged from her father. Works for Doctors Without Borders."

Auntie gave a derisive snort. "No fucking way she's tied into her dad's politics." She snapped her fingers at Bug. "Make sure you pull the names of anyone *suspected* of being connected to the Inner Circle. We need to identify their children and get the word out. *Now!*"

Bug worked furiously and more names began appearing on the main screens and that was quickly followed by biographical data and then contact information.

"No time to get this out to the local authorities," growled Church. "We need to act now."

We all grabbed phones and began making calls. The team leaders from the other DMS shops did the same. Within ten minutes we had three hundred people making calls to families, police departments, the Centers for Disease Control, hospitals, the National Institutes of Health, and a dozen federal agencies. It was a nightmare of urgency, and as we worked reports kept coming in. Six victims. Then it jumped to a nine. A dozen. We kept at it. Fifteen victims. Sixteen.

"Are we too late?" Dietrich asked. "There must be hundreds of Bonesmen. Are all of their firstborn kids being targeted? Or just the children of the Inner Circle?"

"No way to know," snapped Church. "Call everyone. Go beyond the Inner Circle."

The night ground on. Our calls were met with

skepticism and hostility by those people suspected of being in the Inner Circle. None of them denied it. At least none of those who answered the phone in voices that were broken by sobs or screams.

The ordinary Bonesmen were shocked and angry. Most of them didn't believe it. Not surprising, but also not helpful. A lot of people hung up on us.

Some of these people were past presidents. Many of them were generals, corporate CEOs, billionaires. Their combined might could crush even the DMS. And since many of them did not know about the Seven Kings or believe in them, we were the ones bearing the bad news, so a lot of genuine rage was directed at us. Mr. Church got a call from the President, who had gotten over thirty calls from members of Congress and colleagues of such political importance that their calls got through to him without red-tape hindrance.

Between calls I caught a fragment of Church's side of that conversation.

"—yes, Mr. President, I believe that we can call this a terrorist attack. However, I don't think we should say so to the press. A statement to that effect would be exactly what the Seven Kings need—"

Just after midnight we got word of the twenty-first victim. The latest victim had been a fourteen-year-old boy at a military academy. He had collapsed and died during a Christmas party.

God Almighty.

Twenty-one.

By two in the morning we had exhausted all of the numbers Bug could find, but there had not been a new case reported. We made hundreds of follow-up calls.

Three A.M. came and went.

"I think it's over," said Rudy. He was bleary-eyed and gray with pain and fatigue. For the last hour he'd been covertly popping Advil like they were M&M'S.

"Still only twenty-one," said Bug.

Circe gave him a bleak and haunted stare. " 'Only'?"

Church sat back and rubbed his eyes. Even he looked exhausted.

"Now what?" asked Dietrich.

"Now we have to monitor this," said Aunt Sallie. "We need to keep ahead of it in case there's another wave."

"Do we even know the cause of death?" I asked. "Is this a plague? Poisoning? I mean . . . no one else at each of the murder scenes was reported with symptoms. . . ."

"We know the cause of death," said Circe, her dark eyes filled with strange light. "It'll be mycotoxicoses."

Church leaned forward. "And how exactly would you know that?"

Interlude Forty-two

The State Correctional Institute at Graterford
Graterford, Pennsylvania
December 19, 8:42 P.M. EST

Nicodemus lay on his cot, fingers laced behind his head, ankles crossed, and stared at the shadows on the ceiling. The warden had ordered everything removed from his cell. He had no books, no writing paper or pencils, no TV. All that had been left for him was a single sheet, a thin blanket of rough wool, a pillow, and a roll of toilet paper.

It was enough for him.

Nicodemus did not need to be entertained. He did not need to read, not even the Bible. There was no one that he wanted to talk to, no diversion that he required. He had everything that he needed.

It was all there inside his head. In his thoughts. As clear as if he heard it outside his cell. As clear as if *they* were there beside his cot. It did not matter that no one else could hear them. The video recorders trained on his cell would not tape any of the sounds that he heard. That was as it should be. The sounds were for him to hear.

He lay for hour after delicious hour, smiling a small and secret smile to himself. Listening to the screams of the dying.

Chapter Sixty-five

The Hangar
Floyd Bennett Field, Brooklyn
December 19, 8:52 P.M. EST

"The tomb," explained Circe.

Every eye was on her. She looked scared, but she held her ground.

"Spill it, girl," said Aunt Sallie.

"Experts have been trying to scientifically explain the Ten Plagues for years," Circe said. "If there were a series of catastrophes during the time of Moses in Egypt, then there would likely be panic and unrest. During such times raids on food stores would be possible, even likely. After a time of pestilence it's very likely that some of the food stores were contaminated by any number of bacteria or fungi. Any bread made from moldy wheat would carry diseases. The sudden deaths of so many Egyptians could very well have the result of a raid on contaminated foodstuffs. The persons most likely to conduct a successful raid would be the older and more capable members of that society. If not precisely first-born, then at least symbolically the 'first among them.' It's not all that much of a stretch to see how that could have evolved into a more dramatic story of the firstborn dying as a result of a plague sent by God. After all, it was the last straw that led to the liberation of the Isra-elites."

"You're talking about mycotoxins," murmured Rudy, nodding agreement.

Hu looked jazzed by all this. "Right! Mycotoxins can present in a food chain as a result of fungal infection of crops. Human infection can come through direct inges-tion of infected products—bread, livestock, whatever—and even cooking and freezing won't destroy them. Nice call, Circe."

"What are—?" Dietrich began, but Hu cut him off.

"It's a toxic chemical produced by fungi. The toxins enter the bloodstream and lymphatic system, damage macrophage systems, and some other evil shit. Back in 2004, over a hundred people died after eating maize contaminated with aflatoxin, a species of mycotoxin. There have been other cases, too. Mostly in third-world countries."

"The biblical connection is mostly guesswork," Circe admitted. "The Jewish story about Passover begins at the end of the Ten Plagues. Passover celebrates the first meal to mark the escape of the Israelites from bondage *and* from the plagues. The Passover meal consists of symbolic newborn lamb, fresh herbs, and horseradish—and all of these are safe from mycotoxin exposure. The same goes for unleavened bread, which is, by definition, free of any yeasty mycotoxin contamination."

"Makes sense even to me," said Dietrich. "But how's all that relate to a ransacked tomb?"

"Remember the Curse of King Tut?" she asked. "Lord Carnarvon, the Englishman who financed Howard Carter's expedition to find the tomb of King Tutankhamen, died of a mysterious illness after entering the tomb. It's very likely that he became ill after exposure to a fungus that had been dormant in the tomb for thousands of years and reactivated by fresh air. Recent studies of newly opened ancient Egyptian tombs that had not been exposed to modern contaminants found pathogenic bacteria of the staphylococcus and pseudomonas genera, and the molds *Aspergillus niger* and *Aspergillus flavus*."

"Yeah," said Hu, "but the concentrations were weak. They'd only be dangerous to persons with weakened immune systems."

"Oh, hell, Doc," I said, "don't forget who we're dealing with. You trying to tell me that Sebastian Gault couldn't amp up and weaponize one of these toxins?"

Hu sat back and gave me a rueful smile. "Shit . . . *I* could do that."

Rudy said, "So, if Amenhotep II was the pharaoh from the time of Exodus, then his son could have been a victim of the mycotoxin infection. If that's the case, and if we go on the premise that it was Gault and the

Kings who raided the tomb, then are we concluding that they found a more potent strain of mycotoxin?"

We thought about that. Circe chewed her lip and Hu drummed his fingers on the table.

I said, "I may not be a scientist . . . but I *don't* think that's what happened."

"Why not?" asked Church.

"Because it's way too convenient. The tomb was opened what—a month or so ago? That's awfully tight timing for science, isn't it? No . . . Gault's smart, but we *know* that the Goddess is big into misdirection. We also know that the Kings dig symbolism. The tires used to create the Plague of Darkness weren't exactly biblical. Nor are the 'Locust' bombers. Wouldn't it work just as well for them to break into the tomb to establish the mythology and then hit the firstborn of the Inner Circle with something Gault already cooked up?"

They looked at me for a while, then at each other, and one by one they began nodding. Even Hu.

Aunt Sallie grunted her approval, though she clearly found it difficult to believe that Captain Shortbus had thought it up.

The main screen over the conference table showed a collage of twenty-one faces. Young men and women, a few kids. All of them dead now, victims of a modern version of an ancient plague.

I noticed a small red light flashing on Circe's laptop. "What's that?" I asked.

"The Goddess!" she said, toggling over to a Twitter screen. "I have it programmed to signal me if there's a new Goddess post and—oh my God!"

"What?" demanded Church.

"The Goddess . . . she posted something. . . ."

Circe hit a button to send the message to the main screen. We sat there, shocked to silence. The message read:

The Ten Plagues have been visited on the wicked. Witness the fall of the House of Bones.

And then the kicker.

It is complete.

"Dios mio," whispered Rudy.

"Yeah. The Seven Kings beat us," I said. "We lost."

Part Five
Grief's Best Music

The miserable have no other medicine
But only hope.

—WILLIAM SHAKESPEARE, *MEASURE FOR MEASURE*

Chapter Sixty-six

We wrestled and wrangled it and talked it to death, but nothing we said could change the fact that the Seven Kings had set out to murder the firstborn of the Inner Circle and they had accomplished exactly that.

They'd won. Was it a battle? Or had we just lost the war?

We were all so tired, so heartsick and angry, that we were losing perspective. And the great shadowy mass that was the Seven Kings was still moving through our lives. I looked into my own heart and wondered for the hundredth time if this was what I was and who I was: a foot soldier in a war without beginning or end.

Our meeting broke up and we shambled out. Burning with impotent anger, defeated, unable to look at one another.

Circe helped Rudy into the wheelchair and this time he didn't complain. He looked small and used up, and as he sat there he hung his head. Pain had aged him and the loss of so many innocent lives seemed to have sapped away his life force. I walked with him and Circe out into the hall.

"I . . . can't believe it," Circe said in a voice that sounded more like that of a scared little girl than that of a doctor and an expert in global terrorism.

Rudy said nothing. He simply shook his head and refused to look up.

"This isn't over," I said. "We still have some puzzle pieces that don't fit."

She gave a single harsh laugh. "What's the point?"

"Look, Doc, we were starting to make headway when this thing blindsided us. Let's all get some sleep," I suggested. "Maybe in the morning we can make some kind of plan."

"A plan to do what?" demanded Circe. "We've already lost."

I gave her a hard look. "No, we damn well haven't. The Kings are still out there. Just because they won tonight doesn't mean that they'll go away. We need to keep at this. We need to find a way to hit them back."

She stared at me for a moment, then nodded. "If we go after them," she said slowly, "if we can hurt *them*, then—"

"Maybe we can stop them from winning the next war."

Rudy just turned his head away and said nothing. Circe sighed and pushed his wheelchair down the hall. I stood and watched them go.

"Captain?"

I turned to see Church standing a yard away. I hadn't heard him approach.

"Tell me, Captain, do you think that this is what Toys meant when he said that we had to *stop* Gault?"

"No."

"Nor do I."

"I suppose nothing is what it seems with the Seven Kings. Get some sleep." And as if to echo my own thoughts, he added: "The war isn't over."

With that he walked away.

Chapter Sixty-seven

The Hangar

Floyd Bennett Field, Brooklyn

December 20, 1:06 A.M. EST

Ghost was lying amid a heap of gnawed bones, too stuffed to wag. I stepped over him and threw myself onto my bed with every intention of sleeping until sometime in midsummer.

I didn't get a minute of sleep. Not a second.

I lay there for hours. I could feel each minute; I could hear each dry second crack off and fall away.

As soon as I closed my eyes I could hear Toys' voice speaking to me.

You can't trust anyone. Or anything. Nothing is what it seems. It never is with the Kings.

When I'd asked about Santoro, Toys had said, *That psycho prick will be in the thick of it. He wouldn't miss an opportunity to see that much pain.*

And then it hit me.

Nothing is what it seems. It never is with the Kings.

My eyes popped open.

"Holy shit!" I said. I think I yelled it. Ghost woke up and barked in alarm.

Two minutes later I was banging on Church's door.

He opened the door almost at once. He did not look one bit surprised that I was there.

"I was wondering how long it would take you to figure it out," he said.

Chapter Sixty-eight

The Hangar

Floyd Bennett Field, Brooklyn

December 20, 1:19 A.M. EST

This time the meeting was held in Church's office. Rudy, Circe, Aunt Sallie, and me.

Church sat behind his desk in a crisp white shirt with the sleeves rolled up, his tie loosened at the throat. I think this was maybe the second time I'd ever seen him without a suit coat. It did absolutely nothing to make him look less official and imposing.

"Why are we still flogging this thing?" growled Rudy. He looked terrible. His hair was uncombed and he wore pajamas that were too big for him. Circe, in sweats, was only marginally more composed.

"It's the coercion thing," I said. "That's been the problem all along. If the firstborn thing hadn't happened, we might have gotten to it during the meeting. The clue to this thing is there."

"I sure as hell don't see it," Aunt Sallie said irritably.

She wore a bathrobe that had little ducks on it. I knew it was more than my life was worth to comment on it.

"Wait," Rudy said slowly. "Maybe I do." He rubbed his eyes and accepted a cup of coffee from Church. "There are only a few psychological subgroups that are acutely susceptible to suggestion. And an even smaller sub-subgroup who are otherwise healthy and functional. Call it one or two per fifty thousand."

Circe was catching on fast. "No. . . . To do the kind of thing we've seen, it's even more rare. I'd say it's one in two or three hundred thousand."

"Fair enough," Rudy said. "So, measure that against the number of people in the professions that relate to these circumstances. Law enforcement, security, viral research. A few others we haven't identified. That number becomes impossible."

"Right," I said. "It's only possible if we go on the premise that this is not random chance."

"Hold on, dammit," growled Aunt Sallie. "Do you mean that they were deliberately sought or deliberately placed?"

"Either," Rudy said. "Both."

"That's impossible," she said. "The system is too good."

"Yes," Church agreed. "It is." But from his tone it was clear that he meant that Auntie's assessment was wrong.

She gave a stubborn shake of her head. "No one could hack all those records. Not unless they had Mind-Reader. C'mon, Deacon; you're not suggesting that Bug—"

"No," I said. "Not Bug."

Rudy and Circe exchanged a look. Rudy said, "The normal psych profiles used in this level of government work would red flag most of these people. Bug gave me the screener's notes for Dr. Grey, Trevor Plympton, and that other guy. Scofield, the maintenance man from Fair Isle. None of the reports indicated the right kind of psychological vulnerability."

"Then it's bad screening," snapped Auntie. "Who did the screening?"

"Three different companies.

"Same screener working at different companies at different times?"

"No."

"Do we have the psych profiles of the screeners?"

"We do," said Mr. Church. He removed three profiles from his desk and handed them to Aunt Sallie. She opened the covers and scanned the contents. Then she did it again and her eyes were wide.

"No fucking way, Deacon."

Church said nothing.

Aunt Sallie wheeled on me. "Listen, jackass, I don't know what kind of stunt you're trying to pull here, but—"

"Auntie," said Church softly. "Please. I had this suspicion since the Starbucks incident. Very few people knew about that meeting."

She slapped the files down on the desk. I gingerly reached past her and picked them up, opened them, saw what she had seen.

"Ouch," I said.

"What?" asked Rudy, but I shook my head and held on to the files.

"Dr. O'Tree," said Church, "threat assessment is your specialty. Given the facts, work out a scenario for how this is possible."

She chewed her lip and shook her head. "I've been trying to do that," she said after a thoughtful pause, "but I can't."

"You can't?"

"Well . . . I can, but it's impossible." Circe looked like someone had slapped her.

"We seem to be trading in impossible," grumbled Aunt Sallie. "Speak your mind, girl."

But Circe shook her head and it was clear that she was in great distress. Her eyes were filling with tears; she covered her hand with her mouth. "I . . . can't."

"Then I'll say it for you," I said, my voice more brutal than I'd intended. "There's ten kinds of security on places like the London and double that for Fair Isle and Area 51. Everyone gets a background check that goes all the way to their DNA. The people who do the screening are as important or perhaps *more* important than the people they interview for these jobs."

"That's my damn point," snapped Aunt Sallie. "Every screener we use comes with ironclad bona fides. Every damn one."

Tears rolled down Circe's face.

"Yes," said Mr. Church quietly. "And every damn one of them was vetted by Vox."

Circe O'Tree burst into tears.

Chapter Sixty-nine

The American sat behind his desk and smoked a cigar. Beyond the big glass windows the city glimmered with a million jewels. Stars above and streetlights below. He loved the city. He loved its size and its arrogance, its muscle and its swagger. It was like looking in a mirror.

His phone rang. Toys.

"You somewhere safe?"

"Heading back to the castle," said Toys.

"Okay, but keep your head down and your eyes open."

"Why? Because of my call to Ledger?"

"Partly. But mostly 'cause I'm about to piss in the punch bowl here. It's not going to do Sebastian or Mom any good. Not going to do the Kings any good, either. Not in the short term."

He explained what he intended to do.

"God!" said Toys, but there was as much admiration in his voice as fear.

A light flashed on the phone unit on the American's desk.

"Look, kiddo, I got to run. Keep that phone handy. I'll be in touch."

With that, the American pocketed the cell phone and heaved himself out of his chair. He lumbered over to a cabinet and removed a set of schematics. He placed them on his desk blotter, used a red pen to write a note, and then straightened. He cast a last look around the office, sighed again, and went into the bathroom, pushed back the curtain, and stepped into the shower. Then he pushed three tiles on the wall and waited as hidden hydraulics pulled the entire shower wall aside. The American stepped through, tapped another button, and let the wall close behind him. The DMS would find the elevator eventually, but by then he would be long gone.

FOUR MINUTES LATER Sgt. Gus Dietrich kicked open the heavy oak doors of the American's office and surged inside with Liberty Team at his heels. The red pinpoints of their laser sights danced on the floor, the walls, and the big desk.

There was no one home.

Dietrich ordered his men to do a thorough search, and while they were at it he walked over to the big desk and looked at the schematic. And at the note the American had left.

He tapped his commlink.

"Bulldog to Deacon," he called.

"Go for Deacon."

"No one home. But the big guy left us something. You'll freaking love this."

Dietrich bent over so that his helmet cam projected a clean image of the blueprints of the USS *Sea of Hope*.

Written across it in red ballpoint was:

Merry Christmas!
(Tell Circe I'm sorry.)

It was signed: *Hugo.*

Chapter Seventy

I looked out of the helicopter window at total blackness. A full day had burned away since Dietrich found Vox's parting gift. Now I sat in a helo with Circe, Church, Dietrich, and Echo Team. Ghost lay asleep at my feet, his legs twitching as he dreamed of the hunt.

I still felt breathless from the double shock of Vox's betrayal and the plans for the *Sea of Hope*. Vox was someone Church had trusted. Circe O'Tree had worked for the guy for years. Aunt Sallie regularly had Vox over for New Year's Eve parties and the Super Bowl. Now the mask had been peeled away to reveal a villain. A monster. Possibly one of the Seven Kings, and certainly a significant member of that organization.

They are everywhere.

Vox had run Terror Town. He knew the inner workings of every counterterrorism team in the world. That knowledge would ripple through the foundations of world governments like earthquake tremors.

After shock comes planning. We had to make a radical shift in gears with no time to pause at the sheer scope of the Kings' real plan.

"Can't we just off-load everyone?" Dietrich had asked as soon as he returned from Vox's office with the *Sea of Hope* schematics. "We got ships and subs ghosting the cruise ship. Why don't we just frigging *take* it and worry about separating sheep from wolves later on?"

"Because that's the very first thing the Kings would

expect," said Circe, "which means it's the first thing they'll have prepared for. I think that if we order the ship to heave to, or board by force, then some kind of fail-safe plan will be initiated. Bombs would be the easiest."

"And," I added, "we have to keep repeating the mantra 'they are everywhere.' The Kings are going to have agents planted aboard. A firefight would work more in their favor than ours."

"Balls," grumped Dietrich. He loved a plain and simple frontal assault.

I nodded to Circe. "You worked security for the event, Doc. How are we going to get onto the ship?"

Circe chewed her lip. "The problem is that everyone is prescreened."

"We have MindReader," said Church. "Bug can infiltrate the system, plant security profiles, and exit without leaving a footprint."

"We're using the MI6 encryption package," Circe countered. "Not even MindReader can intrude there. Hugo told me—"

"Hugo knew only as much about MindReader as I allowed him to know."

"Why? Were you suspicious of him before this?"

"I'm suspicious of most people."

I hid a smile.

"Then what's our cover?"

Circe gave me a considering stare. "That depends on if you can speak French."

"I speak a lot of languages."

"With the proper accent?"

"Continental or Canadian?"

Circe smiled. "What do you think of Avril Lavigne's music?"

"If it'll get Echo Team onto the *Sea of Hope,* I'll start a fan club."

"She was a late addition to the lineup. She's probably already aboard, but a lot of stars have bumped up their security teams since the London event. You can be a cultural attaché bringing additional security. It'll actually work for us, having DeeDee, because she can be the personal guard for Avril."

"What about the star?" I asked. "She'll need to be briefed."

"Not really. All of the performers have additional security beside the entourage they know. Most of the guards are hired by their record label or studio, so these will be strangers. As long as you don't get chatty with the stars, it'll work."

"Not a problem," I said. "I'm more of a classic-rock kind of guy."

Church stood up. "Then we all have work to do. Circe, you and Auntie will coordinate with Bug to access the right security files."

She nodded and hurried out.

"Captain Ledger," Church said to me, "brief Echo Team and prep for the mission. I want to be wheels up in one hour."

NOW WE FLEW through the predawn sky for a fight that had worst-case scenario written all over it.

The *Sea of Hope* was one of the largest cruise ships afloat. Two hundred and twenty-five thousand gross tons. One thousand one hundred eighty-one feet long, with a 155-foot waterline beam and a 31-foot draft. There were sixteen passenger decks holding fifty-four hundred passengers and over twenty-one hundred crew members. Seven thousand five hundred people in all. That was a thousand people more than live in the average American town. We had no way of knowing how many of them belonged to the Seven Kings. Of those, how many were unwilling slaves, how many were Chosen, and how many were Kingsmen? We did know, however, that scattered through the passengers, rock stars, comedians, and political figures were dozens of the children of the most powerful people on earth. A few were the children of Bonesmen, but most were not. The children of the current president. The two young princes of England. Children of not just the rich and famous but also the globally powerful. Some of these actually were children, the youngest being ten; the rest were adult sons and daughters who were using their parents' positions to make a bid for social change, for compassion, and for basic humanity.

If we made a single misstep, we could get them all killed.

If we did nothing, that was a certainty.

At least we had plenty of backup coming. Two DMS teams in a C-17 Globemaster a few hours behind us. If a fight broke out, they'd swoop down on TradeWinds Combat Motor Kites, which look like batwing hang gliders but with motorized flaps for steering and braking. The kites can support an operator and his entire combat kit. Operators can even fire small arms while flying them.

A hundred feet below the cruise ship was the USS

Jimmy Carter, one of the new Virginia Class attack subs. There were two SEAL teams aboard, plus a platoon of Marines.

"Coming up on her," called the pilot. "Portside."

I peered out the window and saw it. The ship looked like a floating city, and even at night it was ablaze with lights.

I looked over at Circe, who was curled asleep with her head on Dietrich's shoulder. She looked very young. It hurt me to think that she'd be carrying the memory of betrayal and violence around with her for the rest of her life.

I reached over and tapped her arm.

"We're here," I said.

Interlude Forty-three

Chamber of the Seven Kings
December 21, 5:19 A.M. EST

Toys sat alone in the Chamber of the Kings. Now that the second phase of the Initiative was rolling, the individual Kings and their Consciences had all left Mc-Cullough for undisclosed locations. If something went horribly wrong tonight, none of them wanted to be in any predictable spot. Considering what was happening, it was too dangerous to congregate; and trust only went so far, especially bearing in mind the lengths to which Aunt Sallie or Mr. Church would go in order to get information.

Rabbits gone to ground, Toys mused darkly, looking at all the empty thrones.

Gault and Eris were on her yacht, far out to sea. Probably shagging like rabbits, too.

Toys put his feet up on the table, crossed his ankles, and stared at the screens. The wall of screens showed ninety different news channels. The London Hospital bombing was no longer the lead story. Nor was the catastrophic drop in the stock market or even the massacre at the Starbucks in Southampton. Now it was the "Death of the Firstborn." CNN was the first network to put the story together—fed, Toys knew, by agents of the Goddess—that the children of America's elite families were being murdered. All of the other stations had similar titles, rife with biblical references. Most had nice graphics, and Toys wondered if each network had a graphic artist on standby or if titles of this sort were premade and ready for their inevitable use.

He sipped a martini—his third since he arrived—and watched the reporters give hysterical accounts of the mounting death toll. Every law enforcement organization in the country was "being mobilized" or was "racing against time" or "actively hunting suspects." All bullshit. Toys sipped and scowled. No mention of the Department of Military Sciences, of course.

The martini was nearly gone before the ABC News anchor speculated on a connection between these murders and the shootings in Southampton and Jenkintown.

"Took you bloody long enough!" Toys yelled at the screen.

He sighed and set down his glass, and as he leaned forward to do so his gaze fell on the phone the American had given him. Toys' nerves were still jangling from having called Joe Ledger. Few things had ever scared

Toys as much as hearing that psychopath's voice on the other end of the call. Toys snatched up the phone and shoved it into his pocket. With a grunt he thrust himself out of his chair and staggered over to the wall of screens, carrying the half-empty pitcher with him instead of the glass. A glass was too slow.

Toys drank from the pitcher and watched the press chow down on the firstborn story.

"First-bloody-born," Toys said, and then laughed at the slur in his own voice. "I'll bet you're watching this, aren't you, Sebastian? Does it make you feel like a god? You and that wrinkled slut. Gods? What a laugh." He suddenly bent forward and pressed his face against the screen and yelled at the top of his voice, "*This isn't even your fucking fight!*"

He beat his fist on the screen. Over and over and over again until the screen cracked and blood splashed across the hissing, distorted image. Then a fit of laughter rippled through him like an uncontrollable shiver.

He drank a huge mouthful, but the motion of leaning back to drink made him lose balance and he staggered backward five wobbly steps and then sat down hard on the floor. The American's phone fell out of his pocket and the pitcher dropped, too, and smashed, splashing him with booze and broken glass. He stared at it for a long moment, and then burst into tears.

"Oh, bloody hell," he said between sobs. "I've become a sloppy crying drunk." Weeping turned to laughter and back to sobs.

Eventually, drunk and exhausted, his face streaked with tears, Toys climbed slowly to his feet and brushed glass gingerly from his clothes. He picked up the phone and stared at it, suddenly horrified about what he had done.

"I'm sorry," he whispered to the empty room. "Oh, God . . . I'm sorry."

"There are no gods here," purred a voice behind him. Toys screamed and whirled. "Only a fool and a King."

A man stood in the doorway to the Chamber of the Kings. He was tall and handsome, and he was smiling.

Sebastian Gault raised his pistol and pointed it at Toys.

Chapter Seventy-one

The *Sea of Hope*
December 21, 5:26 A.M. EST

The chopper touched down on a helipad that extended out from the foredeck on massive hydraulics. As soon as the door was open, deck crew ran to escort us down a ramp and into a protected receiving alcove. Our gear was loaded onto railed carts that whisked them away. Then the rope was unclipped and the bird rose and headed back across the black water toward Rio, on the mainland of Brazil.

The alcove doors closed and a tall man who had a smile that could burn your retinas and a hairpiece that had no origin in nature entered and shook Circe's hand.

"Dr. O'Tree, so *wonderful* to have you join us," he said in a thick Italian accent. "I thought you had decided not to participate."

"Miss this?" Circe said with a good affectation of genuine surprise. "I wouldn't miss this for the world!"

His smile never wavered. He was of the kind who would roll with anything short of having Ghost hump his leg without allowing his professional demeanor to falter.

"Mr. Alesso, I'd like you to meet my aide, Mr. Kent."

Alesso shook hands with Church, who managed a convincing smile. I wish I had a photo of it. I could win bets with it.

"It is very much my pleasure to meet you," said Alesso. He was probably the real deal, but he sounded like a bad actor in a pizza commercial.

She turned to Gus, who was in a crisp white naval uniform. Ghost sat primly by his side, playing his role. "And this is Chief Petty Officer Wayne. The Navy thought we could use him." She lowered her voice to a confidential tone. "His dog's a bomb sniffer."

"Ah!" said Alesso, arching his eyebrows as if we were all part of a wonderful bit of intrigue. "And these other gentlemen are here for Ms. Lavigne?" He pronounced it "La-vig-ne."

Circe began to introduce me, but I alpha-maled myself into the moment.

"Je m'appelle Jean-François Fieuzal."

Alesso blinked at me. "Perdono?"

I rattled off my full credentials in French, watching to see if he got any of it, but after a sentence or two it was clear I'd left him stranded on the beach.

"I'm sorry. I don't speak—"

"Mr. Fieuzal is with the Canadian Cultural Liaison's office. They arranged for the additional security."

My apparent inability to speak English cut short any need for polite chitchat.

Alesso looked at the "security team." They were really working it. All five of them wore identical sunglasses despite the early hour, none of them had a flicker of expression on their stone faces, and they stood as tall as possible. Even DeeDee looked ten feet tall.

"They're in the security database," said Circe, and handed over a thick folder. "Here are their papers."

"Welcome aboard the *Sea of Hope,*" Alesso said with a bright smile. The only reaction he got was a microscopic twitch of Top's upper lip. Alesso's smile looked like it had become fragile, so I covertly gestured for Circe to wrap this up before the poor guy fainted.

Alesso showed us to staterooms—Echo Team's was a suite directly across the hall from Lavigne's. We carried our stuff inside and closed the door. Circe's stateroom was on another deck, but as soon as she dropped her suitcases she came back. Church and Dietrich, too.

"Welcome to the *Sea of Hope,*" Top said, echoing Alesso. "Now what?"

Dietrich opened one of the cases and handed me a pair of glasses. "First things first."

I put them on. The prescription was fake, and the heavy frames contained an ultrathin receiver that allowed me to get the same lens display intel feed. The lenses worked like one-way glass, so I could see the display, but no one looking at me could. Dietrich tossed me the small pocket mouse that would allow me to scroll the intel. I adjusted glasses, studied the floor plan for this part of the ship, then flicked through some other data to make sure the uplink was working fast.

The shades Echo Team wore had the same technology built in.

Circe and Church were already on their laptops. I was about to kick off a new version of the same discussion we'd been having about what the hell to do now that we were onboard when Circe said, "Oh my *God*!"

"Now what?"Bunny muttered, but we all gathered around her.

Circe said, "This just came in from Dr. Cmar; he's an infectious disease doctor at Johns Hopkins. "He sent these images. Look!"

The first image that filled one lens of the glasses showed Charles Osgood Harrington IV, the rich kid everyone called C-Four. "This was the first victim. Look at the lesions here and here." Little dots appeared on the display and moved to indicate pustules that covered the corpse's face. The lesions were pale, of course, without blood pressure to give them shape and color, but it was clear enough what they would have looked like when the kid was still alive.

"Attractive," I said. "What's it tell us?"

"The symptoms reported by the various first-responder EMTs and police were a rapid onset of pustules that covered the bodies of the victims. Remember in the news, the stories about mycotoxins from the tomb of the firstborn son of the Pharaoh? We're seeing a kind of anaphylactic reaction, like hives. Only the whole thing is amped up. Super-hives."

"So?"

"This isn't nature, Joe, and it's not pure mycotoxins. I'll bet you this is some kind of designer pathogen. Something created to kill very quickly but not spread. Zero communicability."

"Targeted for specific victims," I said.

"Exactly," said Circe. "Now, think about the Seven Kings. What is their defining characteristic?"

"Misdirection." It had become an automatic response by now.

"Right! They want us to think that this was their endgame . . . but it's not. These victims may be firstborn, but that's not what we're seeing. This is the Plague of *Boils*!"

"Okay. But we know their endgame is mass murder on the *Sea of Hope*. What's your point?"

Church cut in. "We're going under the premise that the ship is going to be destroyed by a bomb or something equally large scale. Probably during one of the key speeches. However, remember what Toys told you. Gault is running this show. Gault isn't just a member of the Kings. . . ."

"He's the King of *Plagues*," I said. "Shit."

Bunny said, "Please do *not* say that this is worse than we thought. Do not say that."

Circe looked terrified. The same look was probably on my face.

"Gault is planning something even bigger than the deaths of all these celebrities," she said softly. "He's planning something *huge*."

Church said, "Something the world will never forget."

Interlude Forty-four

"You can't be here!" cried Toys. "You're—"

"Not as stupid as you seem to think."

Gault pointed his gun at Toys' face. "Toss that phone over here. No, put it on the floor and slide it. None of your sodding tricks." His voice was as cold as his eyes were hot.

Toys lowered the phone, weighing his chances of throwing and hitting Sebastian without getting shot. Gault was not a great shot and Toys had a knife, clipped to the back of his belt . . . but at this distance Toys didn't like his chances. He bent slowly, placed the phone on the floor, and shoved it away from him.

"Now back away. Keep your hands where I can see them."

Toys raised his hands and straightened. He took two small backward steps. Gault advanced and crouched, holding the gun steady and looking right at Toys as he fished on the floor for the phone.

Toys whirled and dove for the nearest throne, hitting it with his outstretched palms and knocking it over. The backrest of the heavy seat chopped downward, missing Gault by inches as he spun away and snapped off two quick shots. The first missed. Both shots punched into screens on the wall, killing the FOX and MSNBC news feeds. Toys threw his weight against a second throne and it immediately canted over. Gault pivoted and fired again. The bullet punched red fire through Toys' thigh at the same instant the canting throne of the King of Fear struck the King of Plagues on the shoulder. Both men screamed in agony. The gun went spinning across the floor as Gault collapsed under six hundred pounds of teak and ebony and carved ivory.

Toys flopped to the floor and rolled over onto his stomach as blood poured from both sides of a through-and-through wound. Secondary pain exploded within him as the jagged ends of his shattered femur ground together, pinching torn muscle. Toys screamed and screamed as he clawed his way across the floor toward the fallen pistol. A dozen feet away Sebastian bellowed in rage and pain as he struggled to fight his way out from under the massive throne. The gun was almost in reach, Toys' scrabbling fingers clawed at the wooden grips, and then the world exploded in white-hot agony as Sebastian Gault, free and standing erect, stamped down with all his force on the gushing wound in Toys' leg.

Chapter Seventy-two

The *Sea of Hope*
December 21, 6:01 A.M. EST

"Something bigger than slaughtering all the people on this boat?" asked Top. "Shee-ee-it."

Khalid raised a hand. "Permission to leave the boat."

"These guys keep twisting it, don't they?" asked DeeDee.

John Smith simply grunted, which constituted a long-winded speech for him.

Something occurred to me and I snapped my fingers. "I think the Kings may have thrown us another curveball and I think they did it through their own men."

"How?" asked Church.

"It's more of the twisted logic that they use. Sarducci, the shooter I interrogated. He made a real point of saying how much the Kings wanted me dead. And you, Circe, and Auntie."

"So?"

"What if they didn't? Or what if our deaths are beside the point? What if Hanler was the real target all along?"

"What's the value of that target?" Top asked.

"Silence," I said. "I keep coming back to the disinformation thing. It's *everything* to these guys. Now factor in the fact that we now know Sebastian Gault and Hugo Vox are involved. We know that Vox used his position as a screener and all that, but he wore a lot of hats. He ran Terror Town, and he also had his think tanks. One of those think tanks was made up of—"

"Thriller authors. Like Martin Hanler," Church finished.

"Right. Hanler told me that he talked about his Hospital bombing plot in front of a bunch of other writers. Maybe he mentioned it again—or one of *them* mentioned it during a brainstorming session at T-Town. I mean, think about it. A member of one of the most dangerous terrorist organizations on earth has an entire think tank of novelists cooking up elaborate plots for him. Then he brings in counterterrorism teams from all over the world to run the plots and work out all the details. Sure, they're supposed to be coming up with protocols for stopping them, but if you flip that around, they're also creating worst-case scenarios."

"Like the London."

"And probably Fair Isle and Area 51."

"And the *Sea of Hope*," Church concluded. "I think we can safely assume that Hugo did not share all of the scenarios cooked up by the think tanks."

Church opened his cell and called Bug to order him to hack all of T-Town's think-tank records.

Under my breath I said, "Thanks, Joe . . . damn fine work. Couldn't save the world without you."

Dietrich snorted. "Really? You joined the DMS for all the pats on the back?"

Khalid sat down on the end of the couch. "That think-tank thing is pretty scary. All of those devious brains—authors, CT experts—working hundreds of hours to create the worst possible scenarios. And we're supposed to figure it out by the time the concert starts tonight?"

DeeDee looked at her watch. "Thirteen hours."

"Thank you," he said. "A countdown is very comforting."

"Okay," I said, cutting in, "let's get to work."

That fast they were all business.

One of the suitcases was filled with canvas bags filled with devices the size of shirt buttons. These are one of Hu's very best gadgets: sensors with a microchip inside and a tiny burst transmitter. Peel off the tape on one side and you expose a chameleon chemical. Press it to a wood grain door for five seconds and turn it over and the wood grain is imitated perfectly. Peel off the tape on the other side and press it to the door, and unless you know it's there, you won't see it. Especially if it's set low, below the ordinary fall of the eye. The sensors were designed specifically for bomb detection, and when they finally hit the market it will be possible to position them just about anywhere and maybe give some warning before things go boom!

We each had a dozen multipurpose processor units as well. Those were the size of a pack of Juicy Fruit and had the same chameleon coating. Affix one to a wall or stairway or anywhere in the path of human traffic or airflow and the device collects and analyzes the air for radiation, nitrites, and dense concentrations of viral material. It wasn't as sensitive as the BAMS unit I had at Fair Isle, but it wasn't far behind. And the devices were networked for greater effect.

There were also a bunch of Minicams, and some booster units to collect the signals from the tiny sensors and uplink them to the DMS satellite.

"You each have assigned sections of the ship," I said. They nodded and put their glasses back on, using the pocket mouses to pull up floor plans. "We have time, so place the sensors unobtrusively, but keep your eyes open, too. Report *anything* that looks hinky."

"Hooah," they said, and left one at a time.

I took my batch and followed my map. I headed over to the central main-deck area, which was where the concert would be. It was roped off and there were scores of workers laboring under a hot morning sun. Finishing the bandstand, doing sound checks on the massive speakers, hanging bunting, setting up tapes for line control.

The best angle to see the whole area was by the team working together to inflate several thousand red and white balloons. There were six men, all of them Mexican, seated on folding stools surrounded by big tanks of helium. Huge nets had been erected to catch any stray balloons as the men filled, tied, filled, tied, over and over again. Four other men took netfuls of the balloons aft, where, according to Circe, they would be released as the *Sea of Hope* sailed into Rio. The balloons were all biodegradable and would eventually burst harmlessly in the stratosphere, themselves acting as a symbol of green choices for a polluted planet.

I listened to the Mexicans chatter among themselves in Spanish. Nothing more sinister than speculation on next year's World Cup. One of them noticed me looking and met my eyes. He looked from me to the thousands of red and white balloons and back to me; then he rolled his eyes. I gave him a sympathetic smile and turned away. A few seconds later I heard one of the men speaking in a strangely squeaky voice and turned to see that he had sucked some of the helium out of a balloon and was speaking like Donald Duck. Everyone cracked up.

Then a fussy-looking white man in a cruise line blazer yelled at him and the Mexican pasted a contrite look on his face and tied off the balloon. As I passed, I made a quiet remark about the fussy man's personal hygiene, only loud enough for the six Mexicans to hear. They all cracked up again.

I moved on.

My credentials got me into the VIP area. Behind gates and decorative shrubbery was an entirely separate set of pools and waterside bars. I slouched around trying to look like I wasn't looking. Everywhere I looked, though, was a paparazzo's dream. Movie stars in thongs or Speedos that left nothing to the imagination. I saw Pink, wearing a bikini that could fit comfortably into a shot glass, lounging by the pool reading a Kelly Simmons novel. Two chairs away, John Legend was playing chess with that short guy from *American Idol*. Legend was kicking his ass. There were rock stars and R & B stars and rappers and celebrities from the movies and TV. Some of the Generation Hope kids—daughters and sons of the global power players—were peppered among them, either gawking in starstruck awe or pretending the kind of indolence that only teenagers can pull off.

I moved among them, placing the chameleon sensors here and there, taking my time so that I didn't attract any attention.

I didn't see anyone looking particularly sinister. It's not like on the old *Batman* TV show, where bad guys wore shirts with HENCHMAN, THUG, and EVIL ASSISTANT stenciled on the chest. Would be pretty damn useful, though.

I drifted out of the VIP area and placed the last of my sensors on the major stairways, then headed back to the suite. The others were already there. All of the sensors had been placed, but no one had seen anything.

Interlude Forty-five

The Chamber of the Kings
December 21, 5:22 A.M. EST

"You traitorous bastard!" Gault screamed as he stamped down over and over again. "You Judas!"

Toys felt his broken thighbone shatter. The pain was

so intense, so enormous, that he could no longer scream. His mouth was open, his lungs pushed air out, but the only sound he could make was a thin and nearly ultrasonic shriek that tore itself from each tortured nerve ending.

The world swam in and out of focus as clouds of black and red swirled behind his eyes.

Then abruptly the pain stopped.

The moment was suspended inside a crystal teardrop of time. Toys wondered if this was what it felt like to die. Had the jagged ends of broken bone severed an artery? Was he bleeding out and drifting into the big darkness? Or had he reached the end of pain? Was pain a finite thing, a line drawn in the mind that, once crossed, became an irrelevant concept?

He did not know and did not know how to think about it.

He lay in a cocoon of unfeeling silence for—how long? A second? Hours?

Then feeling returned to him, one unkind bit at a time.

The first thing he felt was a tear breaking from the corner of his eye and falling down toward his ear. It felt cold instead of warm.

"G-God . . . ," Toys whispered. A whisper was all that he was capable of.

Darkness obscured his vision and he blinked. No. Not darkness.

Sebastian Gault stood above him, impossibly tall. Pale and blue-white in the glow of the wall of screens. Not the face Toys had loved for so long. This was Gault's new face. Blond and angular and handsome. The work of surgeons. Nothing that was part of nature. He looked like Apollo. Like the god of the sun.

"God . . . ," Toys whispered again. The pain was an unrelenting fire in his leg. "Please . . ."

Gault stood and looked down at Toys. With his head bent his eyes were in shadows. It gave his face a weird appearance, like a beautiful skull.

"We've had our suspicions, you know. The Goddess and me. She didn't trust her son, and I've lost my trust in you."

". . . God . . . please . . ."

Gault ran both sets of fingers through his hair. He removed a handkerchief and mopped sweat from his face. He folded the handkerchief and returned it to his pocket.

"Last week we planted bugs in Hugo's office. We heard him make a call to someone at the DMS. I wanted to kill him right then and there. We decided that we would let Santoro do it. Goddesses always need new angels."

". . . Sebastian, please . . ."

"And then we heard you in Hugo's office. You, on the phone. Not just with the DMS . . . no, you had to go and call sodding Joe Ledger!"

Gault darted in and kicked Toys in the stomach like a placekicker going for a thirty-yard punt. Toys screamed and writhed. Bloody spittle flew from his mouth and patterned the tile floor.

"I won't ask you why," said Gault, his mild tone completely at odds with what he had just done. "I know why."

"L-love . . . ," Toys croaked in a voice that was barely human.

"Yes. Love. You pathetic little faggot. Do you think I would ever lower myself to love a creature like you? All you've ever been to me is a convenience. Someone to get things. Someone to make sure the dry cleaning is picked up and the wet bar fully stocked." Gault shook his head. "Love? It's not love, Toys . . . it's jealousy. You can't stand the fact that I can love and you're too damaged and twisted to be capable of it."

Toys' lips formed the word again: "Love."

He braced his elbows and tried to heave his head and shoulders off the floor. Instantly there was a burst of unbearable agony from his shattered leg that tore a ragged scream from him. He tried to twist away from the pain, but as he did something hard dug into his opposite hip.

"Don't dare use the word 'love' for what *you* feel," sneered Gault. "I *know* love. Eris *is* love. I know the love of a goddess incarnate."

Breathing through the pain took all of his strength, but Toys fought to get words past his gritted teeth. "You . . . don't understand . . . you fucking idiot. . . ."

The words materialized as a snarl of unfiltered rage.

Gault smiled. "I understand everything."

"No, Sebastian," Toys snarled. ". . . you *never* understood me."

Toys dug his hand under his body, under his hip, to the hard thing that gouged into him. He wrapped his fingers around the pistol, and with a savage growl that was more animal than human he tore it out, pointed, and fired.

Chapter Seventy-three

Circe, Church, and I sat down at the stateroom's dining table. In my absence it had been converted into a full-blown intelligence center, with multiple screens that showed images from the minicams and collected data streams from the sensors. Room service brought in heaps of food. Ghost sat with his head on my lap and I fed him bits of hamburger as we worked.

Circe also had access to the Generation Hope security network, so we prowled that as well. There was an insane amount of movement on every part of the ship. It was confusing and irritating, and probably the least useful scenario for accurate surveillance and assessment. Once, for just a second, I thought I saw Santoro . . . but when I played back the feed it was someone else. Damn. Wishful thinking.

Circe went over the schedule for the event and we looked for holes in it. There were plenty. We made a list of moments when an attack would get the most media punch. There were several of those as well but one that really glared.

"The event gets rolling at seven with the first round of musical guests," said Circe. "The prince of England will take the stage at eight to make his speech. It will be simulcast all over the world. They're estimating an audience of at least three billion. More if China relents at the last minute and allows citizens to watch. After that the ship will head into Rio for a private party with the celebrities and their families."

"How's security for that?" I asked.

"Huge. Over a thousand Brazilian military," she said, "plus three SAS teams and four times as many Marines and SEALs. Heavy support from ground vehicles and helicopters. Gunboats in the water. Plus Secret Service for one-to-one security."

"Can we identify anyone who was vetted by Vox?"

"Way ahead of you," Church said with an approving nod. "I passed along three names to Director Linden Brierly, and he is having them quietly pulled."

"Pulled and detained?"

"Yes. Understand something, Captain . . . a lot of people were vetted by Vox, including Grace Courtland."

I nodded. "Yeah. It complicates things."

Circe touched my arm. "You . . . you don't think that Grace was—?"

"No," I said decisively. "Absolutely not."

Church nodded. "That only complicates things, because it may well be that most of the people Hugo passed are trustworthy."

"Do you think the attack will be in Rio?" asked Circe.

"No," I said, "I think it'll be when the Prince is giving his speech. Killing the Prince and his guests is a solid punch by the Kings. After all, the speech is about disease. It calls on the new generation to unite, to become a unified family, that share money and resources, effort and cooperation, with the goal of eradicating diseases that are perpetuated by extreme poverty. Diseases that did not need to exist, because cures and treatments exist in wealthier lands. That's all key stuff for the Kings to twist. It'll be on every TV in the world. It's the stuff of legends, and we know that part of what the Kings are doing is myth building."

"Agreed," said Church, and Circe nodded. "Let's work out how they'll do it."

Together we came up with about forty really workable scenarios, but the problem was that none of them stood out more than the others.

Finally I looked at my watch. Time was running out.

Circe pounded her fist on the table. "God! I wish we could simply make an announcement, cancel everything, and let the Navy ships take everyone off."

"We could," said Church, "and that would force the Kings into an even more desperate act than what they are planning."

"On the other hand," I said, "we have an obligation to the President, the Prince of Wales, and all of the other families who stand to lose children."

"I'm open to suggestions, Captain."

"We could sabotage the engines. Play it like mechanical failure."

"To what end? That would leave us floating out here with no solution."

I did some math. "There are sixteen operators on board now. Ten from Tiger Shark and my team. I could take the President's daughters under my direct supervision; Top could take Prince William and—"

"And initiate a firefight?"

"Okay, then we cut the number in half and save the eight targets with the highest political value."

Church considered it.

"That might work. But we would need the other teams in the air and in the water right as that happens. That way if you get pinned down or trapped, we'd know help was on the way."

"And what if the ship is rigged to blow up?" asked Circe.

Church said nothing. Nor did I.

Circe sighed.

"Plagues," she said. "This has to be coming from the King of Plagues."

Chapter Seventy-four

The *Sea of Hope*
December 21, 6:30 P.M. EST

The concert was thirty minutes away. A big, cold hand seemed to be clamped around my heart.

"I have to go on deck," I said. I'd already changed clothes again, as had the rest of Echo Team. Circe walked me to the cabin door.

"I don't know whether to wish you luck," she said, "or to hope that you find nothing at all."

"Nothing at all would be nice." But we both knew that was unlikely.

She nodded.

Behind us, Mr. Church was speaking into the phone. "Mr. President . . ."

"God," Circe whispered, "that's going to be a painful call."

"From both ends of the line," I said.

"This is insane," she said.

"Welcome to my world."

But she shook her head. "I was born to it."

Before I could ask her to explain that, she turned and went into her bedroom.

I patted my pockets to make sure I had everything I needed. Yep, everything but a goddamn clue. Then I clicked my tongue for Ghost, who bounded off the couch.

We went out to fight the impossible fight.

Interlude Forty-six

The Chamber of the Kings
December 21, 5:49 A.M. EST

Toys dragged himself across the floor and managed—with curses and tears and screams—to pull himself into one of the chairs. When he realized that it was the throne of the King of Plagues he laughed so long and so hard that his mind nearly snapped. And then he wept for so long that he thought he would never stop.

The tourniquet he'd tied around his leg was probably too tight. Maybe he'd lose the leg. Maybe he'd get blood poisoning.

Maybe he didn't give a damn.

"Sebastian . . . ," he said, and the tears started again. Eventually they stopped. Everything stops eventually.

When he could breathe again he pulled the American's phone from his pocket. He had recovered it during the ten thousand years it took him to crawl across the floor. The casing was cracked and it was sticky with blood. His.

He shivered and he knew that shock was setting in. With all the alcohol already in his system and now the bullet wound and the shattered femur, he figured that his system did not stand a chance against shock.

Toys opened the phone and punched in Hugo Vox's number.

"Toys!"

In his delirium Toys thought he heard the phone ringing and Vox answering at the same time. Then there was the sound of footsteps and Toys turned to see Vox lumber into the room. The big man had a big gun in his hand and he fanned the barrel around the room with a professional competence that Toys admired. Toys tried to say so, but his voice was a slur.

The American holstered the gun and knelt beside him, his face grave with concern.

"Jeez, you're a goddamn mess. Who did this to you?"

"Sebastian."

"Yeah," he said. "What I figured. Shit."

Toys touched Vox's face with the tip of his finger. "Are you . . . real?"

"You better hope so, kiddo." Vox fetched the wheeled leather chair of War's Conscience and gingerly placed Toys' shattered leg on it. Toys screamed.

"Sorry, kiddo." Vox adjusted the tourniquet, which was itself a moment of exquisite agony. He got water and a cloth and mopped Toys's face and then brought over a glass of brandy. "This will help until we can get you to a doctor."

Toys sipped the brandy greedily. It burned through him with a calm fire, pushing back the pain, restoring a measure of control.

"Now," said Vox, "tell me what happened?"

"Sebastian shot me. And I . . . I guess I shot him."

Vox looked around. The room was empty except for them. "The fuck is he?"

"I shot him in the heart. But . . . I think he was wearing Kevlar. Pity."

"Clever bastard."

Toys coughed and winced. "Shame he got away."

"I wouldn't worry about it, kiddo. But . . . if you had the gun, how did he get away?"

"I . . . let him go," said Toys. He drank half of the brandy, coughed again, and drank some more. It seemed to burn more of the pain away.

"Why? Why not put a couple of rounds through that face-lift of his?"

Toys shrugged. "Why bother?" His face was white with pain and trauma, but the brandy seemed to help him focus his thoughts.

The American sighed. "You got a good heart, kiddo. You're lucky it's still beating."

"Sorry."

"Screw it. It's all gone to shit anyway. The DMS know who I am now, so I'm going to have to go way off the radar."

"So where does that leave us?" asked Toys.

"In the wind." He went and fetched the bottle of brandy and another glass. He refilled Toys' glass and poured himself a generous shot. "Ah . . . maybe I've been playing this game too long. My blood pressure could blow bolts out of plate steel and I haven't taken a comfortable shit in five years."

"Well, thanks for sharing."

"It's all stress. I . . . don't think I want to deal with it anymore."

"So . . . what? You're going to retire to Florida and raise flamingoes?"

"Oh, fuck no. I didn't say I was tired of the Seven Kings. I like that shit. I have stuff I haven't tried yet."

"And your secret identity was holding you back?"

Vox chuckled. "No—or not entirely. Mom was the biggest cockblocker in the world. Now she might not be."

"She might escape this."

"Yeah, she might. She's got a lot of clever up her sleeve, too. But you have to think that you're vulnerable before you believe that you should run from danger. She thinks she really is a frigging goddess."

"I know. I got the speech from Apollo."

"Who? Oh . . . got it."

A wave of pain hit Toys and he bared his teeth, then in a very conversational voice said, "Ow."

Vox reached over and pushed a button on one of the computer consoles built into the big table.

"Chang and Kuo will get you to a doctor I own in Toronto. You'll be right as rain."

Toys looked down at the ruin of his leg. "Sebastian enjoyed it."

"Sebastian's a prick," said Vox. "He may have been a great man once, but let me tell you a secret, kiddo: I think that without you he wouldn't have amounted to shit."

Toys said nothing.

"Which makes me wonder what *you* could have accomplished given the right support and freedom of action. Gault never saw you as anything but an employee." He shook his head. "Small thinking."

Toys studied him for a long time. "Why?"

"Why what?"

"Why are you helping me? What's in it for you?"

Vox sipped his brandy. "I told you before, I haven't been able to trust Santoro for years, and I need someone I can trust."

"An 'employee'?" Toys said with a wry smile.

Vox's face was serious. "No. I can always buy more people. But you . . . I think you may have outgrown the point where you can be bought."

Toys nodded and they sipped their brandy.

"I never thought I'd say this," said Toys eventually, "but I hope Joe Ledger lives through all of this. He still has work to do."

"For the Seven Kings," said the American.

"For us," said Toys.

"Sure," said the King of Fear with a laugh. "Why not? For us."

Interlude Forty-seven

Aboard the *Delta of Venus*
December 21, 6:59 P.M. EST

Eris and Gault had a dozen laptops open so they could watch all of the major network feeds. They were naked, both of them covered in welts and scratches.

"This is what I've been working toward since I took control of the Kings from my son."

"You do know with Hugo on the run from the DMS you'll eventually come under scrutiny."

"Eris will," she said. "But that poor woman is going to die tonight."

Gault nuzzled her neck. "So, who is it that I just shagged cross-eyed?"

"I'm not sure. We'll have to think up a new name. Maybe Isis. Or Hera."

"Will you shed a tear if Hugo is caught?"

Eris laughed. "Don't be absurd."

"Would he shed a tear if *you* were caught?"

"Silly questions, lovely boy. Pay attention."

They snuggled together and watched the screen.

The show was beginning.

Chapter Seventy-five

The *Sea of Hope*
December 21, 7:19 P.M. EST

The bandstand was a gorgeous confection of glittering lights, thousands of honey-sweet flowers, mirrored surfaces, and tall vertical posters that showed the faces of smiling children of all races. Healthy children, not the starving and wasted faces used in some charity advertisements. This event was all about rising above sickness and poverty. This was about the coordinated work of tens of thousands of people on six continents who shared a common belief that no child should suffer from a disease that existed only because that child's family lived in abject poverty.

No one associated with the event, except the low-wage staff aboard the ship, was getting paid to be here. The performers even bought their own plane tickets. Many of the celebrities paid to bring friends and guests; others donated money to the charity, recorded songs or public-service announcements, and arranged to have portions of CD and DVD sales allotted to Generation Hope.

The goodwill mega-event was being broadcast all over the world. Thousands of concert venues and tens of thousands of movie theaters were simulcasting the concert. Phone banks in seventy countries were staffed to take what forecasters predicted would be a record number of donation calls. The President of the United States would speak from the tour's end point, Rio de Janiero, as would Prince Charles and the heads of twenty other countries. Even China, a late holdout, had agreed to broadcast the concert, albeit with a ten-second delay to allow "bad messaging" to be censored.

Anderson Cooper probably put it best when he said, "This is what humanity does when we all realize we are one family."

Rafael Santoro found it all . . . so vulgar.

He stood amid the thousands aboard the *Sea of Hope,* a PRESS badge hung around his neck, and watched as the emcee—the actor Hugh Laurie—walked onto the stage amid applause that shook the heavens.

Santoro stood with his hands in his pockets. His left hand caressed a small hypodermic with a plastic cap. The other stroked the beautifully curved handle of his knife.

Chapter Seventy-six

Ghost and I had to fight our way through the crowd. You'd think people would be more considerate of the blind.

I wore heavy sunglasses and Ghost wore a guide dog harness.

We were buffeted and pushed and jostled to the point where Ghost was about to blow his cover as a docile guide by biting someone's throat out and I was almost to the point where I was going to let him.

Like my other pair of DMS specs, this pair had a display on one lens. I had it set to send random crowd images from the minicams. I was looking for someone with a trigger device or a bomb vest. Or a convenient gun butt sticking out of his pocket. Nothing.

And then that changed.

I pulled Ghost to one side and shoved my hand into my pocket to play with the camera control.

Holy shit, I thought.

I tapped my commlink. "Cowboy to team. Check the feed from camera thirty-three. Guess who came to the party?"

Chapter Seventy-seven

Rafael Santoro moved through the shadows, avoiding the party lights, trying to stay invisible. He knew that after tonight his face would have to change. More plastic surgery. Everyone aboard the ship seemed to have a digital camera or a camera option on their cell phone. And all the media. Over three hundred members of the world press were here. His face, even as a noncelebrity in the back of a crowd, would be all over cable TV and the Net. Such a pity. He'd come to like this face.

Ah well, the Goddess would buy him whatever face she wanted him to have.

On the bandstand, Taylor Swift had just finished her set and the audience was cheering and applauding as if the girl had walked on water. Santoro sniffed. He was not a fan of rock or country music, preferring operas or silence. He did, however, enjoy the enthusiasm of the crowd. They were loud and excited and thoroughly caught up in the moment. The daughters of the President were dancing right in front of the stage now as the Jonas Brothers launched into their brand of pop confection. Santoro eyed the children, fingering the handle of the knife in his pocket. Would they become angels, too?

Probably not. There would not be time for that.

Pity.

"Crab puff?" asked a waitress, a beaky-nosed blonde with ice blue eyes who held a tray of hors d'ourves. Santoro smiled at her but shook his head. Now was not the time to nibble on fried muck.

Waiters kept trying to offer him snacks and drinks, and he waved them away, first with grace and then with mounting irritation as the evening wore on. Performer after performer took the stage. Fireworks painted the sky with carnival colors, and the laughter and conversation were almost loud enough to drown out the music.

"Spinach quiche?"

Santoro waved the waiter away without even bothering to look at him. He wished he could hang a sign around his neck: *leave me alone!*

He looked at his watch. Nearly time.

The concert had dragged on. Beyoncé, Pink, Jennifer Hudson, Lady Gaga. None of whom Santoro even knew.

Santoro walked the decks, occasionally slipping downstairs to check on the teams of Kingsmen who were waiting for this moment. As he returned to the deck another waiter accosted him, and another. Santoro had to dig his hands into his pockets and grip his knife in order to calm himself.

Jay-Z finished his set to raucous applause. Santoro consulted his watch again as U2 took the stage. Time was moving along. Nearly eight now. Santoro saw Prince William and Prince Harry go out onstage to shake the hand of each band member. One of the Bush girls was there, too. And so many others.

It was a nice blend of victims and witnesses. Pity that so few would be elevated to angels, but it was not that kind of event.

Santoro wondered what the Seven Kings would be like after tonight. First thing tomorrow morning a team of workers would arrive at McCullough to remove all of the valuables, including the thrones, tapestries, computer systems, and contents of the wine cellars. They would also set the charges. The first subbasement was packed with enough C4 to hurl the stones of the castle for a mile in every direction. There would be nothing left but a crater, and the St. Lawrence River would fill that in within seconds.

Starting over in a new place would be a chore. The kind of fussy busywork that Santoro did not enjoy. He wanted to get out into the field. They would lose a lot of Kingsmen tonight. Many more of the Chosen. The escape craft Santoro held in readiness was designed for one. The rest would die along with the naïve fools who were running this event.

After tonight, after waiting some months for the immediate outcry to die down, Santoro would begin scouting for new recruits, both Chosen and Kingsmen. The thought of that pleased him.

He drifted to the farthest corner of the deck, where it was a little quieter and where he could see everything as the drama unfolded. His active role was done. All he had to do now was enjoy the performance that had taken so many months and so much effort and money to craft. And, of course, to make sure that nothing went wrong. No interference of any kind would be allowed to spoil the Goddess's triumph.

Ahh . . . it would be so delicious. He put his hands in his pockets and caressed the handle of the knife.

Then someone bumped into him and Santoro turned with a snarl, but that changed immediately to an apology.

"I beg your pardon," he said.

The blind man looked in the wrong direction, apparently confused by all the noise. The dog, a gorgeous white shepherd, looked straight at Santoro.

"Ah, jeez, mister," said the blind man. "Did I bump into you?"

"It is of no matter. My own clumsiness. Here, let me guide you to the rail. It's less crowded there."

"Wow, thanks . . . that's very kind."

Santoro took the blind man's arm and steered him through the crowd. The guide dog snarled.

"Quiet," snapped the blind man.

"Your dog is probably unnerved by all the noise."

"Nah," said the blind man. "He just doesn't like scum-sucking assholes."

Santoro blinked. "Sorry?"

The blind man turned and tugged down his glasses and gave Santoro a comical wink.

Santoro sighed. "Hello, Mr. Ledger. I've been looking forward to meeting you."

Chapter Seventy-eight

The *Sea of Hope*
December 21, 8:01 P.M. EST

"Hello, asshole," I said.

"Are you always this crude? It's unbecoming for a person of rank."

"Actually," I said, "I'd really enjoy showing you how crude I can be."

"Do you expect to do something right here and now? With all of these important people around?"

"Only if I have to."

"I could kill you where you stand," murmured Santoro, smiling faintly. His hands were in his pockets; the handle of the knife was hard against his right palm.

"Really? Would be fun to test that theory."

"Are you always this foolish?"

"Do you always wear a dancing red light on your tie?"

Santoro looked down and saw the pinpoint of a laser sight hovering over his heart. He looked up to find the shooter but could not see him.

"Don't bother looking," I said. "He'll find you if you twitch the wrong way. Now—let's go."

Santoro spread his hands. He looked amused. "Very well."

Over the PA system the emcee announced Prince William. The applause was absolutely thunderous. It was probably going to be a great speech; it would probably make me want to grab for my checkbook. But I had other things I wanted to hear more.

A waitress stepped up beside Santoro. Beaky nose, blue eyes, short-barreled Ruger held under her tray. "Sure you don't want a crab puff?"

Santoro smiled with genuine appreciation.

I let Santoro lead the way belowdecks. We passed another waiter and at least fifty passengers hurrying up to hear the Prince. Santoro did not try to escape, didn't grab anyone to use as a hostage, not even when he saw that the laser sight was gone. That worried me a little, because it showed a level of confidence consistent with a belief that he was going to slip this punch.

At the bottom of the stairs I told Santoro to turn right.

He did and we entered another corridor, and this one was also packed with people.

I tapped my earbud. "Find me a clear route."

All I got was a crackle of white noise.

"Cowboy to command."

"It won't work," said Santoro calmly.

DeeDee stepped up and put the barrel of her pistol against Santoro's spine and we steered him into an alcove. She patted him down. Not a thorough job with everyone watching, but she found his pistol and took it, and took the knife from his pocket. She also removed a small syringe and handed it to me, then shifted the pistol from his back to his temple.

"You have one second to tell us how you're jamming this before I blow your shit up right here right now."

"No need for threats," the Spaniard said. "All communications are being jammed by a system even I cannot disable."

"What's the syringe for?"

"It's epinephrine. I have allergies."

"Right," I said, pocketing the syringe.

Above deck I heard the reverb of the Prince's speech.

"Sound's back on, Boss," said DeeDee.

"No. The public-address systems are fine," said Santoro. "We want that noise. But nothing that is happening here is getting out."

"That doesn't make sense," I growled. "I thought this whole thing was to broadcast the Kings' big bonanza event."

He smiled like a crocodile. "What makes you think *this* is the event?"

"C'mon, Boss," growled DeeDee. "Let's drag this shitbag back to the suite. I guarantee you I'll find—"

And Santoro moved. I don't think I have ever seen anyone move that fast. He pivoted and struck DeeDee in the throat with his left hand and then flicked his right so that a sliver of bright metal dropped into his palm. His hand was a blur and then DeeDee was falling against me, blood exploding from her face, a scream tearing itself from her throat.

Ghost and I lunged for Santoro at the same time, no more than a half second after his cut, but his hand was already moving. I felt heat in my chest and then I was falling. I landed hard on Ghost's back and heard him yelp in pain as we both crashed down together.

I heard people in the hallway scream—first in shock and then in pain as Santoro leaped into the crowd, cutting left and right, and then burst through on the other side, running at full speed down the hall.

Chapter Seventy-nine

The *Sea of Hope*
December 21, 8:03 P.M. EST

The video feeds went dead all at once.

"What the hell?" Circe yelled.

Church was right there. "What is it?"

"We lost video and audio—"

Outside the cabin they heard shouts. And then gunfire.

Chapter Eighty

I had two choices: see to DeeDee or chase Santoro. I cut a quick look down and saw that she was still alive. Her face was a bloody ruin and she had one hand clamped over her left eye. Blood welled from between her fingers.

"Go! *Go!*" she screamed.

I hauled myself to my feet. Ghost squirmed out from under, whining and trembling. I couldn't check him out, either.

I ran.

"Clear the way!" I bellowed, and pulled my gun. People slammed themselves against the walls. Some fools turned and ran away from me, obscuring my view of Santoro. I pelted down the hallway. I collided with people. I punched one poor bastard just to get him out of my way. Santoro vanished around the far turn and I ran harder. Behind me I could hear Ghost barking, but the sound was fading. He wasn't following me. How badly was he hurt?

No time to worry about that, either.

I skidded around the corner, going wide in case Santoro was lying in wait. He wasn't, but there was a cabin steward on his knees with his hands clutching a throat that sprayed blood. I had a glimpse of a single wild despairing eye as I ran past.

I had to take two short side corridors. One was empty, and in the other a woman huddled on the ground, hands over her head. I saw no blood as I ran past.

There was a scream ahead. I put on another burst of speed, but as I neared the corner a teenage girl came flying around the bend, propelled by a savage kick from Santoro. I slammed into the girl; her forehead hit me on the mouth, bursting my lips against my teeth.

I twisted as I rolled, pushing the girl away from me, but Santoro darted in and kicked my gun out of my hand, then pivoted and dove for it. He came out of his roll with the gun in his hand just as I hopped to a crouch. I had no choice, so I grabbed the teenager by the collar and the belt and flung her at Santoro's legs. It was a wicked and vile thing for me to do, but the alternative would have been much worse, even for the girl.

Santoro went flying forward and the gun passed me and bounced down a set of stairs. The girl curled into a fetal ball of pain and screamed.

I lunged for Santoro, but he rolled onto his back and kicked up with both feet. Suddenly I was flying backward into the wall. My head struck hard enough to shake loose the moorings of reality, and my sight flickered on and off. Last thing I saw was Santoro coming at me with the short knife in his hand.

Chapter Eighty-one

The *Sea of Hope*
December 21, 8:06 P.M. EST

On the stage a pair of burly SAS men tackled the Prince just as heavy-caliber bullets ripped through the flowers. But the shots were aimed low and they missed the trio as the agents dragged the Prince to safety.

One of the burly bodyguards saw a shooter taking aim at Jay-Z and launched his 340 pounds from the edge of the stage in a diving tackle that crushed the shooter and snapped his spine. The Chosen next to him put his barrel against the bodyguard's head but he never made the shot. A big red hole appeared in the center of his chest and his body was flung backward against the rail. Two other Chosen turned to see where the shot had come from. The sounds of the gunshots that killed them were lost beneath the din.

High above the melee, John Smith worked the bolt and fired. Again and again. Each shot hit the target. Problem was that he didn't have nearly enough bullets.

"Shit," he murmured to himself.

He worked the bolt and fired, worked the bolt and fired.

Then he jerked his head up as a fresh wave of gun-fire erupted from above him. He rolled over and looked into the sky. John Smith smiled.

The sky was filled with TradeWinds Motor Kites. He did a quick count. Forty. No . . . fifty of them. From each harness a DMS agent hung suspended, one hand on the controls, the other clutching a handgun. They rained fire down on the Chosen.

"'Bout time," said John Smith. He rolled back onto his stomach, worked the bolt, and fired.

Chapter Eighty-two

Santoro came at me with a flurry of vicious cuts, and I backpedaled as fast as I could. Even so, I could feel the tip of that little knife ripping away my shirt. Hot lines of agony crisscrossed my chest as he lunged deeper.

He was so goddamn fast.

My back hit the wall at the turning and Santoro smiled and threw himself at me, but his own expression of triumph gave it away. I hit and dropped into a crouch and punched him in the thigh. I wanted to hit him in the nuts, but he brought his leg up. Even so, the blow knocked him back and I dove low and long and caught him around the knees and bore him down. His back hit hard and flat and it drove a *whuuuh!* out of him.

I curled my knees under me to propel my body forward for a downward body slam. I wanted to knock the rest of the air out of him, make him choke, and slowly beat the shit out of him.

But as I lunged, he slammed his elbow down on the crown of my head, then slammed his fist between my shoulder blades. It was the fist that held the knife, and the blade tore through my vest and skin and muscle like a dagger of pure fire.

I screamed.

Santoro released the knife and punched me across the face, once, twice, three times, and then pivoted to kick my deadweight off his legs.

I flopped over. Lines of fire radiated out from the

puncture. I knew the blade was short, but it was jammed in next to my spine. My whole body twitched.

Then Santoro was on his knees, his fingers tearing at my pockets.

"Where is it?" he snarled, first in English and then, as he became more desperate, growling it in Spanish. In my daze I couldn't quite understand what he was doing. He had me; I was completely vulnerable. All he had to do was pull out the knife and cut my throat.

Then he dug his scrabbling fingers into my left front pant pocket and I knew what he was after. The syringe.

He closed his hands around it.

And then Ghost hit him like a white thunderbolt.

Chapter Eighty-three

The *Sea of Hope*
December 21, 8:08 P.M. EST

Top Sims came out of the companionway with his pistol in a two-handed grip. There were scores of men in black masks. The deck was littered with the dead, but there were over a thousand civilians. Top opened fire at every balaclava he saw, going for body shots. Head shots were too risky with so many civilians. The ceramic frag bullets lived up to their reputation. The first one struck a Chosen in the back and the man seemed to explode. It was disgusting, but damn if Top didn't like the effect, because the man next to him stopped to gape at the sudden horror. Top took him in the chest.

Then a shadow passed him and Khalid was there, firing and firing.

"Heads below!" came a yell, followed by, "Broadway! Broadway!" and "Liberty! Liberty!" as DMS agents dropped from their kites into the thick of the fight.

"Welcome to hell!" yelled Top.

THE CHOSEN FALTERED for a moment. This was not part of the plan Santoro had described. Ship's security, some Secret Service, and a scattering of Special Forces from both sides of the Atlantic. Not this. Not men appearing out of the sky, flying on batwings.

One of the Chosen opened up with an M4, cutting three of the agents virtually in half. Then he staggered as a slender steel rod punched through his breastbone and stood out from between his shoulders. He took one staggering turning step and saw more men swarming over the rail. Men who dripped with seawater and who held weapons that looked like clip-fed crossbows.

"Goddess!" the man said, and then vomited blood as he pitched forward.

TWO DECKS DOWN, the second wave of the Goddess's troops erupted from their cabins. These were the Kingsmen. These were the elite of the armies of the Seven Kings. They swarmed into the halls, splitting to head right and left, running with weapons at port arms. Every one of them had been in combat before. All of them were stone killers, and this was the event they had dreamed of.

They pounded up the stairs toward the main deck, ready to join the fight, knowing that they could sweep away any resistance.

Chapter Eighty-four

Ghost and Santoro tumbled backward in a tangle of snarls and shouts and grunts. I struggled to raise my head, fighting to regain control over my arms and legs.

Santoro howled in pain as Ghost slashed him with his teeth; then he punched Ghost hard in the ribs and even from fifteen feet away I could hear bones break. A terrible sharp yelp broke from the dog's throat.

But even that didn't stop him. Ghost bit and tore at Santoro, ripping his left arm, drawing long lines of red down his leg.

I reached over my shoulder and grabbed the knife. It was really a small thing. Not much bigger than a nail file and probably twice as thick. I knew all the rules about not pulling a knife out of a wound. It can make the bleeding worse; it can do more damage.

Fuck it. The thing was pressing on something that was killing my legs.

I tightened my fingers around the handle and pulled. My scream was just as loud as Ghost's as Santoro kicked him in his broken ribs.

Ghost staggered sideways. Blood soaked the fur of his side and there was blood on his muzzle. I prayed it wasn't his. He snarled bravely at Santoro and then flopped down.

Santoro stood hunched over, his chest heaving, sweat and blood running down his face. He stared at me as I struggled to my feet, and spit on the floor between us.

"You will drown in a river of blood," he said, his voice still filled with menace and power.

And then I knew.

He *knew* that I knew.

I looked at the syringe, which lay on the floor by the wall. His eyes followed mine; then he looked at me and smiled.

"Yes," he said, confirming my worst fears. "And there is nothing you can do to stop it."

We both dove for the syringe at the same time.

Chapter Eighty-five

The *Sea of Hope*
December 21, 8:09 P.M. EST

The Kingsmen fought their way up onto the deck, killing everything in their way, even some of the Chosen. They also wore balaclavas, but theirs were white and had a small golden circle on the forehead. The symbol of the Goddess.

Bunny stood with his back to the wall beside the hatchway where he had ducked out of the firefight to reload. He was on his last magazine and would have to scavenge an M4 from one of the Chosen. Suddenly gunfire tore through the hatchway, killing one DMS agent and the two civilians he was trying to protect. A swarm of men erupted from the stairway, firing wildly. They flooded past him, and he was nearly invisible to them, partially blocked by the heavy storm hatch.

Bunny swung his gun around and emptied his magazine into the whole line of them. The dying tripped over the dead, clogging the hatch. They had no angle for return fire. The slide locked back on his pistol and Bunny dropped it without a thought and snatched up an M4. He leaned around the hatch and shoved his arm in, firing as he did so. Holding the weapon one-handed while firing required immense strength. Bunny emptied the whole magazine.

He was grinning.

"Little help!" he yelled as he fished for a fresh magazine. A SEAL ran over to him, assessed the problem, and plucked a fragmentation grenade from his belt.

"Fire in the hole!"

He threw it into the hatch.

The Kingsmen had nowhere to run.

Those who survived the blast were dazed and deafened and bleeding, and they could do nothing when Bunny and the SEAL stood shoulder to shoulder and fired down into the tangled mass of the Goddess's elite.

Chapter Eighty-six

The *Sea of Hope*
December 21, 8:09 P.M. EST

Santoro's hands reached for the syringe. I reached for Santoro. He grabbed the instrument and I closed one hand around his wrist and knotted the other in his hair. The pain in my back was a howling thing, but I took everything it had to give me and bellowed like a fiend as I slammed Santoro face forward onto the deck. His nose exploded. I slammed him again and again.

He stopped trying for the syringe and rolled sideways. I held on with all my strength and tore away a handful of hair and a patch of bloody scalp. Santoro screamed. He lay on his side and tried to kick me, but I blocked the kicks with my bent knees.

I threw the hank of bloody hair in his face and followed it with a punch that shattered bone.

Santoro reeled back, bleeding and dazed, his eyes rolling up in his head. Something abruptly shifted in his eyes and his hands came up defensively to protect his face. I thought it was a ploy . . . but when he spoke the change was there in his voice.

"No!" he shrieked, the single word drenched with terror. "Please!"

No.

God Almighty.

This monster . . . this *thing* dared to beg for mercy.

The very concept of it made me insane with fury. I rolled to my knees and hammered punches down on him. He screamed and screamed, flailing in panic now. Somewhere in his dark mind he had crossed the threshold of combat and entered the territory of defeat. For most people—for warriors—there is a lot of no-man's-land between those two poles. For most people there is a gradual slide from courage to cowardice.

But not for Santoro.

Something in him *snapped* and that fast he lost the belief that he could win this fight. Maybe it was the fact that he knew he could not get that syringe, that even if he could somehow escape the moment then he was still as doomed as the rest of us.

Maybe that was it.

I don't know, and at that moment I didn't care. I didn't even see *him* as I pounded on him. I saw the faces of Zoë and Laura Plympton. Of Charles Grey. Of Mikey, bleeding out on a cold laboratory floor, murdered by his father because the alternative was the possibility that this man, this fucking creature, would find him. And make him into an *angel*.

My fists were a blur. My arms were red to the elbows. I could taste Santoro's blood in my mouth as it flew with each impact.

He kept screaming those two words.

"No."

"Please!"

How many times had he heard them? From his angels. From the people like Plympton and Grey and Amber Taylor, who had been forced by Santoro to look at the photographs and then compare them with the pictures of their own loved ones.

How many times had he heard those two words and gotten an erotic thrill from them?

God.

This man had tortured good people, he had turned innocent people, into weapons of mass destruction. The London Hospital. Area 51. Fair Isle.

This man had ordered the hits on Amber Taylor's family. And on Starbucks.

I battered his face into red impossibility and then worked on his body. My hands were lumps of pain at the ends of my arms, but I didn't care. I staggered to my feet and kicked him, breaking whatever I could break.

"Stop!"

The voice hit me harder than I was hitting Santoro. I wheeled around and saw two figures through a red haze.

Circe.

Mr. Church.

And then I staggered backward, my balance failing, my legs buckling. I fell against the wall and slid down. A few feet away Santoro whimpered like a piglet and tried to crawl away, his hand still reaching for the syringe. Far above us the sounds of gunfire seemed to be thinning, becoming more sporadic.

Mr. Church stepped over my outstretched legs and picked up the syringe. He examined it, frowned, and handed it to Circe.

I flapped a hand toward Santoro. "He . . . he had it. They . . . the Kings . . ."

Circe knelt in front of me, her fingers probing my wounds, her face cut with lines of concern. "Joe . . . oh my God!"

Church looked down at Santoro, who had begun to weep.

Church stepped over and dropped to one knee beside Ghost. His big hands explored the bloodstained fur with a gentleness that surprised me.

"He's alive," he said.

Church turned toward me.

"The syringe. He said it was epinephrine," I mumbled.

"No, it's not," said Circe.

I leaned away from her and spit blood to clear my mouth. "The King of Plagues," I said. "Santoro said we'd all drown in a river of blood. He knows the plan."

Circe gasped and Church's face darkened. He rose and walked toward Santoro, who tried to crawl away.

Church walked past him and then wheeled and with a savage kick tore a stateroom door off its hinges.

"Circe," he said, "Captain Ledger needs medical attention. I think the fighting is about over. Stay out of sight until we know who won."

"What are you going to do?"

Church looked down at Santoro and then slowly removed his tinted glasses and tucked them into his jacket pocket. He squatted and grabbed Santoro by the shoulders and with a grunt of effort hauled him to his feet, spun him around, and thrust him into the room.

"Don't . . . ," she begged.

Church ignored her.

"Dad!"

Church lingered for a moment in the doorway and looked back at her. "Do as I say," he said. Then he walked into the room.

I stared at Circe.

Dad?

From inside the room the screams began. I staggered to my feet and leaned on Circe as we fled.

Chapter Eighty-seven

The *Sea of Hope*
December 21, 8:13 P.M. EST

We didn't go to Circe's cabin. I staggered along with Circe to find DeeDee. She was still in the alcove, sitting in a pool of her own blood. Alive but unconscious and in very bad shape.

"How is she?" I asked. Circe knelt to examine her.

"She might lose her eye. She needs to be in surgery as soon as possible."

"God." I looked back the way we had come and wished ten times as much pain for Santoro.

Footsteps pounded down the stairs and I snatched up DeeDee's gun and spun around.

"*Echo! Echo!*" yelled a familiar voice.

"Come ahead!"

Khalid Shaheed came down at a rush, followed by Glory Price of Tiger Shark Team. Both of them were cut and bloody.

"Sit rep," I said, sagging back.

"The good guys won," said Glory. She appraised me. "You look like shit, Joe."

"Thanks," but I nodded toward Circe. Khalid cursed and pushed Circe out of the way. Circe may have had her M.D., but Khalid was a battlefield trauma specialist.

Others came down. Top and Bunny. They helped carry DeeDee to the sick bay. Cruise ships of this kind have a first-class medical suite, and Rio was close.

My legs buckled and I started to fall.

I'm not sure who caught me, but blackness welcomed me.

Chapter Eighty-eight

It was the goddamn balloons. The syringe had been the clue.

Every single one of them was filled with Ebola. The Mexican worker who had inhaled some helium as a prank was found dead in his shower. He'd gone off shift sick and died alone.

The plan had been for the ship to limp into Rio following the tragic events of the mass slaughter. Once in port, the balloons would be released. They would rise into the sky, drift away on the variable winds, and eventually burst. South America would become a graveyard. The presidents of Mexico and the United States would be forced to cut a safety line across Panama. They would have to burn a no-man's-land with fuel air bombs, napalm, and anything else that would burn.

The stock market would be unstable for years. The Kings would profit.

A workable treatment had been in development for years. Dr. Snow at Fair Isle—who had been an agent of the Kings rather than a victim—had given samples of the vaccine to Santoro, and he to Gault. All of the Kings and their Consciences had been inoculated. Just in case the firebombing didn't work.

How did we find all this out?

Santoro.

He told Church everything. Names. Dates. Places. The identities of the Seven Kings. He told him about

9/11 and dozens of other attacks. He could not tell Church fast enough. He begged to tell him more.

Church listened.

I never learned what happened to Santoro. I doubt he is with the angels.

The Navy pulled the nets of balloons out into the deep blue and hit them with flamethrowers. We all hoped that would do the trick.

It was close to dawn the following day before I got a brief chance to speak with Church. We were alone in Circe's suite. I'd just come from the shipboard vet's office. Ghost was in surgery and I was told to stop bothering the doctors.

I found Church making coffee in the small kitchenette. His clothes were bloodstained and I knew that he had worked alongside the rest of the DMS agents, tending to the wounded. Khalid said that Church seemed to know as much about emergency medicine as any doctor he'd met. I was beyond being surprised.

I limped into the kitchen and fished a bottle of water out of the fridge. Church gave me a quick appraising look, nodded.

" 'Dad'?" I said.

"Don't start," he said quietly.

"No . . . no way am I letting that one go. 'Dad'? Circe's your daughter?"

"And if she is?"

"Why didn't you tell me?"

He poured himself a cup of coffee. "Circe is a formidable person who is making a name for herself. It was her wish that she do so without my help or influence."

"Bullshit."

He almost smiled. "No, it's true. Mostly true." He gave me a considering stare for a moment. "I don't discuss my personal life with anyone. But . . ." He brushed some soot from his chin. "After all this, you get to ask that one question and get a straight answer. Circe's mother and I divorced many years ago. She thought I was another kind of person, and when she found out that I was who I was she wanted out. I agreed." He paused. "We had two daughters."

The word "had" was big and ugly and it hung in the air between us.

"Ten months ago my wife was killed in a traffic incident. Circe believes it was an accident. I know that it was not. I have many enemies and they sometimes choose dishonorable and reprehensible ways to come at me. The previous summer my younger daughter, Emmy, was killed in combat in Afghanistan. Roadside bomb."

"Jesus Christ, man, I—"

He shook his head. "Circe is my only living relative. My father, my brothers and sisters . . . everyone else has died in the service of this country, in one way or another. Only ten people know who Circe is. Hugo Vox is one of them, by the way. Now there are eleven. Don't worry about whether you can keep the secret from Dr. Sanchez. He's known for some time now."

I started to say something, but he shook his head and turned back to making coffee. And just like that he was back to being Mr. Church. It told me something about him, maybe a lot, but it also threw a thousand new questions into the air. Most of them, I knew, would never be answered.

Chapter Eighty-nine

Gault held Eris while she wept.

It had been a long night. The news reports began late in the evening, and by midnight it was all over. The grand centerpiece of the Ten Plagues Initiative had failed. Not one of the celebrities had died. Not one of the children of the rich and powerful had been killed. And there was no report about balloons or Ebola.

No word from Santoro, either, and that was the most disturbing. Santoro had always had an escape plan. Usually two or three of them in reserve.

Nothing.

"We'll start again," Gault soothed. "The Kings are still free. We still have our resources. The Goddess has so many victories to her name."

Eris sniffed and shook her head. She didn't care about the Hospital or the twenty-one dead children of the Inner Circle. She had wanted *this*.

Eris's cell rang and she straightened. "That's Santoro!" she cried, reaching for the phone. She opened it without even reading the screen display. "Rafael, what happened to—"

"Hi, Mom," said the King of Fear.

"Hugo?"

"Yeah . . . saw the news. Thought I'd give you a call."

"It *failed*!" she yelled.

"Yeah, ain't that a kick in the nuts? All that planning.

All those years of scheming, all the work. Hell, Mom, you spent the best years of your life on that thing."

She hissed at him.

"Look," Vox said. "I'm dropping off the radar for a while. Just wanted to let you know that I drained your accounts. Gault's, too. Nice chunk of change."

"What? You miserable bastard!"

"Hey, call a spade a spade. Born out of wedlock and all that, what do you expect?" He chuckled. "But listen . . . I'm not going to cut you off entirely. I left you a nest egg. Whenever you guys reach a safe port, call me on the other cell. My new number's plugged in."

"What other cell?" she demanded.

"I left it in the drawer under the TV. Whenever you want to start over again, use that and give me a call. I'm dumping this phone."

"Wait!"

"Bye-bye, Mom. Hope you two crazy kids can make it work."

"Hugo!"

The line was dead.

Eris threw the phone across the room, where it struck the wall and shattered. "Damn that ungrateful little prick!"

"What the hell was that about?" asked Gault.

She rattled off a quick recap; then she got angrily to her feet and stalked across the room, tore open the drawer, and snatched up the cell Hugo had left for her.

"What are you doing?"

"He took our money! *Our* money." Her voice was a harpy's screech. "I'm going to goddamn well *tell* him to give it back."

She flipped open the phone and scrolled through the stored numbers until she located one labeled: ME.

"He was always an ugly child," sneered Eris as she pressed the call button.

The forty pounds of C4 packed tightly into the hold vaporized the *Delta of Venus*. The blast could be heard for thirty miles in every direction, but they were so far out to sea, no one heard a thing.

Epilogue

(1)

The *Sea of Hope* became a massive floating crime scene.
Everyone who was on board had to be interviewed and
checked. That included the performers, many members
of Generation Hope, and everyone else. There were pro-
tests and threats of lawsuits and actions, but those were
hollow. The DMS had just averted the worst terrorist act
in history. That bought us all the slack we needed. All
of the celebrities and the children of the power players
were off-loaded to the Navy ships. Eventually they'd all
go home.

Home and alive.

I flew home in a big C-140 with Pink, Taylor Swift,
and the guys from U2. DeeDee was aboard, too, with
Khalid watching over her. She would keep the eye, but
it was damaged and so was her face. It was too early to
tell if she'd ever stand in the line of battle again. I had
a couple of dozen stitches in my back, chest, and gums,
but I was deemed fit to travel. Ghost was there, too.
Sedated but alive.

It was all surreal.

The celebs on our plane kept their distance, occasionally shooting strange looks at me. I don't know what stories they'd been told about me, or what rumors had floated around. And I didn't care.

But sometimes you can't tell about people.

"Cuppa?"

I looked up to see who'd spoken and Bono stood there holding two cups of steaming tea. He held one out to me. I took it, hissing at the pain the action caused in every molecule of my body.

"Mind if I sit?"

I tilted my head toward a metal equipment case and he sat down. He was a small man, short and slim. His signature sunglasses were tucked into the vee of his shirt.

"Your name's Joe?"

I nodded.

"Look, man, I came back to say a couple of things, but I'll piss off if I'm bothering you."

"No," I said. "No, it's good. What's on your mind?"

I sipped the tea. It was lousy.

"I made this myself." He sipped his. "God, it's piss."

"It's hot," I said, and we clinked mugs.

"Tell me, man . . . why do you do this sort of thing?" he asked.

I shook my head. "Ask me something I know the answer to."

The plane flew a lot of miles before either of us spoke. We'd drunk our bad tea. Bono stood up.

"Anyway, man," he said. "For me and my mates and, I guess, for everyone . . . I just wanted to say thanks."

He offered me his hand.

I took it. Then he nodded and walked back to sit with the other members of the band. I smiled. A good guy.

Why do I do this sort of thing?

God, I wish I had an answer to that.

(2)

On December 28, Rudy, Circe, and I took a DMS chopper from the Hangar and flew south into Pennsylvania. We landed outside the walls of Graterford Prison. Warden Wilson met us at the gate.

"Has he said anything?" asked Rudy as we shed our coats in the warden's office.

"He hasn't said a word since Dr. Sanchez ordered him placed in solitary," said Wilson. "I had video and audio recorders placed inside his cell and all along the path from cell to showers and back. Nicodemus is always escorted by four guards that I pick randomly, and the time for his shower varies according to a schedule I make up. A schedule I keep in my head. If there was a leak inside the prison, someone feeding information to Nicodemus, these procedures seem to have stopped it."

Rudy and Circe exchanged a look and said nothing. Neither looked pleased. Wilson caught it.

"What?" he asked.

"Nothing," said Rudy. "Except that a little subtlety might have helped us *find* the leak rather than cut it off."

Wilson looked flustered and angry. "Well, you could have *said* that, Dr. Sanchez."

"He shouldn't have had to," I said. Wilson turned aside to hide a face.

"Can we see the prisoner now?" asked Circe.

"Sure," Wilson said with bad grace. He led the way and we followed him through cold, damp halls that felt more like the corridors of an ancient dungeon rather than part of a modern prison. We passed through two heavily occupied cell blocks, and as we passed we saw hundreds of prisoners standing on the other side of the bars. Their eyes followed us, reading us. They watched Circe O'Tree, who wore a tailored suit that hid none of her curves.

The prisoners were absolutely silent.

And that was creepy as hell. I had never heard a quiet cell block before. Not once as a Baltimore cop or during my time with the DMS. There were always catcalls and laughter, the low murmur of conversation, smart-ass remarks. There should have been some whistles at Circe, some off-color remarks.

All we heard was the hollow sounds of our own heels on the concrete floor. Even the warden felt it. He stopped in the middle of one of the rows of cells and looked around. When he made eye contact with the convicts, they returned his stare, but they said nothing.

Wilson cut a look at me and continued leading the way.

Several turns took us through a series of locked doors until we reached the secure area used for solitary confinement. The cells on either side of Nicodemus's cell had been left vacant. The video cameras on the wall were pointed toward his cell. I could see a small figure on the cot, curled asleep under a thin brown blanket.

A guard-supervisor stood at the far end of the row, and he came to meet us.

Wilson said, "Bill, these people are with Homeland. They want to interview Nicodemus."

"Sure, but if you'd called down I could have—"

"Just open the cell," I said.

It was against all protocol, and the guard studied the warden for a moment before complying. He waved to two other guards and they came to join us, bringing waist chains and riot sticks. All three of the guards cut worried looks at the cell. It was the fearful reaction Rudy had described. He was right: these guys were scared as hell by the little prisoner.

"Nicodemus," called the supervisor, Bill. "Rise and shine."

Nicodemus ignored him.

"Come on," Bill said, his tone almost pleading. "Let's not make this harder than it needs to be."

When Nicodemus still didn't stir, the supervisor turned and yelled down the hall, "Open Six!"

There was a metallic clang inside the wall and the door twitched open. The two guards braced the doorway. One opened it, the other drew his riot stick and tapped on the door frame.

"Come on—let's not be screwing around here."

When there was still no compliance, they looked to the warden, who gave a nod, and they entered the cell.

"What the hell? Oh—*shit*!"

We crowded the doorway, watching as one of the guards grabbed the blanket and whipped it away. Circe and Rudy gasped as black and brown roaches scuttled in all directions. Hundreds of them.

There was a pillow and a rolled-up bundle of clothes. Nothing else.

"Dios mio," breathed Rudy.

"Where is he?" demanded Circe. "Where's the prisoner?"

The warden ordered the supervisor to send the alert: escaped prisoner. Horns blared and sirens wailed. The whole place went into hard lockdown. Teams of men and dogs ran through the halls and out into the yards. Teams on ATVs tore through the countryside.

They found nothing.

In the warden's office, Circe asked to see the video surveillance tapes from Nicodemus's cell. When they were played back we watched the little man crawl under his blanket and appear to go to sleep. That was at 4:16 P.M. I knew from when we'd signed in that we had passed through security at 4:18.

At 4:19 the video feed in Nicodemus's cell dissolved into white static. The guards had unlocked the cell at 4:41.

That left a twenty-two-minute gap during which Nicodemus vanished.

The video feed trained on the outside of his cell door, however, showed a continuous picture, and the door did not open. The FBI and investigators from the Department of Corrections spent days going through the stored video files of all of the cameras at Graterford. Nicodemus was not seen on any of them.

Manhunts in three states could not find him. TV alerts and posted rewards resulted in no useful responses. No trace of him was ever found.

But as Rudy, Circe, and I stood in that cold hallway outside Nicodemus's cell, I think we all had the same feeling. It was absurd, impossible, and foolish. But it's what I felt, and when I looked in their eyes I saw the same shadows. The same ghosts.

We did not voice those thoughts. In our profession you don't. Just as you do with pain, you learn to eat your fear. Even fear of something that may not have an explanation.

Rudy crossed himself, though. And that said it all.

(3)

Vox's betrayal hit a lot of people hard. It shook the foundations of our government. So many key people in government, so many people in crucial jobs in labs and nuclear power plants and defense factories, so many of our most highly trained special operators, had been screened and vetted by Vox. Over seventy people in the DMS had been screened by him. Did it make them all guilty or complicit? No. Circe O'Tree had been approved by Vox, and so had Grace Courtland, Top Sims, DeeDee Whitman, and Khalid Shaheed.

What it meant was the start of a witch hunt and a wave of paranoia that would make the McCarthy years seem like an era of tolerance and understanding. Church did not want that to happen and over the next months he would spend more time in front of Congress than he would overseeing the hunt for the Kings.

Vox vanished off the radar. So did Toys and the rest of the Seven Kings. All of the think-tank records had been stolen. That was a sleeping dragon, and we all knew it.

T-Town was shut down pending a review, but absolutely no one wanted to do that review. No one wanted to be known as "the next Hugo Vox."

Rudy, Circe, and Bug spent thousands of hours going over the psychological profiles of people in key industries, looking for those personality types that jibed with Plympton, Grey, Scofield, Snow, and Taylor. They identified 103 possibles. Amber Taylor became part of the debriefing team that conducted the interviews. Aunt Sallie coordinated with Federal Marshals for an unprecedented number of new identities in Witness Protection. With Santoro locked away wherever Church has him it might mean that no one would ever come after the families of the people he had coerced and psychologically tortured—but was that a risk we could ever take?

It was an enormously expensive venture, but somehow the funding always materialized. I wondered if some of the Inner Circle were helping. They were still a pack of evil bastards the DMS would have to take down, but if they wanted to avenge their children, so be it.

As far as I know, the Inner Circle are still on the "to-do" list of Aunt Sallie and Mr. Church. Not a nice place to be.

(4)

The hunt for the Seven Kings wasn't over. We all knew that. It would go on until we found out where they were, and tore them down.

Sounds so easy. Like the War on Terror would be over when we found and killed Osama. But do any of us believe that? Is this a winnable war? It's a fair question, and a hard one, and the answer is probably "no" for both sides.

And yet we have to fight it. If we don't, the bad guys get bigger, bolder, more dangerous, and more destructive. Right now they're jackals nipping at the weak and the unwary. We can't allow them to become the dominant predator.

All of which sounds like a lot of flag-waving, but it's not that simple. We have to be careful not to become what we hunt. We almost did that with the Patriot Act, taking away civil rights in the name of protecting them. That can't happen.

Yet where does that leave guys like me? Where does it leave Echo Team and the DMS?

(5)

I stood at the window of my hotel in Washington, looking out at the green stretch of the Mall, watching the masses of crowds that were already gathering for the big New Year's celebration tonight. The papers said that there would be a candlelight vigil. For the London Hospital, for the *Sea of Hope* and all that it represented, for the victims of the Starbucks attack. I would like to think that some of those candles would be lighted in honor of the DMS agents, SEALs, Delta operators, and shipboard security who had died to keep this from being an international day of mourning.

Now the sun was setting over Washington. In a few

hours this year would burn away. It was crazy. At the beginning of June I was a Baltimore cop. By early July I was fighting to stop terrorists with a doomsday plague. By the end of August I'd fallen in love with an amazing woman, and I lost her to a murderer's bullet. I'd led good men and women into battle with monsters. Actual monsters. And I'd gone aboard a cruise ship packed with people who had gathered for the purpose of easing the pain and suffering of children living in the most economically depressed places on earth. Good people of all races and religions, all colors and political viewpoints, working together for the common good. On that ship, out in the middle of the dark Atlantic, I had moved among the very best humanity has and fought against the very worst humanity can be.

Was this my life?

After Grace died I had planned to leave the DMS forever. Even the Warrior in my head had been glutted from all the blood and death. The Cop had become convinced that all goodness had died with Grace . . . and the Modern Man was adrift, clinging to the last splinter of hope. Then Church had called me and brought me back. To the London Hospital, to Fair Isle, to the gunfight in the coffeehouse, to Jenkintown, to the slaughter of the DMS, and to the *Sea of Hope.*

So . . . *was* this my life? Fighting and fighting and fighting?

It is a horrible moment when you can no longer count the number of people you've killed. I closed my eyes and leaned my forehead against the window glass. It was mild for December, but the glass was cold.

I heard a rising burst of laughter from the adjoining suite. Rudy and Circe. They sounded happy. I felt gutted and empty.

Was this my life?

Was this who I am?

I opened my eyes and saw the first of the candles flare up down in the Mall. A tiny spark in the sea of late-twilight gloom. For a moment there was only that one small light in the darkness, and the loneliness of it was almost unbearably sad.

Then someone bent close and used the flame to light their candle. And others did, and more, sharing out the light so that it spread. Slowly and sporadically, but steadily. An infection of light that did not defeat the darkness—the darkness was too big, too vast, too powerful to ever be completely destroyed—but for now, for this moment, those tiny flames conspired together to drive the darkness back.

I placed my palm on the glass. I don't know why. Maybe it was a romantic or childish need to feel the heat of that light. But the glass was cold.

And yet . . .

I smiled.

The cold was okay. The fact that I was up here in the darkness of my room, in the darkness of my thoughts, was okay. The flame was still there. If this was who I was, and if it wasn't for me to be part of the light, then maybe that was as it should be.

I am what I am. I'm a hunter and a killer. I'm the Cop and the Warrior, and the Modern Man. As I—as *we*—watched the light from the vigil candles spread, the answer to the question was there. It had always been there.

Was this my life?

Yes.

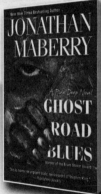

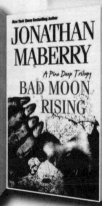